Summer's End

Geraldine O'Neill

D1227577

POOLBEG

Published 2011
by Poolbeg Press Ltd
123 Grange Hill, Baldoyle
Dublin 13, Ireland
E-mail: poolbeg@poolbeg.com
www.poolbeg.com

© Geraldine O'Neill 2011

Copyright for typesetting, layout, design
© Poolbeg Press Ltd

1

The moral right of the author has been asserted.

A catalogue record for this book is available from the British Library.

ISBN 978-1-84223-477-8

Typeset by Patricia Hope in Sabon 11/15
Printed by CPI, Mackays, UK

www.poolbeg.com

About the author

Geraldine O'Neill was born in Lanarkshire, Scotland. She has lived in County Offaly, Ireland, with her husband, Michael Brosnahan, since 1991. She has two adult children, Christopher and Clare.

Summer's End is her ninth book.

Acknowledgements

After nine books I know I should be like many authors and keep this brief, but it never works out!

My usual warm thanks to Paula, Gaye and staff at Poolbeg, and to my agent Mandy Little and the staff at Watson Little.

Thanks to Malcolm Ross-McDonald and the Offaly Writers' Group, and Arts Officer Sinéad O'Reilly, for their continued support.

I'm very grateful to my friend and former teaching colleague, Declan Murray, for his generous and invaluable help in researching the cinemas of the 60s in Ireland for *Summer's End*, and I enjoyed the entertaining chats about it.

Thanks to all the people who helped with the *Sarah Love* book launch, which raised funds for *Dochas* – the cancer support charity in Tullamore – especially Mary Cowen, Des Doyle, Mary Stuart, Siobhán McCormack-Ryan and Pauline Walshe. Thanks also to all the local businesses in Offaly who supported the event.

Much appreciation to all the lovely ladies from Offaly who attended the Acorn night – too many to name – it was a night I will always treasure and be grateful for! I remember and think of each one of you.

Writing *Summer's End* brought back fond memories of our time in Ponteland Teacher Training College and all our old friends. I didn't expect to return there so quickly after re-visiting Newcastle in *Sarah Love*, but I never know where the creative spirit will take me with each book!

I'm forever grateful to the friends and family from Scotland, Stockport and Ireland who continue to support my work and ask when my next book is due.

Congratulations to those with special birthdays this year: brother-in-law John, sister Berni, Mike's mum Mary, sister Teresa, my mother Be-Be and friends Patricia Dunne and Joe Slamman.

Congratulations also to my nephew Tony on his marriage to Lisa!

Thanks to Teddy and Be-Be O'Neill – my parents and my greatest fans.

As always, I owe a debt of gratitude to Mike, Chris and Clare for their love and endless support.

Summer's End
is dedicated to three men who have had a special
place in my life for a long time:
Martin Doherty, Kevin Brosnahan and John Hynes

We shall not cease from exploration

And the end of all our exploring

Will be to arrive where we started

And know the place for the first time.

T.S. ELIOT

1

January 1966

Lily knew she shouldn't feel happy about going to a funeral, but it was a perfect excuse to get away from college for a while. It would give her time to forget the fool she had made of herself the other night.

After months of being curious about him, she had caught the eye of the young-looking history lecturer across the late-night bar. She had noticed him when he joined the staff at the beginning of term, and was immediately drawn to his smooth caramel-toned skin and beautiful dark eyes. And although she knew his colour and culture would have been too different for some of the girls, it made him all the more interesting to her. She had been disappointed that he wasn't teaching her course and had waited for the chance to get to know him.

They got chatting and he bought her a glass of wine. They were still talking and drinking when the rest of her group had gone back to the student halls.

He told her that he had just finished his PhD in London before moving to Newcastle, then he told her about growing up in what he called the 'fusion culture' in the Seychelles with his English mother and Seychellois father. She listened intently as he talked about the art, music and food, and the colourful festivals.

It was unlike any other conversation she'd had before, and it stirred her curiosity and interest about different people and places.

As they walked back to the student houses in the dark, he asked her about growing up in Scotland. She told him about Rowanhill, the small mining village she grew up in, which was happily served with a train service going in one direction to Glasgow and the other to Edinburgh. She described how she had travelled to the cities to shop and mooch around most weekends since she was thirteen or fourteen. They stood outside chatting for a while and then he invited her into his flat for coffee.

That was when she made the mistake. And she couldn't blame alcohol; she'd only had a couple. The all-day hangover she suffered when she first arrived at college had made her wary of it. She couldn't have imagined how the months of wondering about him would evaporate in just a few minutes. A few humiliating minutes when she realised she was well out of her depth.

And now she was desperate to avoid him.

She pushed the mortifying memories away and thought of her escape. She loved travelling, and the fact she was flying for the very first time was a bonus. And it wasn't as if she knew her father's aunt very well. She would be solemn and commiserating with her close relatives.

Lily Grace held her compact mirror up, studying her face and light-brown hair which still had a few streaks of the blonde she had as a child. She supposed she wasn't bad-looking, but there were times she wished she was taller and more curvaceous. Her second cousins in Ireland would see a big change in her. Her last visit was when she was sixteen. She was twenty now, and in her second year at teacher training college, just over the border in Newcastle-upon-Tyne.

She had applied to the traditional Catholic colleges in Scotland, but the exam points were higher than England. Her careers tutor had advised all the teaching candidates to apply to an English college just in case, so she had chosen Newcastle.

Lily had been interviewed at three different colleges, and when the results came out she had enough points for the Scottish ones, but she opted for Newcastle which had also accepted her. It was far more modern than the others and it was mixed. A religious, all-girls teacher training college held no appeal for her. With four brothers,

2

she was well used to boys, and had attended a mixed secondary school in Hamilton, some ten miles from Rowanhill. Another plus was that she would get to live on a college campus in England, whereas if she stayed closer to home she would have to travel from Rowanhill by train on a daily basis.

There was no contest. She had got a taste of the bigger world at her Newcastle interview and wanted more of it.

Her mother, Mona, on the other hand, had been devastated. "Why on earth are you going away to England, when you could go to a college here?"

"I liked it better," Lily said. "And it's only a few hours' journey from home. It would be the same distance if I went to somewhere north of here like Inverness or Aberdeen."

"But you didn't apply to Inverness," her mother had argued. "And it's not even a Catholic college. Imagine going all the way to England! What will the Parish Priest say?"

Lily shrugged. What did it have to do with him?

"Well, that's lovely," her mother had said. "And it'll be me that has to face him every day." Mona had been the priest's housekeeper for over a decade and found herself in the firing-line if any of her children strayed off the conventional religious path.

"Are you sure?" her father, Pat, had asked her later when they were on their own. "You'll be a good distance away from us."

"I'll be home every six weeks," Lily said. "And I'm absolutely sure."

She had remained firm in her decision when Father Finlay called around, and told him that going to an English college wouldn't change her religious views one bit. She didn't elaborate on the fact that she already disagreed with many things about the Church.

"I find it very odd," the elderly Irish priest had said, "that anyone would want go to England if they didn't have to." He raised his eyes heavenwards. "But then I shouldn't be surprised – you're not the first one in the Grace family to go down a different road."

He was of course referring to Pat's sister who had married a Protestant, and her cousin Kirsty who had caused uproar when she took up with an older man her parents had disapproved of.

While Lily was delighted with her choice and happy to explain to anyone why she had chosen the modern college and fantastic campus, her mother had remained tight-lipped.

A few weeks after Lily left – laden down with a huge case and bags filled with Scottish bread, pies and packets of *Oddfellows* sweets – Pat had noticed a change in his wife. Although Lily phoned her regularly, she stood at the window each morning watching for the postman with letters from Newcastle. And he had to stop her phoning the halls of residence every other day to see how Lily was settling in.

Mona's sad demeanour reminded him of the time when Lily had been seriously ill with polio as a child. Her determination had pulled her through, but the slight weakness it left in her legs had put paid to Lily's plans to be a dancing teacher.

One Friday night he phoned the pay-phone in Lily's student house to check that she was free the following day, and then he told his wife they were going to Newcastle first thing in the morning.

"We're driving to England?" Her hand had flown to her throat. The only holidays they took were to Ireland or one of the nearby seaside towns. "We can't . . . it's too far away."

"It's only a three-hour drive. We'll leave about nine and be there after twelve. And then we'll see her. Isn't that what you want?"

By eight o'clock Mona was sitting with bags full of more bread and pies. By midday, they had found signs for the Northumberland college, and a few minutes later were signing the visitor's book at the Porter's Lodge.

"Well, what do you think?" Lily asked, as she walked around the college campus between her parents, linking both their arms.

"It's beautiful," Mona said, as they stopped to study the circle of immaculate Victorian houses situated around a large green oval of lawn and flower-beds. "England is nothing like I imagined."

Lily had laughed. "This is only a small bit of it, and of course Newcastle isn't the biggest city."

"It's big enough," her mother said.

An hour later, after lunch in the dining-room and two sherries in the Students' Union bar, Lily knew that parents' fears about her had evaporated.

She was now in her second year and she had made the journey from Newcastle to Rowanhill so many times she no longer gave it any thought. She was delighted to get a break from college, and since it was for a funeral in Ireland she could string it out to nearly a week. Luckily, it was a term when she didn't have any teaching practices, so she wouldn't be letting any school down.

It was wonderful to be able to fit in a quick visit home to Scotland and then fly over to Ireland. She would also have a couple of days back home after the funeral. A great way to fill the last grey week in January. She had arrived home last night, Tuesday, having caught an evening train to Edinburgh, and her father had picked her up at the station and driven her down home to Rowanhill.

The blustery, wet weather and dark mornings added to the excitement. She felt she was cheating it by travelling, instead of looking at it out of the college windows.

Lily had sat up until twelve with her parents and two brothers, drinking tea and catching up on family news and local gossip. She loved her independent life in Newcastle, and she loved teaching – but she also loved coming home to Rowanhill.

She was surprised to discover she was the only female going to the funeral along with her father and two of her brothers: Seán, who was nearly thirty and married with two children, and Declan the youngest of her brothers, who was single and still living at home. Michael and Patrick were too busy with their own families and working in the family taxi and coach business.

"I thought you were coming with us," she said to her mother.

"Oh, I couldn't face it. The thought of going up in an aeroplane terrifies me, and then driving down those dark wee winding lanes would just finish me off. It's bad enough in the summer never mind the heart of winter."

"But it's all right for me to suffer the terrible trip?" Lily said, making big eyes. "Travelling from Newcastle tonight and going straight to Ireland tomorrow afternoon."

"Get away with you!" Mona gave her a sidelong glance and then started to laugh. "There's no need for you to go at all, and well you know it."

Lily's brother Declan winked at her. "Admit it: you just fancied a holiday off college and the chance to fly in a plane."

"No, I feel I should go to the funeral. She's Dad's aunt."

"What's her full name then? First and second."

"It's Mary Grace."

"Rubbish," Declan laughed. "Her name was Grace before she got married. If you know her well enough to go to her funeral, you surely should know her married name."

An indignant look crossed Lily's face for a second – and then Declan winked again and she started to laugh. "Her name doesn't matter, I just think it's nice for some of us to go to represent the Grace side of the family. And anyway, it's ages since *I've* been to Ireland. I've been working every summer while all you boys went over there fishing."

"Well," her father said, "*I'm* delighted that you're coming with us, Lily. And so would my Aunt Mary be, whose second name is Jordan by the way. At least we won't need to worry about having to make chat to people when you're there. You can talk the hind legs off a donkey."

Everybody laughed.

"I'm really excited about flying," Lily said, grinning. "One of the girls at college goes abroad all the time and she was telling me all about the food and the drink they give you."

"It's only Ireland," Pat reminded her. "It's just over an hour in the air, so you won't have time for much."

"How long will we be there?"

"Four to five days. The removal is tomorrow night and the funeral is on Thursday. We'll travel back on the Sunday. Seán and I can't leave the lads any longer."

"You're entitled to take time off," Lily said. "You're always working."

"We're needed – we've got a lot of runs on with both the coaches and the taxis."

"Michael and Patrick will manage without you and Seán," Mona told him, "and they can always get someone in if they get busy over the weekend."

6

"Five days in Offaly at this time of the year will be long enough," Pat said. "And it will give Lily a day or so when we come back home."

Mona didn't argue. There had been times when her husband had gone to Ireland every chance he got. "It won't do Seán any harm having a bit of a break – in fact, he could do with it." A determined look came on her face. "Eileen has a list of jobs waiting from him every evening he gets in from work. She's obsessed with the house being perfect, and everything has to be the latest fashion. She had him fitting wall-lamps after work the other night and, when the screwdriver made a slight mark on the wallpaper, she told him to watch or they would have to repaper the whole room!" She clucked her tongue. "If it's not painting or decorating, he's running her or the kids over to her mother's house. She hardly gives him time to have a bite after work before he's up and running again."

There was a short silence.

Seán and his highly-strung wife was a favourite topic of Mona's. Once she got into her stride, there was no stopping her.

Lily searched for something to say. "What time is the flight?"

"I think it's at two o'clock," her father took his cue. "I have the tickets in the bedroom."

Some eight years ago Pat Grace, who was a bus-driver for the local company, and his two eldest sons Michael and Seán, who were mechanics, had bought a second-hand coach to do runs at the weekend. The business had taken off quickly and, after several big school contracts and a hectic Christmas driving groups into Glasgow and Edinburgh for work nights and pantomimes, they had bought a second coach.

A year or two later they acquired a couple of taxis as well and were busy enough for Patrick and Declan to join them and for Pat to give up his bus-driving job. The boys had always been mad on cars and engines, and between them all they were able to maintain the vehicles themselves which kept them busy between runs.

Pat came back in with the tickets. "Ten past two," he confirmed. "We'll get into Dublin for half three and pick up the hired car. We should be down in Ballygrace in plenty of time for the removal."

He looked at Patrick who was driving them to the airport. "We'll have to be gone from the house around eleven to be in plenty of time."

"No problem, the school runs will be well finished."

"I'll be up around nine," Lily said, "and then I'll drop over to Sophie's for half an hour."

"Will you have time?" Mona asked. "Don't leave everything to the last minute as usual. And make sure you pack your good black dress and coat for the funeral."

"Mother –" Lily rolled her eyes, "I'm not a teenager any more, I'm nearly twenty-one years old and will be a trained teacher by next year."

"That doesn't stop you being late. You never change." Mona studied her daughter for a moment and then she laughed and shook her head. "Although I think you have us all wrapped around your little finger. I'll bet you do everything perfectly when you're in college or on teaching practice. You must have done it right, or you wouldn't have got all those high marks."

"Of course I work hard," Lily told her, "but I'm entitled to relax and be myself when I'm at home."

"What you mean is you save your laziness for us," Declan said.

Lily pulled a face at him. "Anyone know what the weather forecast is?"

"Cold and wet here," her mother said. "And though it's not as cold, you can always depend on Ireland to be damper." She paused, studying her daughter's trouser-clad legs. "Are teachers allowed to wear trousers in school in England?"

Lily stifled a groan. Her 'outlandish' clothes – her mother's term – were another bone of contention between herself and her mother. "They're allowed in some schools," she said, gazing down at her polished fingernails, "but not in the ones I've been on teaching practice in. All the students and lecturers wear them in college." She knew the fact that she said 'lecturers' would halt her mother for a moment.

"And what about the mini-skirts you wear? Surely you're not allowed to wear them in school?"

Lily saw Declan sniggering and felt like killing him. "I wear longer skirts when I'm on teaching practice."

"I thought so," Mona said. "As you say, you do everything right when you need to."

Lily decided to get the argument over tonight. "I'm wearing trousers for travelling over," she said. "Everyone wears them these days."

Her mother pursed her lips together, a sign she was upset.

Lily looked at her now and immediately felt sorry. What was the point of coming home for a few days to spend it arguing over stupid things like clothes? And, although they had different views on things, she loved her mother with all her heart. Lily leaned over and squeezed her hand. "You don't need to worry," she said. "I won't show you up by wearing anything outlandish, and I promise I'll wear the nice dress and coat for the funeral."

Mona looked at her and smiled. "Good girl," she said. "I know I'm a bit old-fashioned, but I know what people are like and I want them to get the right impression of you. It might not seem fair, but teachers do have a responsibility. They're expected to give an example."

Lily suddenly pictured herself with the lecturer the other night and a heaviness descended on her. She knew exactly what her mother would say if she knew. Him being a lecturer and older would be bad enough, but the fact that he was foreign and coloured would be even worse. And her father's reaction would be exactly the same.

She almost shuddered at the thought.

2

When she went upstairs to her old single bedroom a short time later, Lily sat on the edge of the bed, holding her hot-water bottle tight to her chest. When the rubber got too hot, she picked up her pink nightdress, wrapped it around the bottle and held it close again.

It wasn't because the room was cold, as there was still a glowing fire in the small grate, but rather, a chill within herself.

She looked around the room now, knowing that everything would be exactly as she had left it when she first went to Newcastle. Occasionally, one of her brother's friends might stay the night, or an old friend of her mother's from Galway, who now lived up in Edinburgh. But when the visitors left, the bed linen was immediately washed and ironed, and within hours her mother had the room returned to the same tidy state that Lily had left it in.

She looked over at her dark-wood wardrobe which held her summer clothes, the matching dressing-table with the usual decorative items on top: the porcelain ring-holder and the red musical jewellery box with the twirling ballerina that she got for her twelfth birthday. Her white towelling dressing-gown, with the belt tied neatly, hanging on the back of the door.

As she sat in the silence, she could feel the familiarity of the room and the house settling around her.

It was strange, she thought now, that it would be so easy to find herself living back here again. She had close family all around her, neighbours she'd known since she was a child and her friends from school. It would be easy to pick up the threads of her old life again – pick up a job in a local shop or office, or even start all over again at a Scottish college – but already she knew that it was too late. She had changed too much.

Something deep inside her propelled her out into the wider world. Something she couldn't even put a name to. Was it curiosity, fate or maybe a deep-down dissatisfaction with her old life, she wondered? She didn't think she had been unhappy with any part of it. She loved her family and she had enjoyed her young and teenage years growing up in Rowanhill. She had definitely been happy. Not even her spell in hospital with polio had detracted from that. Her mother and father and brothers and cousins had all rallied round, supporting and spoiling her until she made a good recovery. The only negative from it had been the slight weakness it left in her legs. However, she might not have been able to realise her girlhood dream of being a dance teacher, training day after day in a studio or a college, but still she could dance. She only had to hear music – classic or modern – to find herself swaying to the rhythm or the beat. She could still dance as well as any of her friends, as long as she took a rest when she felt her legs needed it.

And soon, she would be a teacher.

There was nothing wrong with home and nothing wrong with Rowanhill or Scotland. Nothing she could pinpoint to explain her unwillingness to settle for the closest and safest options, for the urge she felt to spread her wings. Whatever the unknown feeling was, the compulsion to keep searching was strong and deep within her and wouldn't allow her to settle for anything less.

She just hoped that if, and when, it arrived, she would recognise whatever it was she had been searching for.

She thought back to the local boys she had gone out with, all friendly and decent and attractive in their own ways. But she had known within a short time – with every single one of them – that she would outgrow them. She would look for something from them that they just didn't have. Perhaps if she could have understood it herself, then she might have been able to explain it better to them when she broke off the romance. All she could say was that she didn't think they were suited.

And it was quite possible, she thought, that she might look back and regret all the nice lads she had turned away. That she might find the fault lay within her and not with them. She was already seeing girls from school getting married and having children. And here was she, when it came to boyfriends, still at square one. Still single and – unlike some of her friends from home and college – still a virgin.

And she was happy to stay like that until she found the right man. If she ever did. A little shiver went through her now. She felt ridiculous thinking back to the evening with the handsome college lecturer. She now made herself picture him and say his name in her head: Gerard René. She thought back to all the times she had spent daydreaming about him, imagining his dark skin against hers. If only she had kept her attraction to him to herself – or restricted to just a few of her trusted college friends. Instead, she had to go and actually *tell* him.

She felt herself cringe at the memory now and moved to lie back on the bed, still hugging her hot-water bottle to her.

When they had arrived at his apartment, he left her in the sitting-room while he went to get them drinks. Her eyes moved around the modern but practically furnished room, taking in the teak dining table and chairs, teak coffee table, square leather two-seater sofa and two armchairs and the teak glass-fronted bookcase. The usual transistor radio, television, various piles of books and files and several framed photographs saved it from being impersonal.

She decided she liked it, and could almost imagine herself living in a place like this in the future. She wondered about the dark-skinned people in the photographs. They were across the room and she couldn't see them clearly enough to ascertain whether Gerard was in the photos, or whether the figures were even male or female.

She had gladly accepted the glass of red wine he poured for her, and she watched him then as he poured his own. Red wine was not the sort of thing she normally drank, but she didn't mind – in fact she felt pleased. The wine and just being there had made her feel different – more mature and sophisticated – as none of her student friends had been invited to the staff quarters.

Earlier on in the bar they had been talking about Scotland and Gerard now continued the conversation, asking what she thought the differences were between Scotland and Newcastle. He had listened intently as she explained about the tensions in Scotland between Catholics and Protestants. He had been most interested in the situation and asked her lots of questions about it. Lily liked the way he gave her answers such considered attention. If it had been a lad her own age, the subject would have moved quickly to lighter things like music or the Scottish football teams.

She had then talked about her mother and father moving from Ireland, while he nodded solemnly, saying he understood what it felt like to live in a strange country, away from your family and friends.

"It is very different, Lily," he told her, "if you are a student. You know you are only leaving home for a certain length of time and you have the long holidays every half-term. If you have to move for work, it could be years before you find similar work at home."

"That's true," she agreed.

"When you qualify," he said, "can you choose where you want to go next?"

"I suppose so," she said. "Although I don't know what I'll do. I have another year to think about it."

"And is there work for teachers back in Scotland?"

"Yes," Lily had told him, "although you might have to travel a distance to another town or village."

"I'm glad for you," he said, "because everyone should have the chance to work in the place they come from."

"But then," Lily said, thinking about her mother and some of her friends, "so many people just stay put where they are, doing the same thing day after day, when there's such a huge fantastic world out there."

"Oh, I wholly agree." His face lit up. "I don't want to give the

13

impression that I don't like travelling – I love it. When I was younger I was lucky enough to travel the whole of Europe and found it amazing. I've also taken a Greyhound trip through parts of America and that was fantastic too." He caught her gaze and smiled. "We went down to New Orleans and heard some wonderful music in the jazz clubs and then we went to California and San Diego." He then went on to explain about the difference in lifestyles between the more affluent areas and the poorer ones there.

His different experiences in life intrigued and enthralled her, and she could have sat there all night listening to him. She could even imagine herself going to all those amazing places with him. "I'd love to hear more about it another time . . ."

The conversation had moved to the courses he was teaching in the college, and he told her how strange it seemed at times to be the only foreign person in the college and with a darker skin.

"There was an Indian lecturer last year," he said, "and I believe he enjoyed his time here." He shrugged. "But having the same colour of skin does not give you other things in common. On the whole, I find the staff and students here very nice, but I do miss my own country."

Lily had felt sorry for him, and said she hoped he got the chance to go back home in the summer to see everyone.

"My family are coming to London in the summer, so we shall have a few months together. London is a wonderful city, and we're all looking forward to spending time there."

"That's lovely," she said. She felt happy for him. She wondered if he meant his brothers and sisters or his parents. He did not volunteer the information and she didn't want to probe in case it made him feel homesick.

Then, she had sat enraptured as he told her all about growing up in the Seychelles, and she pictured him running on the white beaches in cut-off jeans and a T-shirt.

Sometime afterwards things seemed to change. She thought it was when the music stopped and he had moved to stretch out on the sofa. He had checked his watch and then said maybe she felt she had spent enough time listening to him, that maybe she was even bored because he was some years older than her and that she might want to go back to her own block but was too polite to say it.

"You're not old and you're definitely not boring," she told him. "You're the most interesting person I've ever spoken to."

And that was when she had decided he was too shy to make the first move, and maybe unsure as to how she would react. She had put her drink down on the bookcase beside her chair, and then taken a deep breath and quickly moved over to sit beside him on the sofa.

Then – her face burned at the memory now – she had turned towards him and kissed him on the lips.

"Lily," he gasped, sitting bolt-upright. "What are you doing?" He was both shocked and confused.

And that was when she realised she had got the whole situation very wrong.

She felt the blood rushing to her cheeks. "I thought you liked me . . ."

"I do," he said, "but you know I'm a married man and a father of young children."

"Oh, my God!" Lily had said, standing up too and backing away from him. She had her hand over her mouth as she moved towards the door. "I didn't know that . . . I didn't know you were married."

They stood looking at each other for a moment.

"You're a very attractive, intelligent girl but even if I wasn't married, I'm a member of staff and it wouldn't be right . . ."

"Honestly, I didn't know. I would never have . . ." She then turned towards the door. "I'm really sorry!"

"It's okay," he said, and then he said something else, but she didn't hear him because she was out the door and running down the path.

She heard him coming after her and calling her name, but she didn't look back. She just wanted to disappear into the night.

Reliving it now made her feel immature and silly. Both for misunderstanding the situation and for the way she had handled it. Running away had not helped things. She had only postponed having to face him.

She suddenly felt hot and bothered now just thinking about it, and she moved to put the hot-water bottle into her bed, and to change into her nightdress. She would not, she decided, waste this break away worrying about something she couldn't alter.

She had not told a single soul at college about what happened. She would, she knew, have got a sympathetic hearing from some of the girls who were open-minded about foreigners and had commented how handsome they thought Gerard René was. But he was a lecturer, and very few girls would have been brave enough to embark on a relationship with one, knowing that it was frowned on by the college authorities.

Instead, she had written all about it in her last letter to her cousin, Kirsty, and asked her advice. She was the one person who would understand.

*　*　*

The following morning she came downstairs wearing navy slacks, a fine blue sweater with a bow-tie neck and a double row of pearls.

Nothing was said for a while, and Lily thought she had got away with it.

Then her mother came to stand beside her at the sink. "I know it's probably just my own taste . . ." Mona was unable to stop herself, felt she had a moral duty to say it, "but I feel the outfit is a bit odd with the trousers." When there was no response she then added weakly, "I suppose it's smart in its own way but . . ."

"It's not your fault, Mum," Lily said, giving her a mischievous grin, which usually broke the tension with her mother. "It's just that most people your age don't actually know what is fashionable these days."

Then, just as Lily hoped she would, Mona's face broke into a broad smile. "You're the very same as Kirsty Grace – you could sell snow to the bliddey Eskimos!"

After breakfast, Lily walked a few doors up to her Aunt Sophie's house to hear the latest news about Heather and Kirsty. Heather was now married with two children and expecting her third, and

Kirsty and her husband, Larry, were off on one of their long cruises. Kirsty was a popular cabaret singer, while Larry managed the acts. Lily had always been in awe of the girls and still loved to follow their glamorous lives. Heather had gone down the more traditional women's route, working in a shipping office in the centre of Glasgow, but had given up work when she had her first child. She now lived in a lovely big house in Glasgow with her husband, Paul, and kept herself busy with things like painting and learning Italian in the evenings when he was home to mind the children.

Lily was very fond of Heather but Kirsty was her hero.

The girls looked alike, although Kirsty kept her hair blonde with the help of the hairdresser, and they had the same bubbly sense of humour, but Lily often felt a pale imitation of her cousin, and wished she had her slightly fuller figure. Kirsty wrote letters to Lily every other week, telling her about the places they stopped off at on the cruises and the different characters they met on the ships.

She told Lily she would keep her ear open for any work vacancies that came up on the cruises for the summer holidays, and Lily was hopeful of a trip somewhere exotic. So far, nothing had come up.

So, for the time being, a trip for a funeral in Ireland would have to suffice.

3

Lily had two drinks at Glasgow airport. Two more than she would have had if her mother had been with them. She had a *Babycham* when her father was buying and then she asked for a rum and Coke when Declan got the round. She wouldn't have chanced it with Seán, who was older and more serious. If he bought her a drink it was fine, if she asked for one it was a different story.

"Don't make an issue of the rum in front of Dad," she warned Declan in a low voice. "Just pour the Coke into the glass."

"I can see you've learned a lot in Newcastle," he said. "It's a wonder you're not asking for a Brown Ale."

Lily put her head to the side. "It's far too bitter – I prefer the rum and Coke."

"You're some blade," he told her, laughing.

Lily loved the buzz in the airport and the feel of being in a more exciting, sophisticated world. As she looked up at the arrival and departure boards, it amazed her that so many people were flying off to different parts of the world. She could understand it if it had been summer and people were heading off on their holidays, but what kind of people, she wondered, were flying off to Florida, Rome and Sydney on an ordinary day in January?

When they were settled in the bar, her father and brothers got into one of their heavy discussions about sport, so Lily wandered over to the shop and bought a *Woman's Own*. She got chatting to an older woman from Glasgow in the queue who told her she was going to Kildare to see her daughter who had just had a baby.

"She's married to an Irishman, hen," the woman said, "and they have a lovely house and farm. Tom paid for my flight over – he's very good like that." Her eyes had filled up. "I wish she wasn't so far away. That's the only thing . . ."

Lily felt sad, and knew that it was the sort of thing her own mother probably said about her being in Newcastle. But what could be done, she reasoned. Children had to grow up and lead their own lives.

She came back to the bar and sat reading her *Woman's Own* while drinking her rum and Coke. Every so often she put the magazine down to glance around at the other passengers. There were people of all kinds in the airport. Some very ordinary-looking and some more business-like and sophisticated. She studied the women's fashions and felt reasonably satisfied that she had worn the right things to blend in with them.

She enjoyed the short flight and the drinks and sandwiches she was served. Her mother came into her mind again when they hit a couple of patches of turbulence and she caught sight of an older woman across the aisle, sitting with eyes shut tight, silently fingering her crystal rosary beads. The bumps, which gave Lily a little thrill, would have terrified her mother.

Lily wasn't surprised she hadn't come for the funeral. Apart from the travelling, her mother had never seemed to have any interest in visiting Ireland. She sent regular letters and parcels to her sisters at Christmas and that kind of thing, but a visit to or from her family every few years was enough for her. Lily wondered how someone could spend the first twenty years of her life in a place and then forget all about it.

Her father was a different kettle of fish.

He was always keen to go back home and felt it was his duty to attend any Grace family funerals. This one in particular was important to him, as his aunt had only two sons – Kevin who was over in London, and John who had been killed in a farming accident years ago. Her only daughter, Bridget, had always been welcoming to Pat and his family, and he felt honour bound to be there to pay his respects.

Pat's brother Fintan – Kirsty and Heather's father – wasn't able to get away because he was the janitor in Rowanhill Primary School. The winter was his busiest time as he had to keep the boilers stoked over the weekends as the pipes were apt to freeze.

As they came down the steps of the plane at Dublin airport, Lily felt a sense of achievement. She had finally flown – and she loved it. They made their way through Arrivals and then Lily, Seán and Declan waited while their father sorted out the details for the hired car.

When they walked out of the terminal to where the car was parked and felt the biting January wind, Lily was glad she had worn her trousers.

An hour later they were heading down the country lanes that Mona hated. Pat came from the small village of Ballygrace, but since the funeral was in Carraigvale town where his aunt was from, they were booked in a bed and breakfast there. His cousin Bridget had arranged it.

"We'll call in to my Aunt Mary's house to pay our respects first," Pat said, "and they'll be able to tell us where we're staying."

"Will I be okay wearing trousers?" Lily checked.

"I don't think anyone will notice what you're wearing."

"I hope the bed and breakfast will be decent," Lily said, "and with all the proper things like electric lights and an inside toilet."

"Oh, they've had electricity here for years," her father told her. "And the bed and breakfast places will all have inside toilets now as well." He laughed. "Changed days indeed. If you'd seen the small outside sheds that we had to use!"

"Don't remind me," Lily said. "I had to use one last time I was over."

"When you're used to it, you don't give it any thought."

"I'll bet you found a big difference when you moved over to Scotland, eh?" Seán asked.

Pat's brows deepened. "Indeed I did. Most of the changes were for the better, but it was hard leaving a place you love. We had no option of course – we had to move for work."

"Was there nothing at home?"

"The situation was desperate . . ." Pat's voice faltered and he cleared his throat. "Scotland had a lot more to offer, but we missed the old place and the people we left behind. Still do in many ways after all this time." He paused, a thoughtful look on his face. "But . . . that's life. You take one road and you travel too far down it to find your way back."

A silence descended on the car.

Lily felt her throat tighten and she turned to gaze out of the window. She knew her father loved coming over to Ireland for holidays, but she had never thought of him feeling like that. Feeling like his life had taken a turn he had no control over. She wondered if he ever talked to her mother about it.

She felt a little shiver as she imagined her father as a young man, travelling over to Scotland with his brothers, not knowing when he would return. She imagined how her grandparents – both dead when she was little – must have felt waving their sons and daughters off to different parts of the world. And what of the young people? Surely some of them must have felt excited, as she did, leaving home for Newcastle? But maybe not. She supposed it was different times, and travelling on the boat back then would have been expensive and difficult without a car, while aeroplanes were unthinkable. When you didn't know whether you would ever go home again, it must have been frightening.

Lily was grateful that things were so different for her. She knew that she could catch a coach or a train from Newcastle which would bring her somewhere close to home in a matter of hours. Crossing the border between Scotland and England was only a matter of a train stop; in a car, just driving past the sign. The road and the scenery were the exact same either side of it. Even her mother had discovered that.

Ireland was another story. It was the crossing of the water that made all the difference.

The thought of her father and mother leaving this lovely green country behind, never to return to live there again, suddenly made her feel like crying. Lily looked out of the window again, hoping no one would notice the tears that had sprung into her eyes. She didn't normally get upset over things like that. Perhaps, she thought, it was all the travelling she had done and the late night before it. It couldn't be the time of the month as she had finished last week.

Whatever it was, she hoped it would pass

* * *

In spite of the sad occasion, there was a warm welcome for them in the small cottage. Everyone said how great they all were for travelling over from Scotland and how well they all looked. Lily shook hands with relatives she knew, relatives she didn't know and various neighbours. They were plied with tea, sandwiches and drink, and Lily happily accepted a glass of sherry. She was conscious of a few curious glances at her slacks, but didn't mind as she was more dressed up than anyone else.

She listened solemnly as people talked about their memories of Mary, she looked at all the Mass cards and then the tiny old black-and-white photographs that her daughter produced from a rusty biscuit tin. Everything, she noticed, seemed very old-fashioned compared to home. Even the people seemed of a different time, although they were mainly her father's age and older, and she wondered how her cousins would seem when she met them later on that evening.

"I think," her father said after several people left, "we'll head into Carraigvale and drop our bags off at the bed and breakfast and maybe put our feet up for an hour before coming back to Ballygrace for the removal."

They were reassured by everyone that Stewarts' bed and breakfast was one of the best in Carraigvale and that they would be well looked after.

"It's a fine big house, and they've put a lot of work into the roof and the windows in the last two years," Pat's cousin told them. "You'll be in the lap of luxury there."

Lily smiled and said nothing, knowing that things were way

behind the times in Offaly. Pat drove out of Ballygrace along the main road and after a few miles he turned onto the road for Carraigvale.

Ten minutes later they pulled up outside a large rambling house, more imposing than anything they had back in Rowanhill.

"Begod," Pat said, "I think we're in with the gentry."

"It looks lovely," Lily said. "It's a bit like the houses we have in college only bigger. Very impressive."

Pat turned to look at Seán and Declan. "Best behaviour now, lads," he said. "And you can do the talking, Lily. You're well able, being a teacher."

Lily was surprised they had houses so grand in Carraigvale. Or people as grand as the lady who came to greet them at the door. She had silvery-blonde hair cut into a sharp bob and wore a cream twin-set with rows of pearls like Lily's own, and brown slacks tucked into long riding boots. For a brief moment Lily wished her mother could see someone of an obviously higher class wearing trousers.

"Good evening," Lily said, "I believe we have a booking here? Our name is Grace."

The woman held the door open wide. "Come in out of the cold," she told them, and Lily immediately caught the American-tinged accent. "You're here for the funeral out in Ballygrace, of course."

"That's correct." Lily said, stepping into the elegantly tiled and furnished hall. She glanced back at her father and brothers and was disconcerted to see them moving reluctantly, as though they weren't even with her.

The woman held the door open and waited until all four were inside. "Dreadful day," she commented. "And I believe you travelled all the way over from Scotland?"

"Yes," Lily said. "We arrived this afternoon."

"Well, I'm delighted to meet you all." She held out her hand to Lily. "I'm Celia Stewart." She then moved to shake Pat's hand and then Seán's and Declan's.

She walked behind a large black-and-wine leather-topped desk, and lifted some keys from a board on the wall. "You're all on the ground floor. I have Number Four room with one double and one single bed for you men, and a separate room for the young lady." She turned to Pat and handed him a key. "There's a bathroom next door to your room." Then she gave a key to Lily, saying, "And you are in Number Six at the bottom of the corridor, opposite another bathroom." She smiled at them. "I think you'll find the rooms very comfortable, but come back to me if you need anything."

Since the rest of her family were struck dumb, Lily then asked, "Can we just check where we should go for breakfast?"

The landlady tapped the side of her head. "Silly me!" She moved from behind the desk to a door just a few steps further on and opened it. Lily went forward to look into a room with the cream-painted walls with the architectural details picked out in a pale blue, and elaborately fringed, navy swags-and-tails curtains. There were six round tables with four velvet-covered dining chairs at each of them.

Again, Lily looked around expecting her father and brothers to be right behind her, only to see them still standing in the exact same spot by the desk. She wrinkled her brow and gestured with her eyes to tell them to show some interest, but her father only clenched his jaw, gave a brief shake of his head and then looked away.

It dawned on her that they felt completely out of their depth in this house, and inferior to the owner. She wanted to tell them not to be so stupid, and that they were paying the woman good money for her services. She wanted to tell them that if they acted like people who had no right to be there, then that's exactly how they would be treated. She had learned that over the last few years. A spell in England, mixing with all kinds, Lily thought, would do them the world of good.

They had just lifted their bags when the front door opened and a slim, good-looking girl around Lily's age and half a head taller came rushing in. She wore a navy belted woollen coat and a grey felt hat brightened up with a couple of small coloured feathers.

Lily thought she looked smart and elegant but a little old-fashioned – it was exactly the sort of outfit her mother would love her to wear.

"Hello! It's getting wild out there!" The girl's accent was

definitely Irish, clear and well-spoken. She smiled warmly at the group and then went over to the mahogany coat-stand and put her wet umbrella on the tray at the bottom.

"Is the rain still heavy?" Celia Stewart asked.

"It is," the girl said, taking her hat off. Thick, glossy black hair tumbled down around her shoulders. She took off her coat and hung it up, revealing a very slim figure with a full bust. Lily noticed the girl's starched white collar showing under her neat black cardigan and fitted skirt. She wore black leather shoes with a bow and a kitten heel.

The older woman tutted. "Sure, what else can we expect in January?" She looked at her guests. "This is Ava. She's a great all-rounder – she helps out in reception and kitchen, and cleans and tidies the rooms. She'll be on duty this evening and in the morning if you need any help. She's a great girl." She smiled at her helper. "I've a few calls to make – you might show them down to their rooms."

"I will indeed," Ava said, moving quickly to do so.

Lily noticed that her father's shoulders relaxed immediately they set off down the corridor, leaving a safe distance between them and Mrs Stewart.

"Have you travelled far?" Ava asked.

"All the way from bonny Scotland," Pat Grace said, his tone lighter and more jovial. "Although I'm a native of this area myself – Ballygrace. I've been in Scotland the last thirty years."

Ava slowed down and they all came to a halt. "Well, you haven't lost the accent."

"No, I'm not the sort that would. But then, I'd say you're not from Offaly. Do I hear a touch of a Dublin accent there?"

"I thought that myself," Seán suddenly put in. "The minute you opened your mouth I thought of Dublin straight away."

Lily was amazed at the turnaround from their earlier cowed manner.

The girl laughed. "Ah, you have a good ear! No doubt about it. I spent most of my years in a convent just off the city centre."

"And what has brought a lovely young lady like you to the Faithful County?" Pat enquired, using the usual nickname for Offaly whose motto was *Esto Fidelis:* "Be Faithful".

Ava started to move along the corridor again. "A nun who knew Mrs Stewart recommended me . . ." She stopped outside Room Four. "Now, gentlemen, this is your room. It's a good-sized one."

Pat went in, followed by his two sons. "Lovely," he said, looking around at the two high windows, the old dark furniture and the nice beds. "It's grand."

Ava turned to Lily. "And you're just along the corridor, Miss."

"I'm Lily, and this is Pat, my father."

Ava shook hands with them.

"And this is Seán and Declan."

As her brothers shook hands with the striking girl, Lily noticed they both looked flushed and awkward. She wondered how two reasonably confident fellows were suddenly behaving like shy schoolboys. You'd think Seán would know better, being married with children, and Declan was well able to chat to anyone back home. She hoped they wouldn't act stupid like that tonight when they met people at the church.

"You have a double room because we're not busy," Ava said, opening the door to let Lily in. "I hope it's okay for you."

Lily stood in the middle of the room and turned around to have a good look at everything – the dark-wood bed, with the two matching tables at either side covered in lace cloths, and the dressing-table and wardrobe. The bed had a flowery counterpane on it with matching pillows which blended well with the green tie-back curtains. "It's lovely," she said. "And nice and big."

The Irish girl hovered by the door. "Would you like a cup of tea or anything?"

"No, no, thanks," Lily said, putting her weekend case down on the bed. "We had plenty of tea at the house in Ballygrace."

"I'm sorry . . . Mrs Stewart said that you're all over for a funeral."

"That's right. It's my father's aunt. To be honest, I didn't know her that well. I only met her a few times."

Ava smiled. "That's not so bad. Though funerals are sad and depressing whether you know the person or not." She folded her arms over her chest, and something about the gesture made Lily think she was trying to hide the size of her breasts. "Your father and your brothers are very nice. You seem like a lovely family."

Lily rolled her eyes. "Oh, they'd drive you mad at times, but I suppose they're not the worst."

"You're very lucky . . ."

Lily looked at her, wondering what she meant. "Have you any family down here or are they all in Dublin?"

Ava looked over to the window. "I've no family," she said. "I was brought up in an orphanage with the nuns. They found me on the doorstep one morning in a basket, wrapped in three baby blankets. My mother was probably an unmarried young girl who had got herself into trouble." She raised her eyebrows. "Sex causes an awful lot of problems."

Lily sucked her breath in at the casual remark. She had found the English girls at college much more open about sex than her Scottish friends. She had been shocked at their open attitude to the Pill and things when she first arrived in Newcastle, but after a couple of years she had got used to it. However, hearing an Irish girl talking like this was unusual. She had always found her cousins to be old-fashioned and more innocent than any others she knew, and she felt this girl was the exception.

"Well," she said, smiling at Ava, "you seem to have done very well for yourself."

"Oh, the nuns have been very good to me. They're like my family. And Mrs Stewart is a great person to work for."

There was a small silence.

Lily searched for something ordinary to say. "You have a lovely, unusual name."

Ava smiled. "Everyone says that."

"Apart from the actress, Ava Gardner, I've never heard it before."

"I was found on Saint Ava's feast day," she said. "April the twenty-ninth, so the nuns called me after her. She was a famous French saint." She started to laugh. "I was lucky. They sometimes call the abandoned babies after the person that finds them."

Lily hesitated, not knowing whether to be serious or as light-hearted as the girl.

"In my case it was a nun called Sister Theodora! Can you imagine being called that?"

Lily bit her lip. "It is a bit of a mouthful, isn't it?"

"You're telling me! Do you work?"

"I'm a student," Lily said. "I'm training to be a teacher."

"A teacher! You must be very clever. Do you have to do a lot of studying?"

Lily sank down on the edge of the bed. "Not as much as I should. I'm the sort that does it all the weekend before." She gave a little sigh. "I've an essay due in next week, and I haven't even looked at the title yet. Hopefully they'll give me an extension because of the funeral."

Ava started to giggle. "It's a good excuse – your auntie died at a handy time."

Lily looked at her for a moment and then she started to giggle too. "Oh God, we shouldn't be laughing! Sometimes I laugh when something is depressing or makes me nervous."

Ava nodded her head, her eyes watering. "I do the very same."

"Well, I'm glad to hear somebody is as bad as me." There was something about Ava that made her feel comfortable. She seemed the kind of girl who could make a laugh out of any situation.

"Will you be out in Ballygrace for the whole evening?" Ava asked.

"I don't know what we're doing. We'll probably meet up with Dad's relatives and go for a drink. I don't think we'll be too late, with the funeral in the morning." Lily paused. "Do we need a key for the front door or anything?"

Ava shook her head. "I'm here all evening. I'll be up when you come in."

"When do you go home?"

"I am home." She smiled and pointed towards the ceiling. "I have a room up in the attic."

"That's very handy," Lily said. "And aren't you lucky to live in such a gorgeous old house?"

"It is lovely, and if it's quiet in the evenings I can sit and relax and watch television in the lounge."

"Do you go out much?" Lily asked.

"Not really. I don't know that many people my own age in Carraigvale. I've only been here since September . . . I go up to Dublin now and again to see some of the girls from the convent." She glanced backwards to the door and lowered her voice. "To be honest, it's not easy making new friends in the small country towns. They all seem to have their own little groups and they're a bit suspicious of new people."

"I can imagine," Lily said. "We come from a small mining village and everyone knows everyone as well."

"You seem the kind who would make friends easily."

"Oh, I do. I've a lot of nice friends at college and they're from all different parts of England." She shrugged. "It doesn't matter where people come from – once you get to know them they're the same underneath."

"I think you're right. I met all types of people in Dublin."

Lily could tell that Ava was lonely down in Carraigvale, and wondered if she should mention her cousins from Ballygrace, and maybe suggest that Ava meet up with them. But something halted her. She would wait until she saw them tonight to see whether it was a good idea or not.

"You know there's a cinema in Carraigvale?" Ava said. "We get all the latest films. Not as quick as Dublin, but most of them usually come down. We had *The Sound of Music* and *Doctor Zhivago* on a few weeks ago."

"Oh, I love *The Sound of Music,*" Lily said. "I've seen it a few times. I never got to see *Doctor Zhivago* though."

"Oh, it's brilliant!" Ava said, crossing her hands over her chest and closing her eyes. "Omar Sharif is gorgeous!" She looked at Lily. "Do you like him?"

"Yes, he's a good actor, but he's a bit on the old side."

There was a tap on the door and Ava moved quickly to open it. "Oh, it's only you," she said, smiling and moving to let Seán in. "I was afraid it was Mrs Stewart."

"Is she very strict?" Lily asked.

"No, not at all. She's a nice person, but I don't want her to think I'm wasting time."

"Sorry for disturbing you," Seán said. "But we were just wondering whether you had an iron? Our shirts aren't looking the best after travelling in a holdall."

"Give them to me," Ava said, "and I'll have them done in five minutes."

Lily knew that Seán wouldn't know one end of an ironing board from another, as Eileen did all that for him at home. "You probably have enough to do," she said. "If you show me where the iron is, I'll do them."

"Not at all," Ava said. "I haven't much to do at the minute, and it will make me look busy. You can get them for me now." As Seán went off down to his room for the shirts, she looked back at Lily. "I enjoyed chatting to you. I hope I didn't keep you back?"

"You did not," Lily said. "I enjoyed it too."

"I'll go and get those shirts and leave you to get a bit of a rest now."

A few minutes later, Lily heard voices and laughter out in the corridor. She quietly opened her door and saw Ava walking down the corridor with Seán on one side of her and Declan on the other. At least they've relaxed and are obviously more confident here than they were, she thought.

* * *

As they drove out to Ballygrace, Lily was left in no doubt as to the impact Ava had made on the men.

"Isn't that a grand girl back in the old house?" Pat Grace said.

"She's lovely," Lily agreed from the back seat, "and very good-looking."

"Ah, she's too young for me to notice things like that," he said diplomatically, "but she's very well spoken and made a lovely job of ironing and starching the shirts. I'd say she could be anything."

"I thought the same," Lily said, "but you won't believe it – she told me she was an orphan brought up by the nuns in Dublin. She said that she was an abandoned baby, left on the doorstep of the convent."

"Jesus!" Pat said.

"Are you serious?" Declan said, turning around to look at her.

"Of course I'm serious. Why on earth would I say something stupid like that if it wasn't true? We were just chatting and she told me straight out."

Seán shook his head. "That's terrible. She's the brightest, cheeriest girl I've met in a long time. You get the feeling that nothing would be too much trouble for her."

"It makes you think," Lily's father said. "There are girls who complain about everything, and then you get a lovely girl like that who's had a raw deal in life and just gets on with it."

In the short silence that followed, it occurred to Lily just how lucky she was to have such decent parents and brothers. Whilst there was a lot of banter and bickering between them, it meant nothing. And she was lucky to have two sister-in-laws who fitted so well into the family, even Eileen, Seán's wife, who was awkward and fussy at times. Whatever happened, they all stood by each other and always would.

She couldn't imagine how it must feel to be Ava who had no one belonging to her.

4

As Lily shuffled her way back down the aisle of the packed church, she felt someone touch her arm. She looked around and saw her cousin, Marie, smiling at her. Marie was a year older than Lily, and she had two younger sisters and several younger brothers.

"I heard you were here and I was watching out for you. I knew you straight away," Marie whispered, wriggling through a gap in the crowd to be closer.

"I was watching for you as well." Lily kept her voice low, knowing her Scottish accent would draw attention. "How is everyone?"

"Not a bother, we're all grand," Marie said. "We're all going back to our house for a cup of tea. My mother went on ahead, so say to your daddy and brothers to come up when they're ready."

Pat's cousin, Bridget – the deceased Mary's daughter – had a farmhouse a short distance from her mother's cottage. They drove out the mile or so to her house, Pat pointing out significant places from his boyhood to them as they went along. When they arrived, Bridget ushered them towards a table filled with plates of cold meats and salad and home-made bread. Her husband Frank offered the men whisky or beer, and Marie handed around glasses of sherry for the women.

"I thought we'd have more comfort here than back at my mother's place," she explained to Pat. "Kevin and his wife are over from London and Jim and his wife and girls from Manchester, and they're all staying in the cottage. There will be a big enough crowd without us. And I thought we could talk easier on our own, because we won't get much time after the funeral." Bridget suddenly stopped and her eyes filled with tears. "I don't know what we're all going to do without her. My mother was a great woman . . ."

"She was indeed," Pat said, placing a comforting hand on her shoulder. "But at least she was a good age."

Bridget nodded her head. "I know, I know. When you think what happened to our John, and him only twenty-five, and your own poor mother."

A shadow crossed Pat's face. "It never leaves you."

She pulled an embroidered handkerchief from her sleeve. "And you only gone over to Scotland a month. I think you all going one after the other must have broken her poor heart again and again."

Pat shrugged. "What else was there to be done?"

She dabbed her eyes. "I know. There was no work here for men. It was the times. It still is for some families."

Lily and her brothers listened in silence.

"And it's not just our own families that have suffered," Bridget went on. "You heard the terrible news about Helena Casey? It's over two years ago now . . . an awful tragedy altogether."

Lily glanced at her father and saw his face tighten. She turned aside, uncomfortable with yet another conversation about loss.

"I didn't know until it was too late," he said.

"We didn't know anything about it ourselves until after the funeral," Bridget said. "It was one of those weeks in the summer when people were away or busy with visitors. And families keep things very quiet under those circumstances."

"Terrible to think such a thing could happen."

"You knew her well . . ."

"A long time ago . . . before I went to Scotland." He gave a sigh that came from somewhere deep within him. "She was the loveliest girl."

Then, before things got more maudlin, other people arrived and cups of tea and plates and glasses were passed around.

Lily moved into the parlour to chat to her cousins. As Marie and one of her sisters showed off their engagement rings, Lily was amazed by the difference that five years could make. A difference that saw them heading in opposite directions. While she was planning for a life of travel and excitement, her cousins' talk was of weddings and setting up a home in readiness for babies.

It sounded like too much responsibility too soon for Lily.

"And have you a boyfriend?" Marie enquired.

"I've had a few," Lily told her, "but there's no one serious at the moment." The history lecturer's handsome face flashed into her mind. She wondered what they would think if she said she had spent endless nights dreaming of a college lecturer's perfectly smooth, coffee-coloured skin. They would be shocked as would all her friends in Scotland. It would be foreign to them in every way.

"You'll have to get your skates on," Marie laughed, "or all the best ones will be gone."

On her previous visit to Ballygrace, herself and Marie had gone for a long walk and chatted about boys they liked. Her Irish cousin had her sights set on the same local boy – Tommy Keane – since she was at primary school, and had pursued him through her teenage years, refusing offers of dates from any other lads. In the infrequent letters they had exchanged, Marie wrote ecstatically about the dances she had gone to with him and the nights in the back row of the cinema. She also wrote about the heartache she endured when he left her to start courting another girl in her class for a whole year, and then the joy of getting back with him again. And then only two years ago, she wrote of the humiliation heaped on her again when he drunkenly made a pass at her younger sister at a local football match.

Lily didn't add to Marie's woes by writing back and saying the object of her desire had tried to kiss her too, on her last holiday over in Ireland. Instead, she had written to suggest that Marie pretend that she was no longer interested in Tommy, and accept a date with one of his friends and then ensure he got to hear about it.

Lily's advice and Marie's persistence had worked. As soon as the news travelled about her date, Tommy came scuttling back. He said it was time they both settled down, and made it clear that there would be no more nonsense on his side with other girls and he hoped she felt the same about not seeing other lads. The engagement ring followed a short time after.

And so far, Marie told her now, that's exactly how it had been.

A while later, Lily's father went to her and her brothers to say that the men were all going up to one of the Ballygrace pubs. "You're welcome to come," he told her, "but there won't be many women there. Bridget said that she and the girls didn't get much sleep last night, so they can't be bothered going out. If you like, I can drop you back out to the bed and breakfast in Carraigvale. There might be more going on in the town there."

Declan moved to stand beside Lily. "I'll come back with you," he said. "I'm not too interested in the pub here. It's all ould fellas my dad's age. We could take a walk around the town."

"Hi," Pat Grace said, "we'll have less of the 'ould fellas' unless you fancy a good clip around the ears!"

Declan stepped back and held his fists up in a boxing gesture and they all laughed.

Lily thought for a minute. "I suppose we could go to the pictures or something like that. Or do you think it would look very bad? Would anyone be offended?"

Pat shook his head. "I doubt it," he said in a low voice. "It's different if you were a granddaughter or someone very close. No one will even notice where you are."

Declan turned to Lily. "I was chatting to Ava earlier when she was ironing the shirts and she told me there's a film on around nine o'clock. If she can get off, she might come with us."

Lily looked at him. "You've surely got very familiar with Ava all of a sudden! Maybe you'd rather go on your own with her?"

He dug his elbow in her arm and laughed. "Don't be daft, she was only being friendly. Anyway, she might not even get off work . . ."

"It might be *The Sound of Music*, and you won't be laughing then. You hated it."

He shrugged. "I don't care what's on. It'll be a change." Then, when his father went over to speak to his cousin he said, "If we don't go to the pictures, we could always go to one of the pubs there. They're bigger than the ones in Ballygrace and likely there will be younger ones there. You'll be able to have a few drinks without old Pat breathing down your neck. You could even have a Newcastle Brown!"

Lily ignored the jibe. "I don't mind what we do. I'm happy to even go back to the bed and breakfast and watch television."

Declan's eyes widened. "But the owner might be there."

"She won't be," Lily said. "When it's quiet it's only Ava on duty, because she lives there."

"So she was saying earlier. I wouldn't fancy working for that uppity woman, but I suppose it's handy enough for her."

* * *

Ava was sitting in the lounge watching television when they were dropped off.

She stood up when they came in and Lily noticed she looked more glamorous than before.

"I hope your evening went off well," she said. "I hope nobody was too upset." Her face was serious as she looked from one to the other.

"They're all sad," Lily said, "but they're okay."

"Ah, we thought we'd leave the old ones to the local pubs, and see if there was anything more exciting going on in town," Declan said.

Lily threw him a glance, thinking he could have been a bit more reverent about the mourners. She turned back to the girl. It was Ava's eyes that were different, she thought. She had a grey-blue shadow on the lids which accented the blue of her eyes, and she had black mascara. She was also wearing lipstick and a light perfume, making Lily think she must be paid very well.

"We were thinking of going to the pictures," Declan said. "Is there anything decent on?"

"I checked earlier," Ava said. "There's an Elvis film on."

He rubbed his hands together. "That's the game! Me and Lily are big Elvis fans, aren't we?"

Lily made a face. "I wouldn't go that mad – he's all right." She liked Elvis but didn't want to encourage her brother's giddy mood. She smiled at Ava. "Which one is it?"

"*Kid Creole.*"

"Aw, brilliant," Declan said. He checked his watch. "Did you say it started at eight?"

"Half past eight."

"We'll have to get a move on."

Ava looked at Lily.

Lily realised she was waiting for her to say something. "Do you like Elvis, Ava?"

"Oh, I do. I love his music."

"Would you be able to come with us?"

Ava nodded.

Out of the side of her eye, Lily glimpsed Declan winking and holding his thumb up to the girl and she felt like killing him.

"We've only two other guests in tonight, commercial travellers," Ava explained, in a light breathless voice. "They've been coming for years, and have their own routine. One is already settled in his room doing his books, and the other one will be in around eleven. He goes for a few drinks every night and he has his own key for the front door so it won't be a problem."

"So you won't have anyone looking for you, like Mrs Stewart?"

"No, it'll be grand. She won't mind. Your father and Seán have a key for the front door as well." She moved towards the door. "I'll just leave a note for them at the reception desk to say where we are."

Lily followed her out and watched as she wrote the note out in quick neat letters with the names, Mr Pat Grace and Mr Seán Grace, in big block capitals. She thought that Ava was very competent and able. She also thought she had a good head for names, having only met her family once.

"They won't be too long," Lily said, "with the funeral in the morning."

"Oh, we'll make sure to be back by twelve anyway," Ava said. "They'll probably want a cup of tea before going to bed, and I'm sure you'll want one too." She lifted her coat from the coat-stand. "Do you need to get anything from your room?"

"I'll just run down to the bathroom," Lily said, "and then I'll be ready."

When she came back, Declan and Ava were in the lounge laughing loudly at something on the television. She stood and watched it with them for a few moments, but couldn't work out what was so funny. Ava switched the television off and they were just heading out the front door when the phone rang.

She ran back to get it while Declan and Lily waited.

"Yes," Lily heard her say, "I'll be going to the cinema if that's still okay? I've checked with Mr Lyons and he's fine, and Mr Flynn has his own key." There was a silence when Mrs Stewart was speaking and then Ava said, "Lovely. I'll be up good and early and have the breakfast on."

Lily wondered at Ava speaking so confidently to her boss. She also thought she must have been pretty sure that Declan and herself would come back, since she had already organised time off to go the pictures.

5

It was a short walk into the centre of Carraigvale and they walked briskly since it was cold. As they went along, everyone they met nodded or spoke to them as though they knew them. This friendly Irish characteristic was one of the things her father always talked about in Scotland. He bemoaned the fact that, unless they knew you, the Scots would always look the other way.

When they arrived in the main street Declan stopped outside a small pub to check his watch. "We've about ten minutes before the film," he said. "Will we stop off for a quick drink?"

"Grand," Ava said. "There's no big rush. They usually start with adverts or a short black and white film."

The pub was warm and cosy and Lily followed Ava's advice and had a hot sweet toddy to warm them up for the cinema.

When they came out, the three walked down the road to the cinema. Lily was surprised that the outside of the building was newly painted and that it was so well-kept inside. There was a small shop with a cheery woman selling the tickets plus the usual Taytos, sweets and drinks. There was a good crowd ahead of them, and when they eventually got to the counter, Declan, without any big fuss, went ahead and paid for the tickets and some snacks.

When Lily and Ava offered to pay for themselves he said, "I'm hardly going to let a penniless student and a young lady who ironed my shirts pay for themselves."

"Thanks," Lily said, linking his arm. "I won't bother giving you my usual women's lib speech since I'm skint, and I'll buy you an ice cream at the break."

Ava smiled warmly at him. "It's very good of you."

Lily noticed Declan's face turning red and she could tell that he definitely fancied the girl. What Ava's feelings were towards her brother she couldn't tell. He was passable-looking and dressed well, and he was never short of girls back home. But so far, he'd never met one he liked enough to settle down with. But then, Lily surmised, there weren't many girls who looked like Ava back in Rowanhill.

They walked into the three-quarters full hall and went to a quiet row near the back.

"Declan, you can sit at the end," Lily said in a loud whisper. "Ava and I will want to chat." She moved along the row of red-velvet seats. Ava followed and sat between her and Declan.

They chatted about the Elvis films they had seen while waiting for the film to start.

At one point Lily asked Ava, "Do you miss Dublin?"

"In ways," Ava said. "It can be a bit lonely down in the country. You have to cycle or walk here because the buses are so rare and only go to Dublin or Galway. It's easier to get around the city."

"We have regular trains and buses, and it's easy to get from one place to another," Declan said. "I suppose we're spoiled and we don't even know it."

"I heard that Scotland is a lovely place," Ava said. "I'd love to see it."

"You must come over some time," he told her. "Shouldn't she, Lily?"

"Yes," Lily said, "you should. We could meet up when I'm home from college for the summer holidays."

"You could come any time, Ava," Declan said. "There are plenty of us around to show you the sights, and my mother would be delighted to have an Irish girl around the place, wouldn't she, Lily?"

"Yes," Lily said, "I'm sure she would." She actually thought that Declan was jumping the gun a bit, issuing invitations to a girl they hardly knew, but she left it at that. By the time they got home, it would probably all be forgotten about.

Lily glanced at the people around the hall. The girls, she thought, were mainly old-fashioned in dress like her cousins, but there were certain ones who were dressed more stylishly like Ava. There were none as casual as the students back in Newcastle. She turned to ask Ava where she did her clothes-shopping, but Declan was busy telling her all about the plane journey from Scotland to Ireland, so she went back to discreetly studying the groups and couples around her until the programme started.

Although Lily had seen the film several times, she found herself caught up in the story and the music. On a couple of occasions she turned to comment to Ava about the film to find her turned towards Declan again. They were both speaking in animated whispers and Lily sighed to herself, thinking how stupid and obvious her brother was. Lovely-looking and lovely in manner Ava might be, but what, she wondered, was the point in getting involved with someone he would only see for a few days?

At the break she decided to leave the lovebirds chatting and went to buy hot-dogs and ice creams for them. There was a queue at the shop so she went to the ladies' first to check her hair and make-up. When she came back there were only a few ahead of her.

A fellow around her own age, of medium height, and with dark longish hair passed her and went behind the counter. He said a few words to the cheery woman, who promptly put her coat on and left from the side door.

When Lily reached the counter she could see they didn't have a hot-dog machine so she asked for three Cokes and three choc-ices.

He put the bottles of Coke on the counter with straws in them, then stood with his hands on his hips, smiling at her. "It's well known you're not from Carraigvale."

"The Scottish accent?" Lily smiled back at him, thinking his hair was unusually fashionable for an Irish fellow and more like the students back in Newcastle. It had the shaggy look of Mick Jagger's hair but was darker and a bit curlier. She had noticed that her cousins all had the same old-fashioned short-back-and-sides they'd had since they were at school. Like the boys back in Scotland – including her brothers – they had it shorn every few months when it grew noticeably untidy.

"Well, the accent gave a big clue – but it was more the fact that you've asked for ice cream."

She looked blankly at him.

"We don't sell it," he told her. "We wouldn't have the technical advantages of a fridge."

"Ah . . . I'm used to having ice cream and hot dogs in the Scottish cinemas."

"Lucky you, but tonight you're in the backwater of Carraigvale and we don't hold with such frivolities." He grinned and spread his hands out. "You'll have to pick something else from our vast confectionary range."

As Lily looked at the rows of chocolate bars and sweets in the glass-fronted cabinet, she was thinking he was really good-looking. Not perfect, there was a slight cragginess to his face, but Lily reckoned it made him more attractive.

"And what's brought a lovely young lassie like you over the water?" he asked. "I suppose it's our fine Irish weather?"

She looked up and caught his eye, wondering if he was flirting with her, then she dismissed it thinking he was too good-looking for her and probably chatted to all the girls who came into the cinema as it was good for business. "I'm going to make you feel guilty now. We're over for a funeral."

"Oh, we have plenty of those," he said. "No hot dogs or ice cream, but we do a fine line in funerals. It's a national trait." There was a pause and then his face suddenly became serious. "I didn't mean to be disrespectful or anything like that . . . I hope it wasn't anyone close or young . . . It's not anybody from Carraigvale or I would have heard."

"It was an old aunt from Ballygrace, and I didn't know her very well."

"Thank God," he said, pulling a face. "I must learn to keep my big trap closed. *Dún do bhéal* as we say in Irish."

42

Lily rolled her eyes and smiled. "I'll have three Mars bars . . ."

He scooped them up from the cabinet and put them on the counter alongside the drinks. "You're not going to eat them all yourself?"

"No," she said. "I have my brother with me and . . ." she wasn't sure how to describe Ava, "and a friend."

"That's okay then," he said, winking at her. "I think I can sell them to you."

She paid him and then, popping the Mars bars in her coat pocket, gathered the bottles in the crook of her arm and headed back into the auditorium. She was just going out of the door when she glanced back over her shoulder and caught him watching her. He smiled and gave her a little salute and, although she felt embarrassed, she smiled back.

He was absolutely gorgeous, and even better, he was witty and clever.

As she climbed the steps to her seat, she could see Ava leaning towards Declan, her head touching his shoulder. The girl moved quickly when she saw Lily coming back.

Lily gave them each a bottle and a Mars bar. "And don't bother complaining," she said to Declan. "That's all they sell."

"Thank you," Ava said. "It's very good of you, Lily."

On their way out after the film, Declan and Lily waited in the foyer while Ava went to the ladies'.

"You two look very cosy," she commented.

"She's lovely. I'm taking her out for a meal in Tullamore tomorrow night."

"You haven't wasted any time," Lily said.

"Precisely, I'm only here for a few days."

"We're all supposed to be going for a meal after the funeral, you know."

"That's in the early afternoon," Declan told her. "I won't be missed after that." He glanced at his watch. "We'll have to watch the time as Ava said she'd be back around twelve."

Lily suddenly smiled. "You've dropped a bit of chocolate down your shirt and it's all melted on it."

Declan opened his coat and pulled at the front of his pale-blue shirt to check. "Damn it," he said, starting to scrape at it with his nail. He looked at her. "Is that better?"

"Yes, but you can still see it."

He sighed. "I'm just going to the gents' to see if I can dab it off."

Lily moved over to the side of the foyer to let the crowds past. She was bent over, searching in her shoulder-bag for her gloves when she felt someone beside her. She looked up and saw it was the long-haired boy from the shop.

"Well," he said. "Did you enjoy the film?"

"Ah, yes," Lily said. "Elvis films are always okay. Not brilliant, but okay."

"Where are you staying?"

"At the bed and breakfast half a mile up the road."

"Very nice. It's a fine old house."

As the people passed them by, most made a comment or waved to him.

"How long are you here for?" he asked.

"Until Sunday."

"That's good – it will give you a few days around the area." He held his hand out. "I never introduced myself. I'm Dara Ryan."

She put her hand out and was surprised at the firmness of his handshake. "And I'm Lily Grace." She wondered where Declan and Ava had got to, as most of the people seemed to have gone. Surely they hadn't sloped off without her?

"An Irish name for a Scotswoman. I was expecting something like Flora McDonald."

She raised her eyebrows in surprise. "You surely know your Scottish history!"

"Not really," he said, smiling. "Odd bits here and there. I often have time to kill when I'm working in the shop so I always have a few books with me."

"And what are you reading at the moment?"

He raised his eyebrows. "Are you sure you want to know? You might not find it very exciting . . ."

Lily was intrigued. "Go on."

44

"It's a book about architecture."

She raised her eyebrows.

"Have you heard of Frank Lloyd Wright?" he asked.

Lily shook her head. "No, never."

"He's one of the greats, an American architect, way before his time. His work is all inspired by nature."

Lily was wondering what a cinema worker was doing reading books on architecture when a sudden cry made them both whirl around.

"Oh, God!" he said. "It's poor oul' Maggie!"

A small thin elderly woman with straggly grey hair was lying in a crumpled heap at the bottom of the carpeted stairs. Dara Ryan was beside her in seconds and down on his knees checking she was okay.

Lily stood for a moment, then, when she saw the woman starting to convulse, she ran over beside him. "What can I do?" she asked.

"Nothing," he said. "We'll just have to wait until she comes out of the fit."

Lily started to take her coat off. "Here," she said, "put this under her head."

Dara did as she said, murmuring a few words of reassurance to the woman as her body stiffened and then jerked in turn. "It usually only lasts a few minutes," he said in a low whisper.

"Does it happen often?"

"Ah, every now and again. We're all used to it." He looked up at Lily. "Are you okay? I'm glad it doesn't seem to have frightened you."

"There was a girl at school who used to take turns," Lily whispered as she knelt down. "She was actually the cleverest and prettiest girl in the class, so I know it can happen to anyone."

They waited in silence as Maggie's convulsion reached its peak and then started to gradually subside until she was lying completely still.

Lily glanced at the cinema worker's bent tousled head and thought how gentle and easy he was with the woman.

"What about her family? Do you need to phone them or anything?"

"She lives up in the convent with the nuns. I'll see how she is when she comes around. And if she's not well enough to walk home, I'll ring down to the convent and somebody will come for her."

Lily looked at Maggie, who was now still and quiet. She was a strange-looking little woman – the straggly grey hair and the small round glasses made her look old and yet there was something young and innocent about her.

Dara looked over at Lily. "She's not," he mouthed, "a hundred per cent."

Lily nodded, understanding him.

Two figures appeared beside them and Lily looked up to see Ava kneeling down at her side.

"Can I help?" Ava asked.

"I think we're all right," Dara said. "She's had a bit of a fit, but she's over the worst."

"This is my brother, Declan," Lily said, "and this is Ava who works in the guest house."

"Oh, I know Ava, we've met here several times," he said.

There was a small silence.

"Are you sure there's nothing we can do?" Ava asked.

Maggie gave a little groan, opened her eyes briefly, and then seemed to fall asleep again.

"There's not really anything more," Dara said. "We need to wait and let her come around in her own time." He paused. "Actually, I might need one of you girls to take her to the ladies'. She often needs to go there after this happens. My aunt is usually here but she had something on tonight and had to leave . . ."

Lily presumed he was referring to the woman at the ticket office earlier.

Declan looked at his watch and then at Ava. "You need to keep an eye on the time for getting back . . ."

"You go on," Lily told the other two. "I'll wait and take her to the toilet. I know my way back."

"Are you sure?" Declan checked, but Lily noticed the delighted look in his eye. Delighted at the thought of being on his own with Ava.

She nodded at him. "Yes, I won't be long."

After they headed off, Dara said, "That's good of you. Unfortunately, if she hadn't been one of the last to leave the hall, there would be plenty of people she knew who would have taken her back home."

"It's fine," Lily told him. "I'm not in any great hurry. Are you going to let the nuns know about her? I'll be okay if you want to go to the phone."

"I'll give her a few more minutes to see how she is."

Just then, Maggie gave a moan and her eyes fluttered open again. She looked around for a few moments, then she tried to sit up. "My ankle," she said, trying to reach down to rub it.

"You're okay," Lily said. "You just had a wee turn. Do you want me to help you to the toilet?"

"I can't walk with the pain in my ankle," Maggie told her. "The pain is feckin' terrible."

Lily caught her breath at the woman swearing and glanced at Dara, who didn't seem in the least perturbed by it.

"It's very swollen," Dara said. "You must have twisted it when you went down the steps."

Maggie tried to move her leg. "Aah! It's feckin' terrible!"

"You'll be fine, Maggie, when you get it strapped up." He glanced over to the box office. "I'm going to phone the nuns," he told her. "You wait here with Lily. She's a nice girl from Scotland."

Lily chatted to Maggie, who told her all about a nun from Edinburgh who had visited the convent the previous year, and asked her if she knew her.

"I don't think so. Edinburgh's a big place," Lily said, "and there are a lot of convents there."

"Sister Teresa," Maggie said. "She had black hair you could just see under her veil."

"No," Lily said. "I never met a Sister Teresa."

Dara came back across the foyer. "They'll be here for you shortly."

"Grand," Maggie said. "Have you ever been to Edinburgh, Dara?"

"No," he said, "but I'd love to go there. I believe the castle and the buildings surrounding it are stunning."

"It's a beautiful city," Lily said. "The trains run through our village and it's only three quarters of an hour into Edinburgh. They go in the opposite direction to Glasgow. When I'm home, I'm in one or the other city most weekends."

"That close? You're lucky."

"The shops are great, too."

Dara laughed. "Ah, you can keep the shops, unless they're music or bookshops. I would be more interested in the old buildings. You must get a lot of tourists over there. Far more than we have in Dublin."

"In the summer it's crowded with visitors. The Princes Street Gardens are lovely – there's a huge floral clock that actually works and tells the time. When I was at school we used to go for trips up to the castle and we had to walk in lines around the gardens."

Their conversation was interrupted when a black car drew up outside and two nuns dressed in black-and-white habits came rushing in. They thanked Dara and Lily for looking after Maggie, and then they carefully examined her ankle.

"Do you think you'd be able to walk, Maggie?" the older of the nuns asked.

"I don't know," Maggie said.

"If we lift you to your feet, you could lean on us."

"I'll try . . ."

Very gently, they helped her up and then, when she put her weight on her foot, she let out a string of expletives.

Lily bit her lip, waiting for the nuns' reaction.

"All right, Maggie," the nun said, making no comment on the language. "I think that's obviously too painful. We'd be best off carrying you."

"I'll give you a hand," Dara said.

"Thanks, but we have our own way of working with her," the nun said. "And she's not heavy."

Between them they lifted her out to the toilet.

"Maggie is some case," Dara said. "But she's lucky. She has a certain amount of independence and the nuns look after her well."

"I couldn't believe it when she cursed at them."

He shrugged and smiled. "I'm afraid the Irish are known for their colourful language and even the nuns are used to it."

Lily smiled back at him, thinking that not only was he a kind, friendly fellow, he was also very good-looking with lovely hair. She wondered if he had a girlfriend, and thought he was bound to have.

When the nuns and Maggie came back out, they said they thought they should take her to the casualty department in Tullamore Hospital to get her ankle checked out.

They thanked Dara and Lily and prompted Maggie to do the same.

"Lily is from Edinburgh," Maggie said. "But she's never met Sister Teresa." Dara explained about how the Scottish girl came to be helping him, and the nuns offered her a lift in the car back to the bed and breakfast.

"It's in the opposite direction. You go on with Maggie," Dara told them, "and I'll see Lily back home when I've closed the hall up."

Lily waited until the car took off and then she said, "I'll be all right walking back."

"I'll come with you," he told her. "It's after twelve o'clock now. I'll only be a few minutes switching the lights off and locking the place up."

"It's not dangerous or anything here, is it?"

"No, but you can never be sure." He looked straight at her. "Do you have a boyfriend back home?"

Lily caught her breath. He had been wondering the same thing about her. "Why do you ask?"

"Because I wouldn't want to get into trouble with him if I left you on your own."

She put the collar of her coat up. "Well, you're all right, because I don't have one at the minute . . ."

"Well, if you were my girlfriend, I wouldn't be letting you walk home on your own late at night."

Lily laughed now. "Okay, I won't argue any more because we're only going to be standing here all night."

"I won't be a minute," he said, heading into the auditorium.

Lily thought that if it had been earlier in the night she might have asked him to have a look around the cinema. She would love to have seen the film reels and be shown how the projector worked. If she asked him now it might look as though she was trying to spend more time with him.

For all she knew, he had a girlfriend who might be wondering where he was. She felt a small pang at the thought, then she chided herself. She wasn't going to be as silly as Declan.

There was no point in getting notions about someone who lived so far away.

She was busy enough going between Scotland and Newcastle; she didn't need any further complications in her life.

6

When Dara came back down the stairs, he went into the ticket office to collect his coat and things.

As they walked out through the foyer to the front door, Lily's eyes were drawn to his striped university scarf. "Are you a student?" she asked.

"I am. UCD, studying architecture."

"I should have guessed with your interest in buildings, but I thought you worked in the cinema full time."

"I work a couple of evenings and at the weekends." He let Lily out first and she waited on the steps while he locked the heavy wooden door. "Half the family work here. My aunt is usually in the ticket office and the shop, and myself and my brothers work the projector, or help in the shop when it's busy and show people to their seats and that kind of thing. My father is the caretaker."

"That's amazing," Lily said. "I never thought that a family could run a cinema. It's a great idea – very handy."

"Well, it means there's always someone there," he replied. "And it also means we get to see the new films first, although it was more of a novelty when we were younger."

"I would have loved it when I was a teenager. I couldn't imagine anything more exciting than working in a cinema."

"How about a chocolate factory?" he said. "I always fancied that."

Lily laughed. "Well, I suppose that might just have had the edge on it."

They walked out into the silent street, their breath forming small clouds in the cold night air.

"What do you do?" he asked.

"I'm at teacher training college."

"In Scotland?"

"No, in Newcastle-upon-Tyne, just over the English border. I'm doing Primary teaching."

He studied her for a moment. "You don't look old enough or cross enough to be a teacher. Do you enjoy it?"

"Yes, I do, very much. I really like the children."

"I suppose it's hard enough work."

"The planning and the marking is the hardest part. A lot of it's easy enough if you enjoy the subjects and the projects you're teaching, and you get a good laugh with the kids most days."

"And how do you find living in England?"

"Great. The Geordies are very friendly people. It's a great city, and it's only a few hours from home on the train." She stepped sideways to avoid a break in the tarmac path and brushed up against him. She quickly moved away in case he thought she had done it deliberately. "I like college but I like to get back home whenever I can."

"I travel up and down on the train to Dublin most days," he told her. "But I often stay with friends who have flats there on the weekends I'm not in the cinema, and the odd night during the week. It depends on what's happening."

"Would you not like to stay in Dublin full time?" she asked.

"Yes, I would, and I was supposed to, but my mother died the summer before I started." He paused. "I didn't feel it was right to leave the rest of the family, especially my younger sister. They'd lost enough with her going."

Lily's throat tightened. "Oh, I'm sorry . . . That must have been very hard on you."

"Harder than anything I could ever have imagined."

She thought back to the jokes they had made earlier about funerals and knew that his sense of humour was a defence.

They walked in silence for a few moments and then she said, "You were very good with that woman earlier tonight."

"Maggie's a harmless soul. Films and the stars in them are all she talks about. She loves her nights at the pictures. She'd live there if she got the chance."

"It's a lovely old cinema," Lily said, "nice and cosy. And it's a cheery place to work. You're lucky. I work in a baker's shop during the holidays."

"Are you doing that this summer?"

She rolled her eyes. "I hope not. The staff are nice and everything, but I'd like to do something more exciting. My older cousin is a cabaret singer on the cruise ships and she said she's going to look for something for me. I hope she does, otherwise it will probably be back to selling bread and pies at the baker's!"

"You sound as though you get about a lot, travelling to college in Newcastle, over to Ireland for holidays and planning foreign cruises."

"I wish I could travel a lot more," Lily said. "There are loads of places I'd like to visit – Paris, Rome, Florence. When I read about places in books or see them in films, I want go and see them for myself."

"It's the buildings for me," he said. "Hopefully, when I'm qualified I'll have the money to get out into the world more."

"Same here."

They walked at a relaxed pace, talking first about films and books and then music, and laughing every time they discovered they had things in common.

After a while Dara's pace slowed down and Lily recognised the driveway of the bed and breakfast.

"Oh, it's a lot closer than I remember," she said, with some surprise. "Thanks for walking me back."

"I enjoyed it. And I very much enjoyed talking to you . . ." He looked at her and then looked away. "When do you go back to Scotland?"

"Sunday," she said. "We have a few days after the funeral."

There was a pause, and for a few moments she thought he was going to suggest that they meet up again.

"Well," he said, "it was lovely meeting you, Lily." He put his hand out, and this time his eyes met hers. "And thanks again for helping me out with Maggie."

Lily felt a stab of disappointment as they shook hands. This was the second time in a week where she had read things wrong with men. And of course she knew that it would have been a pointless exercise as they lived too far away to keep a relationship up. But it would have been nice to have been given the option, instead of feeling rejected. Especially since they had found so many things in common.

As her indignant footsteps crunched up the driveway, she was aware of his heading off quickly in the opposite direction.

She passed the car they had hired and thought that her father and Seán were back. She hoped they had gone to bed which meant she could just go straight to her room, but when she pushed the heavy front door open she could hear muted laughter and chat coming from the lounge. As she walked along the carpeted hall, for a brief moment she considered sneaking past, but knew they would be waiting up for her. They wouldn't leave her out in a strange town without knowing she was safe.

She turned in the doorway to see her father and brothers sitting playing cards with Ava.

"Ah, here she is," Pat said, a light beery glaze in his eye, "Florence Nightingale herself! We heard all about the drama at the cinema."

She smiled. "Och, it wasn't that bad."

Ava put her cards down and went over to Lily, her face serious and concerned. "How is she? Did she come around okay?"

"She did, but it was her ankle that was the main problem," Lily explained. "She fell down the few steps, and she's hurt it. We don't know if it was twisted or broken. The nuns collected her and took her straight to casualty."

"There's always something," Pat said. "Just when you think

things are going well, something always happens. But it was good of you to stay and help the poor soul."

"Can I get you a cup of tea or a sandwich or anything?" Ava offered.

"No, thanks," Lily said. "It's late and I'm tired now."

"I could make you hot milk or cocoa to take to bed with you," Ava said, walking towards the door. "It would only take a few minutes and it might help you to sleep. You must be chilled after the walk back. I'll do you a hot-water bottle as well."

As a wave of weariness washed over her, Lily suddenly felt in need of the comfort offered. "Actually, I'll have a cup of cocoa if it's not too much trouble."

"No trouble at all," Ava said, smiling kindly. "If you come down into the kitchen with me, I'll give you the bottle to put in your bed now, while I'm making your drink." She opened the door and gestured to the corridor opposite. "The kitchen is just down at the bottom."

"That's great, thanks." Lily turned to her father and brothers. "What time do we need to leave in the morning?"

Pat thought for a few moments. "If we just go straight to the church, I'd say half nine would be fine."

"So, if we're up and ready for breakfast at half eight?"

"Fine," Pat said. "Ava said she'll have the breakfast on from eight o'clock."

Lily gave them a little goodnight wave and headed down to the kitchen.

"You were so good there tonight," Ava said, holding the neck of the pink rubber bottle under the boiler tap. "I felt bad leaving you, but I had to get back here."

"It was no problem." Lily put a hand to her mouth to stifle a yawn.

"Dara's a lovely fellow, isn't he?"

Lily nodded. "Yes, he seemed very nice . . ."

Ava looked at her as though waiting to hear more, and when there was only a short silence, she turned to find the top of the hot-water bottle.

When Lily came back up from her bedroom, the cup of cocoa was waiting for her on a small tray with two small coconut biscuits.

Ava's kindness struck Lily. It was over and above her job. "That's very good of you, Ava. I appreciate it."

"It's nothing at all. It's been a long day for you. Travelling over and then out at the church and everything tonight and then the cinema."

"I suppose it has," Lily said.

"Thank you for inviting me to the cinema with you and Declan. I don't get out that often, and I really enjoyed it."

"It was nice to have your company," Lily said.

Ava turned towards the darkened window. "You're very lucky . . . your father and brothers are lovely, so nice and welcoming. And from what I've heard them say, I can just imagine what your mother and other brothers are like. That's what I've missed growing up in the orphanage." She turned back.

"They've all been good inviting me over to Scotland, so I'm going to chat to Mrs Stewart about getting some time off."

Lily tried not to show her surprise. "Will you come in the summer?"

"Actually," Ava said, "I'm hoping to come over for Easter. Declan said he can take time off then and you would be home from college too."

"Lovely," Lily said, wondering what her mother would make of it.

7

Lily woke with a start. For a few moments she stared into the darkness, not knowing where she was. And then it came to her. She lay back on the pillow, her heart thudding. She had been dreaming. She sat up in the bed and switched the lamp on.

She had been dreaming that she was walking alone on a deserted beach. And then another figure had appeared in the distance. Somehow, she knew it was a man. They had walked towards each other and then the figure had suddenly disappeared. Lily could recall that she had turned around and the figure had appeared again in the distance. She started walking towards it again, and once again it disappeared. This time, when she turned around, she was face to face with Gerard René.

Although she knew it was a silly, obvious dream about not wanting to see him, muddled in with meeting Dara Ryan, it unsettled her.

She lay back on the pillow for a few minutes, and then reached for her watch to check the time. It was ten past three. Still a long way to go until morning. She put her watch back and then lifted a magazine to distract her racing mind. She flicked over pages of fashion and music and then made herself focus on an article about The Beatles.

Shortly afterwards she threw her magazine down on the floor and turned the lamp off. She lay straight in the bed for a while, then tossed and turned, and eventually put the light on again.

She decided to go to the bathroom. She padded across the floor, opened the door quietly and went down the corridor. When she returned a few minutes later, she was just closing her bedroom door when she heard the murmur of voices in the reception area. She listened and recognised one voice as Ava's. The other was a man's. She looked back along the corridor towards reception and Ava came into view. Then she caught a glimpse of a man with his arms wrapped around her. He whirled her around and, as they moved out of sight again, she thought she heard a Scottish accent.

God, she thought, Declan isn't half taking this little holiday romance seriously.

They moved into her view again, with Declan's back to her, and she noticed that he had changed his shirt. The plain blue one with the chocolate stain had now been replaced with a patterned shirt in blue and green. It crossed her mind that it was an unusually modern style for Declan, who was the most conservative of her brothers. It wasn't the sort of shirt that he would buy for himself, nor, she imagined, the sort her mother would pick. She deduced it was probably a Christmas present he'd got from their fashion-conscious sister-in-law Eileen. The boys often took the mickey out of Seán about the loud clothes she bought him.

Not wishing to witness anything more intimate, she quickly closed her door. She read for another ten minutes and eventually fell into a deep, dreamless sleep.

When she woke to the sound of her father tapping on her door to say breakfast was in fifteen minutes, she moved out of bed and down to the bathroom for a quick bath. As she lay back in the hot water for a few minutes, she began to feel back to her old self. It was a surprisingly sunny day for January and she was going to make the most of it. Dara Ryan was already fading from her mind. She couldn't even remember what he looked like apart from his long hair.

She would put on her good black fitted dress with the three-quarter sleeves and the matching coat with the fur collar that her mother had insisted on. She would go to church and join in with the prayers and singing and do everything that was expected of her.

* * *

The funeral mass and the burial at the cemetery and then the meal back in a small hotel on the outskirts of Carraigvale all passed in a seemly but busy haze. As the day wore on and the elderly people drifted off home, the crowd moved out to the public bar, where there the subdued mood gradually lifted and an almost celebratory feeling took over. Lily met and spoke to so many people that she found herself being introduced to some people several times.

She enjoyed the first few drinks she was bought but when she began to feel the effects, she asked for glasses of red lemonade. Declan came to her at one point to say he was getting a taxi back to the bed and breakfast if she wanted to come with him. He said she might be better going soon because, just in case she hadn't noticed, their father was knocking back the pints. He also reminded her, however, that if she did go back to Carraigvale she would be on her own for the rest of the evening as he was taking Ava out for a meal. Lily thanked him but said she would stay a while longer. There was no point, she thought, in being stuck in the lounge with Mrs Stewart or maybe even one of the commercial travellers.

She went to check on her father but before she got the chance to corner him, Bridget's husband, Martin Kennedy, was over to her asking what she wanted to drink. She waved away the offer saying she had two drinks waiting back at the table with the girls. She chatted to Martin for a while, keeping one eye on her father, who she noted was talking in the halting way he did when drunk, and gesturing with his hands.

When she got the opportunity, she pulled him to the side. "I think you've had enough to drink."

He looked at her with wide, surprised eyes. "Sure, I've only had a couple of pints. What's the harm in that?"

"You've had more than a couple," she told him.

"I'm only keeping up with the other lads," he said. "It's the tradition to have a few . . ." He paused. "I'm only enjoying the chat and the bit of craic."

"It's a funeral, not a wedding."

"Ah, don't be giving out to me," he said, shaking his head. "You're sounding like your mother now!" He nodded to himself.

"I'd have thought twice about you coming if I'd known you were going to be so critical."

"I'm not criticising you," Lily said. "I'm only looking after you." Although she was really annoyed with him now, she knew this wasn't the time or place to have an argument with him. She took a deep breath and then squeezed his hand to show she wasn't falling out with him. "Just take it a wee bit easier, that's all I'm saying."

She went back to the table where her cousins were. Various people came to speak to her and when they went someone else quickly appeared. A local lad came over to introduce himself, and within minutes he was asking her to go to the cinema the following night. She could see he was nice in an old-fashioned way, but she declined as he definitely was not her type. And if he had been, the last place she would have gone with him would have been the cinema.

Shortly afterwards, a good-looking, small curly-haired fellow – definitely the worst for wear – came over to ask her to go to his brother's wedding in Kildare on Saturday with him.

"A *wedding*?" she repeated incredulously.

"Ah, sure I know it's short notice," he explained, "but the girl I was going to bring along is just a neighbour. She knows well that I only asked her because there was nobody else."

Lily gasped – half amused and half shocked. "I can't believe the cheek of you. That's a dreadful insult to any girl."

"Ah, don't be giving out to me," he said, holding on to the table to steady himself. "I can tell just by looking at you that you're a lovely girl."

Lily was now trying to keep a straight face. "But you don't even know me! We might not get on."

"Aren't you lovely-looking with the same curly hair as myself? And you have a lovely smiling face." He staggered back. "And wouldn't the wedding give us time to get to know one another? We'd have the whole day."

Lily looked at him. The state he was in after a few hours' drinking, she could just imagine what he would be like after a whole day.

Just then her cousin Marie appeared, and when Lily laughingly explained the situation to her, her face tightened and she took the fellow by the elbow off to a quiet corner.

She came back a few minutes later. "The nerve of that Frankie Doherty," she said to Lily. "He's been going out with Sinéad Lynch for the last few months." She leaned forward so no one else could hear. "Now it's well-known he's only making an eejit out of her, and has no serious intentions at all, but it would look fierce bad if he turned up at his brother's wedding with a total stranger on his arm." She shook her head. "Poor Sinéad has spent a fortune on an outfit for the day."

Lily could see the potentially explosive situation. "Well," she said, her face now suitably serious, "I wouldn't be interested in going anywhere with him even if he was single. She'll be lucky if he's sobered up by the time the wedding comes around."

"You have it in one," Marie said. "And imagine him carrying on like that at a funeral. Some people have no respect at all."

A sing-song began, and another while passed as a variety of singers – both good and bad – took their turn.

When Lily heard the overloud clapping she took little notice but when she heard some loud, overenthusiastic cheering her heart quickened. She craned her neck to look over to the corner where her father and Seán were, but she could only see the tops of their heads. When the next singer came on, her fears were confirmed when the loud shouts of encouragement started up again and she heard Pat's unmistakable Scottish accent.

It was time, she thought, for them all to head back to the bed and breakfast.

She excused herself from the group and made her way over to the men. Her father was engaged in conversation with three or four others and she knew by the dull heavy look on his face and the jerky mannerisms that he shouldn't be drinking any more. She managed to get Seán away from the group and whispered to him that they should be thinking of going back before her father made a show of himself.

"I was just thinking that myself," he said. "Give us another five minutes to finish our drinks. And before you say anything, I've already told him I'll drive. I've only had three or four pints and I know the road well enough."

By the time they got outside, Lily could see that her father was in one of the worse states she'd ever seen him in. If he wasn't flinging his arms around her and making halting statements about random, nonsensical subjects, he was staring off into the distance and muttering to himself.

Between them, she and Seán managed to get him into the passenger seat of the car while Lily sat in the back. Once settled in, Pat began his ramblings again, gesturing at houses they drove past and calling out names they had never heard of. A few times she caught the words 'my mother' and 'Helena Casey' and she knew he was thinking again about all the people he knew who had died.

And then he suddenly went quiet.

Lily leaned forward to tap his shoulder. "Dad?" she said. "Are you all right?"

"It's okay," Seán said. "He's asleep."

"Thank God!" Lily said, and heaved a sigh of relief.

Getting him out of the car at the bed and breakfast was another hurdle, and it was only when they got to the door, each taking an arm, that Lily remembered that it was Mrs Stewart on duty.

"Have you the front-door key?" Lily said to Seán, her heart thumping.

"Aye," he said, taking it out of the top pocket of his jacket and handing it to her. "You open the door and I'll hold him up."

Lily held her breath as they entered the hallway, her eyes darting from side to side. There was no sign of the landlady, so they quickly and quietly helped Pat stumble his way down the corridor and into his room. After closing the door behind them, they put him on the bed and Lily took his jacket off, unlaced his shoes and slid his socks off. He closed his eyes and was silent.

"You can do the shirt and trousers," she told her brother.

"Ah, I'll leave him for a while," Seán said.

"They're his good suit trousers and hard to press. They'll be ruined if you let him sleep in them."

"I'll sort him later," Seán said. He went to the door. "You keep an eye on him while I go to the bathroom."

Lily glanced around the room. "I hope he doesn't get sick. That's all we need ..." Her eyes lit on the plastic wastepaper bin. "Pass me the bin over, just in case."

"He'll be fine," Seán said, heading out of the door. "I've never seen him be sick with drink."

"There's always a first time," Lily said. "I've never had to carry him home before, and I'm not taking a chance while we're in this place tonight."

Seán closed the door behind him.

Lily viewed her father, lying dishevelled on the bed. "God almighty," she said aloud.

Pat suddenly shifted in the bed. "I'm grand," he said, moving into a semi-sitting position.

"You're anything but grand," she hissed, in a low tone that she knew sounded exactly like her mother's.

He turned to face her, his eyes glazed. "It's been a hard day . . . it's been . . . well . . . it's been one of the worst days."

"It's nearly over," she said

"It might not have happened . . ." he paused, ". . . if I hadn't left Ireland."

Lily sucked in her breath. "She was an old woman," she said, trying to keep her patience. "She would have died whether you were in Ireland or not."

"She wasn't old . . . not when I left and not when she died."

Lily's forehead creased. He was obviously starting his ramblings again.

"Go to sleep."

Pat was still turned towards his daughter, but his gaze was vague and wandering. "I told her I would come back. I wrote and told her I would come back . . ."

"It doesn't matter," Lily said. "Forget about it."

"But you don't understand!" He was shaking his head. "I was sending money home and I was saving a bit every week to come home. I always meant to come home . . ."

"That was good you sent money back." Lily had always known about the money Pat and his brothers sent back to help their parents in Ireland. "But things don't always turn out the way you think. And you've done well in Scotland."

He looked over to the window. "I never forgot her . . . I thought about her all the time."

Lily looked down at her hands, wishing this night was over.

"I wrote and told her I would come back." He was shaking his head again. "I can't remember now . . . It doesn't matter. But somebody told me that she was stepping out with somebody else. She was seen in Dublin arm in arm with another lad."

Lily was totally confused and frustrated now. "Who," she asked, folding her arms over her chest, "are you talking about? Are you saying my granny in Ireland was going out with another man?"

"Helena Casey," he told her.

Lily's throat tightened. Something told her she didn't want to hear any more. "Forget about it, Dad. Turn over now and go to sleep."

"She was the loveliest girl in Ballygrace . . ." His voice broke now. "I always thought I'd marry her . . . I always thought it."

She felt a hot rush in her face. "Dad, you're talking rubbish now. Stop it. If my mother could hear you!"

"You're my daughter . . . a grown woman now, Lily . . . things in life aren't always straightforward."

"I'm not listening to any more," she said, turning towards the door.

"When I met your mother I thought Helena was spoken for. We got together very quickly . . . and next thing I knew the oul' shotgun was over my head. Six months down the line we got married . . ."

Lily's hand came up to cover her mouth. Since she was a teenager, she had known her mother was cagey when talking about her wedding date. Eventually, she had worked out that her eldest brother, Michael, was born five months after her parents married. It was information she had put in a little box somewhere in her mind, to maybe discuss with her mother when she was older and married herself. To have it confirmed now by her father and framed in such a cold and loveless manner shocked her.

"I don't know why you're telling me this old rubbish," she snapped. "You've obviously had far too much to drink."

"But you don't understand . . ." He rubbed his hand over his face. "When Helena heard I'd got married she wrote to me. The lad in Dublin was only her cousin."

His voice was so low she could only just make out what he was saying.

"He was at the seminary. She was only up visiting him ..."

Tears slowly formed in Lily's eyes. Her father had just told her that he had never planned to marry her mother. That he had got stuck in Scotland with her and Michael and then with the rest of her brothers. He hadn't wanted any of them. He had been in love all these years with another woman.

How was she to deal with this knowledge now?

"Go to sleep and I'll see you in the morning, Dad."

Lily closed the door behind her.

She left her own bedroom door open until she heard Seán coming down the hallway and then went out to motion him into her bedroom.

Seán took one look at her face. "Are you all right?" he asked.

"No," she said, "I'm not . . . I've never seen my father in that state." She took in a big gulp of air. "And I've never heard him say such horrendous things before." She couldn't stop herself. "He said he never meant to marry my mother and that he was in love with another woman."

Seán's eyes widened in shock. "Jesus Christ!"

"Imagine him saying that!"

"He's drunk."

"Has he ever said anything like that to you?"

He looked away.

"Has he?"

There was a silence.

"He's never said it in so many words," Seán eventually muttered. "But a week before I got married to Eileen he asked me if I was a hundred per cent sure . . ."

Lily stared at him.

"He said that marrying the wrong woman was like serving a life sentence. That it was better to walk away before the wedding, no matter what kind of uproar it caused, than be stuck for the rest of your life." He looked up at the ceiling. "I've never forgotten what he said, and I wondered why he was so serious saying it." He shrugged. "I know he and my mother are not that gone on Eileen – that they think she's too bossy, and I know myself there are times when she is. But I always thought that what he said wasn't entirely to do with her."

"Well," Lily said, "now you know."

8

Lily lay looking at the ceiling for a long time during which the darkness in the room had turned to a watery early-morning light. Every time she thought of the events of last night, she felt something that was close to a stabbing pain in her heart.

Eventually, at half past eight, she decided that whether she was ready or not it was time to face her father. Quietly, she headed across the corridor to have a quick bath. She heard movements out in the corridor as she was drying herself and wrapping her curly hair in a towel, and presumed that Ava was busy about her duties.

Back in her room she dressed in her pale-blue jeans and a blue blouse with a grey sweater on top. At college she would have taken a few minutes to put on mascara and lipstick and some foundation to even out her freckles. But this morning she was not in the mood and didn't even put on her beads or earrings.

She gave her hair a last rough towelling, then brushed it out and left it to dry. Then, with a heavy heart, she went down to the dining-room.

There were three occupied tables. What looked like a family of five – a man and woman in their forties and three teenagers – sat at the biggest table in the centre and a lone businessman in a suit was in the top corner.

She gave them a smile and a "Good morning" as she passed

them on the way to the table in the far corner near one of the big bay windows.

Her father, looking fresh and hearty, beamed at her. "Here she is," he said, pulling a chair out for her. "The lovely Miss Grace!"

Lily sat down, then looked up at him, waiting for something to be said.

"I knocked on your door earlier but there was no answer, but then I heard the water running in your bathroom. I said to the lads here that you'll be washed away with the amount of baths you have."

"It's nice to be clean," Lily said, her voice terse.

"We've already ordered the full Irish breakfast," he handed her the menu, "and I told Mrs Stewart no doubt you would probably have the same. She's actually a very nice woman. I was up and about early this morning."

Lily looked at him, wondering how he could act as if nothing had happened the night before – and how he could seem so well.

"I walked down into the town for a newspaper and I met her on the way in," he went on. "She was full of chat, asking me all about Scotland, and saying how lucky we were to have such a beautiful city as Edinburgh so close. I told her that we have people from all over the world visiting it, especially the Americans."

Lily knew now that he was deliberately putting on a show of normality for her. He was talking for the sake of it, because he was usually scathing about all the tourists in Edinburgh, maintaining that Glasgow was a far friendlier, more down-to-earth city. She decided she wasn't going to let him off the hook, and merely raised her eyebrows instead of joining in the conversation.

She looked over at Declan. "How was your meal last night?"

"Great," he told her, and the glint in his eye said it all about Ava.

Lily guessed he knew nothing about last night's carry-on. Seán wasn't the kind to rock the boat. He probably hadn't even mentioned it to her father. She looked down at the menu. If her father was going to play the innocent about it all, then she would play along with it. Why should she take on her mother's role? He must remember some of what happened, and Seán would certainly remember it all.

A feeling of sadness and loss crept into her chest. Then, she felt her father's hand covering hers. She looked up at him and saw the regret in his eyes. She gave him a small smile. Enough to let him know that she wasn't going to spoil the rest of their time in Ireland. She would act her old self and let him do the worrying.

Ava and Mrs Stewart brought their breakfasts and, when the other guests had gone, Ava took off her apron and joined them for a cup of tea.

Lily was glad to have the friendly girl's chat as a distraction from her depressing thoughts. She noticed her lovely tight plum-coloured sweater and pink-and-blue crystal necklace and matching earrings, and wondered how a girl brought up in a convent had developed a taste for such classy clothes.

"Have you any plans for the day?" Ava asked, smiling at everyone. "It's lovely and sunny outside." She gave a wry smile. "Of course being Ireland it's cold, but still lovely."

Lily rolled her eyes. "Don't forget you're talking to people from Scotland," she said. "We know all about cold."

Everyone laughed.

"We haven't decided yet," Pat said, "but I think we'll have a break from Ballygrace – we've spent enough time there."

Declan leaned his elbows on the table and gazed at Ava. "Have you any ideas?"

"It depends on how far you want to travel," she said. "Athlone or Mullingar are nice places or, if you don't mind the journey, you can catch the train to Dublin or Galway."

Lily thought for a moment. She didn't fancy spending the whole day with her father. She looked at Ava. "I don't suppose you have the day off?"

"Not the whole day. I have two o'clock until six o'clock off, but it wouldn't be worth going further than Tullamore for that length of time."

"We could kill time around the place until two, couldn't we?" Declan said, looking at the others hopefully.

Pat ignored him and turned to Seán. "We might head over to Mullingar. I have a second cousin there, on my mother's side, that

I haven't seen for a while. He has a fine big farm with horses and everything, and his wife always gives us a good welcome."

Just then, Lily noticed Mrs Stewart coming into the dining-room. She stood for a moment and cleared her throat which made the others look up.

"Sorry for disturbing you, but you have a visitor," she said, looking directly at Lily.

"Me?" Lily asked, her brow deepening. Marie, she thought, she must have decided to take the chance to have a look around the bed and breakfast.

Then she noticed Dara Ryan standing in the doorway, in a short black coat with his long hair tucked under his university scarf.

"It's the lad from the picture hall," Declan said. "I wonder if something has happened with the woman who took the fit."

For a moment Lily didn't know quite what to do, then she realised if she didn't move to meet him he would have to walk over and speak with them all at the table.

She got to her feet. "I won't be a minute . . ." As she went towards the hallway, she remembered that she had no make-up or jewellery on. It was too late – there was nothing she could do about it.

He had walked across the hallway, to stand by the outside door. He came to meet her. "Sorry for catching you at your breakfast . . ."

Lilly stared at him. "You wanted to see me?"

"I need to talk to you . . . to explain."

"Explain what?" she asked.

"Why I let you go the other night without saying anything." He gently took her arm and guided her through the door to stand at the bottom of the steps outside, where no one could hear them. "You must have known that I'd want to see you again."

Lily raised her eyebrows in question.

"It's just . . ." he said. "Well, it was complicated, but it's sorted out now."

She stood looking at him, her heart beating quickly. Afraid to say anything in case she picked him up wrong.

"Could we go for a walk? It's a bit early to do anything else . . . even to get a cup of tea. There's nowhere open until after ten."

"I don't feel like more tea," she said. "I've just finished my breakfast, but a walk would probably do me good. I've been constantly sitting for the last few days."

"Funerals are like that," he said. "A lot of sitting in houses and churches."

Lily glanced back at the big house. "I'll have to let my father know where I am."

She had gone up the steps when he said, "I've got to go to Dublin later. If you were free we could go this morning and have the day up there."

She halted, wondering if she had heard correctly. "*Dublin?*" she repeated.

"I have to take the cinema reels back and get the new ones. We do it every week as the films are changed every few days. I have my father's van." He looked uncertain now, unable to gauge her reaction. "I know a pub with a great jukebox, and we could maybe drive out to the sea."

She hesitated. Dublin was a good drive away. "I'm not sure . . ." She wondered what her father would say, and then she remembered last night again and suddenly didn't care what he thought. But she wasn't going to agree too quickly and look like she had been hoping Dara Ryan would come back. "Let me just check if there's anything planned."

As she walked back to the dining-room, Lily could feel her heart quickening. Apart from his obvious good looks, there was something about this curly-haired lad that she really liked. And whilst it seemed a bit pointless wasting time on someone she would never see again, it was better than spending a day trekking around a farm in Mullingar with her father who she could hardly bear look at.

When she looked in the door of the dining-room she could see there were only the two boys and Ava at the table, so she went down the hallway and tapped on her father's door. When he called to her to come in, she stuck her head around the door and quickly explained.

"You're going to Dublin with a lad you met at the cinema?" His brow wrinkled. "That's a bit odd, isn't it? I didn't hear you mentioning him."

"He's the one that we met the other night when the woman had the fit. He only works there part-time. He's studying architecture up in Dublin."

"Begod, he must be clever enough, so."

"I don't fancy the visit to the farm in Mullingar," she said in a flat but firm tone, "so a drive to Dublin will pass the day for me."

He looked at her and their eyes locked. His hand moved to nurse his chin. "I'm sorry about last night . . . I think I drank a bit too much."

She said nothing for a few moments then her eyes narrowed. "There is no thinking about it." Her voice was sharp and cold. "You were completely drunk and made a holy show of yourself."

"Oh, God!" he groaned, his hand sliding up to cover his face.

"And," Lily said, turning away, "I hope you're happy now, because you've made me doubt everything about our whole family life back in Scotland and any feelings you have for my mother and the rest of us."

"God almighty! I'm sorry." He couldn't look at her now. "It was nonsense . . . all down to the drink. She was only a woman I knew when I was young."

So he does remember, she thought bitterly. "I don't want to talk or even think about it." She went to the door. "I'll see you and the boys later."

9

Lily went back to her room to collect her coat and bag. Dara Ryan and a day up in Dublin, she decided, would be a welcome distraction from her thoughts about her father. She didn't really care what his reasons were for not seeing her before now, and she didn't mind what they did when they got to Dublin. Anything would be fine compared to the alternative of plodding around a farm, trying to keep her face fixed in a smile.

She was glad she had confronted her father, and took some comfort from the fact that he said his ramblings had been nonsense. She wanted to believe him, so that all the good memories and ideals she'd held about their family would still be true.

She studied herself in the wardrobe mirror and then reached for her make-up bag. It wouldn't take long to put on a bit of foundation, lipstick and mascara, and she knew he would wait. She busied herself with the make-up, then brushed her hair out into long loose spirals. A few minutes later she was heading back to the front door wearing her coat and shoulder bag. As she walked along, she fixed the clasp on her silver locket at the back of her neck and then took three thin silver bangles out of her pocket and pushed them over her hand to her wrist.

As she approached him, she could see his eyes moving from her head all the way down to her feet.

"You look really lovely," he said, as they strolled down the driveway together.

"Thanks . . ." She slid her bag down from her shoulder, and to cover her embarrassment pretended she was checking for her purse.

"I really like your hair."

She closed her bag and looked up at him. "That's funny, because I was just thinking that I really like yours!"

"Well, that's a good start," he said. "We can be the founding members of the Mutual Hair Admiration society."

They both laughed, and she knew she was going to have a good day with him.

As they walked along Lily remarked how quiet Carraigvale was at this time of the morning and told him that in either Rowanhill or Newcastle there would be people all around.

"It is quiet here," he said, "but I never noticed it until I started spending more time in Dublin."

As the cinema building came into view, Dara slowed down.

"I want to explain why I didn't see you until now."

"You don't owe me any explanations." She didn't want to give the impression she cared one way or the other.

"I had been seeing this girl," he said, "and I didn't think it was right to ask you out until I broke it off with her."

They were dawdling now, hardly walking.

"And did you?" she asked. "Did you break it off with her?"

"Last night. It was the first chance I got to see her as she lives out in Kildare."

Lily looked at him and his face was serious. "You didn't really break it off because of me, did you? You hardly know me."

"Well, you were definitely the deciding factor." He smiled at her. "I liked you from the minute I saw you standing in the queue in the cinema."

Lily needed to know more. "How long had you been going out?"

"Since last summer – about seven months." He sounded vague and uncomfortable talking about it.

"That's quite a while . . ." Lily had gone out with a local boy for nearly a year before going to college and, when she broke up

74

with him, everyone acted as though they had almost been married. Both their families had been upset, and Lily had been terrified of meeting his mother and sister for months afterwards. If the truth be told, she still felt awkward meeting them now.

"Seven months is a long time if you're seeing someone regularly, but not when you're only seeing each other every few weekends. It wasn't that serious, but still, I didn't think it was right to see you behind her back."

"So how did you tell her?"

"I drove up to see her last night. I could have phoned, but I thought I should do the decent thing and tell her face to face."

She was impressed with his need to do the right thing, but said nothing. "Was she upset?"

"A bit . . . but I had been straight with her all along. She knew I wasn't planning to settle down for a while. We'd had a big discussion about it at Christmas, but she wanted us to keep going out."

Lily felt intrigued. "Did your family know her?"

He hesitated as if it was something he hadn't thought of. "I suppose they met her a couple of times."

She bit her lip. There were a lot of questions she wanted to ask that would help her to know him better, but she knew it would seem nosey or odd.

"So," he said, "what about you?"

She shrugged and smiled. "What about me?"

"You told me the other night that you didn't have a boyfriend – is that true?" He halted and turned to face her.

She nodded. "Yes. I'm not going out with anyone just now." She didn't tell him that she hadn't been going out with anyone because she'd had a crush on the Seychellois history lecturer. She cringed now at the memory, and how naïve she had been.

"In that case, is it all right if I kiss you?"

Lily caught her breath. "Now? You want to kiss me here in the middle of the street in the middle of the morning?"

"Yes," he replied, moving to put his arms around her waist. "There's nobody around, and I've been wondering what it would be like to kiss you for the last two days." Then, when she didn't step away, he pulled her towards him and put his mouth firmly on hers.

For a few moments Lily didn't move, then she found herself swaying against him with her arms wrapped around his neck and her lips moving against his, and little ripples of excitement racing through her.

How long they would have stayed glued together she didn't know if a loud wolf-whistle hadn't broken through their passion. She jerked her head away to see an older man across the road on a bicycle, laughing and winking at them.

"Howya, Jimmy!" Dara called, and waved over to him.

"Early for it!" Jimmy called back.

"Never too early," Dara laughed back.

When the bike moved off, he turned to her and caught her hand.

"That was lovely," he said. "Even better than I had imagined."

"I'm glad you enjoyed it!" she said, laughing. She sorted her hair back in place and pushed her bag up on her shoulder. Her mind was absolutely whirling at the sudden speed of everything, and her stomach felt full of butterflies. She had felt something akin to this with other boyfriends but it had always started slowly.

He took her hand, then clasped it tightly as they walked towards the cinema. "That's the van there," he said, pointing with his free hand. "I've got the cinema reels in it and crisps and chocolate and drinks to keep us going until Dublin."

"I'm impressed – you're very organised," she told him.

"I was up early this morning, so I thought I might as well sort things out and save time now." He grinned sheepishly. "To be honest, I hardly slept. I was lying awake wondering whether you'd still be in the bed and breakfast and whether you'd already made any plans for the day. I was afraid if I didn't move early that you'd be gone."

"I almost was," she said. "If you hadn't turned up I'd be wandering around a farm in Mullingar."

"A fate," he laughed, "worse than death."

He opened the doors of the small white van and she climbed into the passenger seat. It was freezing inside, even though, Dara had informed her, he had poured a kettle of lukewarm water over the frosty windscreen and had run the engine for a good ten minutes to heat it up.

"It will be fine in a few minutes, when it gets going," he assured her. "It's got a good little heater."

Lily hugged her coat around her and tried not to shiver as he started up the engine and got the windscreen wipers going to remove the small lumps of melting ice.

"That's it," he said, his breath coming out in white clouds. "It's warming up now. We'll be grand and warm in a few minutes, like two little bugs in a rug."

There was something about the earnest look on his face that reminded her of her brothers when they were concentrating on something and she started to giggle, quietly at first, and then it gradually built up into a full-scale laugh.

He turned to her, a look of utter bemusement on his face. "What's so funny?"

"You," she said, shivering and shaking with laughter at the same time, "acting all chipper when it's like bloody Siberia in here!"

He raised his eyebrows in a mock-serious manner. "You have to think positive."

"Why? Will it help to melt the ice on the inside of the windows as well?"

"You're a real skit, aren't you?" He started laughing too, then turned around in his seat towards her and pulled her into his arms. "I can think of other ways to warm you up . . ."

"As long," she giggled, "as it doesn't involve taking off my coat and scarf."

He put a cold hand on either side of her face and looked straight into her eyes. "You are," he said, in a low and serious voice, "the most gorgeous girl, but it's not just your looks. I know it might sound strange and weird, but I knew there was something special about you since I first laid eyes on you."

Lily felt elated at him saying she was gorgeous. She knew she wasn't, but as long as he thought there was something attractive about her she was happy. "That's nice of you to say," she answered, "because you didn't escape my notice either . . ."

He looked at her for a few moments without saying anything, his face serious. "I know it's all very complicated with you being Scottish and at college in Newcastle," he continued, "but that doesn't mean we can't enjoy each other's company for the time we have now, does it?"

His words were like a sting. Was that all he wanted – a couple of days? She lowered her eyes, not wanting him to see the disappointment in her eyes.

"I know we've only really met," he went on, "but if we're still keen when you have to go back, we could visit and write. What do you think?"

She couldn't tell him that she suddenly felt much happier. "Yes . . ." she said, in a deliberately vague manner.

"I don't want to say too much in case it puts a jinx on things – but plenty of people manage to work through far worse things, don't they?"

For a moment she thought of making a funny remark about him jumping the gun a bit, but something stopped her. Something told her that, in spite of his modern clothes and Rolling-Stones hairstyle, he was a serious and genuine fellow and she might actually hurt his feelings. Instead, she just nodded.

Then, he bent his head closer to her and started kissing her again and all thoughts of being cold or being funny drifted away. After a few minutes, when his mouth became harder on hers and his tongue parted her lips, she realised that she could quite easily envisage them starting to take their clothes off in this freezing, damp little van, and she pulled back.

"Sorry!" he said, smiling and moving to arm's length. He jokingly tapped the back of one of his hands. "Enough!" He swung around in his seat to reach into the back of the van. "I've a surprise for you, something to keep us company on the journey to Dublin." He pulled out a small Pye transistor radio. "We keep it in the cinema, and I often bring it with me to pass the time when I'm driving." He rolled his eyes. "Niall, my older brother, will go mad when he realises it's missing. He's a big Country music fan and has it on the same stations all the time. When he's not around I switch it to the ones I want! He's always giving out to me."

"Brilliant!" Lily said. "It's like the one I have at home. What's it tuned into?"

"Luxemburg."

As they drove out through the small winding country roads, they chatted about music and discovered they both preferred the Rolling Stones to The Beatles, loved Bob Dylan and Simon and Garfunkle. They then went through the albums and discussed and compared favourite tracks. Dara told her about a record shop he knew off Grafton Street called Vic's, and said they might drop in there.

They had switched to talking about films by the time they hit the outskirts of Dublin and the better roads, and Lily pretended to take umbrage when he mocked her for liking *Seven Brides for Seven Brothers*. The conversation had moved to books by the time he parked the van on the quays just down from O'Connell Street.

As soon as they set off walking, he took her hand and held it tightly as they went along. Every so often Lily caught him looking at her, and he just smiled at her each time.

"Do you know Dublin at all?" he asked as they came towards the Ha'penny Bridge.

"Not really," Lily admitted. "I've been up a few times, but I just followed my cousins around the shops. They weren't great either – old-fashioned compared to the ones in Scotland and Newcastle."

"You didn't go to the right places," he told her. He lifted their joined hands and pointed over to the right of the bridge. "I know some good shops around what's called the Temple Bar area, that sell unusual second-hand American clothes and Indian beads and necklaces – you know, the hippie style that girls like. Well, the styles that a certain type of student girl might like."

She gave him a sidelong glance. "And how would you know what girls like?" She said it in a light and breezy manner, to cover up the tinge of jealousy which she suddenly felt.

"Because I have a younger sister who buys stuff there and so do some of the girls at university. And I take notice of things. I like things that are different." He squeezed her hand. "That's why I like you."

"You know all the right things to say," she said wryly, "but don't forget I have four brothers, so I have more than a fair idea of what guys are like too."

"Well," he said, "that must make us a very wise pair."

She gave him a playful dig in the ribs.

"Right," he told her. "You must be ready for a cup of tea or coffee?"

"Aye," she said, momentarily lapsing into her Scottish vernacular, "I mean *yes*."

"I like it, the Scottish words and accent."

"I've had to tone down the way I speak since going to college in England," she admitted. "I used to rattle on in my usual way, but then I discovered that neither the kids I was trying to teach nor the other students could understand me. A bit of a handicap when you're trying to explain things." She shrugged. "I've got used to going a bit slower now, although I often slip into my usual ways when I'm back home."

"You have a lovely, musical voice."

"I'm glad you think so, because I can't sing a note."

"I don't believe it," he teased. "You seem to do everything else so perfectly." They began to cross over the old cast-iron bridge.

"This is beautiful," Lily said, pulling him to a halt to examine the beautiful and sort of delicate construction properly.

"The people who had to pay a ha'penny to cross it when it was built in 1816 didn't think so," he told her.

"Really?"

"Yep, there used to be turnstiles at either end of it, so you couldn't cross it without paying. Apparently the builder was entitled to charge a ha'penny for a hundred years, and there was uproar when he increased it to a penny ha'penny. I don't know the exact details, but in 1919 the charges were completely abolished, and it's been free ever since."

She liked the easy and interesting way he explained things. He would, she thought, make an excellent secondary school teacher, although the long hair and the casual clothes would have to go.

"You've got a great memory for details," she told him. "I'm terrible at dates. I have to keep checking back, although history is my second subject at college and when I get into studying a particular period I find it really interesting, especially the social history." She laughed. "I became almost obsessed with Henry the Eighth and all his wives, especially Anne Boleyn. I even went on a weekend trip to London to see the Tower of London where she was beheaded."

"My God," he said in mock-horror. "I can see a macabre side to you coming out now that I would never have guessed. My course is beginning to sound a bit boring compared to yours. I'm studying all the buildings and constructions in Dublin this year."

"But that's interesting too," Lily said. "I thought all the old buildings in London were unbelievable, so old and still perfect, and I've always loved the ones in Edinburgh. There are some gorgeous old houses up by the castle, really unusual in colours like pale pink and green. I'd love to live in one of them."

"I'm very impressed you like architecture, not many girls do," he said in a mockingly high-handed tone. He put a finger to his chin. "So that's yet another thing we have in common. We'll be morphing into the same person if we're not careful."

"I wonder," Lily mused, taking on the same tone, "will my browny-blonde and your dark hair mingle together or will it be one side dark and one side light?"

"That," he said, "depends on which character dominates."

"You're completely daft," she said, shaking her head. "Everyone knows that women always dominate."

"Right, on a sensible note, I think we should start off at Bewleys café in Grafton Street, then we'll go down to Vic's."

When they arrived at the coffee shop, Lily reckoned that he had deliberately underplayed how lovely the place was to see her reaction. Then, satisfied with her response, he tucked her arm in his and gave her a guided tour of the café, pointing out the beautiful stained-glass windows, the Oriental features, the marble sculptures, the dark mahogany wood tables and chairs and the unusual architectural details that made it like no other café she had never been in.

As they walked upstairs to look around the other rooms, he told her that it had been a favourite haunt for some of Ireland's most famous literary and artistic figures like Patrick Kavanagh, Samuel Beckett and Seán O'Casey. James Joyce, he said, even mentioned the cafe in his book *Dubliners*.

She loved the picture he painted of all those well-known figures congregating in the exact café they were now standing in, although she felt she had to confess her ignorance. "I'm embarrassed to say that I haven't read any of their work. We studied Shakespeare and Dickens and Thomas Hardy, and before that we did some of the Scottish authors. We never got around to the Irish authors apart from a couple of Oscar Wilde's books."

He shrugged. "You can't study everything at school and college, but when you get time later you can always pick them up. I've read a good bit of Dickens and Hardy as well. My favourites are *Oliver Twist* and *The Mayor of Casterbridge*."

Lily held her clasped hands to her chest. "Oh, I cried at *The Mayor of Casterbridge* – I felt so sorry for him at the end."

Dara raised his eyebrows. "He was," he said in a dramatically censorious tone, "the author of his own misfortune."

"I know, I know," she said, emotional at the memory of it. "He did terrible things like selling his wife and child, and I don't know why but I still felt sorry for him."

He winked at her. "You obviously have a good and forgiving heart."

As they made their way back down the empty staircase, Lily was taken by surprise when Dara swept her up in a great hug and kissed her again. As her fingers tangled in his hair, she felt a surge of heat rush through her body that left her quite breathless. And as they stood wrapped in each other's arms, she suddenly wondered what would happen when the weekend came to a finish, and how she could go back to her normal life.

When footsteps and voices could be heard coming up the stairs they pulled apart and walked back down, trying to look all innocent as though nothing had happened. Then, as they waited to be shown to a table, he told her quietly that she was to pick anything she fancied.

"I'll pay half," she said. "It's only fair since we're both students."

"You will not," he said firmly. "I'm working part-time so it's not a problem." He smiled. "And even though I have the long hair and everything, I'm still a bit old-fashioned about things like that."

"Well," she said, thinking that he had scored another impressive point with her, "that's very good of you." For all she liked her boyfriends to be up to date with clothes and music, she still thought it important that they do all the gentlemanly things that she had been brought up to expect from all the males at home. Her father would think it sacrilegious if either she or her mother suggested paying for meals or drinks when they were out.

There was nothing worse, Lily thought, than a mean man. She had no problem about married couples pooling resources as time went on, as that was only natural, but at the beginning of a courtship she felt that it was the man's place to pay for things.

As she looked at the menu now, she became aware of the butterfly feeling in her stomach again, and by the time the waitress came to take their order, she felt so jittery that she thought she wouldn't manage to eat much. She knew it would be foolish to eat nothing so she scanned the menu for something small.

"I think," she whispered to Dara, "I ate too much at breakfast, so I'm just going to have a scone."

"Are you sure?" he checked. "I was thinking of having soup and a sandwich."

"A scone," Lily said to the waitress, "will be perfect."

And as she sat there watching the woman writing down the order, the word *perfect* echoed in her mind. This day, she thought, has been perfect. Being with Dara felt perfect.

When she thought back to the events of the previous night, she wondered at how things could change so dramatically in twenty-four hours.

She no longer felt the terrible anger with her father. It was already becoming a distant memory, clouded by his excuses and apologies this morning. By the time they got back home she might have almost forgotten it.

But the funny, intelligent, hugely attractive Dara Ryan was an entirely different matter.

How, Lily wondered, was she ever going to forget about him?

10

Pat Grace was exasperated. Lily, in an unpredictable and unusually distant mood, had disappeared this morning with a scruffy-looking long-haired beatnik, and now Declan was telling him that he had invited Ava to come to Mullingar with them.

"What, in the name of God, did you go asking her to come with us for?"

"Because," Declan said, his jaw obstinately jutted out, "I want to spend as much time with her as possible."

"Well, why don't you go off on your own with her?"

"Because we've already walked the legs off ourselves in Carraigvale and Ava fancies a wee trip to Mullingar. I want you to drop us off in the town and then come back and collect us."

"I'm not a taxi service," Pat said. "I might be one back home, but I'm not one here in Ireland."

"I'm only asking you to drop us into the town," Declan repeated. "I don't know what you're going on about taxis for."

Pat looked over at Seán who was sitting on the bed, keeping out of the argument, then back at Declan. "I hope you're not making a fool of yourself with that girl."

"How do you mean?" Declan's hackles were plainly rising.

"She's a lovely girl . . . too lovely . . ."

The unspoken words '*for you*' hung in the air.

"Believe it or not," Declan said, "she really likes me too. She told me. And, she's already looking into coming over to Scotland at Easter."

"Aye," Pat said, "if she doesn't meet anybody else between now and then."

"Aw, for God's sake!" Declan went over to stand by the window. "That's nice. Can you not think of something better to say? Is it that unusual that a lovely girl might like me? You wouldn't say that to Michael or Patrick or Seán. What's so odd about me?"

"Nobody said you were odd," Pat challenged.

"Nobody's saying anything like that," Seán suddenly interrupted. "He's just saying that she seems, well – the type who could get any man she wanted."

Declan put his hands on his hips, his face white and earnest. "She might be lovely-looking, but Ava has had a hard life. She's not looking for some fly-by-night playboy, even though she would only have to click her fingers to find one. She's looking for somebody ordinary and decent, to make up for the family she never had."

"And you reckon that's you?" Pat asked.

There was a pause.

"I don't know . . . it might be. We've just got to give it a chance."

"How are you going to keep it going when you're in Scotland and she's here?"

"There's such a thing as postage and telephone these days."

Pat took a deep breath. It wasn't often that Declan used a sarcastic tone.

"Right," he said, "we'll drop the pair of you off in Mullingar and then we'll head out to the farm. I don't know what Nora will say, because when I phoned her this morning I told her you were coming."

"I don't mind stopping off to say hello to them," Declan said.

"Tell you what, Dad," Seán said, "we'll go straight to the farm, Declan can see them and then he can take the car and go into town for a couple of hours." Before his father had a chance to argue, he added, "They won't mind if he doesn't stay. It's you they'll really want to see." He held his hands open, palms up. "There," he said, his voice sounding as though he was talking to one of his own young children, "that's it all sorted."

Pat looked from one to the other now, feeling completely defeated. He had been well and truly put in his place once again. Lily had done it already this morning, walking out with that Irish hippie or beatnik or whatever people called those long-haired lads, and now the normally docile Declan had done the exact same thing.

He had thought that escaping to Ireland for a week would give him a break from his dependable but demanding wife. A week where he could have a few drinks and walk down a few old memory lanes without having to answer to anyone. But, it seems, he had been mistaken.

And worse still, he suddenly felt old.

It seemed everything was about the young ones. This one getting married and that one having a baby and the other going off to university. The old ones – like his Auntie Mary – who were plain and simple and who had talked sense – were all gone. His cousins, he thought, at least were on the same wavelength as him. The men went one way and the women went the other. Everyone knew their place and how they should behave. But now, it was getting all mixed up. Declan was happier to go off shopping and sight-seeing in Mullingar like a Mary-Ann, while Lily was off living her own life in Newcastle. If she could go off to Dublin at the drop of a hat, he thought, God knows what she got up to at college. He dreaded to think.

God be with the good old days, he thought.

* * *

The conversation in the car was stilted to begin with, but Ava unwittingly hit on a subject that helped liven things up.

"The difference between Scottish soccer and Gaelic football?" Seán repeated, turning around in his seat to look into the back of the car.

"There's a mighty difference," Pat said. Since he was on a straight and empty road, he half-turned in his seat – one hand on the wheel

– to join in with the conversation. "The Gaelic football is far rougher, they have fifteen players and the points are different, but the main difference is they can handle the ball."

"I wouldn't say it too loud while we're in Ireland," Seán said, "but I definitely prefer our own soccer. There's nothing to beat a good old Celtic and Rangers match."

"Ah, well . . ." Pat's voice trailed off, as he turned his attention back to the road ahead. "I don't think you've had a chance to really compare them. You've only heard the odd Gaelic match on the radio and seen one or two games over the years. It's a far more exciting, physical match altogether. I know where I'd be every Saturday afternoon if they played the Irish games in Rowanhill." He turned around again, smiling and holding his thumb up to Ava.

"Maybe –" Seán said. Then, he turned around and saw a tractor slowly pulling out just a few yards in front of them. "Jesus, Daddy!" he yelled, leaning over his father and pushing the steering wheel to the right.

Pat, stunned into a shocked silence, reacted quickly and managed to steer the car onto the opposite side of the road. Amidst screams and shouts from the passengers he then tried to straighten up, but they had gone too far and the car bumped its way up onto a high ditch before coming to a shuddering halt.

"What the hell was that all about?" Declan said, thumping his fist on the back of his father's seat. "You nearly killed us all!" Fear and shock made him speak without monitoring his words.

Pat whirled around, unused to being challenged so openly by one of his sons. Lily was a different matter. Girls got away with much more, and she somehow managed to put a humorous touch to her criticisms.

"It was the bloody tractor – it came out of nowhere!" he said.

Seán cut him off. "No! Don't try to wriggle out of this one." His face was white and his eyes blazing. "If you'd been watching the bloody road it wouldn't have happened. Declan's right, we could have all been killed."

"Calm down now, we're fine." Pat's trembling legs belied his words. "These things happen."

Now he had support, Declan wasn't letting go. Being the youngest, he was the one taken least notice of and it irked him at times. "You wouldn't be saying that if it was one of us driving your precious coaches or taxis. You're the one that's always telling us we drive too fast."

"I wasn't driving fucking fast!" Pat roared now. "It was the bloody oul' tractor's fault for pulling out on us."

"You weren't looking!" Declan couldn't stop himself. "What if there had been something coming on the opposite side of the road? It would have been a head-on. We'd all have been killed for sure." He suddenly remembered Ava. He turned to look at her and saw she had her face buried in her hands. "Are you all right?"

She nodded, then said in her usual quiet way. "I'm grand, thanks." Then, when she felt him stroking her back, she took her hands down. "But I'd be much better if you all stopped arguing."

There was a sudden silence.

"Is everyone else okay?" she asked, leaning forward to touch a hand on Pat and Seán's shoulders.

"Aye," Pat said, and then the other two echoed him.

"Well, thank God for that, and thank God the car is okay too," she said, in a calm, quiet tone. "So we should be grateful." She turned back to pat Declan's hand. "It was a pure accident, one of those things that just happens. Your father was driving perfectly until the very second the tractor pulled out, *and*," she emphasised, "Seán's quick reaction and then your father's good steering made sure none of us were hurt."

"Exactly!" Pat said. He sank back in the driver's seat, his arms crossed.

"So we'd all be best to forget it now," she said, "and let us carry on and enjoy the trip to Mullingar."

"True enough," Declan said, squeezing her hand.

"Aye, you're right, Ava," Seán said, nodding his head.

All three men stared at the road ahead now, each one grateful for the girl's intervention and secretly thinking what an asset she would be to the family.

11

The car bumped its way up the long stone-littered driveway.

"I'm sure this is the place," Pat said, looking first at the field on his right and then the one on his left.

"If this isn't the right one," Declan said, "then you'll have to drop me and Ava straight into Mullingar, otherwise it won't be worth our while going. She's got to be back to work for six."

"It's only two o'clock!"

"I know, but it took us over an hour finding this place and we'll obviously need to allow time for getting lost again on the way back!"

The previous tension descended on the car again.

"We'll be fine," Ava said reassuringly.

"I won't bother coming in," Declan said. "We'll just get going. I'll see them when we come back." He made eyes at Ava to agree with him, but she just looked out of the window.

"Suit yourself," his father replied. "Seán and me will be just fine on our own." After a few wrong turns and a few wrong bumpy laneways, Pat was wishing he had never mentioned visiting his cousins in Mullingar. He wondered why he had bothered now, as they had never made the effort to even write to him in Scotland, never mind visit. He should have gone back out to Ballygrace today, where he would have had a warm welcome from his cousin Bridget.

The car came to a halt at the side of the house.

"I'd put a hundred pounds on this being the right house," Pat said, getting out of the driver's seat. "Yes, two-storey farmhouse with outbuildings behind. This has got to be the place. But – I'll just go and check to be sure to be sure."

As he walked to the front door, Declan tapped Seán on the shoulder. "The description he just gave would fit all the other houses we stopped at."

"Don't I know?"

"Well, there's no point in me getting into the driver's seat until we know for definite we're at the right house."

"The way things have gone so far today," Seán replied in a droll voice, "I wouldn't be surprised if the door opens and a hoard of fucking leprechauns come leaping out of the house."

"At this stage," Declan said, "neither would I!"

Seán looked back at him and they both started to roar with laughter. Then one would stop, and the other would start laughing harder again until tears were streaming down their faces.

"Oh, don't!" Ava said, laughing along with them too.

"Oh, where's my hanky?" Seán said, rooting in his trouser pocket. He wiped his eyes and then he pointed over to the door where Pat was still standing, with his hands behind his back like a schoolboy. "D'you see the vague look on his face? He hasn't the foggiest notion where he is. If by any chance we are at the right house, they're probably all inside hiding from him."

They all started laughing again.

"Here he comes," Declan said, reaching his arm out to Seán. "Give me that hanky before he sees the state of me and thinks I've been crying."

"We'll all be crying," Seán guffawed, "if we find out we've come all this way for nothing!"

Pat came towards the car, and just as he put his hand on the driver's door handle, a woman's voice called out from the side of the house.

"Pat? We're here! We're around the back."

Pat's face lit up. He turned back to the car and held his thumb up to let them know the good news, and then he walked to where the voice was coming from. Less than a minute later, he came running back from the side of the house with an agitated look on his face, beckoning them to follow him.

Declan looked at Ava. "We'll move into the front now and head off."

They all got out of the car.

"They need a hand over here, boys!" Pat called to them. "They're having a bit of trouble with the oul' bull. It's got out of the main field and it's stuck in the holding pen. There's only Nora and Joe there, and they're not fit to move it on their own."

Seán's eyes widened. "I'm not going near a bull. They're dangerous big things."

"Would you come on!" Pat demanded. "I've told them you'd help. It's only an oul' docile thing, Nora said it wouldn't hurt a fly." He pointed back. "She's out there petting it on the head. Get your coats off and come on."

"If I go in," Declan said, "me and Ava will never get away. We've been hours trying to find this flaming place and now you want me to go chasing a bull."

"Never mind that," Pat said, going red in the face now. "Just get yourself over here and give these poor people a hand!"

Declan stuck his head back in the car. "I won't be long," he told Ava. "And I'll buy you a nice bottle of scent to make up for the delay."

"Oh, Declan, that's very kind of you," Ava said, smiling warmly at him, "but there's really no need . . ."

"I want to do it," he told her.

"Come on!" Pat yelled again, gesturing wildly now.

"We'd better go before he bursts a blood vessel," Seán said.

He and Declan took their coats off and reluctantly followed their father, leaving Ava safely in the car.

When they got around to the back of the house, it was plain to see what the trouble was. The middle-aged couple were stuck in a ten-foot fenced area with the heavy white bull. It had a rope through its nose which Pat's cousin, Joe, was pulling on to guide the bull through the gate, while his wife Nora was unsuccessfully trying to push the huge animal from behind.

"Ah, lads, lads!" Joe Power called, completely out of puff. "Are we glad to see you? You've come just at the right time." He took his cap off and rubbed the bull's head affectionately with it. "I don't know what's got into poor oul' Billy today. He got himself into this pen and now we can't get him back out. He's usually so easygoing, but we can't get him to budge."

Pat introduced the two boys to his cousins, and they shook hands over the fence. He then went on to explain that Declan wouldn't be staying as he was going off into town with a friend who was waiting in the car outside.

"Oh, that's an awful pity," Nora said, looking at Declan. "I have a nice piece of ham all cooked with potatoes and cabbage. Surely ye can stop and have a bit to eat with us before you go?"

"I don't think we have time," Declan said lamely. "We're running late as it is . . ."

Pat's eyes widened in a warning to say nothing about getting lost or the near-miss on the journey over. He turned to smile at his cousins. "Don't worry about dinners or anything like that," he told them. "We only came to see you and Joe. Now, let me and the boys give you a hand with the oul' bull." He rolled his sweater sleeves up and gave a chuckle. "We might not come across too many bulls these days, but we're well used to pushing and pulling heavy cars all the time when the brakes stick, so between us all I'm sure we'll manage to move poor Billy. Isn't that right, lads?"

There was a silence and then Declan gave a reluctant, "Aye . . ."

Seán surveyed the muddy, dung-mixed-with-hay-laden pen with some apprehension. Apart from being wary of the bull, he was wondering how he would position himself in order to keep his decent clothes someway clean. Eileen had packed one sweater, a shirt for each day and a spare one, and two pairs of trousers. But he had only brought his good black shoes – having slid the other ones his wife left out under their bed – and had no other footwear to change into.

"You and Declan get around the back there, Seán," Pat commanded, "and I'll help to coax him at the front." He looked over at Joe and laughed. "Seán's not so keen on the bull, so I think we'd be better keeping him at the rear end." He shook his head. "When I think of all the cattle and bullocks and bulls we used to handle when we were half their age! They don't know they are born these days with the easy life they have."

"True for you," Joe said, smiling benignly over at the boys. "True for you, Pat. Sure, our own are the very same."

Seán threw his father a black look for showing him up in front of everyone.

Pat ignored him and went in through the gate at the far end of the pen to position himself at the front. Declan climbed over the fence and went in at the back of the bull, anxious to hurry the procedures up and get back to Ava.

Seán hesitated for a few moments, weighing things up, then before his father got the chance to make any further disparaging comments, he took a run at the fence and hopped over it to join his brother. Once in the pen, he hoisted his trousers up at the waist so the hems wouldn't trail in the muddy mess.

"Well done, lads," Pat said, in an encouraging tone. He turned to his cousin,

"We'll take over now, Nora. You have four strong men here, so you can leave oul' Billy here to us and head back to your nice warm kitchen."

"Are you sure?" Nora asked, glancing back at the boys.

"Are we sure?" Pat laughed. "Wasn't I brought up with bulls and cattle all me life?" He patted the docile Billy on the head. "It's like riding a bike, you never forget."

Nora went out of the gate and Pat looked at her husband.

"Now, Joe," he said, "you call the shots here. Tell us exactly which way you want us to move and we'll all follow."

Everyone suddenly became serious, listening intently as Joe instructed Pat to hold onto one end of the rope that ran through the bull's nose while he held the other. He then told the two lads to put their shoulders against the animal's rear end, and then push as hard as they could when he called the signal.

Seán went to move forward, but one of his feet was glued to the ground and when he looked down, he saw it was stuck in a lukewarm cowpat. He quickly eased his foot out of it, but the thought of having to clean his good shoes later suddenly made him want to heave. Then, when the animal let out a steaming spurt of urine which pooled around his and Declan's feet, he closed his eyes and wished he was anywhere but on this freezing, stinking farm.

"Are you ready, lads?" Pat called. "Joe's counting to three and we'll pull on Billy, then you give the most almighty push."

The first three goes were successful, as Billy was propelled several feet further towards the gate leading from the pen to the field.

"Keep him there, lads!" Joe called. "Pat will hold him at the front while I open the gates now and then we'll push him through."

"Well done, so far, boys! We'll make farmers out of ye yet." Although Pat sounded short of breath from the effort, his spirits were high with the excitement of it all. Many a happy evening he'd had with his Scottish friends back in the local pub, recounting boyhood memories of activities such as this. He would keep them well entertained with this particular event when he got back home.

The pulling and pushing continued for a few more minutes, and then, just as all seemed to be going well, the bull dug his hooves in and refused to move.

"Come on there, boys!" Pat yelled back to them. "Will ye push him harder?"

The bull suddenly let out a loud roar, startling everyone, then it threw its huge head in the air and pulled the rope out of the men's grip.

"Jesus!" Joe shouted. "Catch the rope now, Pat, or we're in trouble!"

The bull moved backwards, a hoof catching Seán sharply on the foot. Distracted with the pain, he lifted his weight off the bull and suddenly it swerved sideward, taking Declan along with it and throwing him against the fence.

"Grab him! Grab him!" Joe yelled.

Pat made another dive for the rope and, just as he pulled on it, the bull reared up causing Pat to skite in the watery mess and land on his backside. "The bastard!" he shouted as he attempted to get back on his feet, his hands grappling in the farmyard debris.

Then, as the end of the bull careered towards the two boys again, Seán decided he'd had enough. "C'mon, Declan!" he called, reaching a hand out to the top of the fence and starting to clamber up it to make his escape.

Declan went to follow him, but had only put his foot on the first wooden bar when the bull backed into him again, this time pinning him hard against the fence. Seeing his brother in distress, Seán instinctively leapt back down and with both hands pushed against the side of the beast, shouting at his father and Joe to keep on pulling.

But the bull wasn't to be moved.

Once, twice, three times Billy jerked against Declan with his heavy might.

Then, as the sound of the wooden fence cracking behind him could be heard, Declan let a scream of pain out before collapsing to the ground.

"It's gone mad!" Seán called, putting his shoulder to the side of the animal to steer it away from his brother. "Pull it back! Pull it back – before it tramples him to death!"

Pat and Joe dived forward again and pulled the rope with all their might, Joe making unintelligible noises as he tried to calm and soothe the bull. Then, Seán found a strength from somewhere and gave an almighty heave, pushing the animal a few steps forward and away from Declan, who was still lying groaning on the ground.

Then, just as quickly as he had erupted earlier, all the bull's energy and strength suddenly seemed to evaporate and he turned back into the old, docile Billy, allowing Pat and Joe to lead him by the nose into the field.

The men closed the gate on him and then ran back to the end of the pen where Seán was kneeling by his younger brother.

12

Lily and Dara spent an hour wandering around the indoor market, and Lily was delighted when she came across a pair of black PVC stretch boots. "Brilliant," she said. "The last time I saw this type of boot was just before Christmas and I couldn't afford them, what with having to buy presents and everything." She gave a delighted smile. "I got my student grant at the beginning of the month, and since I'm not totally skint yet I'm buying them!"

A short while later she came upon a stall that had the new-style cheesecloth smocks, and she bought a grey one which she thought would go well with jeans.

"I'm glad I brought you here," Dara said. "I had a feeling you might like it."

On they way out she stopped at another stall and she bought some long, dark grey beads to go with the smock, and an Irish headscarf with designs from the Book of Kells which she knew her mother would like.

They walked up to Vic's music shop and stood together looking through the racks, after a while separating to look at different sections. Then, while Lily was busy reading the back of a Kinks album, Dara came up behind her and put his hands over her eyes.

"I have a present for you," he said, putting a familiar square-shaped package in her hand.

When Lily opened her eyes she saw it was the Donovan album he had told her about earlier in the day. "Is this the one with 'Catch the Wind'?" she asked.

"Yes," he nodded, "but you'll enjoy all the other tracks as well. It's called *What's Bin Did and What's Bin Hid.*"

"I'm looking forward to listening to it." She folded her arms over the album, hugging it close to her.

"He's really good, although I don't think he's the British answer to Bob Dylan. I think they're quite different. Dylan is a one-off – out there on his own – but I think Donovan is very good in his own way."

She stood on her tiptoes and kissed him on the lips. "You shouldn't have, but thank you – it was really thoughtful."

"Now," he said, his face serious, "I'm giving it to you under one condition . . ."

"What?"

"That as soon as you've listened to it, you write me a big long letter telling me what you thought of each track."

"I will," she told him. "I promise." She had already pictured herself lying on her single bed in college with her record-player on the side of her desk, listening to it and thinking of Dara.

After their tour of Dublin city centre, he drove them to the depot to pick up the new films. Lily waited in the car until he and a lad helping him returned with the reels.

She turned to him when he got back in the driving seat. "What did you get for tonight?"

He held the reel to his chest. "Guess!"

She shrugged. "I haven't the faintest idea."

"I'll give you a clue. It's a fairly new cowboy film," he said. Then, he held his hand up and made a wiggling gesture. "Well, sort of cowboy. A mixture of cowboy and war."

"I don't think it's the sort of film I would really like."

"Ah, you would." He kissed her on the side of the head. "Sure there's women and everything in it. It's called *Shenandoah.*"

She raised her eyebrows and smiled. "I've never heard of it."

"You soon will," he said. "You'll get a chance to see it tonight or tomorrow night." Then, he caught himself. "That's if you don't have any other plans . . ."

Lily lowered her eyes so he wouldn't see the relief in them. She had been afraid that this might be the only time they would have together. Afraid that she might have said or done something today, something she was unaware of, that might have put him off her. Afraid that although he was still very attentive and taking her hand and kissing her every chance he got, that it was all an act.

"I'll have to see," she said thoughtfully, "when we get back to Carraigvale."

If any plans had already been made, she would do her best to un-arrange them. Having spent the most enjoyable day so far that she could ever remember, she didn't want it to end.

"Would you like to come to the cinema tonight?" His face suddenly grew serious. "Or am I being too forward or pushy with you?"

She looked up at him, and realised it wasn't fair to keep him guessing. "No, you're not being at all forward, and I'm pleased you want to see me."

"That's okay then," he said, grinning. "It's the type of film your father and brothers would like as well."

"I'm not bringing them with me," she said. "Can you just imagine it? Me and the three of them sitting in a row like crows on a fence."

Dara started to laugh. "I thought the Irish had some sayings but that would beat a few of them."

"Oh, the Scots have their own," she said lightly.

He looked at his watch. "We have a few more hours. Would you like a drive out to Malahide? It's a lovely seaside place. We have relations there, not that I'm going to visit them today or anything. I know it's not the time of year for sitting on the beach, but it's a nice place to have a look around."

"Fine," Lily said. "It sounds lovely."

When they arrived in Malahide, Dara parked the van on the road closest to the seashore, then they got out and walked down to it. Although it was cold, it was bright and the sea was calm. They walked along the damp sand, Lily's arm through his, then they sat on a bench, huddled close together to keep warm. They chatted about trivial things and he told her a bit about the village and its history and then for a while they sat in silence, staring out over the greyish-green wintry sea and watching the crashing waves.

When it became too cold to sit any longer, Dara pointed to an old building that stood at the head of the village. "That's the Grand Hotel – do you fancy a walk around the grounds?"

"Fine," Lily said. She loved the seaside village, and by now knew that whatever he suggested would be exactly the sort of thing she would like.

They walked around the hotel grounds, her arm through his, stopping occasionally to look through the big wide windows into the luxurious hotel.

"Would you ever like to stay in a place like that?" Dara asked her.

"I'd love to," Lily said. "But I could never imagine being able to afford it."

"Maybe," he said, "if we keep in touch . . ." His face grew earnest. "I don't know how to say it without sounding like a total eejit because we've only known each other a few days . . ."

Lily's heart lifted, but she said nothing. She just waited.

"Maybe if things work out with us for the future, we could come and stay here some time."

If, she thought, was a little word with a big meaning. And yet, at this moment in time, she couldn't imagine finding anyone else who was so similar to herself. She pulled his arm tighter to hers, and laid her head on his shoulder. "Who knows?" she said. "Maybe we will."

13

Declan lay on the sofa in the parlour of the farmhouse surrounded by a sea of concerned faces.

"I think," Nora said, her brow furrowed with guilt and anxiety, "it would be best to get him down to the hospital and get him checked over. We'd never forgive ourselves if it's anything serious. You could go to the one in Tullamore – it's nearer to where you're staying."

Nora felt bad enough that Pat and the lads had got their clothes and shoes all messed up – and she had helped clean them – but Declan's injuries were a more serious matter altogether.

"I'm fine," Declan said bravely, looking over at Ava. "I don't need to go to the hospital." Then, he closed his eyes as another wave of pain hit him. "I think it's my ribs."

"The aspirins will work soon," Ava said, touching a soothing hand to his forehead, "and you'll feel a good bit better."

"And wasn't it unbelievable how Seán suddenly got the strength to push the bull off?" Pat said. "The weight of him!"

Nora joined her hands together as though in prayer. "God works in strange ways."

"I came around the corner of the house just as it happened," Ava said, "and I was sure the bull was going to turn on Seán as well."

Seán looked both awkward and yet pleased at the same time

with the praise. "I suppose I was just lucky." He looked down to check Nora had got all the cattle muck off his shoes.

"No," Ava stated. "I think it was a very brave thing to do, especially since you were wary of bulls to start with. You often hear of people being killed by bulls."

Seán looked at her and gave a wink of appreciation, thinking it was nice to get praise from a woman for a change. Eileen rarely said anything nice about him.

"Or even a rogue cow," Nora said. "When they've just calved, some of them can be very dangerous."

Pat clapped a hand on Seán's shoulder. "You as good as saved your brother's life in there – and maybe saved me and Joe as well. It could have gone berserk and us all stuck in that small pen." His eyes widened. "It could easily have killed the lot of us."

"I still can't imagine," Joe said, glancing anxiously at his wife, "what got into oul' Billy." He gestured towards the door and the field beyond. "He's out there now as meek as a lamb."

It was agreed that they would give Declan until after they'd eaten their bacon and cabbage, and then if he was no better they would head into the hospital at Tullamore.

They started eating and just as they were almost finished Declan limped over to the table, his hand under his breastbone, and sat down. He ate a few forkfuls and then he started to cough.

"Ah, Jesus!" he said, pressing two hands to his ribs.

"I think," Nora stated gravely, "it's hospital for ye."

"We won't wait for tea," Pat told them, getting anxious now.

There were quick goodbyes all round and then Pat's cousins followed them out to the yard to wave them off, still apologising for the bull's behaviour.

"Don't be apologising," Pat said, getting into the car. "And thanks again for the lovely dinner. It was great to catch up with ye both again. You must come and visit us in Scotland some time – everyone would love to see ye."

"Did you notice," Pat said, as they drove away from the farm, "that there was no mention of getting rid of the bull or putting it down?"

"Do you think they should have?" Seán asked. "They said it was usually fine, like a tame pet."

"Tame, me arse! It's a dangerous big bastard of a thing!" He suddenly remembered Ava. "Sorry now for the language, but you can understand."

"Of course," Ava said, nodding in agreement.

"And don't forget," Pat added dramatically, "he was acting up before we even arrived. If we hadn't turned up it could have killed Joe and Nora stone dead."

"That's true . . ." Declan said in a weak voice. "I was lucky he only pinned me against the fence."

"And with his arse – it would have been a whole different matter if he had whirled around and caught you with his horns. You've seen what happens to matadors in the bull-ring." He suddenly stopped. "That's all I have to say."

"Do you not think they'll put him down?"

"Not – at – all." Pat's voice was scathing. "Sure, they'll never get rid of Billy, not unless he kills someone, that is, and I'll tell you why." He held his hand up and rubbed two fingers against his thumb. "Money. Pure and simple. For all Joe and Nora look as ordinary as you and me, money is their God."

"How do you know that?" Seán asked.

"Because I can tell."

"I thought you only met them a couple of times."

Pat gave his son a long look. "That's all it takes. You would know by the looks of them. They'll still have the first penny they ever made at the cattle mart."

*   *   *

The casualty department was busy and after sitting for a while in a row on hard chairs, they were told by an officious stout nurse that it could take several hours before Declan was seen by a doctor and then taken down to the X-ray department.

Declan looked at Ava. "You can't wait all that time, you'll be needed in work –" He broke off, holding his chest again.

"I don't like to leave you . . ."

"We won't be too long now," Pat said, folding his arms.

"But they said it could be a few hours," Declan said.

Pat pulled a face. "Never mind what Hattie Jacques says," he whispered. "That lovely young nurse I just spoke to says she'll do her best to get us seen to soon."

A short while later Declan was brought in to see the doctor and then he was taken off in a wheelchair by a cheery young porter to have his X-ray done.

Half an hour later they brought him back.

"Two cracked ribs," he said, holding out the X-ray folder. "But they said there was no damage to the lungs or anything like that."

"I had half an idea it would be that," Pat said solemnly.

"And you're not going to believe it – they want to keep me in overnight." He looked over at Ava and shook his head. "What a bliddey disaster and a waste of a day!"

Pat looked over at Seán. "You take the car and go on down to the bed and breakfast with Ava. I'll see to Declan."

"I'll drop her off and come back again so," Seán said.

Ava stood up and lifted her bag. She put her hand on Declan's shoulder. "I'm sure you'll be back first thing in the morning."

Declan carefully turned sideways to look up at her, but even that small movement caused a pain to shoot across his chest. He closed his eyes and nodded. It was just his luck, he thought, that just when he had met the girl of his dreams, something as ludicrous as being attacked by a bull would go and spoil it all.

As he watched the elegant Ava walk out of the casualty department with his brother, he made up his mind that he would do whatever he could to make up for the time he had lost.

He reckoned that the Irish girl was the one he had been waiting for, and he was determined that nothing was going to come between them.

14

Seán pulled the car up in front of the bed and breakfast just as the Angelus Bells started to strike in Carraigvale church.

"That's grand," Ava said, opening the passenger door. She swung her long legs out. "I'm dead on time. Thanks for the lift."

"It's not been much of a day out for you," he said, getting out. He stood leaning on the edge of his open door. "In fact, it's been a total disaster . . ."

"It doesn't matter," she said, smiling. "I enjoyed the drive over and all the company. It's nobody's fault what happened, and if it hadn't been for your bravery, it might have been a lot worse."

"Anybody would have done it – Declan would have done it for me."

"Your family are very nice – you are all so lucky to have each other."

"Aye, we're not bad," he said. "We have our ups and downs, but we get on most of the time."

She turned to leave, then paused. "Why don't you come in for a cup of tea? Mrs Stewart will be gone in a few minutes and I only really have to keep an eye on the desk and tidy up the kitchen and the lounge. We're quiet again tonight – the family that were here this morning have gone and there's just yourselves and Mr Flynn."

Seán hesitated.

Ava reached a hand out to touch his arm. "Please don't feel awkward about the other night. It was just one of those things that sometimes happens – and it won't happen again. Nobody will ever know."

"We took a chance," Seán said. "We were nearly caught."

"I'm sure your sister didn't see us because she's been nice and friendly to me since."

"She *definitely* didn't see us," he said. He thought back to the fuss Lily had made about his father's drunken ramblings. "Because Lily's not the sort to keep her mouth closed. I nearly died when I saw her out in the corridor at that time of the morning." He turned away to look out over the garden. "I've never done anything like that before, Ava . . . I don't want you to think I'm the kind of man that behaves badly when his wife is not around."

She moved close to him and put her finger to his lips. "I don't think anything of the sort." She lowered her eyes. "And I hope you don't think I'm the type of girl who goes after married men?"

"Of course I don't. You're an amazing girl. You make me wish I was single again."

She looked up and caught his gaze. "That's a lovely thing to say." Her eyes glistened a little. "It's just that when we were on our own the other night and I started talking about my childhood, I got upset. I feel so embarrassed about it now. I'm so sorry . . ."

"Don't be sorry," he told her. "It was lovely to talk to you." He gave a little sigh. "I wish Eileen, my wife, could talk as honestly as you do. All she talks about is decorating the house and about the piles of ironing she has to do." He shook his head. "You're so honest and open . . ."

"I feel bad about Declan. I'd die if he knew what happened between us. He's such a lovely lad."

Seán lifted his eyes heavenwards but said nothing.

"And it wasn't as if we did anything really terrible," she said softly. "We were sensible enough to stop before . . ."

Seán tried to stop the pictures of what they had done coming back into his head again. It had all happened so quickly – had escalated from that first kiss so amazingly fast. How such a virginal convent girl knew exactly what to do with her hands the first time she had ever touched a man astounded him. Those sorts of skills definitely hadn't come so naturally and easily to his wife, who often made him feel he was overly demanding in the bedroom department and was shocked if he suggested they vary things even slightly.

And although he certainly felt guilty about Eileen and Declan, there was a tiny part of him that felt no regret at all.

"We were sensible," Seán said. "And we can put it all behind us."

A noise came from the back of the house and they moved apart.

"Come in and have a cup of tea," she said. "You need to have something."

He looked at his watch. "I don't suppose they'll be expecting me at the hospital just yet, and I doubt if they would let two of us in with him anyway."

"I wouldn't think so. It will be a while yet by the time Declan is taken up to the ward and all the admittance business is gone through."

He looked at her again and thought it might be the last time they spent alone in each other's company. What harm could it do? "I might as well come in then. I could do with getting a wash and changing into a fresh shirt." He rolled his eyes and gave a shudder. "When I think of being up against that filthy big bull! To say nothing of the state of my shoes before I cleaned them!"

He closed the car door and they walked up the front steps.

"I thought you were wonderful."

"Oh, forget about that," Seán said, his tone slightly brisk. "You're making me all embarrassed." If the truth was told, he could listen to her saying the same thing again and again. He couldn't remember Eileen ever saying anything like that to him; she wouldn't want to make him big-headed. "Once I'm sorted, I wouldn't actually mind a cup of tea. It might help keep me awake."

"Are you tired?"

"A little bit – between the travelling and the late nights and the few drinks, I suppose it's all catching up on me."

"It's terrible," Ava's voice had a quiver in it, "that you all came over here – out of kindness – for a funeral, and this has happened. It makes me upset just thinking about it."

Seán reached his hand out and gently patted her arm. "Now, don't you be getting all worried about it. Declan will be fine, it's only a couple of cracked ribs. Fellows get injuries like that playing football and sports all the time."

"You're right. He will be fine." Her gaze moved to the glass on the door. "I must get moving now or Mrs Stewart will wonder where I am." She opened the door. "I'll leave you to have a rest for a while," she said in a low voice, "and then I'll knock on the door when the tea is ready."

Ava went straight to the kitchen while Seán went down towards his room. He used the bathroom first, having a quick strip-wash, and then he came back into the bedroom with his coat loosely buttoned and carrying his shirt. He took off the coat and threw it and the shirt on the single bed and then he lay down, bare-chested, on the double one he and Declan had been sharing.

He woke some time later when Ava came to the door.

"Aye?" he called, sitting up and trying to gather himself together. "Can I come in?"

He looked around the room, checking it was tidy enough. "Sure, sure," he said, running a hand through his hair in case it was sticking up.

Ava opened the door and came in. She looked flushed and flustered. "Oh, sorry!" she said, when she noticed he wasn't wearing a shirt.

"It's okay," he said. "I'm going to put on a clean shirt now." He lay back, holding his stomach muscles taut to show off the bit of body-building he did.

There was a silence as their eyes locked, during which Seán wondered what it would have been like to finish what they'd started the other night.

"Can I ask you a really big favour?"

"What is it? Do you need something lifted?"

Ava shook her head. "Would you go out to the reception desk . . . ?"

His brow wrinkled in confusion.

Her eyes darted towards the door. "There's a man there – well-dressed and quite a bit older than me – that I don't want to see." She put a hand to her mouth. "If he asks where I am, will you just tell him that I'm not here and that I've gone away for a few days?"

He got to his feet. "Is there something wrong? Are you afraid of him?"

She took a deep, shuddering breath. "It's all complicated . . . I know him from Dublin. He's driven down here a few times, but I don't want anything to do with him." The wavery note was back in her voice. "Thank God Mrs Stewart isn't here or I'd be in trouble."

He went to the wardrobe and took his shirt off the hanger. Ava watched him as he put it on.

She had said the man was well-dressed, so he would have to look decent himself to show some kind of authority. He buttoned it right up to the neck and then lifted his tie from the back of the chair. "Will he be awkward or anything? Will I have to sort him out?" He made his voice casual, as if he was used to sorting people out every day.

"No, no. I wouldn't think so. He was very polite to Mrs Stewart when he called last time."

Seán stifled a little sigh of relief. He made a tidy knot in his tie. "Has he been harassing you, like?"

A pained look crossed her face. "It's difficult to explain. If you wouldn't mind just saying that I'm not here and that I've gone away for a few days."

"Will he ask who I am?"

"Maybe if you say you're a friend of Mrs Stewart's filling in for me . . . something like that."

Seán nodded, thinking that he would have to handle this awkward situation well. After the bull incident, Ava obviously saw him as some sort of hero, and there was something strangely gratifying about that. Eileen, his wife, was a very competent girl with a razor-sharp tongue, and if she found herself being harassed by anyone, she would have gone rushing down the corridor to sort the nuisance out herself. Ava was a different kind of girl, he thought. There was something innocent and vulnerable about her.

He supposed she was bound to be, given her early tragic life. As he looked at her now, he also had to acknowledge that she was stunning. Where Eileen was definitely attractive and well-groomed, in a girl-next-door way, Ava was actually beautiful.

He had been approached by girls before – one ex-girlfriend in particular – but he had always been able to hold them at arm's length. But the other night with Ava was different, and they had been a whole sea away from Rowanhill. Between the few drinks he'd taken and the emotional late-night conversation, things had got a little out of hand between them. It was a one-off incident, and he had tried not to think too deeply about it.

He reminded himself again that he was a married man and, even if he wasn't, Ava was already tied in a way to Declan. But there was no denying that she was in a different league from any other girls he had ever met. And whilst he could only admire her from a very safe distance, he knew, as a matter of self-pride, he couldn't let her down now when she needed him.

Seán strode along the corridor, his shoulders back and his chin high. As he came to the desk he could see a man around his father's age with well-groomed thick grey hair, wearing an expensive navy winter coat over a dark pinstripe suit.

"Can I help you?" Seán asked. He wondered what a man of his age would want with a young girl like Ava.

The man's eyes narrowed. "I'm actually looking for Miss Lowry." His voice was low and well-spoken.

Seán held his hands out. "I'm sorry, but you've actually missed her. She's gone away for a few days."

"She's gone away?" he repeated in a sharp tone.

"I'm filling in for her while she's gone. Doing it as a favour for Mrs Stewart . . ."

"Indeed . . ." The man looked around him with narrowed eyes.

"Would you like me to take a message?" asked Seán.

The man turned away now, looking out towards the door without speaking.

"Who should I say was looking for her?"

The silence continued, then eventually the man turned back.

"Tell her William called. Tell her I was in the area and thought I'd check up on her. Tell her I'll call again."

"And that's William . . .?" Seán waited for his surname.

"She'll know," he said. "She'll know who it is all right."

15

Dara dropped Lily off at the bed and breakfast just before seven o'clock. "I'll be murdered by the brothers," he laughed, "disappearing with the van and the transistor all day."

"Are you going home first?" Lily asked.

"No," he said, "they'll be waiting for me down at the cinema, so I'll go straight there now and get this all set up as I'm on the projector tonight."

"At least you've eaten," she said. Then she laughed. "Lucky you did, because these Irish cinemas don't even have hot dogs or ice cream for sale!"

"Ah, don't," he said, shaking his head. "I'll have to come over to Scotland to see how it's done right. You never know, I might give up the architecture idea and set up a chain of cinemas all over the country."

They sat talking nonsense and laughing, both reluctant to let the day end.

Eventually, Dara looked at his watch. "I'd better go. So, will I see you down at the cinema later?"

"I'll have to see what's happening," She gestured towards the bed and breakfast. "My dad and the others must be here as the hired car's parked in the drive."

"Come down as soon as you can get away. It doesn't matter how late it is. My brothers will probably be there and Aunt Carmel will be in the ticket office. I'll tell her you'll be calling in and she'll show you where the projection room is."

"Should I buy a ticket?"

"Are you mad? You're coming to help me at work."

"How?"

"If you don't come I won't be able to concentrate. I'll be thinking about you all night. I might get the film reels all mixed up."

"Don't be daft." She thought for a moment. "I think I might be a bit self-conscious just walking in on my own and introducing myself in front of your brothers and aunt."

"By the time you come down, the film will probably have started, so there will only be my aunt in the ticket office and she'll be fine. "

Lily hesitated. "Did your other girlfriend come to the cinema to see you?"

There was a small pause. "Yes," he said. "Just once. Do you mind?"

She didn't like knowing that someone else had done the same things with him, but she was glad he had told her outright. "Have you brought a lot of other girls there?"

"No, and I'm glad you said 'your other girlfriend', because that sounds as if you're my girlfriend now."

She raised her eyebrows. "Am I?"

He moved quickly to take her in his arms. "You are," he said, looking deep into her eyes. "And the most beautiful girl I've ever seen."

"I really wish," Lily whispered, "that we didn't live so far away from each other."

The door of the house opened and they sprang apart.

"It's Seán," Lily said. "I wonder where he's going." She lifted her bag and shopping from the floor of the car. "I'll catch him before he goes." She gave Dara a quick kiss. "See you later."

Seán drew to a halt when he saw his sister.

"Well," she said, "how did the day in Mullingar go?" She

suddenly remembered all the trouble from the night before with her father, and felt a sinking sensation in her stomach. She was just going to say she hoped her father hadn't been drinking again today, when something about Seán's face made her pause.

"You're not going to believe what happened," he said. "Declan got crushed by a bull."

"You're joking!" She put her shopping bag down on the ground and waited for him to laugh and say he was only kidding, but he didn't.

"I wish I was. The big bastard pinned him up against a wooden fence."

Her hand flew to her mouth. "By – by the horns?"

"No, not by the horns, thank God. It backed into him several times. He's got two cracked ribs and he's in the hospital in Tullamore. It's lucky you came back when you did. I'm going there right now."

"I can't believe it! Poor Declan – is he all right?"

"Aye, he should be fine when the ribs heal. But he was in a bit of pain and was finding it hard to breathe. They're keeping him in overnight for observation."

"My God," Lily said, "did he get a terrible fright?"

"We all did." He took the car keys out of his pocket. "Are you okay to come with me now, or do you need to get something to eat?"

"No, I'm fine. I had something earlier on, and even if I hadn't I'm more bothered about seeing Declan." She lifted her shopping bag. "I'll just throw this in the boot."

*   *   *

When they arrived in the casualty department, there was no sign of her father or Declan. They went to the desk and were told they could go upstairs to the ward and see him for a few minutes.

A nurse showed them down the corridor to a room with eight patients. "He's in the bed with the curtains drawn," she told them. They waited outside the ward while she checked. She popped her head through the curtains and beckoned them to come in. The other men in the ward who were awake gave them a sign or a greeting as they passed.

"The Irish are so friendly," Seán said in a low voice. "It makes all the difference."

When they went in to see him, Declan, eyes closed, was lying back in the bed wearing pyjamas more suited to an elderly man, while Pat was sitting in a chair by the side of the bed reading *The Irish Independent*. He put it down on his lap when the curtain opened.

Lily looked at her brother and took a deep breath. "I can't leave you for five minutes and look what happens!"

Declan opened his eyes and gave a lopsided grin. "Can you believe it? A bliddey bull!" He pointed his finger at her. "Don't dare try to make me laugh, it kills me."

"Don't," her father repeated, winking over at her.

Lily moved her gaze away from him. She knew he was only trying to curry favour with her and she wasn't giving in that easily. She looked at Declan. "That's the last thing I would do, I'm just glad you're okay." She paused, her face serious. "Was it very sore?"

"Terrible," he said. "I thought it was going to kill me."

"A bull of all things – trust you!" Lily's gaze met her brother's.

"Don't – " He bit his lip and closed his eyes. Then, his shoulders started to shake. "I told you not to –"

"Ah, now," Pat's manner was grave, "don't be kidding around with him. He was told to keep quiet – any laughing or coughing might make it worse."

She looked alarmed. "I didn't do or say anything!"

Pat made a face at Seán and Lily. "The nurses gave him some strong painkillers, and said they would help him to sleep and it would give the ribs a chance to heal."

They were all silent and serious as they waited for the spasm to ease.

"I'm okay," Declan said, opening his eyes again, "but the tablets have definitely made me feel a bit tired . . ."

"Have a sleep now," Pat told him, "and you'll be grand when you wake up."

They were all quiet for a while until Declan dropped off.

Lily looked over at her father. "Is it okay," she mouthed, "if we stay?" She pointed to either side of the curtains. "Do you think the other patients will mind?"

Pat shrugged, then leaned across the bed, making sure he avoided touching Declan's legs. "I don't think so," he said in a low voice, "but I don't think there's a whole lot we can do here either."

They were all quiet for a while, just watching Declan as he slept.

Then Pat said to Lily quietly, "Did you hear about your brother being a hero?"

Lily looked blankly at him. "Declan?" she whispered.

"No, Seán," he said, pointing at him. "If it wasn't for him, we could all have been killed. He got right in behind the bull and gave him the greatest shove."

"Well done, Seán," Lily said, rubbing his arm. "But tell me, what on earth were you doing near a bull in the first place?"

Just after they had finished telling her the whole story, the nurse came back to check on Declan, and asked if they didn't mind leaving now, as the patients were going to have their last cup of tea.

"Can we come back in to see him in the morning?" Lily asked.

"After the doctor has done his rounds would be best," she suggested. "We'll know whether he's getting out then."

"You don't think," Pat said, "that he could be kept in?"

"I doubt it, but we need to be completely sure."

The nurse woke Declan and they all said goodnight to him, and told him they would see him in the morning when the doctor had done his rounds.

As they walked back to the car park, they all remarked on the sudden frost which had fallen while they were in the hospital.

"Have you any plans for tonight?" Lily asked them.

"We thought we would go for a couple of pints into Carraigvale," Seán said, "as we'll all be out in Ballygrace tomorrow night to say goodbye to everyone."

Lily stared coldly back at him to remind him about the previous night.

"We'll probably get something to eat in town too," Pat said.

"We've had nothing since early on this afternoon." He looked at her. "I'll treat you to a meal if you want to come." He saw her hesitate and knew she still wasn't letting things go. "We won't be long. I don't know about Seán, but I'm for an early night. All that country air has me knackered."

"I think I'll go on down to the cinema. I told Dara I would unless we had definite plans." She said it casually, not looking at either of them.

"You haven't wasted any time," Seán said, grinning at her. "You and Declan." He started to laugh. "The Irish must be desperate, waiting for people to come off the boat. You think they'd be able to find somebody a bit closer to hand!"

Pat gave him a nudge with his elbow. "Never mind mocking the Irish, you! Don't forget you're half-Irish yourself. And I'll tell you something for nothing: Declan would go a long way to meet a girl as nice as Ava in Scotland. An awful long way." He looked straight ahead. "And the young lad from the cinema looks nice enough, and wouldn't he look grand if he got a half-decent haircut, don't you think?"

Lily smiled in spite of herself. "I won't be very late, and if you're gone to bed I'll see you in the morning.

Pat put his arm around her now. "Look after yourself, won't you? After what happened to poor oul' Declan today, I wouldn't want anything happening to you. Not my only daughter."

She turned and looked him in the eye. "You don't need to worry. I'll be fine," she said, "honestly."

"Well, you're a grown woman now and you know your own mind. All I would say is just be careful."

Whatever doubts she had about her father's past, she knew how much he loved her – and always would.

16

Dara's aunt was busy refilling the stock at the shop from boxes full of chocolate bars and bags of crisps. When she saw Lily she smiled. "You must be the Scottish girl Dara told me about?"

"Yes," Lily said, feeling her face flush a little.

She put the boxes down and came to shake Lily's hand. "I'm Carmel," she said. "Dara's aunt. I'm delighted to meet you. He said you were studying to be a teacher."

"That's right." Lily smiled, wondering what else he had said about her. Whatever it was, his aunt looked happy about it. She wondered what the woman had thought of the other girl Dara had brought to meet her, and how she compared.

"He said you were over for the funeral out in Ballygrace."

"Yes, it was an aunt of my father's."

"Dara's father is my brother, and we're originally from Westmeath, so I don't know the families from this area too well."

Lily nodded. It was similar in the small villages back in Scotland.

Carmel looked thoughtful. "His mother was from one of the local villages around here originally, you know, and when she and Dara's father got married she moved out to Westmeath. When we lost her a couple of years ago, Jimmy took on the running of the cinema in Carraigvale so we all moved into the town here." She paused. "Did Dara tell you about his mother?"

"A little bit," Lily said.

"Losing her hit him hard. It hit all of the family hard. Dara's a good lad. He works hard and he looks after everyone. You wouldn't meet many lads who would travel up and back from Dublin every day to make sure the family are all right. His younger sister, Rose, took it especially bad." She suddenly stopped now as though she had said too much. She guided Lily across the foyer and pointed up the stairs. "If you go in the first doorway to your right, that's the projection room and Dara's in there."

Lily felt slightly alarmed, the projection room in a cinema always seemed like a very private, out-of-bounds place. "Will I disturb him in the middle of running the film?"

"Only if he's changing the reel, and he'll tell you the minute you walk in if he's doing that."

"Are you sure it's okay to go in?"

"Do you want me to take you there?"

"Thanks, if it's not too much trouble . . ."

Carmel put the boxes on the counter. "No trouble at all."

They went upstairs and when Carmel opened the door and Lily could see Dara sitting back in the projectionist's chair. His face lit up when he saw her.

"Thanks, Carmel," he mouthed to his aunt, and then he went to the back of the small room and lifted a chair over beside his for Lily..

As soon as the door closed, he leaned over to pull her close to him and then he kissed her.

"Is this okay?" she asked in an anxious whisper. "Can people see us or anything?"

He laughed softly. "Not at all." He spoke in a low voice too. He pointed to the window the projector worked through. "But they might hear us if we talk too loud at a quiet bit in the film." There was amusement in his eyes. "Did you think we might show up on the screen?"

"Well . . ." She felt silly now. "Maybe our shadows or something like that."

"No, no." His face grew serious. "I suppose it seems strange when you've never been in a projection room before. We've been used to it for years. I'll show you how it all works after the film."

She looked around her. "So what do you do in here?"

"Do you mean while the film's running?"

"Yes."

"I either watch it through here," he pointed to a small window adjacent to the one that the projector worked through, "or, if it's a film I'm not interested in, then I'll glance at a book for a bit." He pointed to a shelf at the side of his chair. "I've got to keep an eye on the film, because you have to change the reels every so often. There are six reels with this one, and we're on reel three at the moment." He looked up at the clock on the wall. "It will need changing again in about fifteen minutes." He looked at her. "I'm delighted you got away. I can't stop thinking about you."

"I'm the same."

He came close to kiss her again. "So, what have you been up to in the long drawn-out hours since I last saw you?"

"You won't believe it." She kept her voice low. "Declan, my brother, got attacked by a bull!"

He stared at her for a moment. "You mean gored? You're not serious?"

"Well, not exactly gored – but attacked, crushed by a bull at my dad's cousin's farm." She went on to explain the incident in detail as her father and brothers had reported to her. "He has two cracked ribs. I've been at the hospital in Tullamore for most of the time since I last saw you."

"Christ almighty! How long will he be in?"

"Just overnight, I think."

"He's lucky – his lungs could have been punctured, you know. There's nothing much they can do for the ribs except let them heal."

Lily nodded. "That's what they said."

"So," he put his head to the side, "there's no chance of you staying in Ireland a bit longer."

"I doubt it. They all have to get back to work and I have to get back to college." She pushed away the picture of Gerard René that came into her mind. It was more fleeting and less real than it had been before, as was the usual sinking feeling in her stomach when she thought of him.

When the time came, she watched with some fascination as he changed the reels over, switching from one projector to another. He did it with easy dexterity, ensuring that there was only a flicker of a gap between the film reels. When he finished, he came back to sit beside her, his arms around her. "Some people," he told her, "think when they see an obvious break in the film that it's been censored. It's actually only a badly joined reel or one with a flaw in it, but they're convinced a chunk with some forbidden content has been cut out."

"And has it?" she asked.

He laughed. "Not at all! Usually any cuts by the Film Censors are seamless – well, technically anyway – they can sometimes make the story a bit difficult to follow!" He leaned closer. "We've even had people complaining that we've cut them here in the projection room in Carraigvale. They've accused us of being censors."

"They must think you have great authority."

"Not as much as a cross schoolteacher," he whispered.

When the film ended there was the loud noise of the red velvet-covered chairs banging into place. A knock came on the door and then two lads Dara's age came in.

"Howya, Dara," one of them said. "We thought you might be here at the projector . . ."

He went to the door to chat to them and Lily could see them looking around him to catch a glimpse of her. She turned away, looking at Dara's book on old Irish buildings. She heard one of them say 'She's *Scottish*?' with some surprise, but she didn't lift her head.

When Dara came back in, he was grinning from ear to ear. "Two lads I'm friendly with. They spotted you at the break and they thought they'd come and have a gawk at you. You'll be glad to know they were mad jealous when they got a good look at you. They think you're gorgeous." He kissed her. "Which you are."

When all the cinema-goers had left, they walked out to the foyer to see that Carmel had closed the shop up and left.

"I need to check that everyone is gone from the toilets," Dara said. "Would you have a look in the ladies'? And I'll check the gents'."

Lily went and checked but everyone had gone.

When she came back out and told him so, he said, "No sign of poor oul' Maggie in there tonight?"

"No sign of her."

"Now," Dara said, "would you like the grand tour of the place while we have it to ourselves? And while it's still warm."

They started off in the main hall, and he held her hand while he told her all about the history of the cinema and how it had been a dance-hall previously, up until the 1950s. He described how it had looked before and the great expense that had been splashed out on it by the local owner, putting in the wine velvet-covered cinema seating and the red carpeting, and the blue velvet curtains that covered both walls. He showed her how the black curtains at either side of the projection screen could be moved to fit the width of each film, as they came in various sizes.

She observed him closely as she listened, and liked that he enjoyed talking about it so much. She liked his voice, which had a rich quality to it, and was impressed by how easily the right words came to him. And yet he wasn't pretentious, he picked the simplest, shortest words to explain things, and the best thing about him, she thought, was that he was actually interesting.

With other boyfriends, she had spent most of the time pretending to be interested, so as not to offend them or appear rude. Even with students on her own course, who had lots of things in common with her, she often found them to be bland or boring. And that, of course, had led her to focus on someone she found immensely interesting – but immensely out of bounds.

She realised now she found Dara much more on her wavelength than the older lecturer could ever possibly be. She also realised – after months of mooning after him – that she really knew nothing about Gerard at all. The attraction had been his physical appearance, his intelligence and the fact he came from an exotic, wider world.

She realised it was early days – *very* early days – but something told her she had now found all the things she had been looking for, in the boy beside her. The only problem, so far, was that they were separated by the Irish Sea.

He saw her looking thoughtful and paused. "Tell me if I'm being boring about all the cinema stuff, my family are always taking the mickey out of me for going on about things . . ."

She hugged his arm tight to her body. "You're not, I'm enjoying listening to you. Now, tell me, what about the big curtains at either side of the stage?" She pointed up to them. "Do they stay tied back all the time or do you close them sometimes?"

He led her by the hand up the stairs at the side of the stage, then he showed her how they operated from a switch.

Afterwards they went backstage and, as they were walking around, Lily heard a shuffling noise. That, he informed her, was probably the mice that they fought a constant battle with due to ignorant people throwing food – which they had sneaked in – on the floor. It was rare, he noted, that anyone threw sweets or chocolate they had bought from the shop on the floor. It always seemed to be stuff they had bought and hidden in their pockets.

"It sounded bigger than a mouse," she said, looking with great suspicion back to where she had heard the noise.

"It might well have been," he said, with a mischievous grin.

"What do you mean?"

"What I said. That it might well be bigger than a mouse."

"You don't mean . . . you don't mean a *rat*?"

He shrugged. "They've got to live somewhere and they're clever creatures – they know to gravitate where they might find food."

When Lily realised he was serious, she shrieked and ran back to the front of the stage and down the stairs.

"They don't come out when there's anyone here!" He followed her laughing as she ran up the aisle, glancing anxiously between the rows on both sides in case there were any signs of the invading rodents.

He caught up with her in the foyer, where she was standing facing the wall with her head in her hands.

"Are you okay?" he asked, putting his hands on her shoulders.

"No," she said in a muffled voice.

His face suddenly changed. "Oh, God, have I really frightened you?"

She whirled around and yelled, "No!" then collapsed into giggles. Then when he moved back, she said in a high voice, "Who got the fright now?"

He gathered her into his arms. "Thank God you're okay. I thought you were really upset."

"Well," she said, "I'm still not in love with the idea of the rats – or even the mice – but I don't think I'll let them come between us."

After taking her to have a look at the balcony upstairs, Dara locked up and they decided to walk into one of the pubs in town for a drink. As they passed the chipper opposite, Lily said the smell of the fish and chips was lovely.

"Not allowed from here," he said, ushering her past. "If you still want them when we reach the chipper near the pub we can stop then."

"I didn't even say I was hungry. But if I was, what's the problem with buying them here?"

"The problem is I'm banned. Actually, all our family are banned."

"So you're not allowed in?" she said in amazement. "Why?"

"They won't physically stop us going in, and they will actually serve us, but nobody behind the counter will speak and the food will be banged down in front of us."

"Why?"

"Well, I hate to bring it up again, but it's the rat situation."

She lightly pinched the back of his hand. "Explain it in plain, straightforward English, please."

He looked up at the dark sky. "They won't serve us because my father made a rule that no takeaways were allowed to be eaten in the hall because of the dropped chips and the mess it made on the floor and the stink of them . . ." he was trying not to laugh, "and . . . because of what it attracts. And the chipper owners were blazing, because they had a great trade going from people queuing for the cinema. Of course some people stopped buying them altogether then because they had to either eat them outside or dump them in the bin. It caused ructions between the chipper people and my father."

"Oh," Lily said, nodding, "I suppose it's possible to see both points of view, but I don't know any cinemas in Scotland that would let you eat fish and chips in them. And the people who want chips probably buy them on the way home anyway."

"That's exactly what my father said, but it didn't make any odds. That was last year and they're still ignoring us."

"I think your father could compromise . . ." .

"How?"

"Well," she said, "he could start selling hot dogs and then you'd be the same as the cinemas in Scotland!"

Dara shook his head. "You're mad."

She looked up at him. "All joking aside, you've got me worried now. People do throw all their rubbish and uneaten hot dogs on the floor – I'm now beginning to think that our local cinema might be teeming with rats too." She shuddered. "Ohhhh, you've ruined it for me by telling me that! I'll never relax in it again in case there's a mouse or a rat under my chair."

"Why," he said, "did I ever say anything?" He bent his head so his mouth was at her ear. "I won't mention the unmentionables any more, if you don't mention hot dogs!"

17

Later when they were settled in a corner of a small, almost empty pub, Lily was surprised when Dara asked her opinion on religion. She told him that she was Catholic and she usually went to Mass every week.

"Even at college?"

"Well . . . I miss the odd Sunday," she said, "because I'm often with friends who aren't Catholic and the church isn't near. It's not a Catholic college – much to my mother's disapproval."

"And how do you feel about religion in general?"

"I think everyone is entitled to their own religion, but it can be hard at times when you live in Scotland and people are either Catholic or Protestant. The bigotry is awful, as bad as the North of Ireland." She paused. "I do pray, but I think it's more important to listen to your conscience and try to help other people, rather than be running back and forward to church all the time."

He listened carefully to what she had to say, and she noticed that he looked more serious now than he had since they met.

"I think we're on the same track." His gaze moved away from her eyes. "I used to go to Mass every Sunday without fail, I never questioned anything. I thought if anything bad happened, I would always have my faith to help me through it. But when my mother died . . . I began to wonder what type of God would allow a mother to leave a family behind? When things started to go really wrong, I discovered that there was nothing there to help me, no matter how many hours I spent in the church and no matter how hard I prayed. There was still nothing there."

Lily covered his hand with hers, but she stayed silent, sensing how hard this was for him.

He looked at her now. "And it's been the same ever since. I've never felt the same about religion for the last two years."

"I can fully understand how that experience would affect your views," she said quietly. "Have you spoken to anyone about it?"

He nodded. "My father and the local priest – they both told me my faith would come back, but there's no sign of that happening yet. To be honest, I'm not that bothered. My thoughts on it might have gone that way without my mother passing away. I think, before I just believed without questioning things. I'd never had my faith put to the challenge. Now, I think you've got to rely on yourself to know the right thing to do."

"Do you ever go to church?" She suddenly thought of her mother and how she would react to bringing a boyfriend back who didn't go to church.

"If it's going to cause anybody else a problem then I go – and for special occasions like a funeral or christenings or First Communions. I also go some Sundays with Rose."

"And how would it be if you were visiting me in Scotland and my mother's the priest's housekeeper?"

"That," he said, smiling now, "would qualify as a special occasion."

They had another drink and as they walked back to the bed and breakfast Dara asked her what plans she had for the next day – the family's last day in Ireland. Lily told him it all depended on whether Declan was let out of hospital and how he felt after that. Probably, she thought, they would go back out to Ballygrace in the afternoon or evening – to say their goodbyes. They would go to Bridget's house and then visit the rest of their cousins who were staying in the cottage, and then it was likely they would end up in one of the local pubs for a final drink or two.

He told her he had arranged to work in the cinema in the afternoon for the children's Saturday matinee so he would have the night off to be available to see her. He had also asked to have the van in the evening in case she wanted to go out somewhere.

"I think," she said, "I'll be out visiting relatives with my dad and Seán and Declan in the afternoon."

"That's understandable." He paused. "Do you think you'll get away for a few hours for us to meet up? Or, if you can't, would they mind if I join you all later in the evening wherever you end up?"

She hesitated for a few moments, wondering if it was a good idea to introduce them all properly. What harm, she thought. If the romance came to nothing then they would quickly forget about him. If they kept in touch and he came to visit her, he would have already met them.

"No, I'm sure they wouldn't mind if you came. But it might be a bit boring for you."

"Nothing could be boring if *you're* there," he told her.

"That's nice," she said, giving him a little kiss. "I'll tell you what – I'll ring you when I know what's happening. If I can get away I will."

"I'd prefer that, as I don't really want to push in if it's all family."

"I wouldn't be surprised if Ava joins us – that's if Declan gets out of hospital," she mused. "She seems to have taken to him in a big way. It's funny, because I would never have imagined them as a pair."

"I wouldn't have thought it either," Dara said. "He seems young for her."

A puzzled look came on her face. "How do you mean? They're around the same age – in fact he's a year or two older than her."

Dara shrugged. "I didn't really mean anything. I don't know the girl at all, and I don't think many do in Carraigvale. She's been in the cinema a few times with different people, but she's not the sort you would have a big chat with. She just seems a serious type of girl who strikes me as being more at ease with older people."

"Do you mean Mrs Stewart?"

He started to laugh. "I don't really mean anything, forget that I said it. It's great that she and your brother are getting on so well." He paused. "Listen, Lily, why don't you call in for five minutes to my house tomorrow evening? I'd like you to meet my father and my sister, Rose, in particular. I'm going to be talking about you a lot, and I want them to know who you are."

Lily looked at him. "Will they not think we're mad? That we're making a big deal out of things? It's only been a few days." As she said it, she knew her voice and the way she said it had lacked conviction. She wanted him to persuade her otherwise.

"That's all it takes when you meet someone who is so like yourself." He said it so easily and was so self-assured. "It's like you know most things about them already. You don't have to waste time."

She leaned on his chest now. "It's complicated, with me in Newcastle most of the time and you here. We can't pretend it's not . . ."

"Come here," he said, pulling her into his arms again. "What's complicated about this?" And he kissed her with an intensity she had never felt before.

* * *

It was after midnight when Lily quietly let herself in the front door of the guest house. She was surprised to see a light still on in the lounge. Then, she could hear voices – and was sure one of them was Scottish. The voices were so low she thought she might have been mistaken about the accent, so she gave a quick glance as she went past the door. Then she came to a sudden halt.

She stood there, open-mouthed, staring at her older, married brother Seán – who was sitting on the sofa with his arms wrapped around Ava.

18

As Lily walked into the room they both looked up at her and then sprang apart. She closed the door after her so no one else could hear.

"What the hell's going on?" she demanded.

Seán got to his feet. "There's absolutely nothing going on – it's not how it looked."

"Well, it looked bad!" Her eyes were flaming. "You're a married man with children, and I don't think Eileen would take it too well if she walked in and saw you cuddling another woman!" She looked at Ava. "And neither would Declan. I can't believe it – carrying on like this, especially when he's in hospital."

Ava was holding a screwed-up hanky tightly in her hand. "Honestly," she said, her face looking as if she'd been crying, "we weren't doing anything!"

"I told you," Seán said. "You've got it wrong, Lily."

"Explain it then." Lily folded her arms tightly over her chest and waited.

Seán looked over at Ava. "She had a frightening experience just a short while ago. A man she doesn't like came into the bed and breakfast to see her and when she asked him to leave he wouldn't go. He was so belligerent I had to put him out on the street. I nearly had to call the cops."

Lily looked from one to the other, not sure what to make of it. "Who was he?"

Ava brought the hanky up to dab her eyes. "It's a man I know from Dublin . . . He's called down here a few times, and I've told him I don't want anything to do with him, but he won't take 'no' for an answer."

"Do you mean he fancies you?"

Ava rolled her eyes to the ceiling and said, "I suppose so."

"He's old enough to be her father," Seán said scathingly. "Imagine thinking a girl like Ava would even look at him!"

Ava lowered her head now but said nothing.

Lily looked at her and suddenly remembered that Dara had said she was the sort of girl that would be more suited to an older man. She wondered now if there had been more to his remark.

"He was here earlier this evening," Seán went on, "just before you arrived that time and we went to the hospital. Anyway, Ava told me about him then – she came running down to my room to ask me if I would tell him she wasn't there. I went down to the desk and told him that Ava was gone away and I was covering for her. I said I was a friend of Mrs Stewart's from Scotland. I was pleasant enough to him, so he wouldn't think otherwise. He didn't seem too happy but he went off in his car and we thought that was him gone."

Lily sat down in a vacant armchair. Her gaze moved from one to the other, not sure what to think. She was also aware that Ava was letting Seán do all the talking. "So, what happened then?"

"He obviously didn't believe me," Seán said, "and I didn't realise until it was too late that he actually knew Mrs Stewart, so he would probably know she didn't have a friend from Scotland staying."

"He must have gone down into the town, into one of the pubs," Ava said in a shaky voice. "I could smell the drink off him."

Lily turned to Seán. "Did my father get involved?"

Seán shook his head. "No, he had gone to bed. I just happened to be in the corridor – I was on my way up looking for a cup of tea and I recognised his voice. The minute he saw me he started saying that I was a liar and an impostor who, according to reliable information, didn't work in the bed and breakfast. I just told him that Ava didn't want to see him and he got so bad I had to tell him that if he didn't leave we'd call the police. I had to walk to the door and hold it open to make him go."

"I don't know what I would have done if I hadn't had somebody as strong as Seán here to deal with him." Ada bit her lip. "If it had been one of the commercial travellers it would have been very awkward."

Lily looked at Ava. "Have you phoned Mrs Stewart?"

She shook her head. "I don't want to involve her, because she knows him. It's very awkward because he helped me get the job down here."

"But if he causes you more trouble you'll have to tell her."

"She might not believe me," Ava said, lifting her hanky again. "And I don't want to be out of a job as there aren't too many places in Carraigvale or Tullamore."

"Do you think he'll come back again?" Lily asked.

Ava shrugged. "I don't know. He probably won't come back if he thinks that Seán is still here."

"Well, I don't think he'll stay away too long," said Lily. "He doesn't sound like the type to give up easily." She looked at Ava. "How long have you known him?"

"I suppose a few years . . . I used to work for them in Dublin. They have a bed and breakfast out in Ballsbridge, one of the expensive areas." She gestured around the room. "Not like this one, it's much bigger, like a hotel. They own a lot of other properties too."

"Is he married?"

Ava nodded, but didn't elaborate. "I have a feeling that Seán gave him a good fright threatening him with the Guards. I'd say he won't come back."

"He better not come back," Seán said, "and especially not while we're still here."

There was a pause.

"Would you like a cup of tea, Lily?" Ava asked, standing up.

"I'll take a cup of tea back to my room with me, if that's okay."

Lily knew the girl was hoping the awkward conversation was over. By slipping into her role of caring for them all – something she did very well – she was quietly putting everything back into place. Underscoring the fact to Lily that there was nothing more to be said.

Ava looked at Seán. "Would you like a last cup before you go to bed?"

"Aye, that would be great."

Lily noticed his eyes and voice had immediately softened, and she realised that – whether he knew it consciously or not – Seán was responding to the striking, dark-haired girl the way most males did. And it was obvious to Lily now, that Ava's old-fashioned – almost servile – attentiveness made them feel special. Even her father, she thought now, had had that same beguiled look in his eyes as Ava hovered around the table at breakfast checking everything was all right. Reassuring them that nothing they could ask for could be too much trouble.

And it struck her now that this attentiveness was received with a sense of disbelief at first – that they could be thought worthy of it – then gratitude that it set them out as being so special. And she knew that Seán – who was used to being bossed and harried by Eileen – had fallen for it too.

The men were fools, Lily suddenly thought, that they actually believed that Ava's fluttering around was because of some individual quality they possessed, and that only she – being unusually perceptive – had noticed. It hadn't dawned on them that she treated everyone – including women – in the exact same manner. She had seen it with the way Ava anticipated what Mrs Stewart was going to ask her to do – and was already moving in the direction she might need to go – before it was even made explicit. In the way she complimented Lily's hair and clothes and was happy to run and make tea or do anything else requested of her.

It could easily seem like a well thought-out plan to gain favour with people, and yet Lily wasn't sure that it was. There was something about the look in Ava's eye that made her think that her pleasantness might well be genuine, that she was an unusually generous and giving girl.

When Ava went out to the kitchen, Seán lit on his sister. "What did you think you were doing accusing us of getting up to all sorts?"

She viewed him with a cold eye. "What else was I to think? It looked really bad. Anybody would have thought the same thing."

"She was upset," he said. "She's a very sensitive girl."

"And Eileen," Lily reminded him, stabbing a finger for emphasis on the arm of her chair, "is a very sensitive wife!"

Seán walked towards the window, running a hand through his hair. "I don't need this," he said. "I was enjoying my few days' break here, even if it was for a funeral, and you're causing problems where there's none." He turned back to her. "Even the business with my father last night . . . you couldn't let that go either. He's not been himself all day, waiting to see if you were going to bring it up again."

"You know what he said." Lily's hand moved to the hollow at her throat. "I told you that he kept going on about being in love with another woman, and that he'd never have married my mother if he'd known the other woman was free."

"For Christ's sake, Lily, it was just the drink talking!" Seán said, his voice rising now. "Would you just let it all go? He was at a funeral and he drank too much, which in Ireland I would say is a common occurrence." He sucked his breath in. "We're only here for a few days and we don't need to feel every move we make or every word we say is being watched over and scrutinised. You're not the moral guardian of us all, you know!"

Lily was shocked into silence, and he still wasn't finished.

Seán narrowed his eyes. "And maybe I should remind you that there was nobody in the van with you this afternoon watching everything you did with the long-haired cinema guy, and there's nobody down in Newcastle watching every move you make there. You're the very lady that wouldn't take any questions or criticisms about it either."

Seán was the deepest and quietest of her brothers, and she'd never heard him voice such strong feelings before.

"It seems to be," he said, "that as far as you're concerned, there's one rule for you – and another rule for everyone else."

A jagged, silent tension filled the room.

It was one of the rare occasions in her life when Lily felt bereft of words.

She had never been spoken to in such a manner by any of her family. She was the one who was always quick off the mark with words, and, being the only girl in the family, and the youngest, she had always been allowed to.

In the silence it crossed her mind for a moment that he might just be right, making her, therefore, in the wrong.

Maybe, she considered now, she had jumped the gun a bit, but the situation had definitely looked bad, and something about Ava's too-good-to-be-true manner made her feel uneasy.

She looked at her brother now and decided there was no point in having a head-to-head argument while he was in this unusually defensive mood. But neither, she suddenly decided, was she going to completely capitulate and let him think he could speak to her as he liked.

"Well," she eventually said, "thank you for putting me well and truly in my place. Now I know how you feel about my concerns for your wife and family, I'll certainly keep my opinions and advice to myself." She looked over to the window. "That'll be the last time you need to worry about me saying anything to you."

Seán stared at her for a few moments, as though not quite sure how to proceed. On the one hand, his outspoken sister seemed to have taken his point on board, but, on the other, she was reminding him that she had criticised his behaviour in the best interests of his wife and family.

"I think," he said, his voice lower and without all the anger, "we should forget about it all now." He held his hand up. "I accept it might have looked bad but, now you've heard the reason, you can forget about it." He moved across the room to sit on the edge of the sofa next to her, lowering his voice further still. "And you can rest easy in the knowledge that both my father and myself are quite content with how things are back home, and neither one of us would be so stupid as to risk our families."

"I wasn't saying that," Lily argued, "but careless words and actions can tarnish things. I'll say no more tonight, but I'll tell you, it will take me a long time to forget what my father said."

Seán shrugged. "Be that as it may, I don't feel as strongly about it as you do, and I bet none of the other brothers would. Women and men have different ways of going on, and there are times when my mother drives us all to distraction – you included. I think it was a hundred per cent the beer talking. I don't think he even remembers half of what he said."

Lily turned her head away.

He moved from the sofa to get down on one knee beside her chair. "I don't want us to fall out, Lily, and I'm sorry if I blew up at you earlier. I know you only mean well." And when she turned to look at him with tear-rimmed eyes, he patted her hand and said, "I know you feel hurt and let down by him – but my advice is to treat it as a load of drunken rubbish and forget all about it."

They heard footsteps out in the corridor and Seán stood up, then Ava came in carrying a tray with tea and buttered toast.

"This will make us all feel better," she said, smiling at them.

19

The atmosphere over breakfast in the dining-room was light the following morning. Whether it was the sunny, frosty weather or the fact they were all determined to make the most of their final day, Lily didn't know, but she was happy to enjoy it.

"I had a great sleep last night," Pat stated, "and I definitely feel the better of it. I hope poor oul' Declan feels the same."

"I think he'll have been well looked after in the hospital," Lily said. "The nurses were all lovely."

Seán clapped his hands and rubbed them together. "So what's the plan for the morning?"

"A walk into the town to get a paper," Pat said, "and I might go mad and bet on a few horses. After that, I think we should drive into Tullamore and see what the story is with Declan. They said the doctors would be doing their rounds after eleven."

"Better leave it until closer to lunch-time so," said Seán. He turned to Lily. "And have you plans made with the long-haired student today?"

Lily looked down at her plate. "Maybe tonight. I thought we'd be visiting people today to say goodbye."

"And we will," Pat said. "But we just need to get Declan sorted first."

Lily looked out of the window now. "It looks lovely with the trees and bushes all white. I wonder if it's frosty back home and in Newcastle?"

"There's a more than fair chance it will be," Pat said. "The further north you go the colder it is."

Lily's gaze lingered on the white scene as she thought about her room and her friends back in Newcastle. Her room in the lovely old house with her desk and books, the view of the circular campus she had from the front door and of the playing fields at the back, the corner of the long teak desk she always sat at in the lecture room.

She thought of the Students' Union Bar and the great nights she'd had with her college friends, and the Saturdays spent shopping in the city. She liked Fenwick's department store, but she particularly loved the shops in the small backstreets like Pilgrims Lane which had a nice bookshop, a funny old sewing and knitting shop, Harrison's, and her favourite boutique, Love. Strangely enough, the girl who owned the shop and made most of the clothes, Sarah, came from Offaly. She must call in and tell her that she had been to her part of Ireland for a funeral.

Her thoughts then moved to tomorrow, when she would leave Ireland and Dara Ryan behind. How sad it was that they should be parted already, she thought, when she felt closer to him now than she had felt towards any other boyfriend. If she had known how hard this was going to be, she might have thought more carefully about spending the day in Dublin with him.

She felt something touch her hand and she suddenly jumped.

"Lily," her father said, "are you all right? You looked as if you were a million miles away."

She turned to him and smiled. "I'm fine, I was just thinking about college and all the things I have to do when I get back."

*　*　*

They took the morning easy, walking down to the shops for newspapers and a magazine for Lily, and then all three went into a pub and had two sweet hot toddies each while they chatted and read.

Then they went back for the car and drove out to the hospital. They found Declan all dressed and waiting for them in the ward. He had bandages strapped around his chest and had been given enough painkillers to keep him going until he saw his own doctor back home.

"Is that it?" Pat asked. "They didn't do anything else?"

"No," Declan said. "They said if I find the bandages too tight or uncomfortable or if they make it hard to breathe I can take them off. The doctor said, apart from putting ice on my ribs to reduce any swelling, it's just a case of letting them heal on their own."

"How do you feel?" Seán asked.

"As if I've been hit by a bull," Declan said, and then he closed his eyes to stop himself from laughing.

They drove out to Ballygrace to see Pat's cousins again. They sat chatting for a while, and the story of Declan and the bull was recounted in great detail which led on to a variety of stories involving incidents with bulls.

Bridget then insisted they all sit down for an early afternoon dinner of roast chicken. When Pat told them of their plans to go to one of the bars in the evening, she said she hoped they didn't mind if she wouldn't join them as she wasn't really a pub kind of woman and she was behind with ironing and various chores on account of the funeral.

Later they made their goodbyes then moved on to visit the relatives from England who were still at the auntie's cottage. After a couple of hours there, again recounting the story about the bull, they, along with some of the relations drifted on down to the local pub.

Marie and some of the girls had said they might call down later, so Lily found herself as one of only three women in the pub. At first she felt a bit self-conscious, but as the time went on, she didn't mind as the men and lads all included her in the conversation.

When it came to seven o'clock, Lily thought she had better phone Dara to let him know she was still in Ballygrace if he wanted to join them. When she asked her father if he knew where the nearest phone was, Declan cut in.

"I'm going to head out to Carraigvale in a taxi if you want to come with me."

He looked at Pat. "There's no point in her hanging about here with a bunch of men."

"It's up to yourself," her father said. "You've seen everyone really, so if you want to go and meet the young lad, then do."

When the taxi called for them, Pat had a quiet word with Lily and assured her that he was taking things a lot more slowly, and she needn't worry about him drinking too much that night. In fact, he said, he was deliberately drinking the small bottles of stout instead of pints.

"That's fine," Lily said. "I'll see you back in Carraigvale later."

When they got to the bed and breakfast, Ava let her use the phone and she called Dara. He was delighted she was back and asked if she would like to call up to the house and meet whoever was in, and then they would go into town to hear a band playing in one of the bigger pubs by the canal.

Lily told him she felt a bit shy coming up to the house on her own, so he said he would call for her and they'd walk up together.

They arranged a time and then Lily went off to have a bath and wash her hair.

As she lay in the comforting hot water, Lily realised she felt apprehensive about meeting Dara's family. She didn't know whether having only one female – his sister, Rose – to meet was better or worse. She tried to think how her brothers' girlfriends might have felt when they came for the first time to their house, and then she had a pang of guilt as she remembered giggling at one girl in particular. It was a girl that her other brother Patrick brought home and Lily could not remember now what had been so funny. Something trivial to do with her hair or something she was wearing. Lily knew now that it must have been awful for the girl – and more awful for Patrick who had gone mad at her later for her bad manners. She hoped Dara's sister was more mature than she had been at that age.

Her thoughts moved back to her own family again, and she wondered whether Ava had said anything to Declan about the unwelcome visitor from the previous night. Whether she had or not, Lily decided she wasn't going to interfere.

An hour or so later she went down to the lounge wearing the grey cheesecloth smock over a crimson miniskirt, black tights and the stretchy PVC boots she had also bought in Dublin. As she looked down at her legs, she kept wondering if they looked a bit too outlandish for the small town. As she approached the open door she was surprised to find that Dara was already there waiting for her in one of the armchairs and appeared to be totally relaxed chatting to Declan.

His face lit up when he saw her. "We're just saying that it's been a very eventful few days for your family."

Lily lifted her eyes to the ceiling. "You can say that again."

"It's been different," Declan said, giving a lop-sided grin. "A trip we won't easily forget."

When they were on their way up to Dara's Lily told him about the incident with the man who had called looking for Ava the night before.

"What was he like?" Dara asked.

Lily repeated the description that Seán had given.

He hesitated. "I didn't like to say anything before, but she was in the cinema one night with an older man who sounds exactly like that."

"That's why you mentioned about her liking older men, isn't it?"

"Well, I was reluctant to say anything because I don't know her well enough to make any judgements. For all I knew it might be her father or her uncle. I couldn't tell anything from the way they were with each other. She was always polite but distant any time she came to the cinema, and my aunt and my brothers all said the same thing."

"And you only saw her once in the cinema with the older man?"

"Yes . . ." He paused. "Although one of my brothers saw her in a car with him, and said he was sure they were arguing." He shrugged. "The other times I've seen her around is with Mrs Stewart or another girl who sometimes helps out in the bed and breakfast. I didn't want to tell you about the older man in case you thought I was making too much of it – as I say, he could be a relation."

"According to Ava he's definitely not," Lily said. "She said he's some man she used to work for who now seems to be obsessed with her. I don't know why she doesn't just sort him out or threaten him with the police. I know I wouldn't put up with it."

Dara laughed. "Everybody isn't as confident as you, Lily."

"Well, Ava doesn't strike me as lacking in confidence. She seems to have all the men in our family fighting her corner. And I think it was all a bit dramatic, crying in Seán's arms about it. I felt a bit uncomfortable the way she was acting as he's a married man." She looked at Dara and rolled her eyes. "I know it sounds as if I don't like her, but in a lot of ways I do. She's really nice and helpful and I'm sure if it works out she'll be a lovely girlfriend for Declan."

"I suppose that's the main thing."

"You're right," Lily said. "I'm not going to say anything more about it to Declan or Seán."

Dara's house was much bigger than Lily had expected, a tall old-style semi-detached house on three floors. It was only a few streets away from the cinema, tucked down a laneway. He told her that his Aunt Carmel, whom she had met at the cinema, owned the one next door.

"That's the way our family are," Lily said. "My aunt Sophie lives only a few houses up from us. They're not as big as yours though – only about half the size."

"Our last house wasn't as big," Dara said. "And I should warn you that this one is a bit dilapidated. My father's always saying he's going to do work on it but he never gets around to it. He did a lot more in the other house, when my mother was alive. I think he just doesn't have the heart for this house just yet."

"I suppose it takes time," Lily said.

"It does . . ."

Lily could see exactly what Dara had meant about the house. The hallway they arrived in seemed more suited to an old farmhouse than a town house. There was a big antique hallstand with a square marbled centre beneath an ornate but mottled mirror, and a dark wood panel on either side with coat hooks. It was over-burdened with coats and the marble top was dusty and cluttered with a mountain of mail and cinema tickets. Underneath it there was a collection of boots and shoes and wellingtons.

Lily immediately liked the old building and the lived-in feel of the house, but as they walked down a few steps into a big old rambling kitchen, sweet with the smell of baking, she knew her mother would have a heart-attack at the casual state of affairs. There was a family-sized pine table with a mixture of wooden chairs and stools around it, a tall cupboard with glass doors, and two white-painted dressers full of crockery. The surfaces were cluttered with ornaments and an assortment of random objects like scissors, maps and a home-made clay pot filled with pens and pencils

"Is there no one in?" Lily asked, looking around her. Then she noticed the worktop by the sink, with the round loaf of soda-bread which was cooling from the oven, and the dozen fruit scones which also looked newly baked.

Dara moved towards the hall. "I'll just give a shout upstairs."

Lily heard him calling, "Rose!" and then "Joe!"

A few seconds later she heard noises from upstairs and then footsteps coming down. A tallish, smiling fellow who looked a bit older than Dara came in and was introduced as Joe. Lily noticed that his hair was thick like Dara's, and even though it was quite a bit shorter, it seemed much more unruly. He shook Lily's hand so enthusiastically that she thought her fingers would be crushed to pieces.

"Lovely to meet you, Lily," he told her, his head nodding up and down.

He was just asking her which part of Scotland she came from when a small, slim girl with shiny black bobbed hair and a serious face came into the kitchen.

"Lily, this is Rose," Dara said. "She was upstairs studying as she has exams next week."

Lily smiled and went forward to shake the girl's hand. "Hello, Rose," she said. "I was just thinking you're the same as me, one girl living in a house full of brothers."

Rose's face brightened a little. "Are you an only girl too?"

Lily nodded, thinking the girl had lovely brown eyes like Dara's but that there was a sadness in them. "I am, and I'm the youngest as well. I bet your brothers don't drive you as mad as mine do." She was trying to keep things light. "They're always working on cars or my dad's coach and they're in and out of the house, leaving oily rags and fingerprints on everything."

Rose smiled properly now. "Oh, mine can be just as bad when they're doing work on the van." She glanced over at Dara, then she said, "Will you have a cup of tea? I baked some scones for you and my Auntie Carmel left in a fresh loaf of soda bread as well."

Lily put her bag and gloves down on the table. "That would be lovely," she said, surprised and delighted that the girl had made such an effort. "And so good of you to go to the trouble of baking. Can I give you a hand?"

"You could butter some bread if you don't mind."

"I'd like to make myself useful," Lily told her. "I'm used to it at home." She was about to say, 'My mother has me well-trained' when she just stopped herself in time.

She noticed Dara over by the window fiddling with a transistor radio, and when some low music came on, she knew he was trying to make things more relaxed for her.

Rose went over to the cupboard and brought out some side plates and a dish of butter. She put them down on the table beside Lily, then went and got a plate of sliced ham, some tomatoes and a jar of home-made strawberry jam.

They were sitting round the table drinking tea and Joe was telling Lily all about his day job in a local Veterinary Suppliers when the door opened and Dara's father, Jimmy, and his other brother, Frank, came in. They all, she noticed, had the exact same thick hair, although Frank's was the shortest of the brother's and a lighter brown and his father's was mainly grey.

They were equally as pleasant as Joe and when they were settled with their tea and bread and ham, they asked her about Scotland and she repeated all the information she had already given Joe and Rose. They asked her about Celtic and Rangers and Hamilton Academicals and she smiled and told them she didn't follow any

143

particular team herself but that her father and brothers were big Celtic fans.

She then explained all about the funeral they had come over for and told them about the Grace family's relations. Dara's father said he vaguely knew them and Joe and Frank said they thought they knew her cousin Marie and her boyfriend. She then told them about the area her mother came from in Galway and about that side of the family.

"Ah, sure you're Irish through and through," Jimmy Ryan said. "Even though you have that lovely Scottish accent."

Lily was helping Rose with the washing up at the sink when Dara said he was going to have a quick wash and change his shirt and would be ready to go out in five minutes.

When she had first arrived, she would have been anxious if he had left her on her own, but she now felt relaxed enough with his family to chat away without him.

"That fella will have himself washed away," Frank laughed. "If he's not in the bath, he's ironing shirts and even T-shirts. So much for the long-haired unwashed students!"

"I think Lily would prefer him like that to somebody who can't be bothered having a bath," Rose said.

"You're a hundred per cent right there," Lily said, and she was delighted when the girl laughed along with her.

"Sure I have a bath once a year whether I need it or not," Joe said and they all laughed.

As she dried the mugs and plates, Lily thought about Dara's family and it struck her that in many ways they were very like her own. The men were all very friendly and had that same initial over-respectful manner that her father and brothers had. The big difference, of course, was the fact they were missing a mother, and Lily instinctively knew that that was the reason for the quietness in Rose.

When they were sitting on their own, Lily asked Rose what she was going to do when she left school at the end of the year.

"I'm hoping to get into nursing," she said, "but I'm worried I won't get a place near home. My two best friends are planning to go over to Manchester. They have relations there." She made an anguished face. "But I don't feel brave enough to travel that far. I'd rather be at home if I could get a place in Tullamore Hospital."

"Is that the only one nearby?" Lily asked.

"No, there's Portlaoise General."

"Would that not suit you?"

She lowered her head. "It's next to the mental hospital and I don't think I'd like to work so close to it. I think I'd find it too upsetting."

Lily nodded. "Well, hopefully you'll get a place in Tullamore."

*　*　*

The Canal House was a big bustling bar, nicely furnished and well laid-out. It wasn't a dance night, but the band was good to listen to and they got chatting to a couple that Dara knew from school called Liam and Maura.

Other people came over to stand at their table and Dara introduced Lily to everyone, and she could tell by the way everyone greeted Dara so warmly that he was well thought of.

Later, as they walked back to the bed and breakfast, Dara turned to Lily.

"I have your address and college phone number," he said, "and you have my number at home and at the cinema."

She smiled. "Who will write first?"

"Me," he said. "I'll write tomorrow and it will get to you early in the week." He paused. "What time did you say you get back to college?"

"About five."

"I'll ring you after six," he told her, "when I get into the cinema." He laughed. "There's a chance my call won't be noticed on that bill as easily as the one at home."

"I'll miss you," she said.

He put his arm around her and hugged her close. "If we write and phone regularly the time will pass quickly until we meet up again."

20

As the almost empty coach rolled up the wide, curving drive of the college towards the main campus, Lily felt a little knot in her stomach – a mixture of apprehension and excitement. The familiarity of the wide curving fields that swirled around the college and the tall swishing trees, the circle of perfect grass with the flowery border and then the elegant houses, made her feel like she did when she first arrived.

As she made her way down the coach steps, bumping her case as she went, she felt the same air of possibility around the place. The feeling that drove her away from the stifling predictability of things back home.

Several students who were waiting to board the coach called out to her and asked if she'd had a good trip. She smiled and gestured to them and said it had been fine and she would catch up with them later.

She moved a safe distance from the crowd and then put her case down for a few moments to catch her breath and reacclimatise herself with the place that would continue to be her home for the next year and a half. Her gaze moved to the white patches of snowdrops on the lawn and then to the purple and yellow crocuses which now covered the small hillocks and the areas under the tall beeches.

The snowdrops were in their final flourish, some of them already flat to the ground and brown at the edges, while the crocuses were fresh, straight and new.

It struck her then that she had seen few flowers in Ireland. The bed and breakfast had been the only colourful garden she'd noticed.

Here, she was surrounded by them. The well-tended but naturally rambling grounds and the colourful flower-beds had caught her eye when she first arrived for her interview. She had also noted the respect the students had shown the place, walking around the groups of flowers and small hedges, and the friendly banter between them and the gardeners who tended them.

The thought of waking up in this beautiful setting daily – to wander from her living quarters to the state-of-the-art lecture rooms, the well-stocked library or the restaurants or bar – had given her the determination to secure a place.

The semi-formal interview with the course lecturers – which she had dreaded after the dour Scottish interviews – had been almost enjoyable. She had relaxed and allowed her natural affinity with children, her love of reading and her curiosity about the learning process to speak for her.

Within a few weeks an offer of a place at the college had come with the proviso she pass her English and History Higher Examinations at no less than a 'B' level.

Relieved they had been happy enough with her Maths at an 'O' Level grade, Lily had immediately knuckled down to her British and American history studies and her English course books. Over the next few months, any time she felt like throwing the books aside to go to a disco or for a day rambling around Edinburgh, she only had to picture the college and she was back with her nose in the relevant pages.

Eighteen months later, the novelty of being in such inspiring surroundings had only slightly dimmed.

She was sorry now, as she looked around the campus, that she hadn't properly explained all this to Dara. She knew he would have immediately understood – she knew he would love this place.

There had been so much to talk about and so little time to cover everything. If things worked out between them, she thought, they would have all the time in the world to talk.

Her gaze moved along the houses to the one where her room was – across the circular lawn – and she started walking towards it, carrying her case. She would write a long letter to Dara tonight, describing the place to him in detail so that he would get a complete picture of it – be able to imagine her in these surroundings. She would enclose one of the small college brochures which had pictures in it and would better explain certain things.

She had gone about twenty yards when she heard a male voice calling her name, and she turned to see one of the students from her history class coming across the lawn towards her.

"A wee lassie like you can't carry that big case," Bill Toft said, putting on a Scottish accent.

Lily laughed and dropped the case. He was a friendly Yorkshire chap – a bit gawky with studious, large circular glasses – who was always glad of a valid excuse to visit girls' blocks. He lifted the heavy case, made heavier with the addition of Scottish bread, pies, pancakes and Empire Biscuits – onto his shoulder.

"Thanks, Bill, that's good of you. I was struggling a bit."

"No problem. Have you been home?"

"Scotland then on to a funeral in Ireland. Any news since I've been away?"

He thought for a moment. "We had the big rugby match on Saturday and we slaughtered the opposition."

"I meant real news."

They both laughed.

"Not much," he said. When they got to the other side of the lawn, Bill put the case down and then carried it by the handle. "There's a band playing in the bar tonight," he told her.

"Is there? I've got to stay in and get that essay on the Industrial Revolution finished . . ."

"It's two third-years on guitar and vocals and a brilliant first year on the keyboard."

Lily screwed up her nose. "Not a real band then?"

"They're good, not your usual college band, and they're all music students." Bill's voice was authoritative – he was an expert on bands.

"I'll see how things go with the essay."

"It's on until twelve, so you could come down for the last hour."

"I'll see . . ." Her tone was vague and noncommittal.

She was also expecting the phone call Dara had promised around seven o'clock. They went up the path to the house she shared with seven other students, four of the rooms upstairs and four down. She pushed the main entrance door open and held it open for Bill and the case, then she did the same with the interior fire door.

"You're upstairs at the back of the house, aren't you?" he said, hoisting the case on to his shoulder again.

"Yes." She forced herself not to smile. It was a running joke with the girls on the course that he talked with great knowledge of where all their rooms were, obviously hoping to give the impression to the other lads that he was often invited in.

One of the girls on the upstairs floor came out now – Lily's closest friend, Ann – and looked over the banister. She was wearing a turquoise dressing-gown and had a towel wrapped around her hair.

"Hi, Lily!" she called. "Welcome back! I've got a copy of the notes I made on Martin Luther King from the history lecture on Friday. I'll drop them in to you when I sort them out."

"Oh, thanks, Ann. I'll catch up with you when I've got a bit further on with the essay I'm running late with."

"Did everything go okay with the funeral and everything?"

"Yes, I'll tell you all about it later."

Ann suddenly looked alarmed when she caught sight of Bill and the appreciative smile on his face.

"Are you going to hear the band tonight, Ann?" he called. He went up the stairs two at a time now, showing how fit and strong he was to do this with a case on his shoulder.

"I'll have to see," Ann said, clutching her dressing gown tightly to her chest, and stepping backwards into her open door.

Bill put the case down on the landing. "They're brilliant, they can do Status Quo, Bowie, Dylan and all that kind of stuff."

"I'll see . . ." Ann said, giving a weak smile to Lily before sliding back into her room and closing the door.

Bill looked at Lily. "When you get settled back in, it might be a good idea to knock on all the doors and let them know about the band. The women always need a bit of encouragement – they don't realise that these guys are really putting themselves out there. Their own student audience can be the most critical."

She smiled at him. "If I get my essay sorted, I promise I'll come."

Bill was a decent sort. To Lily's knowledge, he had gone out with two girls in the eighteen months since they had been on the course, and both romances had finished after a few weeks. He was a fixture in the discos in the Students' Union bar every weekend and, while Lily and her friends liked him, none of them were interested in him other than in a platonic way.

But that didn't put Bill off, and he was openly hopeful that by being friendly with the different groups of girls, one of them would introduce him to another who might be interested in him. In a way Lily admired his cheerful optimism. If it had been a girl in the same boat, they would have pretended that dating was stupid and they were too busy concentrating on their studies.

And maybe, she thought now, that wasn't such a terrible attitude either. Dara had pointed out that the distance between them might well be a positive. It would allow them both to concentrate on their courses and forthcoming exams without the distraction of seeing each other every day.

Lily thought it was one way of looking at it, but she didn't like the idea of him being surrounded by lots of attractive girls in the university. She was somewhat heartened by the fact that there were few females studying architecture, so at least he wouldn't be sitting with them during classes.

She unlocked her door and let Bill and the case in. He set it down by the window, then went to stand beside it, his two hands splayed out on the deep, white-painted sill.

"You've some view here," he told her. "You can see the running-track and the football fields. You could watch the matches here without leaving the room. I must remember that."

"The houses further up have a better view," she told him. "You'd be better off making friends with some of the girls in one of those."

She wandered over to stand beside him. There were the usual few eager PE students running around the track in shorts or tracksuits and people taking the path down to the student shop. A tall figure went past and Bill started waving and gesturing to him.

"D'you know him? Gerard what's-his-name? " Bill asked.

"Who?" When she looked down, she met the gaze of the dark-skinned lecturer she desperately wanted to avoid. She drew back into the room, her heart racing.

"The guy below, he's one of the lecturers. Don't you know him?"

"Not really . . ." Her voice was falsely bright.

"He's a really nice guy. I was chatting to him in the Union bar the other night." He laughed. "You must be one of the few girls that haven't noticed him. All the ones that are on the course he teaches think he's great. It's a pity he doesn't teach on ours."

She looked at her watch; it was nearly half past five. "I need to get started on that essay, or there will be no chance of me making it to the band tonight."

Bill moved towards the door. "Don't forget to ask around."

"I won't," Lily said, "and thanks for carrying the case."

After he left, Lily went over the window to stand at the side of the curtains. There was no sign of Gerard. She was sure he had seen her. And worse still, he had seen Bill Toft in her room. Whatever he thought of her before, God knows what he would think now.

She stood for a good ten minutes just staring out over the playing fields and the patchwork of fields beyond. What, she wondered, if he had told anyone else? What if he'd gone to her student rep or even her personal tutor? She'd never heard of another student being in this position. Although the lecturers were friendly and helpful to their students, they were professional and kept their distance socially. She should have known that and not pursued him. Just thinking about it gave her huge butterflies in her stomach.

She would have to sort this situation out with the lecturer, she suddenly realised, and sooner rather than later. The next time she saw him passing by or saw him in the bar, she would ask if she could have a few private words with him. That decided, she made herself take several deep breaths, then, she lifted her case and put it up on the bed and started taking things out of it. She put the foodstuff her mother had packed in a big Tupperware box, sorted out the things that needed washing and put them in her laundry bag and then put the rest of the stuff in her wardrobe or chest of drawers.

When the case was empty, she dragged her chair over to the wardrobe and stood on it to put the case in the luggage shelf above. After that, she went to her bookcase and picked out the books she needed for her studies that night. She decided she wouldn't bother with the evening meal in the student refectory, as she would only get chatting to people and it would delay her getting back to her work. She would work straight through now until quarter to seven and then she would open her door so that she could hear the phone ringing downstairs.

She went to the big shoulder-bag she had travelled with and took out the carefully wrapped Donovan LP. She slid the album out of its sleeve and held it with a finger in the hole in the middle and a thumb at the edges. Then, she flicked the wall-switch on, lifted the lid of her record-player and positioned the record on the spike.

A few moments later Donovan's voice filled the room singing "Catch the Wind". She sat back in her chair, listening to the music, and thinking of the day she and Dara had spent together in Dublin. When it finished, she stretched over to the record player and lifted the arm with the needle back to the start again. This time she closed her eyes, concentrating on the words.

It was beautiful, she thought, and the lyrics were like poetry. The opening line about *chilly hours and minutes of uncertainty* brought to mind all the ups and downs of the previous week, then when he sang *to take your hand, along the sand,* she felt a little pang as she remembered the walk along the seashore outside Dublin hand in hand with Dara.

Whilst the relaxing melody was lovely, some of the lines saddened her with descriptions of longing and a sense of loss. She listened a few times, moving the needle back and forth, and wondered about the girl it had been written for. Whoever she was, Lily concluded, she was special enough for Donovan to take the time and care to pen such a beautiful song.

She let the needle move unhindered on to the other tracks while she turned her attention to her essay, and worked away for a while.

A sharp knock on her bedroom door startled her. She froze. Then, just as she moved to open it, she saw a large envelope being pushed under the door.

She picked it up and opened it and then her shoulders dropped in relief. It was only the lecture notes that Ann had promised her. She heard Ann's voice in the distance, saying to one of the other girls that Lily was either asleep or must have gone out as there was no answer. Lily hurriedly opened the door to thank her, and found herself face to face with Gerard René.

"Hi, Lily," he said. "I hope I'm not disturbing you. Do you mind if I come in for a few minutes?"

21

As Lily opened the door wide enough for him to come in, she caught a fleeting glimpse of Ann watching from halfway down the stairs and knew that she would have to give some explanation for his visit later.

When she closed the door behind him, she moved to the middle of the room.

She gestured to the chair at her desk. "Do you want to sit down?" Her voice sounded hoarse and odd, and she could feel her legs starting to tremble. The way they did when she'd attempted a driving lesson with her father, and couldn't control the pedals. She had never tried again.

"No, no . . . I'll stand, thank you."

He stood by the door, which made her feel even more anxious. Did he think she was going to pounce on him again?

She folded her arms over her chest. "I've just come back."

"I know," he said, nodding his dark head vigorously. "I was looking for you and the office told me that you'd gone away."

She caught her breath. Had he been to the office and reported her inappropriate behaviour? Would she be thrown out of college? She felt sick to her stomach.

"I was relieved when they said you'd gone for a funeral, as I was worried that it was something to do with the night in my apartment."

"No . . ." Lily could hardly get the words out. "I went to Ireland for the funeral with my family."

"I'm sorry about that," he said. "I hope it wasn't too sad for you."

"She was old . . ."

He twisted the door handle. "I came to say I'm very sorry for what happened."

Lily looked at him now. "*You're* sorry? But you didn't do anything . . . it was me. I'm the one who should be saying 'sorry' to you."

He shook his head. "I'm the lecturer – the person with responsibility. I should never have asked you back to my apartment."

She knew she should feel better that he was shouldering the blame, letting her off the hook, but she didn't. It just made her feel even more like a silly teenager.

Memories of the night came back in bits and pieces, flooding her with embarrassment. She turned away. "I really didn't know you were married. I would never have – I'm not like that – I'm so embarrassed."

"Don't be," he said in a low voice. "I should never have allowed us to get into that position. It has really wakened me up to the great risk I took. If it had been another type of girl, I could have been in a lot of trouble."

She folded her arms even tighter. "I've never done anything like that before," she told him. "I don't know what I was thinking . . . I am so sorry." Tears filled her eyes and she turned towards the window.

"It's me who should apologise, Lily." he told her. "I'm the one who is older and I'm the one who is married. I should have said that straight away."

"But you didn't know what I was thinking. You thought I was just being friendly . . ."

"No, Lily," he said. "I knew."

There was a silence and then she turned back to look at him.

"I was foolish and vain." He gestured towards her. "You are a very beautiful young girl, and I was flattered. And when you kissed me, I reacted so strongly because I was afraid I might be tempted."

He looked up to the ceiling. "If I am truthful, I was tempted, and I feel very bad because of that."

She bit her lip. "I gave a very bad impression of myself – I really wouldn't have done anything that night. I didn't think I'd drunk that much, but it must have gone to my head anyway." She gave a teary smile. "Believe it or not, I've never slept with anyone . . ."

He nodded. "Oh, I believe you. It's easy to tell what kind of girl you are. I knew that when we first talked. You were so nice and friendly and interesting – and very attractive . . ."

"That," she said in a low voice, "is what I thought about you."

There was a pause. "I was so very wrong inviting you back."

Lily looked at him now and he caught her gaze.

"I have a beautiful, intelligent wife and two children," he told her. "The problem is, I miss them. I get lonely. But that's no excuse for my behaviour that night. I was just so lucky that it was a girl like you with good morals."

She suddenly felt like crying with gratitude. She was so grateful to have the burden of guilt lifted from her shoulders. "You behaved like a gentleman and a faithful husband when I . . ." She looked away and then back at him. "When I did that stupid thing. No matter what you say now . . . you really got a shock. I could see it in your eyes."

"I didn't handle it well at all."

"You're being too hard on yourself," she told him. "I'm sure everybody at some point thinks and imagines what it would be like to be with other people. But it's only certain married people who will take the risk." Her voice was softer now. "And you didn't consider that. The minute you saw that something might happen between us you told me you were married. You're punishing yourself as if you've actually done something wrong and you haven't . . ." She paused and then added, "We haven't. I think we both need to stop blaming ourselves."

He looked at her for a few moments. "I'm glad I came to see you because I'm actually beginning to feel better about this. I was very anxious when I realised you had gone away. It's been on my mind all that time . . ."

"I was the same," she told him. "I felt so bad that when I heard about the funeral, I took the chance to have a few days off so I wouldn't have to face you . . ."

"I'm sorry you had to do that, but I think maybe we've both learned from this incident. I was wallowing in self-pity about being lonely and away from my family. When I spoke to my wife this weekend I told her how much I missed her and she said she felt the same. She has booked a week's leave and she's coming over next month for the half-term holiday with the children."

"Oh, that's lovely," Lily said. "I'm delighted for you."

"It's a pity I didn't think about it before making such a fool of myself."

"Don't," she said. "Both of us need to forget about it."

He put his hand out. "Can we be friends? I like you very much, Lily. I think you're a very wise young woman, and I would hate us to be awkward with each other."

She came across the floor towards him and took his hand. Then, on impulse, she stood on tiptoes and kissed him lightly on the cheek. "Thank you, Gerard."

He looked at her. "Thank you, Lily – you're very kind."

Their eyes locked for a few seconds and in that short space Lily knew that if circumstances had been different, they would probably have been together – even for a short time. Gerard smiled at her and something told her that he was thinking the same thing. In time to come, she thought, she would look back on this small episode in her life and feel good about herself, knowing that she had attracted someone like Gerard.

But she was now very glad that fate had intervened and allowed her to go to Ireland and meet Dara.

She felt lighter, almost giddy with relief now. "Can I tell you something before you go?"

"What?"

"Well . . . maybe all this was meant to happen to give us both a jolt, because when I was over in Ireland I met this lovely guy and we got on really, really well." She couldn't hold back the beaming smile as she thought of Dara. "He's studying architecture in Dublin, but we're going to keep in touch. He's ringing me tonight."

"That's great news. I believe there are only a few people we meet that we could spend the rest of our lives with and, if you meet one of them, Lily, try to make it work." He held his finger up. "If you lose them, you could spend the rest of your life searching for someone like that and never find them. That's what I was so frightened of when I thought of doing something dangerous that would make me lose my wife. I know I would never find anyone like her again."

"You can put it completely out of your mind now."

"Oh, I will, but I've learned from it." He turned to the door. "And you, Lily, try to see your nice Irishman as much as you possibly can."

22

As Lily hung the phone up in the downstairs hallway, a feeling of euphoria ran through her. Dara had sounded exactly as he did when they were talking face to face. He had been funny, serious, complimentary and romantic – all of the things she remembered and liked about him.

She ran back up the stairs, hoping not to bump into anyone, as she wanted to rerun the entire conversation in her mind from start to finish. When she reached her room she threw herself on the bed and then lifted one of her pillows to hug tightly to her chest.

She closed her eyes and tried to remember the sound of his voice and all the lovely things he had said to her. As she recalled each topic they had touched on – most of them light and ordinary – she hugged the pillow tighter.

He told her tonight's film was *Comedy of Terrors* and they expected a good crowd for it.

"I hope none of them will be eating chips," she said, and they both laughed. They had then gone on to talk about a series of unrelated, random subjects, stopping only when Lily reminded him that it was time to go and sort the film reels out.

The comforting pleasure she had from talking to him had been intensified by the overwhelming relief she had felt after Gerard René left. Today, she thought, has been one of the best days of my life. She was grateful that things had turned out with the lecturer as they did. It could have been so very different. And whilst she knew she had been naïve and clumsy about it all, and had embarrassed herself, a little part of her felt grateful to know that someone as intelligent and fascinating as Gerard had been attracted to her.

Although she believed one hundred per cent that she would never act on it – would never consider an affair with a married man – her self-confidence had grown from knowing that in a different time and in a different situation something could well have happened.

And she had learned so much from the incident that the dreadful anxiety had almost been worth it. She would now put the experience away in a little box at the back of her mind.

With the guilty sword of Damocles now lifted, she could focus her attention on the exciting, new relationship that might possibly come to mean something more in the future. Dara had told her that he missed her and that when he was in Dublin at university earlier in the day, he had seen constant reminders of her everywhere. He had passed Vic's record shop when he was in town in the afternoon and then had walked across the Ha'penny Bridge.

A few times she had the urge to ask him if he had been talking to any girls or sitting next to them in lectures, but she stopped herself. He sounded so warm and sincere, telling her several times that he couldn't stop thinking about her, and it would only cast a doubt over his feelings. She reminded herself of the situation she had just escaped from, and it made her realise that Dara could easily question her.

Later, when she had endlessly run the conversation over in her mind, and picked out all the parts that made her feel warm and tingly, she put the Donovan record back on and got stuck into her essay.

She stopped after an hour or so when her mind drifted back to Dara. She could picture him, quite clearly, sitting in the projector room, watching the film through the small square window, and then moving to the projectors to change the film reels.

She was still thinking of him when she realised she hadn't eaten anything all evening. She went to the Tupperware box to get one of the favourite pies her mother had packed for her, ran downstairs to heat it in the Baby Belling cooker in the kitchen, and then came back upstairs and worked for another twenty minutes until it was ready.

Around nine o'clock her friend Ann and some of the girls in her block called to see if she was going down to the Students' Union to watch the band Bill had been going on about.

"It'll probably be more of a laugh than anything," Ann said.

"I'm going to work on for a while longer," she said, "but I might catch up with you later."

Ann held back while the others went towards the stairs. "What did the gorgeous Gerard René want?" she whispered.

Lily trotted out the answer she had thought of earlier. "Oh, nothing important. I was chatting to him before I went away and he said he would loan me a book."

"Oh!" Ann said, making eyes. "Maybe he was just using it as an excuse. You don't often get tutors coming up to the rooms. Do you think he fancies you?"

Lily laughed. "I don't think so! He was actually talking all about his wife and children."

"Really? I didn't know he was even married. But then, he's rather quiet and reserved. Really sexy –"

"Anyway," Lily said, changing the subject, "I've got some news for you in the romance department after my week away."

Ann clasped her hands together. "Did you meet someone?"

Lily nodded. "In Ireland. He's lovely."

"Tell me, tell me, tell me!"

The phone suddenly rang, echoing through the hallway.

"Lily," Beryl Hammond called, "it's your mother!"

"Oh God," Lily said, running down the stairs. "I forgot to ring her when I got in to say I got back safely. She'll kill me!"

"What about the guy you met?" Ann called after her.

"I'll tell you all about it later when I've finished my essay!"

Lily listened to her mother telling her all about her cousin Kirsty's latest trip to Spain and then they talked about various other things.

Then Lily brought up the subject of Dara. "Is it okay if he comes over at the Easter break?" she asked.

There was a short silence, then her mother said, "That seems awful quick after you just seeing him . . ."

"But it's weeks away!" Lily said. "And because we're students, we have to plan things around the college and university holidays."

There was another pause. "Well, if you want him to come and stay then we're not going to argue with you."

Lily bit her lip. "You don't sound too keen . . ."

"No, no," her mother said, sounding brighter now. "It's fine. You can tell him it's fine to come."

Lily gave a small sigh of relief. She knew it was all a bit too much too soon for her mother, but she was often like that when things were landed on her. She would be fine when she met Dara and got to know him.

When Lily came back upstairs she worked on a while longer in the silence of the empty house with Donovan's songs for company. At half-past ten she put her pen down and decided that the essay was in good enough shape to submit in the morning. She would set her alarm for seven and get up early and do a last edit and then a tidy rewrite before handing it in.

She went to her wardrobe and took out the cheesecloth top she had bought with Dara and put it on with her jeans and matching beads. She checked the smock in the wardrobe mirror – anxious in case her mother had shrunk it in the wash – and was glad it looked fine.

It was cold outside so she wrapped up in her duffle coat and student scarf. As she walked along the edge of the lawn, her breath came out in cloudy puffs. It was every bit as cold as Scotland, she thought.

She could hear the electric guitars and the thumping of the drums as she approached the hall, and when she got inside the entrance lobby, she could see that it was packed. She was going to have to work her way through the crowds in the smoky, dimly lit bar. Had she known it was going to be so busy, she might not have come. She usually hated the self-conscious feeling she got as she edged her way past groups – most of them taller than her. Between the dark corners and the jerky lighting from the rotating disco ball, it was hard to make out who individuals were and try to guess where her friends might be sitting.

But tonight she didn't feel self-conscious or awkward. After her phone call, she still felt so close to Dara that it was almost as if he was walking beside her, holding her hand.

In the midst of the banging drums and the beyond-amateurish screeching guitar, Lily thought she heard her name being called. She looked to the left and the right, craning her neck to see where her friends were. Then, one of the taller lads in her history class came smiling towards her and gently caught her by the shoulders and guided her to her friends at the side of the bar.

"We were trying to catch your attention," Ann said. "We were waving and jumping around. Did you get the essay finished?"

"Yes, thank God."

"I'd almost given up on you. I thought I'd have to go back to the house and bang on your door to hear all about this new boyfriend."

Lily took off her coat and scarf and then reached into her pocket. "I'll get us all a drink first," she said to the three girls. She smiled and waved a ten-pound note. "It's courtesy of my dad." She didn't say that it was guilt money, and that her father was still trying to be really nice to her to make up for that awful night in Ireland.

It was almost one o'clock when she got back to her room. The band had been useless but the night was great. She had enjoyed telling the girls all about her time with Dara, and Ann with her gunshot-like questions had made sure that not a single detail was left out.

"He sounds almost too good to be true," Ann stated. "Gorgeous-looking *and* has great taste in music and books."

"Everything about him is perfect," Lily said airily, "apart from the fact that he lives in Ireland."

* * *

Dara rang again on Thursday night as arranged and Lily told him all about the essay she had completed and about the teaching practice she was due to start after the Easter break.

163

"I'm really pleased," she told him. "The teaching-practice tutors were working out the lists today and I found I've got the top class, the eleven and twelve-year-olds, which is the one I was hoping for. It's for a full term starting after Easter and I'll be going in every day apart from a Friday when we meet up with our Education tutors and get our evaluation from the previous week, and show her our plans for the week ahead."

"Sounds like hard work," he said.

"It is, but I love it. I'm doing a Viking project and one on the history of the markets in Newcastle, so we're going to be going out for day trips to visit two of them."

He told her all about the work he was doing at university, and then she asked him about the film he was working on later that night.

"I hope it's not another horror." There was a mock-disapproving tone in her voice.

"No, it's billed as a comedy musical film, it's called *So This is Paris.*"

"I've seen it," she said. "It's got Tony Curtis in it. It's a bit on the ancient side."

"How many times have you seen it?" he asked.

"Once."

"Lucky you," he said. "It's my fifth time watching it."

They both laughed and then Lily said she liked the bits about Paris, and that she would love to go there some day.

"We'll add it to the list of places we're going to see." His voice was lower now. "I miss you," he said. "I miss kissing you and touching your hair. You're absolutely gorgeous, you know."

Lily felt her stomach tighten. "I miss you too."

They talked for a while longer, Lily lowering her voice when any of the girls or a visitor went past. When he asked why she was talking quietly, she explained, and then he asked her to describe the house she lived in and what the other girls were like.

"I want to picture where you are and what you're doing," he explained. "You know where I am because you've seen college and you know where I live and what I'm doing in the cinema."

During one of his phone calls the following week, he said he had his college diary with him as he wanted to check a few dates with her. "When is your half-term?"

She thought for a moment. "The last weekend in February."

"I'm off then too," he said. "What are you doing?"

"Going home probably." She wondered if he was going to suggest coming over to Scotland. They'd already tentatively arranged that.

"Do some of the students stay in the halls of residence during the breaks?"

"Yes," she said. "I know a few who don't go home for one reason or another."

"I was wondering . . . if we could work it so that I could come to Newcastle during the mid-term break? Easter seems too long."

Lily's heart quickened. She couldn't think of anything she would like more. "Oh, Dara, I would absolutely love you to come, but I think my mother would have a fit if I don't go home, and I think she would have an even bigger fit if she knew you were coming here and we'd be on our own."

"Maybe you could do both, keep your mother happy by going home and give us some time to ourselves."

"Go on," she said, "I'm listening."

"Well, I was just thinking that if I came on the Thursday before the half-term and stayed until the Monday or Tuesday, then you would still have nearly a week after that to go up to Scotland."

"Sounds good, but how would I explain it?"

"You could say you were doing an extra course or there were activities going on in the college over the break that you'd like to be involved in." He suddenly realised what he'd said and started to laugh. "I can easily think of a few activities I'd like to involve you in."

Lily laughed along with him. "How do you know I'd be a willing participant?"

"Well, I think I'll have to wait and find out."

She became more serious now. "I think it's a brilliant idea! I would love you to come here and see all the things I've told you about."

"I keep looking at the college brochure and trying to picture me there with you."

"Be warned that it will be very quiet over the weekend when everyone goes home, but if you could get here on the Thursday night there will be a disco or something on in the Union bar."

"Sounds great, but I don't care if we don't see another soul. It's you I'm coming to see."

"I can't wait." She calculated. "Do you know that it's only about ten days away? Will you be able to sort out the boat and everything in time?"

"No problem, in fact it's the easiest part. I've got to know a lad from Manchester who's on the Maths and Science course, and he has a car, and he's going to bring me over on the morning boat to Holyhead and then drive me as far as Manchester, and I'll catch the train up to Newcastle in the late afternoon."

"Will it be expensive?"

"No, it doesn't cost any more when you're already paying for the car, and he was happy when I said I'd split the petrol money with him." He laughed then. "It'll work out cheaper than all the phone calls I've been making. I had to give my father a donation towards the last bill. He says if the next one is as high I've got to start using the local phone box."

"I told you it would be expensive. After this, I'll phone you every second time when you're at the cinema. It's only fair."

"We'll see," he said. "We can chat about it when I come over."

"I can't believe it," Lily said, her voice high with excitement. "Are you really going to come?"

"Yes," he said. "I've been thinking about it since you left, and I can't wait until Easter to see you, it's far too long."

"I keep reading your letters over and over again and listening to Donovan and all the music we talked about."

"I bought you another album in Vic's at the weekend."

"What is it?"

"You'll have to wait and see."

"All the girls are dying to see you. I've been talking about you all the time since I came back."

166

"That's great – I'm looking forward to meeting them." He paused. "Lily . . ." His voice was serious now. "Where will I stay when I come?"

Lily caught her breath. She had been waiting on this since he mentioned about coming over. "Where do you want to stay?"

"If you want me to be honest, then I really want to stay with you. Would it be a problem?"

"God, Dara . . . we'll have to think about it," she said. "What it would mean . . ." She was in no doubt that she wanted him to stay with her, but how would it work when they had spent so little actual time together? They had talked on the phone regularly and written long rambling letters about everything and anything. But they'd had little physical contact – only those few days in Ireland. To jump from kissing and cuddling to sharing a room – possibly sharing a bed – terrified her.

They had swapped photographs in their first letters, and she had bought a frame for his. It was a lovely picture, taken by a photography student friend of his, and he looked just like she remembered him in it. Dark-haired, beautiful brown eyes – really good-looking. But there were times when it worried her that she couldn't remember how he looked when he was talking and laughing.

"I don't want to put any pressure on you," he was saying, "and I'm not suggesting anything you don't want to do."

"I think I just feel it might be rushing things to share a room the first time we see each other like this. I've never done anything like that before . . ."

The unspoken question hung in the air.

"That's good, because I haven't either," he said. "I've stayed over at parties and slept on floors and that kind of thing, but never visited a girl on my own before. Not like this . . ."

Lily felt much better instantly. "We'll work it out."

"Honestly," he said, "I'd be happy in a sleeping-bag or on a mattress on the floor." He hesitated. "Or I'll go in a separate room if that's what you want. I don't care where I sleep . . . I just want to be with you as much of the time as possible."

Lily's mind worked fast. She could ask Ann if she could borrow her room for Dara from the Thursday. Ann was going home to Durham Friday lunchtime as the classes finished for the holidays then, but Lily knew that she would be all packed on the Thursday night and wouldn't mind staying in Beryl's room.

All the girls, including Lily, on different occasions, had done this to accommodate friends or relatives staying and the occasional boyfriend from back home. There was a more formal system for visitors staying, but most of the students Lily knew just had them stay on the quiet. Whilst it was without a doubt breaking the official campus rules, there was an unspoken agreement that as long as students were discreet – and didn't blatantly flout the rules – then nobody would come banging on the door.

She would explain to Ann that Dara would only use the room at night, and that he would keep his bag and stuff in her room, and that she would change the bed and leave everything perfect for her coming back. She was sure her friend wouldn't mind.

"Don't worry about the details," Lily told him. "Just come. That's all that matters."

"I'll start counting the days," he said. "And the hours and the minutes."

23

The following Sunday afternoon when Lily was on the phone to her mother, she broached the subject of the half-term break.

"What weekend is that?" Mona said. "Let me just check the calendar."

There was a pause when Lily could hear paper rustling and her mother talking to someone in the background, presumably her father. When she came back on, Lily rushed in with her prepared speech.

"Now, I won't be coming for the whole week this time," she said. "There are some art courses running over the first weekend, for the students who are going on teaching practice after Easter." She crossed her fingers. "I'll probably come home on the Tuesday and come back here the following Sunday."

There was a silence, then Lily could hear paper rustling again.

"So that's the last weekend in February?" Mona checked. "Believe it or not, we have a wedding that Saturday up in Dunfermline – you know Peggy Ingles's son, James? Well, it's his wedding and the bride is from that area. Your father and I are booked into a bed and breakfast on the Friday and Saturday night."

"So you wouldn't be there anyway?" Lily said, unable to believe her luck. It was amazing because her parents hardly ever stayed overnight anywhere. "Well, that's fine, you'll hardly miss me."

"We'll still have most of the week with you," Mona said. "And it's more important to do all the courses you can, to make sure you get a teaching job when you come back home."

Mona had never for a minute presumed that Lily might decide to stay on in the Newcastle area as many of the college students were inclined to do. If a vacancy came up in one of the schools where a student had done very well, it was often suggested that they might like to apply for the post.

Mona talked on for another ten minutes, bringing Lily up to date on any local news and then told her that Kirsty and Larry were coming home the following weekend, a quick stopover with Lily's aunt and uncle before flying out to Florida for a fortnight's holiday.

"Isn't it well for them?" Mona said in a high voice. "You'd think they've had enough of travelling being on the cruise ships, but oh, no, Miss Kirsty said that's their work, and the trip to Florida is a proper holiday."

"The lucky things!" Lily was only half-listening now as she couldn't wait to get off the phone to tell Ann that all her worries about the half-term had been for nothing.

"Declan's long-distance romance seems to be going well," Mona continued. "He has letters every week with the Irish stamp on them." She paused. "Your father and Seán have assured me she's a lovely girl and will get on fine with us all." She paused. "And are things still going well with you and the lad from the cinema in Carraigvale?"

"Dara?" Lily's voice was deliberately vague. "Yes, he phones and writes regularly. He's still hoping to come over for Easter."

"So is Ava I think. I must check with Declan. Trying to get information out of that fella is like trying to get blood out of a stone."

The main door of the house opened, and then the fire door, and Ann came in. Lily gestured for her to wait as she wanted to tell her about the unbelievable turn in events.

"I'll have to go, Mum," Lily said. "There's somebody waiting now to use the phone."

"I'll ring at the same time next Sunday," Mona said. "Look after yourself and work hard."

"I will," Lily said. "Give my love to everyone."

After she came off the phone, Lily felt a wave of guilt. She couldn't ever remember being dishonest with her mother before. But, she was a grown-up woman now and she had never been in this situation before. She wanted to see Dara before Easter and she wanted to see him on her own. If she told her mother that he was coming to stay at the college – even as a bona-fide visitor – she would never hear the end of it.

She decided that she would just have to live with the guilt.

*　　*　　*

The next week and a half slipped by quicker than any other time since she had been at college. Her main lectures in Education and History – on 'Bonding in Early Childhood' and 'The Impact of The Kennedy Family on US History' – gripped her interest and she found herself flying through the books on her term's reading list. In the afternoons and during any breaks she made her way over to the college library to return or borrow more books, or to study information in the Reference Library.

Back in her room in the evenings, she settled down to make notes for the essays due in before the half-term break on both subjects.

As interesting as she found her current topics, she often found herself drifting off into daydreams about Dara and what they would do over the five full days they would have together. At other times – when her head was too full of dates and names – she would wander off the main subject and become engrossed in sections that focussed on the glamorous President's widow, Jackie Kennedy.

She loved studying pictures of her clothes and hair and the big sunglasses she wore, and pictures of her and her late husband and their two lovely children – casual pictures of them on holiday and more formal ones of them at home in The White House.

During those breaks from her formal books, she also leafed through the monthly subscription magazines the college had casually dotted around on the tables. She would flick over the pages of *Good Housekeeping*, glancing at the fashions that were just that little bit too old and formal for her, and lingering on the knitting patterns, the food recipes and the interior design sections.

Sometimes the domestic details sent her off into a little fantasy, imagining the sort of house she would have if she and Dara got married, the sort of furniture and curtains she would choose and even the bed linen.

She felt he was there with her all the time, an ever-present shadow living her life alongside her. Everything she did, whether it was studying, eating in the refectory or walking down to the local shop for shampoo and biscuits, he was there on the edge of things.

And then there were the phone calls and letters which she replayed in her mind and reread in any empty, spare moments that left her feeling he was too far away or if she couldn't remember exactly how his hair looked and the exact tone of his voice.

And then it was the Thursday afternoon and she was going in circles around her room checking that the bed was made perfectly, checking that she had enough coffee and biscuits for him, checking that she had all the music that she knew he would want to listen to – and then checking how she looked once again in the wardrobe mirror. She had tried on half a dozen dressy outfits – skirts, jeans, blouses, sweaters, a dress – even though it was only a Thursday and nobody else would be wearing one – and nothing looked right. And then she had come to a halt and made herself think, and gone back to one of her old favourites – a fine black angora sweater – which fitted her perfectly and looked good with her jeans and silver jewellery. When she looked at herself in the mirror, her whole body relaxed and she knew it was the right thing.

And when she had finished with all the checking, she threw her grey woollen jacket on and went downstairs to chat to her friends until the five o'clock coach from Newcastle rolled into the campus.

Several of the girls were standing around in the kitchen sorting laundry for going home or making drinks. She took Ann to one side and repeated again what would happen, in the worst-case scenario, if she was caught having Dara stay in Ann's room.

"I'll make out I borrowed your key to use your typewriter, as you often let me use it – and when Dara turned up I thought it was better to let him stay there than in my room."

"It will be fine," Ann said. "Just say that Dara turned up as a surprise, and with it being half-term you couldn't go to the office to book him in officially."

Lily put her arms around her friend. "Thanks, I really appreciate it, and I'll make sure you don't get into any trouble."

Lily made a cup of coffee and then went to stand by the window. The light was just beginning to fade and she could see the groups of people assembled at the bus-stop area, all heading into Newcastle for the evening or heading home early for the weekend.

"I bet you're really excited," Ann said. "Imagine him coming all the way over from Ireland just for a few days. He must be completely mad about you!"

Lily rolled her eyes and smiled as though she was completely relaxed about the whole thing, but inside her stomach was jittery and her legs were starting to feel weak.

What if, she wondered, he seemed completely different to the boy she met in Ireland? What if she didn't fancy him any more? How would they pass five whole long days on their own if things didn't work out?

"There it is!" Ann said, gesturing towards the window. "The coach, it's just passing the Porter's Lodge now."

Lily's hand flew to her mouth, all attempts at being cool and poised suddenly gone. "Oh, God," she said, heading towards the door, "what if we don't know what to say to each other?"

Beryl let out a screech of laughter. "Lily – you have got to be joking! You're never off the phone to each other and any time I've passed, you certainly never seem lost for words."

"Oh, God, God – God!" Lily said, rushing towards the front door.

"Bring him back and introduce us," Ann called. "We'll wait in here."

"No," Lily called. "I'll be too embarrassed with you lot."

The coach was making its usual circular turn around the green to come to a standstill at the stop back at the college entrance. As she crossed the grass in the gathering dusk she tried to relax and breathe deeply to still the fluttering in her stomach and chest. The queue of students waiting to board did the usual slow shuffle forward – lifting cases and hoisting rucksacks up on their shoulders, as the coach came to a halt.

Lily was aware of a figure coming close behind her to join the queue, and then she felt a light tap on her shoulder.

"Hi, Lily!" Gerard René's manner was bright and cheery. "Are you going into Newcastle?"

She deduced from the holdall he was carrying that he was obviously heading off somewhere for the mid-term break.

"No, I'm here to meet my Irish friend. He's coming for the weekend."

A warm smile crossed his face. "That's wonderful for you," he said. "I hope you have a great time." He moved to join the queue. "I'm off to Liverpool for the week, I have relations living there and they asked me over."

Lily smiled back at him, feeling sorry for him that he couldn't go home for the break to his wife and children. "You have a great time too!"

The coach doors gave a great sigh and opened, and the few passengers coming into the college disembarked. And then she caught sight of him coming down the steps, rucksack on his back, his curly hair moving in the breeze. Then, as he came towards her, the fluttering feeling suddenly escalated and filled her whole body.

When he threw the rucksack on the ground and swept her up in his arms, all the tension seeped out of her and she buried her face in his neck, her hands moving through his thick dark hair. And suddenly, she was back in Ireland, back in the cinema, back in the van with him – and with all the lovely, familiar feelings that had started then.

"I can't believe you're actually here!" she said, half-laughing and half-crying.

He tightened his arms around her again, holding her as close to him as was physically possible. "I can't believe it either." He reluctantly loosened his grip and stepped back a few feet to take a good look at her.

"You look fantastic," he said. "Better than the photographs and even better than I remember."

The anguish over what to wear was but a dim, distant memory, and delight at the compliment now slid into place. "Oh, thanks – and so do you! Your hair is even longer than before!"

He reached to the back of his head and caught a handful of it. "I thought about getting it cut. I wasn't sure whether the male teacher-training students would be all smart, short back and sides."

"A few of them have long-*ish* hair," she said. "And I'm glad you didn't get it cut, it's gorgeous."

They both stopped at the same time, having run out of breath or excitement or something.

Dara looked around him. "It's fantastic," he said. "Bigger, better . . . everything."

"I knew you'd like it."

Then Lily took his hand and he lifted his rucksack and threw it over his shoulder. She pointed across the green at the house straight on the diagonal.

"My room is in there, at the back. We're going there first to drop off your stuff and then we're going to the refec – I've booked you in for an evening meal as I thought you might be starving."

He looked at his watch. "I'm okay just now. What time does it finish?"

"Seven," she said. "The food is quite good, but the later you leave it the less choice you'll have."

"I'll chance it. I'd rather have a look around first."

They walked across chatting, Lily explaining the layout of the campus and pointing out each of the individual houses, and telling which were male and which were female.

"No mixed?" he asked.

"Nope," she said. "Although some third-years live out in shared houses in Newcastle and travel in here every day."

He looked at her. "If no males are allowed, will there be a problem with me staying in your house?"

She shook her head. "Definitely not this week, because there's hardly anyone around. And during the terms, people break the rules all the time, but as long as they don't draw attention to it, nobody really says anything. The trouble starts when the male students start seeing somebody in a shared room and the other person doesn't like them being around all the time." She rolled her eyes. "And the other problem is when students in a single room have a boyfriend or girlfriend there too often and they stop others from using the baths or showers."

He smiled. "I suppose that would cause a problem."

"I'm lucky," she said, "because I'm on a floor with a bathroom, a shower room and two toilets, so you never really get held up waiting on other people." They were getting nearer the house now and she felt she was babbling a bit, but couldn't stop herself. "And if they do happen to be busy, there are more bathrooms downstairs."

They came onto the path now, stopping to let two cyclists by, and then they walked the few yards up to her house.

"Do a lot of the students have bikes?" he asked.

"Yes, they use them for cycling down into the village. We've got a couple of old ones in the house. I bought an ancient second-hand one with a basket, which is handy for carrying books and shopping."

He grinned at her. "I can just imagine you cycling along with your hair blowing in the wind."

She laughed. "I don't use it as often as I should – I'm more inclined to catch the coach if the weather is bad."

"This all looks great," he said. "The accommodation I've seen in the universities or colleges in Dublin is nothing compared to this."

Lily stopped at the door. "Some of the girls might be around, so I'll have to introduce you."

"No problem," he said, smiling reassuringly at her.

She went ahead, holding the main door and then the fire-door open wide to let him and his rucksack through. They were just heading for the staircase when the kitchen door opened and Ann stuck her head out.

"Hi!" She stood smiling and waiting.

"This is Dara from Ireland," Lily said.

"Hi, Dara," Ann said, coming out to shake hands with him. "Lily mentioned you were coming."

Lily made eyes at her in case she laughed and gave away the fact that he had been the main topic of conversation all week.

"Hi, nice to meet you," Dara said, dropping his rucksack and shaking hands with her. "What a fantastic place!"

"Yes, it's lovely, isn't it?" She looked back to the kitchen. "If you hang on for a second . . . there's a few more of the girls here, and I know they'd love to meet you."

Lily shook her head and made eyes at her again. "It's okay, we'll catch you later!"

Ann moved quickly to open the kitchen door. "C'mon, girls!" she called. "Lily's friend from Ireland has arrived."

"I'll kill her!" Lily hissed.

Dara shrugged and smiled and just waited.

The other girls came out now, looking too quiet and demure for Lily's liking. She introduced each one to Dara and they shook hands and said and did all the right things, and then when Lily said they were going up to her room, they all stood and watched as the couple ascended the stairs.

"My room's along here," Lily said quietly, conscious that the girls were still standing below. "It's just at the back . . ." Then, just as she reached the door, she heard all the girls starting to cheer and laugh.

"What's all that?" Dara looked back with a bemused look on his face.

"Just ignore them," Lily said, searching for her keys in her pocket. "They're just being silly." Then, as she went to put the key in the lock, she heard Ann's voice.

"Oh, Li-ly!" she called up in a theatrically thin voice, "I've just had a premonition . . ."

Lily looked at Dara. "What the hell is she going on about now?"

"I have a very strange feeling . . ." Ann went on in the same high-pitched voice, "that you will not require the use of my room over the weekend!"

Lily closed her eyes and leaned her back against the door. "I am so embarrassed . . . I'll kill her!"

There was more laughter now and the sound of scuffling as the girls all retreated back into the kitchen.

177

24

Lily opened the door and switched on the light.

"Wow!" Dara said, walking into the middle of the room. "It's fab!" He slowly turned around taking in the bed, the bookshelves, the desk and angle-poise lamp, then he turned again to the large fitted wardrobe and built-in dressing table.

He put his rucksack down by the window and then stood looking out. "You have a great view of the sports field and the running track."

"Everyone says that, especially males."

He looked over his shoulder at smiled. "I hope you haven't had too many in here?"

She went over to stand by him. "Only the maintenance workers," she said, Gerard René guiltily crossing her mind for an instant. "You're the first real visitor."

He turned towards her, his eyes searching hers. "I've missed you." Then he placed his hands on either side of her face and bent to kiss her – a slow, gentle kiss. After a few moments he moved back. "That was beautiful. I've been waiting for weeks to do that."

Lily lifted her head and, without saying a word, she kissed him firmly on the lips. His arms circled her waist and then moved up her back. Instinctively, her mouth opened and seconds later she felt his tongue searching for hers. Then they stayed locked together like that until any tiny uncertainties or unfamiliarities had all faded away.

When they stopped for breath, she moved her fingers along the side of his face and then traced over the slightly rough evening stubble. He caught her hand and brought it to his mouth to kiss every inch of it.

"Your skin," he said, "is beautiful and not like any other girl's I've known. I was thinking about it all the way over on the boat, and I was imagining how it would feel to touch you again."

"And how does it feel?" she whispered.

He tilted her chin and looked into her eyes. "It feels exactly as I knew it would." And he kissed her again.

"I think," she said at one point, "we could take our coats off now . . ." And their laughter broke the intensity in the room.

Lily took her jacket off and threw it on the armchair and then Dara put his coat on top.

She looked at him now, at his pale blue sweater and his faded jeans. "I've never seen you in that colour before," she said. "It really suits you."

"Thank you, I have to confess I actually bought it for coming over."

"Did you buy it in Dublin?"

"No," he said, smiling in bemusement, "I bought it in Oliver Gayle's men's shop in Tullamore."

"Why are you smiling?" she asked.

"Because girls are so funny about clothes – my sister, Rose, asked me the exact same thing."

"How is she?" Lily asked. "She's a lovely girl."

"She's grand," he said. Then, he suddenly remembered. "I brought you a couple of small things." He went to his rucksack and brought out a package she immediately recognised as having come from Vic's.

She opened it and it was a single record of 'Unchained Melody' by The Righteous Brothers.

"I have a copy of it and I like both the tune and the lyrics," Dara told her. "And I think of you when I'm playing it."

"That's really lovely," Lily said, trying to recall the words of the song, but it wouldn't come to mind. She kissed him and thanked him and then turned to the other small package which she guessed was a book.

"Oh, that's lovely!" She held up a small framed picture of the Ha'penny Bridge. "You remembered how much I loved that bridge. That is so thoughtful . . . I'll hang it on the wall above my bed." She was thrilled with the presents and thought that she must look for something suitable to buy him in return. She lifted the record again. "I think I'll play this now –"

Before she had a chance to say anything more, he took her hand and wordlessly led her over to the bed. Then he went over to switch the main light off, leaving the room in a shadowy twilight.

As he came to lie beside her for the very first time, Lily moved to rest her head on his chest. He pulled her close to him, and they lay there in the darkened silence. After what seemed like a long time he turned towards her again and kissed her deeply. Then, without saying anything, he gently moved her so she was lying back on the pillow and then he moved to lie on top of her.

When she felt his hard body pressing against hers, Lily felt a hot urge building up inside her that she'd never felt with anyone else. But then – she had never wanted anyone so close to her as Dara was now. And as his kisses became harder and more passionate, he started moving against her and she suddenly felt the extent of his arousal.

She halted, unsure what to do. She was afraid that if she continued he might think she was prepared to move their relationship onto a whole different level. But then something inside started to move things along, and a longing came in the pit of her stomach which made her body move naturally to meet his. And she knew then how difficult it would be if they did not have the barrier of clothes between them.

"God, Lily . . ." he said, burying his face in the hollow in her neck. "I can't describe how being so close to you makes me feel. You are just the most beautiful thing – I can't believe I actually have you in my arms."

He pulled her tighter to him now and, in spite of her anxiety, she felt a sense of confidence knowing that he wanted her so much.

As they continued to kiss, his hands moved around her face and neck and shoulders, and then Lily caught her breath as his hand moved down to caress her breasts. He must have sensed her sudden tension because he moved to lie beside her again and went back to kissing and holding her.

"You don't need to worry," he whispered in her ear. "I won't expect you to do anything you're not sure about or not ready for."

She lay silent for a few moments and then she looked into his eyes. "I don't know what to say. This is just lovely, and it feels so right, but I never thought I would feel like this with anyone so soon." She lowered her gaze. "I've never had strong feelings like this for other boys, so it's never really been an issue . . ."

He sat up. "And it's not an issue between us either," he said. "I know things seem to be racing along, but they don't have to." He touched a hand to her hair. "Being this way with you feels beautiful and natural and right – but it is very soon and I understand that you want to take it slower." He smiled. "And believe it or not, there's a tiny sensible bit of me feels the same. So –" he stretched his hand out and took hers, "up you get, Miss Grace, and you can take me to see more of this fine college of yours."

When she stood up she wrapped her arms tightly around his neck, and tried to stop herself from shaking. She was grateful to him for reacting in such an understanding manner and yet disappointed they had to stop. She had never felt so physically aroused, and it was all she could do to stop herself pulling him back on to the bed. She wanted to tell him how disappointed she felt that they couldn't go further, but was afraid he might presume she wanted to have sex at some point very soon. Maybe in the next few days. And his presumption would be right, because her body certainly felt that, but a sensible little voice in her head was telling her something very different.

Darkness had fallen by the time they went outside and it seemed much colder than it had just over an hour ago.

"I think," Lily said, as they walked along hand in hand, "that we shouldn't waste that visitor's meal ticket I bought you. We might as well be sensible and go straight to the refectory now as it will close in half an hour."

He tightened his hand around hers. "I agree," he said light-heartedly. "We have to be sensible in all areas."

25

Lily was conscious of eyes being on them as they walked into the refectory, and she didn't doubt that Dara would meet with approval from the females. His hair, she knew, would draw attention, although not quite as much here as it did in Ireland.

As Lily had predicted there wasn't much choice left, and, after checking out the dried-up chicken casserole, they both picked up plates of cold meat salads and bread and glasses of milk. They chose a table in the far corner of the large hall and were only sitting a few minutes when Bill Toft and another fellow from her history group came to join them. Lily introduced them and was pleased when she saw how relaxed Dara was chatting to them, telling them how great he thought the college was, and then discussing football and rugby. The boys then asked him to explain exactly where he came from in Ireland, and he drew them a map on a paper napkin and pin-pointed Offaly for them.

When it was established that Lily and Dara were an item, and had met up the previous month Bill looked incredulously at her and said, "All the fine lads that are here in the college and she has to go all the way to Ireland to find one that suits her!"

Lily laughed and said, "I'm very particular, Bill – very particular!" And Dara caught her eye and winked at her.

Afterwards she took him on night-light tour of the college and grounds, pointing out the old main house and giving a quick history of the building, then showing him the new gym area and the building where she had her main lectures.

Dara was hugely impressed with it all, and when they finished up back at the Students' Union they went in for an early-evening drink while it was still quiet and they could chat.

Lily insisted on buying him his first drink, and when they clinked their glasses of lager together she was delighted when he said, "May this be the first of many drinks in here!"

They went to the jukebox and picked five tracks between them. Dara picked a couple of Rolling Stones songs and Lily picked "Yesterday" by the Beatles and Bob Dylan's "Like a Rolling Stone". And then, when they were picking the last track they laughed when they both stabbed their fingers on "I Got You, Babe".

When the first song – "The Last Time" – came on they went back to their table to listen and talk again.

They stayed for a second drink, and then they walked back to Lily's room by the back lane, pausing to look at the running track and the games field.

While Lily was fixing "Unchained Melody" on the record player, Dara looked through her record collection and after that he checked her bookcases.

As he leafed through one of her education books, Lily listened to the words of the song.

She looked over at him, and was struck again by the way she felt about him and all the physical longings he had. She was afraid to ask if he really meant all the words in "Unchained Melody" in case he said he did, because she knew it would only bring up another discussion about things moving too quickly. And yet, there was another part of her reluctant to bring it up in case she was reading too much into the lines . . . *I need your love* . . . and he told her that he hadn't chosen it for the lyrics and that it was the general feel of the song he liked.

When he asked her what she thought of it, she said she really liked it without going into any details. They also skirted around any more physical contact apart from the odd kiss and sitting together on the bed, backs leaning on the headboard, flicking through *The Mayor of Casterbridge* to find their favourite chapters and discussing other books they had both read.

When it came to nine o'clock Lily said, "I haven't asked you whether you like dancing or not?"

He looked bemused. "Why are you asking?"

"Because we said we might go to the Students' Union and there's a band playing in it."

"Do *you* like dancing?" he hedged.

"I love it, but we don't need to go if you're not keen. The only thing is, it's going to be very quiet around the campus after tonight. There will be nothing on in the bar apart from the juke-box."

He shrugged. "I don't mind either way. I'm happy enough to go." He got up from the bed now and went over to his rucksack. "Is it okay if I use the shower?" When Lily told him of course it was fine, he said, "Will you check that none of your housemates are using it?"

While he was showering, Lily went through her wardrobe and picked out a purple tunic she had bought in her favourite Love boutique which had two black patch pockets and a long black zip which went all the way from her neck to the hem which ended three inches above her knee. The zip had a large black, circular pull-tab in the shape of a flower with purple petals. She wore it with a skinny-rib black sweater, black tights and her stretchy boots.

Although the tights were definitely more practical with the new shorter styles than stockings and suspenders, she found them hard to get used to. With Dara out of the room, she had tried the outfit with stockings, but was afraid that when she sat down her tunic would ride up to reveal the band at the top of them.

She had opted for the tights, as she felt awkward enough with the physical issue between them without having to worry about the hem of her tunic riding up and exposing the top of her stockings.

She brushed her blonde hair out straighter than usual and sprayed it to keep it in place, then did her make-up. Then, reasonably satisfied with her appearance, she went over to the record-player and put a Kinks album on to make things feel more relaxed, and then switched the main light off and put on her bedside and study lamps.

She told herself that the sex thing wasn't a big problem between them. It was simply that she had expected the problem to be all Dara's. She had expected she might have to make it plain to him that she wasn't ready for any kind of a sexual relationship, and that they would have to be going out for a long time before anything like that happened. That's *if* she decided to let it happen before she was married. But what she hadn't taken into account – or even imagined – was the intensity of her own physical reaction towards him.

She had not considered that it would be an issue at this stage. She had thought that those strong feelings only came after having some experience of sex after marriage. She had presumed it was something to be learned, not something that came as naturally and automatically as the feelings that had engulfed her when lying on the bed with Dara earlier in the evening.

As she went over it all again, a feeling of dread stole over her. What have I done? she thought. I've put myself in a terrible situation – I've put Dara in a terrible situation, agreeing that he could stay here where there's not going to be anyone else. I should have just asked him to come to Scotland. A picture of her mother flew into her mind. If my mother knew what I've done, she would kill me!

The feeling became so intense she almost felt sick. She decided she needed to switch off her uncomfortable thoughts, so she lifted a *Honey* magazine from her bedside cabinet and forced herself to concentrate on a feature about fashions for professional women.

A short while later she turned towards the door when Dara came back into the room wearing a fitted striped shirt and jeans, his dark hair still damp from the shower. He hadn't fully buttoned up the shirt and when she saw the smooth triangle of skin on his chest showing, a little ripple ran through her making her feel slightly flustered.

"Wow!" he said, looking at her outfit. "You look amazing – and look at those legs!"

Lily felt herself flush. "Thanks," she said, going over to take the damp towel from him to put it on the radiator to dry. "You look really nice too. I like your shirt."

When he came over to take her in his arms and kiss her, she loved his fresh Pear's Soap and shampoo smell, and was glad it wasn't the pungent scent of Old Spice or Brylcreem. Growing up with her father and brothers, the familiar smells permeated the house any time there was a special occasion on. She could picture her father now, standing in front of the bathroom mirror, grimacing as he splashed the overpowering lotion onto his newly shaved skin.

They stood kissing for a while with the music playing low in the background, and again, after a few minutes of delicious closeness, she felt his body hard against hers. She tried to ignore the urge to lean against him, and became anxious when she found it difficult. Then, when she finally pulled away from him, she imagined she could feel a tension again between them, and she wondered how she was going to get through the rest of the evening and the whole weekend.

Although Dara gave no sign of being annoyed, she knew he must be. She had heard the other girls talking about how frustrated males got when girls led them on part of the way and then pulled back. While most of the girls at the college were sensible and had quite strict moral values, she knew several girls in the house who had their boyfriends stay over regularly and they were quite open with their friends about being on the Pill. She wondered if Dara had thought she was one of those modern types – especially with her living in England – and if he now regretted the effort he had made to come to see her.

If that was the case, Lily thought, it was all her fault. She should have thought about it properly instead of taking such a chance with someone she hardly knew.

But, she told herself, there was no point in panicking about it. He was here now and the situation would have to be managed.

26

The bar and even the entrance were packed and Lily held on tightly to Dara's hand as they made their way through the crowd towards the bar. Every now and then she tugged on his hand to make him come to a standstill while she spoke to people and introduced him. He chatted easily to everyone he met, and then stood at the bar with his arm around her while they were waiting to be served. Lily had glimpsed Ann and some of the other girls through the crowds, and thought she would catch up with them later as it was unfair to drag him into a circle of girls for the whole night.

On the first round Lily decided to have a half of lager, then, when she insisted on buying the second round, she ordered a Babycham. The band came on and they both agreed they were actually very good, playing a mixture of all the bands they liked. Dara ordered them both another lager and then they took their glasses and moved up towards the stage and the dance floor.

They stood for a while then a couple left a table beside them and they got two small stools at the end of it. They sipped their drinks and chatted when it wasn't too noisy, then Dara positioned his stool behind hers so he could slip his arms around her waist. Feeling more relaxed, she leaned back against him, her hands clasping his. They were sitting like that for a while when he moved his lips to her ear and said in a quiet voice, "Are you all right, Lily? You seem quieter and more thoughtful."

She turned towards him. "I'm fine," she said, a touch quickly. Oh God, she thought, I've made him feel awkward. He's come all the way from Ireland and he's been kind and generous and because of this sex thing I'm making him feel awkward. "Honestly, I'm fine. I didn't think I was being that quiet."

"Good," he said, squeezing her tighter. "I'm glad there's nothing wrong."

The band moved into quicker numbers now and groups of people moved onto the floor to dance. Lily waited a while, then when "Sugar Pie – Honey Bunch" came on, she turned to Dara. "Shall we dance?"

He laughed and rolled his eyes as though he would be too embarrassed, and it suddenly struck her how strange and odd she would find it to have a boyfriend who didn't like dancing. It was something she loved and she had always thought music and dancing went hand in hand. Whether she was at home or in her college room, if there was a tune – any kind of tune – playing on the radio, she found herself automatically moving in time to it.

She didn't force the point with him, and they sat for a while longer watching the other people on the floor, and making odd little comments.

Then, the band struck up with the familiar opening bars of The Stones "Satisfaction" and Dara leaned forward and said, "Do you want to get up now?"

"Okay," she said, but she had a little sinking feeling in her stomach as they stood up.

She knew it was stupid and that being a good dancer didn't really count for much, but if he was one of those awkward or jerky dancers she knew she would definitely be embarrassed or even worse, might start to laugh with nerves. And she supposed there was every chance he wouldn't be that great because there were quite a few awkward movers amongst the male students. If she had thought earlier, she would have checked him out on this, and found out whether he liked dancing or not – instead of just assuming.

The bar was so packed now that they had to shuffle along

slowly, Dara behind her, to find a space on the dance floor. The song had gone into full swing when she felt him moving closer to her and then placing his hands on her shoulders. As the beat got quicker she felt herself being moved from side to side in perfect time. She turned and looked back at him and he was singing along to it and moving naturally. Then, a space appeared on the floor and they shifted in opposite each other, both moving in the same way.

Lily's face lit up and she leaned towards him. "You can dance!"

He started laughing. "Of course I can! Did you think I had two left feet or something?" He took both her hands and started to move with her in a combination of The Twist and a jive.

"My God!" she said, laughing along with him. "You really can dance!"

"Irish people love dancing," he called over the music. "Another national trait!" Whether he realised how important it was to her or not, she didn't know. But it was another item ticked off on the unwritten list of things she would have asked for in the perfect boyfriend.

They stayed on the floor for the next few numbers and then just as they went to sit down the band started "Yesterday".

"One of your favourites," said Dara.

She smiled as Dara moved closer to her for a slow dance. There wasn't much room on the floor so they just circled around slowly moving between the other couples.

"This is a fantastic place," he said. "I'm really glad I came – it's a great change from the projector room on a Thursday night."

"I'm glad you came too," Lily said.

He moved back a little. "Are you really? I hope you're not regretting meeting up again."

"No," Lily gasped. "Not at all!" She couldn't let him think that. "It's just the thing about the rooms and everything, I'm just afraid I've given you the wrong impression about me."

His brow deepened "How?"

The music stopped and they went back to their places at the table. Lily took a sip of her drink, trying to find the right words. She really thought she had sorted it all out in her mind and was relaxed again, but Dara obviously didn't think that. Then, she saw Ann coming towards their table.

She gave Dara a cheery smile then bent to speak to Lily. "Pamela went back to the house to phone Edward, and he's just broken up with her." She nodded towards the doors. "She's in the ladies' now, crying her heart out."

"Oh, no!" Lily said.

Pamela had been going out with Edward since they were at secondary school – over five years. He was at Durham University studying Geology and had been coming up to Newcastle to stay with Pamela every other weekend. Lily thought he was okay, but he was old-fashioned in clothes and hairstyle, and inclined to be a bit pompous at times about things like religion and politics. He was also openly elitist with regards to food and wine which the other students hadn't even heard of and couldn't afford to buy.

Pamela clearly adored him, hanging on to his every word, and lived for his visits, fussing around him, and making sure she had his favourite Earl Grey tea, and little pots of jam for his toast in the morning. And any time she was in Newcastle she went to a special stall in the market to buy pâté and a fancy salmon mousse that he liked.

Naturally big-boned and hefty, Pamela had come back to college last September, after the summer break, over a stone lighter and determined to lose another stone by Christmas. Edward, it seems, had said he would prefer her to be more slender so she could wear some of the new short fashions that the female students in Durham were wearing.

Pamela had stuck rigidly to her diet and had taken a walk around the campus every morning after breakfast and in the evening after dinner, and by the time the time the Christmas holidays had come around she had lost another stone and a half.

She confided in the girls that she had been hoping for an engagement ring at Christmas but had come back quiet and disappointed, showing them a small silver locket he had bought her instead. She had raised her hopes again when they went off to spend the night together in a hotel in Newcastle for Valentine's Day, but she had come back to college ring-less yet again.

And now it seemed, after all her efforts, the romance was completely off.

"What happened?" Lily asked.

Ann pulled a face. "He's been seeing somebody else, a girl from York who's on the same course as him. Can you imagine what they must be like? Two boring geologists trying to impress each other with their pâtés and fancy teas."

"Poor Pamela," Lily said. "But Edward was always a bit of a pain, so she's probably better off without him. Do you think we should we go in and check on her?"

"I've been with her for the last ten minutes, and Beryl is still there trying to console her. Maybe if you went in it might help." She gave a sigh. "She's had a bit too much to drink which isn't a bit like her. I think she's downing her sorrows. She downed a double rum and Coke and then she went up and bought a double sherry."

Lily put her hand to her mouth. "Oh, no, not *sherry* – too much of that is lethal." She looked at Dara. "Will you be okay if I go out to see one of the girls for a few minutes?"

"You go on, I'll be grand."

Pamela was sitting in one of the toilet cubicles, rubbing her mascara-ringed eyes with handfuls of tissue. "How can I go home?" she sobbed. "It's only a small town and everyone knows us. He told me that he's bringing her home to meet his parents next weekend. All the girls knew I was hoping to get an engagement ring and they all probably knew he was seeing that slut on the side." She brought the tissues up to her eyes again. "It's a total humiliation for me after losing all the weight to please him." She sniffled into her hanky. "We were perfect together – all my family loved him and all my friends. I'll never meet anyone like him again."

Lily wondered what on earth they had seen in the pompous boorish Edward. "If he would do such a terrible thing," she said, "then you don't want to meet anyone like him again."

"You don't understand," Pamela snapped. "We had the exact same background and the same school friends – the same religion and politics. We had plans to buy a house in York and we'd even talked about the furniture we wanted. How will I find someone like that again?"

"You just have to give it time," Lily said in a soothing voice.

"How could he do it to me? How could he be all nice and normal one night on the phone and the next tell me that it's all over?" She shook her head. "I don't know how I can face seeing everyone!"

"Edward and this new girl will be keeping a low profile," Beryl said. "They know people will be annoyed at what they've done, so you probably won't see them around at all."

"It's a small place," Pamela repeated. "I'm bound to run into them."

"Why don't you come up to my parents' for a few days?" Ann suggested. "I'm not doing much over the holidays, and we've got a spare room."

Pamela thought for a few moments. "Thanks, but my parents are expecting me home." She gave a weak smile.

"If it gets too much for you with Edward around you could come for the last weekend.

"I will think about it."

Lily stayed a while longer, throwing in a few words of sympathy or encouragement where it was required. When she felt there was a bit of an improvement and that Pamela was now looking at how she was going to handle things, she left them and headed back into the main hall.

The band were playing a Beach Boys' number that she liked and she was just going to the table to get Dara up to dance again when she halted in her tracks. He was sitting with two of the most glamorous third-year girls, one on either side of him.

They were girls Lily didn't know that well, but they were so striking that everyone noticed them and she had been told they were first cousins. The blonde one, Pippa, was from London and the brunette, Moya, she now remembered was from Dublin. Lily had been surprised when she discovered that the very sophisticated dark-haired girl was Irish, but since she was in the year above them and didn't move in their circles, she had forgotten about it.

They were always dressed in the latest fashions with bright pink lips and false eyelashes, and were usually to be seen on the arms of the college rugby team players or one of the male students who owned a sports car. She watched them now, as they both talked animatedly to Dara, giggling and constantly touching his arm or his shoulder as if they'd known him for years.

Lily took a deep breath and walked over to the table.

"Hi," she said, looking at Dara, "will we have a dance?"

The girls looked up at her as if she were intruding on a private conversation.

"Grand," he said, standing up. "I'll see you later, girls."

"Don't forget," the Irish one said, "we'll be gone tomorrow afternoon."

Lily waited until they were out of earshot. "How did you get stuck with them?" "They were passing the table when I was chatting to the lad next to me," he explained, "and they heard the accent. They thought I was on my own so they sat down for a few minutes."

They started to dance.

"Did you tell them you were with me?"

"No," he said. "I thought it was best not to."

She stopped dancing. "Why not?" Did he want to give the impression he was unattached, she wondered, or had he got so carried away talking to a glamorous Irish girl that he had forgotten about her?

He stopped dancing now too. "They were talking about going to London for the half-term and they wanted to know where I was staying and all that kind of thing. I didn't say anything about us because I was afraid it might put you in an awkward position if they guessed I was staying with you. I didn't know whether they might tell someone or report you."

Lily looked at him now in relief. "You were right to do that."

"Good," he said. "I didn't want to put my foot in it. I feel you're strained enough with me being here without making it more awkward for you."

The same look came on his face that had been there earlier and she now recognised it as dejection, and she realised if she didn't sort this situation out he was going to go. He'd never stick out the weekend in Newcastle and would probably just go back to Ireland. Or he might even hook up with Pippa and Moya.

The thought of it galvanised her into action. She moved to put her arms around his neck. "Dara, you've done nothing to make me feel awkward. It's me. It's all my fault."

She felt his arms tighten around her waist, swaying to the music and then she felt his mouth close to her ear. "As long as we're both okay, Lily," he whispered. "We can sort this out. We can work together and make sure we both feel okay."

And then suddenly it all made sense. The whole thing of them being together. She wasn't carrying this thing all by herself. She was now with Dara and he was with her. Without knowing exactly *why*, she knew that they had a special connection that not many people ever found. It didn't matter how long they had known each other or how near or far they were from each other. The bond was there. And even what her mother might think now or later didn't matter either. This was her life and her future. The choices she made had to be hers and hers alone. Whether she ran to meet Dara halfway or whether she ran in the opposite direction.

If they continued down the path they had already started on, they would find their way together. It might not always be easy, but it would be worth it. If she took cold feet now about what other people might say or do, she would lose him. And she would forever regret giving up at the first hurdle, because she knew that he would not make this journey twice to be rejected.

It was suddenly crystal clear. She alone had responsibility for her future and, at this moment, for their future together. As the realisation dawned on her, she knew she would remember this moment for many years to come.

She tilted her head and looked up at him, and in the darkness of the smoky hall he kissed her passionately – and she kissed him back.

All the fear and uncertainty had gone. She wasn't going to waste any more time worrying about imaginary repercussions.

Tonight, and for the next four nights, Dara would sleep in the same room and in the same single bed as her.

27

They had enjoyed the rest of the night, dancing to the band and then chatting to her housemates who came to join them for the last hour. They were followed a short while later by Bill Toft and some of his friends who brought their stools over to their table.

Every so often Lily had glanced at Dara to check he was okay, and was pleased and relieved to see him joining in with the friendly banter.

He seemed completely at home, as if he had known them for ages, and had no trouble throwing in the odd comment or joke, and later, when Bill asked him about his course, he held the attention of the whole group.

It was only at the end of the night that she felt the awkwardness again, and it was neither of their faults. Dara had been angled towards Bill as they discussed the music scene in Dublin, while Lily had pulled her stool in the opposite direction so she could join in the discussion with the other girls about the letter that Pamela now planned to write to her cheating boyfriend.

The incident might have passed unnoticed if Ann hadn't gestured to Lily to look behind her. When she turned, Lily caught sight of the two girls who had been chatting to Dara earlier, and saw the dark-haired Irish one passing a slip of paper to him.

She watched as Dara held the paper out to her and shrugged –

as though trying to give it back – but the girl had just bent down and whispered something in his ear. By the time Lily had closed the gap between her and Dara the girls had gone off.

"What did they want now?" she asked in a low voice, hoping that she didn't sound as suspicious as she felt.

He shrugged. "Your guess is as good as mine. They asked me how long I was over here for, and when I told them I was leaving on Tuesday, they said if had nothing on next weekend there was a party in London in a big Irish bar." He handed Lily the note. It had an address and phone number on it.

Her face reddened with annoyance. "The bloody cheek! They know you're with me."

He put his arm around her. "Lily, they are not worth bothering about, and even if I wasn't with you, they're not the type of girls I'd be interested in. I said that in a polite, roundabout way."

"I don't care," she said. "They still shouldn't have done that."

He took the note off her now and tore it up into tiny pieces and put it in the ashtray. "There you go," he said, "that's the end of it."

She could see that he meant it. She decided to say no more for fear of coming across as insecure and jealous.

He squeezed her hand now. "That kind of thing might well happen to either of us during the times we're apart. I'm quite sure you get approached by lads all the time." He shifted his eyes in the direction of Bill and the other lads. "I can tell by the way they all talk about you that most of them wouldn't mind a chance with you."

She laughed. "You must be joking! I wouldn't be seen dead with any of them."

He raised his eyebrows. "Exactly my point," he told her, gently but firmly. "And even though you're going to be here on campus with them all during the term-time while I'm back home – I believe you're not interested in them and I trust you."

Lily looked at him and smiled. "Point taken."

It was after twelve when they walked back to Lily's house with the other girls. Pamela had gone quiet again, her earlier euphoria at all the things she would put in the letter to Edward having seeped away as the effects of the drink she had taken wore off. She also said she felt a bit sick.

Ann and Beryl said they would go back to the room with her to make sure she was okay, and when they were in the hallway Lily whispered to Ann, "I'm going to make coffee for Dara and me, and I'll make a strong one for Pamela and bring it down to her room."

She made Pamela's coffee first and delivered it, then she made some for herself and Dara and they carried them back up to her room.

Things felt very relaxed between them now and they both sat on the bed with their backs against the wall, drinking their coffee and going over the evening.

They talked about their plans for the following day. When Lily finished lectures at one, they were going to catch the coach out to Morpeth, a local market town about eight miles away and spend the afternoon there. They would come back and have their evening meal in the smaller café on site as the main refectory was closing at lunchtime for the half-term break.

"I'll get up and go over to breakfast," Lily told him, "and I'll bring you back a bacon sandwich or something like that."

"That's great," he told her. "You said the cleaners will be around the house in the morning while you're at lectures, so I thought I would take a walk down into the village and get a newspaper and maybe find a quiet pub to sit and read it in."

"It's a good half an hour's walk," she warned him.

"I know," he said. "I saw it on my way in here on the coach. It looked a nice village so I'll pass a couple of hours easily until you're finished."

"There are four pubs in it," Lily said, "so you can try them all out and see which one you fancy for us to go to tomorrow night."

"Great, sounds like a good plan." His suddenly looked serious. "It's getting late and I think it's time you decided where you would like me to sleep tonight."

"Here," she said, patting the bed. "I've thought about it and I want you to stay here with me."

His face softened a bit. "Okay," he said. "But it's on one condition."

She looked at him. "What?"

"That we both agree nothing serious happens between us." He smiled. "Well, nothing *very* serious happens."

Lily bit her lip, not sure what to say.

"I've been thinking about it a lot this evening, and I think it would be best for both of us if we know where the boundaries are. That way, you don't have to feel that things are going too quick for you, and . . ." His tone was very serious now. He took her hands in his. "And it means that we're not going to make any serious mistakes that we might regret for the rest of our lives."

She pondered his words for a few moments. "You mean me getting pregnant or something like that?"

"Exactly." He was smiling now. "It's the last thing either of us needs at this stage in our studies and so early in our lives."

Lily looked up at the ceiling. "My mother would absolutely kill me!"

"Well, we can't have that either," he said, laughing. "So until we've been together for a while longer, and until you're absolutely, one hundred per cent sure, I think it would save you worrying – and me wondering – if we just say we won't get ourselves into a situation that's too dangerous for us."

Her head was lowered now and she looked at him from under her eyelashes. "You're right, and I think you're very mature and sensible to have thought it out like this." She paused. "Knowing myself as I do, I would probably get cold feet doing anything we shouldn't – especially so early – and that would only cause problems between us."

"I thought that," he said. "And I also thought that we can't take any risks." He gave a self-conscious smile. "And I don't want to embarrass you or anything, but talking along those lines, even if we agreed to let things take their natural course, I haven't any protection with me. You know things like Durex are illegal in Ireland?"

Lily's hand flew to her mouth. She'd never talked this way with anyone before. "No, I didn't know that!"

"Well, they are. So I suppose I thought we'd talk about it when I got here and then decide whether they were necessary or not." He shrugged. "But I think that deep down I knew that we would only be rushing things."

"If it was different circumstances, would you like us to . . .?"

He looked at her incredulously. "Of course I would." He laughed and made a pantomime of grabbing her now. "When I'm close to you I can't think of anything else."

She laughed now too. "I wonder if this is the kind of conversation all couples have when things start to get serious? I just can't imagine some of my friends talking like this."

He nodded. "Neither can I, but that's the problem. If you don't talk about it properly then that's when things happen that shouldn't happen."

28

The alarm clock startled them both when it rang. Lily was on the inside of the bed at the wall and she tried to stretch over Dara to switch it off, but her arm wouldn't reach that far. She ended up having to lie across him and, as she was moving back to her former position, he put both his arms on hers and guided her to lie on top of him.

She nuzzled into his bare chest. "Did we get any sleep at all last night?" she asked him.

"I think," he said, "we might have got a few hours."

"I don't want to move," she told him. "I want to stay like this forever."

"So do I, but there's the small matter of your lectures to consider." He pulled her closer now and started to kiss her.

As she pressed against him, Lily felt the familiar longing starting again in the pit of her stomach and she took a deep shuddering breath. "This is so, so hard," she whispered.

"Not really," he said, pushing his lower half tight against hers, "but I think it's about to get a whole lot harder now."

She dissolved into giggles as she realised what he was referring to. "You are terrible! "

They lay for another while, kissing and caressing and whispering to each other, Lily wearing her pink and white baby-doll nightie and matching knickers and he in inoffensive black-and-white patterned underpants. His choice of underwear had earned him another tick on her list, as she had secretly dreaded seeing him in the fluorescent Y-fronts that were all the rage just now, or the ones with cartoon characters or cars on them that Declan had taken to wearing.

Looking back on the events of the previous night, Lily wondered at how easy and natural things had been between them. Since they had sorted things out, it was as if a great weight had been lifted off her. She felt relaxed now that she knew that nothing too serious was going to either happen between them or cause a row between them, and it let them concentrate on getting to know each other better.

And they had spent a good part of last night doing exactly that. She had never spent a night lying beside a male before – had never really allowed herself to imagine what it would be like. And it had been a complete revelation to her. One of the best experiences of her life to date.

And it had all happened so easily, she could hardly remember how they had got from lying on top of the bed to lying under the covers together with his lovely warm skin against hers. Of course the drinks in the Students Union had helped things along a bit, and then the reassuring conversation.

While Dara was brushing his teeth, she had turned all the lights off apart from the small bedside one. Then, with only the slightest apprehension, she had got changed into her night things and slid into bed.

And after that, everything has just fallen into place. Dara had switched the lamp off and then they had naturally gravitated into each other's arms. They had spent hours wrapped together, kissing and cuddling and enjoying the touch and the feel of their skin so close together.

Now Lily instructed him to go back to sleep while she showered and dressed and ran over to the refectory to grab a quick breakfast and bring something back for him.

After her breakfast she woke him and gave him a mug of coffee, which she had made in the downstairs kitchen, and a large roll with bacon and egg that she had brought from the refectory. Then she sat on the end of the bed drinking her own coffee while he ate it.

"I was chatting to Ann on the way back to the house," she told him, "and she said you might be best getting the coach down to the village rather than walk past the Porter's Lodge on your own. Apparently, if he doesn't recognise someone, he could stop and ask them for their college ID and if you don't have it, he might not let you back in."

Dara nodded his head. "They're like that in the university in Dublin as well."

"It will be fine whenever the college closes tomorrow, because the usual porter has the week off too, and the temporary one doesn't know the students. He just waves you past."

She then went on to explain that the coach from Morpeth would pull in around ten o'clock and drop him off in the village, and that there would be one coming back at quarter to one. The cleaners would be gone by then and most of the students would be heading home.

"No problem," he said, "I'll make sure I do things right so you don't get into trouble." He paused. "Did your friend ask if I used her room last night?"

"No, and I didn't say anything either." Her face was serious now. "This is different from anything I've done before – you and me – and I want to keep it private. I didn't mind chatting and giggling about other boys before, because it didn't mean anything, but I don't want to do that about you."

"I was the same with my brothers," Dara said. "We would sneer at each other and make stupid remarks about any girls the others were going out with. When I told them about you and they started the same nonsense I told them to shut up and stop being so immature and they fell about laughing at me."

Lily grinned at him. "Did they? They were really nice to me when I visited your house."

"That's because you were Scottish and so different, and very good-looking. I think they were lost for words, plus I'd threatened to kill them."

They both laughed and then they chatted a bit longer while they finished their coffees.

Then Lily checked her watch. "I'm going to have to go – my first lecture is at half nine." She went over to the hook on the door to get her jacket, then to pick up her shoulder bag and folder with her lecture notes and notepad.

"I'll get ready to go to the village now," he told her, "and I'll see you back here around one."

She came back over to sit on the bed. "It's stupid, but I'm going to miss you. I'll be thinking about you all during my lecture."

"Good," he said, "because I don't want to imagine you sitting in a lecture room surrounded by lads."

She laughed at him and then gave him a quick kiss before heading out the door. And as she went down the stairs she thought that even though she knew he was half-joking, how lovely it was that he was just the tiniest bit jealous.

29

The rest of Friday went off just as planned, with a busy afternoon spent in Morpeth, the capital town of Northumberland, looking around the old castle ruins and the old churches and buildings. They found an old coaching inn and spent an hour there, then later headed back to college for their evening meal. Then, around eight o'clock they wrapped up in coats and scarves and gloves and took a walk out to one of the lovely old pubs in the village.

As there were no cleaners around the residences at the weekend, they lay in bed late on Saturday, and then they went down to the kitchen and Dara helped her make coffee and omelettes. Around lunchtime they ran across the green for the coach to carry them from the quiet of the campus into the bustling centre of Newcastle city.

As Lily had anticipated, Dara's main interest was the old buildings in the city. Since it was a nice day they spent a couple of hours wandering around the streets, looking at Grey's Monument and the towering old buildings in Grey Street and Pilgrim Street, and then Lily guided them down more side streets and lanes to the smaller shops she liked.

They visited the old Catholic Cathedral and, while Dara was wandering around looking at the inside roof design, Lily went to a side altar and lit two candles. She prayed that things would work out well for them with the first candle and that she would be forgiven for not telling her mother about Dara's visit to Newcastle with the other.

They walked down to the railway station, a Grade 1 listed building. Its distinctive roof with three arched spans was the first example of its kind. After a quick look around it, they headed back into the city centre and found a cosy old pub that sold food. They went in and had fish and chips and a couple of drinks each.

"It's a great city," Dara told her. "I can see why you picked it."

Lily nodded. "I love it. Next year I'll be doing a full term's teaching practice in one of the city schools, so I'll be living in lodgings somewhere around here. I'd actually love one of the seaside schools. Do you know we're near Whitley Bay?"

"I'm ashamed to say I don't know the North of England at all," he said. "I just had time to look up Newcastle on the map and then work my journey over from Manchester." He gave her a hug. "Hopefully I'll get to know it much better over the next year."

"I hope you get to know it too," she said. "And I hadn't a clue about it either before my interview." She gestured with her hand. "Anyway, Whitley Bay is the biggest seaside place and it has a huge funfair. I had a great day out there last September with a crowd of the girls. We really had a laugh. It's a pity it's winter now, because it would have been nice to visit it."

"We have plenty of time to see all these places," he told her.

"What do you want to do tonight?" Lily asked. "We could stay in town and catch one of the late buses back. They don't go into the college after nine, so we would have to walk back from the village."

"I'd be happy to stay in Newcastle," he told her. "It's fantastic. And it's a dry enough night to walk back to the college." He thought for a moment. "I thought the cinema looked great – will we have a look and see what's on?"

Lily looked at him in amazement. "Don't you get enough of cinemas back home? Talk about bringing coals to Newcastle!"

He looked at her and they both laughed. "I know it sounds a bit mad, but it's different over here from Ireland. We're in a big city that will have all the brand new films. We don't get them down the country for at least six months or a year later. It would be great to tell the lads that I've seen one of the films that's just come out."

They found The Queens cinema first.

"I don't believe it!" Lily said, "It's *The Sound of Music*."

"Great film," Dara said, "but I know it so well I could act and sing all the parts."

They walked up to the Odeon on Pilgrim Street and saw all the signs advertising *Thunderball* and found out the next showing was in half an hour's time.

"If you don't mind James Bond, I think it's a good one," Dara said.

Lily shrugged and smiled. "I quite like James Bond."

"Great!" He rubbed his hands together. "The lads at home will be raging I've seen it before them. I can't wait to get back and wind them up about it." He checked his watch then pointed to a pub across the road. "Time for another drink before it starts."

As they sat in the one of the rows at the back of the cinema, Lily whispered to him that it was amazing that they were together in a cinema in Newcastle only weeks after meeting in one in Ireland.

"That was the luckiest night of my life," he whispered back, and she buried her face in his neck.

Lily thought the film was fairly good and she was pleased that Dara enjoyed it so much. She liked the romantic parts and the setting in the Bahamas, and covered her face at the breathtaking chases and the frightening scenes when people were thrown into a pool of sharks to be eaten alive.

Towards the end it crossed her mind that the time had flown by so quickly and they had only two days left together. The thought of it brought a tightness to her chest and she found it hard to imagine that he would be gone back over the sea and she would be in Scotland. But, she knew, that's how things were and nothing could change it. She would have to then wait another five or six weeks until Easter to see him again.

She worried what would happen in that time. She knew from the reaction of the girls in the house and the two third-years that she wasn't the only one to find him good-looking and to admire his lovely long hair. What, she wondered, would happen if he actually realised he could have almost any girl he wanted?

Then she thought again of all the girls at the university with him in Dublin. The girls who would see him day after day, while she was back in Newcastle counting the hours until she saw him again.

She hugged his arm closer to her and then closed her eyes and laid her head on his shoulder.

His hand immediately came to touch her face. "Are you okay, Lily?"

"I was just thinking how quickly the time has gone and how I'll feel when you're gone back."

"You must be telepathic," he said in a low voice. "Because I was thinking the exact same thing. We'll just have to do what we did these last few weeks, writing and phoning all the time until I come over to you at Easter."

She moved her lips to his ear. "You'll have to share a room with Declan."

He shrugged. "As long as I can see you I don't care where I sleep."

Then they heard a loud *"Shhhhhh!"* coming from a man in the seat behind and they both huddled in close together trying not to laugh.

* * *

As Lily had dreaded, the last two days flew in and then it was Tuesday, and they were both standing at the college green waiting for the coach to take them to Newcastle.

She had timed her train up to Scotland to coincide with Dara's train back to Manchester. He arranged to meet the friend he had travelled over with at the station there and would travel back with him in the car to Holyhead to catch the overnight boat to Dublin.

They had a coffee in the station and then when the time came, he walked her to her platform and waited with her until the train pulled in. As it pulled up alongside them she felt her chest tighten and tears springing in her eyes.

Dara gathered her up in his arms one last time and held her close to him and she breathed in the sweet familiar scent of his hair and face and neck. Then the train doors started to bang open and she knew she had to move. She lifted her case and shoulder bag and then turned for one last kiss. Then she stepped on the train, feeling as though a part of her had been ripped away.

When she got in she quickly closed the door and rushed to put her luggage in the rack, then she came back and pulled the window down and leaned out.

He stood close to the door, his rucksack at his feet, and held her hands in his. "I wasn't going to say this, because I know it's going to sound all gushy and stupid . . ." His voice trailed away.

"What?" she asked, conscious that the train was going to move any minute.

"You might think it's too soon and it probably is, but . . . I think I love you, Lily. You're like no other girl I've ever met . . . and I'm going to miss you so much that it hurts."

A wave of joy tinged with sadness washed over her. It was more than she had hoped for. Tears sprang into her eyes and ran down the back of her throat. She nodded, unable to speak.

A whistle blew and then the train shuddered into life. It started to move and Dara moved alongside it for a moment, still holding her hands, and then he let go.

Lily suddenly found her voice as it pulled away. "I love you too!" she called. "I love you too."

30

Everyone commented on how quiet Lily was back home, and she kept having to reassure her mother that she wasn't sickening for something. She couldn't tell them that her mind was constantly being pulled back to her room and single bed back in Newcastle. And she was afraid to mention Dara's name in case she said something that gave away their stolen days together.

And so she had moved about the family house in Rowanhill with a small smile pinned on her face, trying not to show the loss she felt.

Her mother's talk filled the silences as she told Lily all about the wedding in Dunfermline, going into great detail about the bride's and bridesmaids' dresses and the wedding cake and the meal they'd had. She then gave long descriptions about the bed and breakfast they had stayed in and re-enacted conversations she'd had with people at the wedding and the owners of the guesthouse.

Shortly after she arrived home her mother had asked about Dara.

"He's definitely coming at Easter if that's still okay?"

"He's welcome, the same as all your friends." Her mother's brow had creased. "I was worried when you went to college in Newcastle that you might meet an English lad and want to go and live there, but I never imagined you'd meet an Irish one."

Lily looked at her. "What about it?"

"Well, if you're just friends then it's fine. But if it goes deeper then you could run into all sorts of problems with him over there, and you back in Scotland, when you finish college."

She shrugged. "Who knows what'll happen, we'll have to see."

Her mother's eyes had narrowed in thought. Then, after a while she asked Lily what she had thought of Ava.

Lily had looked blankly at her. "She was nice."

"Maybe too nice by the sounds of it," her mother said.

"What do you mean?"

"Well, I saw a picture of herself that she sent to him, and you can tell a mile away that she could do an awful lot better than him. And Seán and your father have said as much. So I'm just wondering what it is that she wants?"

"Poor Declan," Lily said. "That's not a very nice thing to say about him."

Mona had glanced over her shoulder, checking that no one else was listening. "It's the truth," she stated. "He's my own son and I love him the same as I do the lot of you, and in a lot of ways he has the kindest nature. But I've seen her picture and heard what you've all said about her and it doesn't add up."

"Is she still coming at Easter?"

"As far as I know. She'll be staying at your Auntie Sophie's because there's no room here for a girl. Sophie is delighted to have company because the house is so quiet these days. She still misses Heather and Kirsty, and she's getting the bedroom all decorated for Ava coming. I told her not to go to any trouble, but she says it needs doing and having a visitor gives her the perfect excuse."

"Well, you'll see Ava for yourself when she comes," Lily said, "and you'll find what everyone thinks about her is true. She's a lovely girl and for some reason she thinks our Declan is the bee's knees."

* * *

Heather, Lily's cousin, came out from Glasgow to catch up with Lily on the Friday. She called at her mother's house first and then came the few houses up to Mona's house. She had left her two children at home with a friend so they could have a good chat without being disturbed.

"You're looking great," Lily told her pregnant cousin when they were in the kitchen on their own.

Heather smoothed her maternity smock over her growing bump. Over the years she had changed very little. With shoulder-length dark hair, she was naturally curvier than her younger sister, Kirsty, but she kept herself trim with all the walking she did, taking the children to the park or down to the local shops.

"I feel great," she said. "I usually do at this stage when I've got past all the morning sickness." She smiled at Lily. "I hear from various sources that there's an Irish fella on the scene. Is it serious?"

Lily went over to close the door properly. "Yes." She spoke in a low voice, her eyes sparkling. "I suppose in a way it is serious, although I don't want to talk about it too much in front of my mother."

Heather's brow knitted together. "Why? What's the problem. He's not a Protestant or anything?"

Lily shook her head. Her mother's obsession about people from the same religion sticking together was well-known throughout the family. That particular problem had raised its head on a number of occasions, especially some years back when their dad's sister, Clare, had married an older Protestant.

"No, he's from a Catholic family. It's because he's from Ireland – she thinks it's too far away and too complicated."

"Odd, with her being Irish herself. Ah well . . . and do you feel it's too complicated?"

"It's not easy," Lily admitted, "but we've been keeping in touch by phone or letters every few days."

She had a warm glow about her now – talking about him made their relationship seem more real, brought him closer to her. She told Heather how Dara was not only gorgeous, but that he had lots of other great qualities such as intelligence and a good sense of humour. She explained he was studying to be an architect, and said she had never met anyone like him before and, even though it was early days, she couldn't imagine finding anyone nicer.

"That really is serious," Heather said. "Does Kirsty know?" She knew that Lily and her sister were that little bit closer but she didn't mind.

"Yes, I've written and told her all about him."

She hadn't mentioned anything in the letter to Kirsty about Dara's visit. She wasn't quite sure how Kirsty would react to hearing how she had organised him to come to the college without her parents knowing. She was also unsure what her older cousin's view would be on them spending days on their own together in a house. Either way she felt, whether Kirsty approved or disapproved, that it wasn't fair to swear her to secrecy over it, because it was difficult not to blurt things like that out by mistake. If everything went well in the coming months with her and Dara, she thought she might take her into her confidence then.

Heather was lovely, but an entirely different kettle of fish from her sister, and Lily couldn't imagine talking to her about such personal things.

"Why don't we go over to my mother's?" Heather suggested. "She said that Kirsty is going to ring this afternoon, so we can all have a few words with her."

"Oh, that would be great," Lily said, getting up from the table. "I'd love to hear all about the cruise and the places they've been visiting. Have you any idea where she is now?"

Heather said she thought she would be somewhere in Spain or Greece. "I'm sure she said Athens was one of the ports she'd be in this week or next."

They walked a few houses along to Heather's mother's and Lily got her usual great welcome. Sophie insisted that all three of them have a small sherry, telling Heather it would be good for the baby's blood. Heather wasn't so sure and only took a few sips from the glass.

Sophie also asked about Dara, and Lily was delighted to have another opportunity to talk at length about him. Sophie said she thought he sounded lovely, and advised her to enjoy the friendship and the letters and phone calls while it lasted, and not to worry too much about how things would pan out in the end. Lily felt a little deflated and thought her aunt didn't seem to hold out much hope for their future, but she said nothing.

When they started talking about Kirsty's travels, Sophie went off to get her latest postcard collection to show to the girls, then she brought out the entertainment brochures from the cruise-ship. There were pictures of Kirsty looking her most glamorous, wearing tight, low-cut sparkly dresses and matching high heels. Larry, her husband and manager, had his name and photograph on the bottom of the brochure.

Lily's voice was breathless. "Oh, she is absolutely gorgeous!"

Sophie looked at the clock. "She said she would ring around three, so hopefully she will and we can all have a wee chat with her."

Kirsty's voice came across the line loud and clear. She chatted first to her mother and then wanted to hear how Heather's pregnancy was progressing. It crossed Lily's mind that Kirsty had been married a number of years and there was still no sign of children. She wondered if it was deliberate, since having a baby would have a huge impact on her career – or whether they actually wanted children and were having problems conceiving.

It wasn't that she couldn't ask Kirsty, because her cousin was open about most things, but more that she didn't want to hurt her by raising a subject that might prove painful for her.

When the phone was passed to Lily, Kirsty immediately started quizzing her all about Dara. "I can tell by your letters that you're very keen," she laughed. "And from your descriptions of him, I don't blame you."

They chatted about him for a while and then Lily asked her all about the ship and the places she had visited recently.

"The ship is amazing, very luxurious," Kirsty told her. "The restaurants and the theatres and the cinema are exactly what you would see in an American movie. Some of the cabins aren't huge but the more expensive ones have their own balconies and are done out in a fabulous art-deco style."

"It sounds fantastic," Lily said.

"But of course it's only for the very wealthy people who can afford it, the staff cabins are much more basic."

"Is the food nice?"

Kirsty had laughed. "Wonderful for the passengers! Ours is nice but not quite so exotic."

"What else do they have on the ship?"

"Well, they have their own beauty salons and hairdressers, and rows of shops. It's so big you have to see it to believe it."

"And where have you stopped off?" Lily asked.

"On this cruise we've been to lovely sunny places like Gibraltar, Malaga, and Barcelona in Spain, and we're going to several Italian ports and then on to Athens. I'll write all about it in my next letter."

Even the names of the cities made Lily catch her breath, it all sounded so exotic and interesting.

"I suppose you won't be interested in work on the cruise-ship over the summer now you're courting so seriously?"

Immediately Lily realised that she wouldn't want to be separated from Dara for a whole summer, but she didn't want to explain that while the others were around. "Why?" she hedged. "Has anything come up?"

"Nothing definite yet. I heard there might be a few vacancies in the shops, but we won't know for a month or two yet. "

Kirsty then asked her how things had worked out with her college lecturer.

Lily glanced over at her smiling aunt and cousin who could hear her side of the conversation. "That was all sorted," she said. "And we've become good friends."

"Take it as a compliment he liked you. As he said, he's flattered that such a lovely girl would like him. It would probably all have been different if he hadn't been married." Kirsty laughed. "I've done a lot more embarrassing things than that. I cringe when I think how hard I ran after Larry, when he thought I was too young for him."

"In your case, it was worth it," Lily said. "But I'm over it now and Dara's much more suitable for me in every way."

"Oh, it sounds as though life is varied and exciting for you at the moment, with all these men in your life, Miss Grace. It makes me think back to when I was your age."

"You wouldn't change places though," Lily laughed. "You wouldn't want to be studying and writing essays and teaching a class of thirty-five children."

"No, I suppose not," Kirsty said. "And I can't complain. I get to travel all over the world with the man of my dreams."

"How is he?"

"Larry is great," Kirsty said. "He's just signed up a new Scottish band called *Dynamite*. They're absolutely brilliant. Larry reckons that in time they could be as good as the Beatles. They're joining us on the June cruise."

Lily suddenly had a thought. She didn't want to be heard so she moved towards the window, stretching the phone cable. "Do you have any summer vacancies for male students," she murmured, "like waiters or maybe working in the kitchen?"

There was a pause. "And who did you have in mind? Anyone in particular?"

"There might be . . ."

"The Irish architect student by any chance?"

"It could be." Lily's voice was light and easy.

"I'll keep it in mind," Kirsty told her. "Wouldn't it be fantastic for you to have the summer together in the sunshine? And your mother wouldn't be able to say a word with me and Larry there to chaperone you."

"I never thought of that." Her mind suddenly filled with all the possibilities. She could see herself and Dara standing on the deck of the luxury ship at night and seeing the lights all glinting in the water. She could imagine them walking around all the sunny Mediterranean cities hand in hand, he in shorts and her in glamorous dark glasses. She glanced over at the other two women but they were chatting away, oblivious to what she was saying. "I don't know what plans he has for the summer. But you never know, it might just work out."

"Exactly," Kirsty said. "Give me a bit of time and we'll see what comes up."

*   *   *

On the Saturday morning Lily was tidying up and sorting out clothes for her return journey to Newcastle the following day, when

Declan came up to her bedroom, an envelope with an Irish postmark on it clutched in his hand.

"I was wondering," he said, closing the door behind him, "if you'd ask the cinema fella – Darren –"

"*Dara*," Lily cut in. "I don't know how many times I've told you, his name is Dara."

"Right, *Dara* then," he said, his brow knitted irritably. "When you're talking to him next, will you ask him if Ava can travel over with him at Easter? It's just that she's a bit nervous about coming over on her own. She's never travelled outside of Ireland and doesn't know how to go about booking her ticket, and with it being an overnight boat she'd rather have company." He gave a knowing look. "With such a fine-looking girl you never know who'd be trying to chat her up."

"She's a nice-looking girl," Lily said, "but she's not exactly Marilyn Monroe or anything."

Declan ignored the jibe. "She's very modest, she would never think of herself that way. It's just my opinion and, being a man myself, I know how other men think. You might not realise it, but she's not as confident as she appears and I think she's had a few bad experiences with men."

Lily thought back to the night in the bed and breakfast with Seán and Ava when the older man had caused all the trouble. She had never mentioned it to Declan since he had only come out of hospital, and she didn't know whether the other two had said anything about it either.

"That's fine," she said. "But wouldn't it be easier if she just went down to the cinema to see Dara herself and made arrangements instead of us being the middlemen?"

Declan shrugged. "I said that to her in my last letter, but in the one I got from her this morning, she says she feels a bit awkward going down to ask him herself."

"I don't see why," Lily said. "Dara's very easygoing and she's met him several times when we were in Carraigvale."

"She can be shy at times, and I'm worried she might change her mind about coming." Declan tapped the envelope against the back of his hand. "So, will you ask him?"

Declan didn't ask her many favours and he was good in his own way. Whilst they had their own silly ways of going on, the bottom line was that they could always depend on each other. She could tell he was really keen on Ava coming and had probably told all his friends about her. "Okay," she said. "I'm going to ring him this afternoon while my mother's over at the priest's house. He'll be doing the children's matinee so I'll catch him before it." Dara had sent her a list of all the performance times so she could ring before or afterwards.

Declan grinned now, delighted that things were working out for Ava's visit. "You're lucky that the phone bill doesn't come in until you're safely back in Newcastle. My mother will have a fit with all the calls you've made to Ireland."

"I'll give her something towards it," Lily said, batting her eyelids in an exaggerated way. "I'm only home at the holidays, and she would have a lot more to complain about if I was living here all the time and using it more regularly."

"You're some blade," Declan said, heading towards the door. "You've always got an answer!"

*　*　*

When she rang Dara later, he was his usual talkative self, asking her about the time of her train back to Newcastle on Sunday and what her plans were for her last night. Lily told him that she was going to a dance with a few of her school friends, and that she was catching the two o'clock train from Edinburgh so she would arrive at college for her evening meal around six o'clock.

He told her that he wished he was back there with her, and she said she couldn't imagine being in the college house and in the room without him. She didn't tell him that she thought those five days with him seemed longer and more real than all the time she had spent there on her own.

He went on to tell her all about the recent happenings in the cinema, which included a fight between two lads over a girl. One, it seemed, turned up at the film with her, after she had cancelled a date with the other. When the lights came on at the end of the film, the lad spotted the couple and all hell broke loose. Dara described the events in great detail, and Lily laughed out loud when he told her how the lad that was spurned jumped over two rows of seats to get to them. Dara and his brother, Frank, had been in the projector room at the time, and when they heard all the commotion had come running out to separate them. Frank had received a box in the jaw for his trouble and had given a harder one back in return. By the time they all got outside, and the lads had calmed down, the one who had been with the girl said he knew nothing about any cancelled date and had been going out with the girl for a month. The other lad said that was impossible as he had been going out with her for the last year.

It was then they all realised that the girl in question was nowhere to be seen.

Lily and Declan had a laugh over it and then Lily had gone on to tell him any news she had. She thought it was too early to mention the idea of them both working on the cruise together, and since there was every chance it might well come to nothing, she kept quiet about it. Then, she told him that Declan had asked about Ava accompanying him on the journey over at Easter.

"Do you think she's really serious about coming over?"

"Oh yes," she told him. "Declan just received a letter from her this morning asking about travelling with you."

"I'm surprised," he said. "I didn't think that would last too long."

"I'm surprised too," Lily said. "But it seems we were both wrong."

"Is she going to call to see me nearer the time," Dara asked. "Or do you want me to go up to the bed and breakfast and see her?"

"I think," Lily said, "Declan was hoping you might go and see her. He says she's a bit shy."

There was a silence.

"Do you mind?" Lily asked. "I know it's a bit awkward when you don't know her very well."

"No, I don't mind. I'm sure it will be fine. I'll go down and see her at the bed and breakfast tonight and I'll write to you tomorrow," he told her. "So you'll get my letter in a few days' time."

31

The following evening when she got off the coach and walked across the college green to her room, Lily felt a sense of despondency, knowing it would be weeks before she saw Dara again.

When she went into the house Ann came to the kitchen door and beckoned her.

Lily dropped her case in the hall and followed her friend. "Have you been back long?" she asked.

"About an hour ago. I was waiting for you." Ann checked to see there was no one in the hallway then closed the kitchen door. She turned to Lily, her face serious. "Pamela took an overdose and she's in the hospital."

"What?" Lily gasped. She put her hand to her mouth. "Oh, my God – when did she do it?"

"Last Thursday night. She did it after Edward came around to see her face to face. Apparently he told her there was no chance of them getting back together and she went hysterical. It was after he left that she did it. I rang her mother and she told me."

"Was it serious? I mean, did she really try to kill herself or was it just a cry for help?"

"Her mother thinks it was serious. She took a packet of aspirins along with a pint glass of really strong rum and coke. If her mother hadn't found her God knows what might have happened. She gave her a glass of salty water to make her sick then she rang an ambulance. They took her to hospital and pumped her stomach out."

Lily closed her eyes at the thought. "Is she okay?"

"Well, the doctors said she was really, really lucky that they caught her in time. They've kept her in for a few days as they want her to see a psychiatrist."

"A psychiatrist?" Lily paused for a few moments to digest it all. "Have they let the college know?"

"That's the thing," Ann said. "Her family don't want anyone else to know, but I had to tell someone and I knew I could trust you. You won't say a word?"

"Of course not," Lily said.

"They're terrified that if the college find out, she might lose her place. They think they might say she's not fit to be a teacher or something like that."

"That's rubbish! Teachers are the same as anyone else and have the same problems and feelings." She shook her head. "Poor Pamela."

"That bloody Edward! I could kill him. I don't know what she ever saw in him." She lowered her voice. "All the weekends he came down here to stay with her. The porters got so used to seeing him here they thought he was one of our students. And you know, even though Pamela let him stay with her and was on the Pill and all that sort of thing, underneath it she was quite old-fashioned and felt guilty about it. She kept saying it wasn't so bad because they were going to get married, and now Edward has done a bunk and gone off with somebody else."

"I still don't see why she did something so horrendous," Lily said. "It's not the end of the world to break up with somebody." She halted. "It's not as if she was pregnant or anything."

Ann bit her lip.

"She wasn't . . . was she?"

"No, no," Ann said quickly. "She wasn't pregnant. But . . ." She went back to the door and checked there was no one around again. "Last year she had a miscarriage. It was during the summer holidays and she had missed a period and then she had stomach pains and very heavy bleeding. When she went to the doctor he told her that from what he could tell, she'd lost a baby."

221

"I can't believe it," Lily said. "I never imagined she'd gone through all that."

"Well, now she's gone through a lot worse, and it's all down to focussing her whole life on trying to please Edward and then discovering that he wasn't worth it."

"Can we do anything?"

Ann shrugged. "I don't know. It's a bit awkward with me not supposed to tell anyone. We'll see if she tells you all about it when she comes back. I know Pamela really likes you and trusts you, but it's her mother who's asked me not to say anything about the overdose."

"I think she'll probably want to keep it to herself," Lily said. "If she didn't say anything to me about the miscarriage, she probably won't want to tell me this either. I don't blame her, she's entitled to her privacy about such personal things."

"You're probably right." Anne paused. "How did Dara's visit go?"

"Great, thanks," Lily said. "And thanks for the use of your room. I changed the bed. He didn't touch anything else so it's back just the way you left it."

"It looked perfect," Ann said. "I actually thought he hadn't used it at all." She paused and looked sharply at Lily. "Did he not stay with you at all then?"

Lily moved her gaze just a fraction away from her friend's. "No, I decided I wasn't ready for that just yet." A little warning voice at the back of her mind told her not to tell her friend the whole truth. If she told anyone that Dara had stayed in her room, they would automatically assume they'd had sex and she didn't want that getting around.

"Really? I thought you two wouldn't be able to keep your hands off each other. All the girls thought he was gorgeous and that the two of you are really suited."

Lily decided she couldn't be a total hypocrite. "I have to admit it was hard, but I just felt it was too soon and Dara didn't have a problem with that. If things work out we've all the time in the world to start sleeping together."

Ann looked at her for a moment, as if she wasn't quite sure. "So what did you do?"

"We went into Newcastle and we went to Morpeth and all that sort of thing." She smiled at the memory. "We had a great weekend and the time just flew by. It really gave us the chance to get to know each other much better. And thanks for the loan of your room again. I'll pay for all your drinks tonight."

"You don't need to do that." Ann said. "I'm glad it went so well for you."

Lily gave a sad sigh. "The only thing is, I really miss him. I couldn't stop thinking about him when I was in Scotland. I'm going to have to throw myself into my college work to try to forget him."

"You'll get used to it. You'll get into a routine again and the time will fly and before you know it will be Easter."

"I hope so. I really hope so."

Ann gave a little wry smile. "Just think, you could be me – still hoping to meet someone."

Lily waved her hand towards the window. "There are loads of them out there – you just have to make the effort to meet them all."

"Or go to Ireland like you."

"Try here first," Lily laughed. "It's definitely handier."

When she spoke on the phone to Dara a few days later, Lily decided to say nothing about what had happened to Pamela. She was afraid she might be overheard, and she was also reluctant to bring up such a sensitive subject on the phone as she knew the suicide attempt might lead on to discussing the miscarriage. She felt that might then sound as though she was making a point about what could happen to couples who weren't careful.

* * *

The following days passed slowly to begin with, then began to pick up speed as they turned into weeks with the routine of phone calls and letters and college work.

In his first letter Dara told her that he meant what he had said at the train station in Newcastle, and that he was now quite sure that he loved her.

Lily felt a great sense of relief as she had wondered if it had been something he had said without thinking and that he had since regretted. As she now studied the words, written down in ink in his small tidy handscript she felt it made it official and marked another milestone in their relationship.

She sat down that same afternoon and wrote a letter to him saying she loved him too, and couldn't wait until they met up again.

Pamela returned a week later, telling people she'd had a bad chest infection which was taking a while to clear up. Lily just said she hoped she was feeling better now and Pamela nodded and smiled, but said nothing about the real reason for her absence.

The other girls commented on how pale and tired and thin she looked and no one mentioned Edward. Lily thought she must have been put on some sort of medication because she slept every afternoon and went to bed early at night. Any evenings they were in the bar she avoided alcohol, and Lily wondered whether it was because she didn't want to make a fool of herself getting drunk again or whether she was on medication she had been told not to drink with. As the weeks went on Pamela got a bit brighter and gradually seemed to be coming back to her old self.

Then Lily realised that the Easter break was just around the corner.

As her longest teaching practice – a full term – was looming, her mind moved to focus on class timetables and lesson preparation. She had to meet her teaching practice tutor every other day to show the work she had planned for the term ahead. She drafted out daily lesson plans for English and Maths, twice weekly for History and Geography, and once a week for Nature and Art and Crafts and Science. She had asked for the top class – the eleven-year-olds – as she felt it gave her great scope with the subjects. And, when she cleared her mind and got down to concentrating, she really enjoyed subjects such as the Viking project she was working on. She found it a great challenge to make the lessons as exciting as possible, and loved integrating it with art and creative writing.

She spent long afternoons in the education department making outlines of Viking longboats which would be painted, let dry, and then have all types of materials glued to them. She drew large male and female Viking figures and then sorted out sacking and fabrics for clothes and yellow wool for their hair and metallic paper for their horned helmets.

She went into the school where she would be teaching just off Newcastle City Centre and took samples of the Maths and English books she would be teaching from. She sat with the teachers in their lunch hours and after school going over worksheets in grammar and punctuation, and fractions and decimals with them, to make sure she was up to speed on the latest methods of teaching them.

As the nights lightened into spring, she spent hours in her bedroom sorting out her teaching practice files and timetables, and studying books on child development and the different systems of discipline.

* * *

Both Lily and Ann were relieved to see Pamela more or less back to her old self. Like the others, she was busy preparing for her teaching practice, in the same school as Bill Toft. The small ones like Lily's only had one student, but Pamela's was one of the bigger schools and had agreed to take two students if one of them was a male to help out with sports.

Initially, Pamela had moaned about being with Bill, wishing she had been given a female student. And she had complained when he started turning up at the house in the evenings to discuss some aspect or other at school, or cornering her in the refectory or bar.

Then the other girls in the house noticed that Bill was visiting her practically every evening and Pamela was complaining less about him. When they were spotted on a Friday night dancing to a slow number on the dance floor, everyone realised they now seemed to be a couple.

"Can you believe it?" Beryl had said. "Bill and Edward are like chalk and cheese. Edward was so stuffy and formal and Bill has scruffy hair and drinks pints of Newcastle Brown Ale."

They had all gossiped and giggled about it as they watched them smooching in a dark corner.

"I actually think they're quite well suited," Lily said, "Pamela is a kind well-intentioned girl and Bill is a really nice guy, and they're both very studious. I heard them talking last night about the maths projects they were doing and Bill was offering her great suggestions."

Ann started to laugh. "The way they're wrapped around each other now, he looks as if he's offering suggestions in more than maths!"

Lily looked over at them and felt a tinge of apprehension. After all she had gone through, it wouldn't be the wisest thing for Pamela to get involved in another physical relationship so soon. And for all she liked him, she hoped that Bill wasn't sort to think that Pamela was an easy touch because she'd had Edward to stay at weekends.

"He wouldn't be my sort with that scruffy hair," Beryl said. She glanced over at Lily. "Bill doesn't keep himself nice and groomed like Dara. It's more like a haystack that needs a good clipping."

"Well," Ann said, "I think we'll see a change in him after Easter as the teaching practice guidelines have reminded all the male teachers to be smart and dress in a shirt and tie, and to be sure to get a tidy haircut for the teaching practice."

As the term wore on Lily received letters and cards regularly from her family, and postcards from Kirsty and Larry. Every so often a large boxed package would arrive from Scotland and Lily would open it eagerly to see what goodies her mother had sent. Her housemates would cheer with delight when she produced packets of Oddfellow sweets, Scottish Tablet – a hard creamy fudge – coconut icing and Macaroon Bars, confectionery items only available in Scotland. Mona had even packed mutton pies and Morning Rolls in Tupperware containers which Lily would then warm up in the Baby Belling oven.

Every so often she would run across Gerard René in the refectory, café or Students' Union and they would chat about their families back home or discuss their plans for the next college break. Now and again she would be aware that there was still a little spark between them – a spark that would never be acted upon – and she felt flattered that such a handsome intelligent man found her attractive.

Dara was consistent with his letters and calls and occasional gifts of records and books. He had sent her a collection of Robert Frost's poetry which she loved, and he had marked the poems which he particularly liked. In the evenings, when she had finished her work her thoughts and memories turned towards him, and she would bring him closer to her by rereading his letters and listening to Donovan or another of the albums they both liked.

He sent her a letter giving her the times of his journey over to Scotland, from the coach leaving Tullamore which would take him and Ava to the bus station in Dublin and then the times of the bus which would take them to the docks for the overnight boat. They would arrive in Glasgow the following morning to be picked up by Declan.

Lily's mother had phoned more often as the time grew nearer for the two Irish visitors. She checked on Dara's eating habits and wondered whether he preferred tea or coffee and hoped he didn't mind sharing the twin room with Declan. Lily reassured her each time, saying that he wasn't a bit fussy and she really shouldn't worry. Then, just when Mona was confident that she had everything in order for Dara, she would then start the same procedure again, checking Ava's likes and dislikes on behalf of Sophie who would be hosting her.

"Stop worrying, Mammy," Lily told her time and time again. "Ava is a really nice girl and she'll be grateful for anything you give her or do for her."

"I know, they're all telling me that," Mona said, "but whether the girl was brought up in an orphanage or a palace, I still want to do it right and so does Sophie. I'm sure there will be no complaints there as she has decorated the girls' old bedroom from top to bottom with pink roses on the walls and even on the new candlewick bedspread."

"It all sounds lovely," Lily said, trying to keep her patience, as she had heard all about the pink roses at least a dozen times. "I'm sure Ava will love it."

"I'm sure she will . . . but I just wish he could have found a girlfriend nearer home," her mother always ended up saying.

The conversation would eventually come to an end with the unspoken thought that her mother wished she had found a boyfriend nearer home as well.

32

Lily made her way down the narrow train corridor, stopping every few minutes to drop her heavy case to the floor. A few times she almost lost her balance as the busy train gathered speed, and then she recovered and started dragging it again. Eventually, she found a carriage that had only two people in it – a middle-aged man and a woman who looked a few years older than herself. She put the case down to slide the heavy door open enough to get through, and heaved the case into the gap. The door slid closed again, jamming the case halfway in, leaving Lily standing in the corridor.

The man immediately got to his feet and held the door open with one hand and took the case with the other. Lily thanked him and was even more grateful when he lifted it up onto the shelf above the seats.

She moved past the woman to sit opposite the man at the window. She could tell by their dress and distant manner that they were not together. After passing a few remarks about how busy the train was and the nice weather, she dug into her duffle bag for her current book, *Peyton Place.*

She read halfway down the page and then gave up. She couldn't stop wondering how things would be when she arrived in Edinburgh. Dara would be there waiting for her. She checked her watch. He would be on his way now, travelling on the train from Rowanhill. They only went every two hours so he told her he would catch an early one and have a walk around the immediate area while he was waiting for her train.

He had arrived from Ireland the previous day and told her that instead of her father driving to the city, he would catch the train to meet her. Her mother had phoned last night and said what a lovely lad he was and she could see why Lily liked him. She told her that when he arrived in the late morning he had eaten a good cooked breakfast and then after meeting everyone he had gone for a lie down and now he was back up again and chatting to everyone.

"He's a great mixer," Mona had said. "Able to chat about anything. And I had to tell him off for coming laden down with presents. He brought me a lovely Waterford Crystal vase in a beautiful box, and he brought your father a good bottle of Tullamore Dew which, as you can well imagine, he was delighted with."

"Oh, that was nice of him." Lily was pleased as her own family were very generous and it was great that Dara had that same spirit about him. And she knew it would go a long way to making her mother warm towards him.

"Ah, it was very good of him," Mona said. "And then he and Ava put together and bought fancy boxes of chocolates for all the others. Wasn't that very decent of them?"

Her mother had then said in a low voice what a lovely girl Ava was, and how she had brought nice tea towels with the map of Ireland on them for her, and that Declan had taken her out to meet all his friends. Dara, she reported, had decided to stay in as he wanted to get up early to get the train for Edinburgh.

"I thought Seán would have been down to meet them, seeing as he knows them from Ireland, but Eileen came down on her own this afternoon and said he wasn't feeling too good and that he'll see them later."

"What's wrong with Seán?" Lily asked.

"I think she said it was a kind of flu, a headache and sore all over – that kind of thing."

"I hope he's feeling better soon."

"Eileen only saw Dara as Ava was up at Sophie's. I suppose Seán has plenty of time to see them."

There was a short pause then Lily spoke in a low voice. "Nobody asked Dara about his mother, did they?"

"No, no," her mother said, and Lily could tell by the tone of her voice that Dara was near and she couldn't say anything more.

"Good," Lily said.

Then her mother's voice had suddenly lifted. "Dara!"

Dara had come on the phone then and reassured Lily that he was fine and that her family had made him very welcome. He hadn't talked as freely as he usually did because the house was busy and he could be overheard. But he did tell her that he missed her and was really looking forward to seeing her the next day.

Lily was part worried, part excited about seeing him again.

She was worried on two fronts. One, the recent photograph cut from the newspaper he had sent her didn't look at all like the boy she remembered. It was one of him playing in a hurling match. His lovely dark curly hair looked shorter and straighter, and – wearing a striped jersey and shorts – he looked totally different.

Her second worry was Ava – who had travelled over with Dara and would be waiting for her when she arrived home. Ava, with her stunning good looks and big bust. Ava, who had won the hearts – and gained the sympathy – of her father and brothers at the funeral in Ireland.

She was a nice girl, Lily thought, but something about Ava made her feel a little uncomfortable. She seemed to have latched on to everyone in too big a way. Since Dara had gone to see her about their travel arrangements a month or so back, Ava had started sending letters to Lily in Newcastle every week. At first Lily had thought it was nice, but when the conversations about the travel arrangements ran out, she found it hard to think of new things to write back. She knew it was partly because her mind was full of school things, but she felt it might also be due to the fact they didn't know each other that well and might not have that much in common.

She wondered what Declan and Ava would have to talk about during the fortnight she was over in Scotland, but presumably they must have something between them to still be in touch.

She then found herself wondering if Ava might actually prefer someone like Dara. And, it would of course be far handier for them both because they lived in the same country and even in the same town.

Although Lily had been out and about at parties and concerts, she had kept her promise to Dara and hadn't got romantically involved with anyone else.

Most of the time it had been easy, but there had been several occasions when she had questioned the merits of a long-distance romance. Especially when the handsome top rugby player in her year had asked her out. She hadn't given him any encouragement and had told him about her Irish boyfriend, but she could easily see that others in her position might have been tempted.

She told herself she was being silly and that Dara hadn't shown any interest in Ava the night she met him in the cinema. In fact, he had been quite disinterested in her . . . but he couldn't ignore her when they were travelling all the way from Tullamore, sitting beside each other on coaches and on the boat. They would have had plenty of time to get to know each other on the boat trip over. It was a long, overnight journey from Dublin to Glasgow. They would have sat together, eaten together and probably had a drink together. And of course, her mother told her that they had picked fancy chocolates together on the boat to bring to her brothers and their wives.

She had been trying not to think of this since the travel arrangements had been made, but now she couldn't stop herself. She kept imagining Ava as some sort of femme fatale movie star. With her striking face, silky dark hair and voluptuous bust, she couldn't help but draw men to her like a magnet.

Try as she might to ignore it, pictures of people sleeping on the couches, chairs and even on the floor of the boat drifted into Lily's mind, and she wondered for the umpteenth time where Dara and Ava had slept.

She forced herself to go back to *Peyton Place* in an effort to keep the disturbing thoughts out of her mind.

33

Lily was standing by the door, holding her case steady and waiting for the train to come to a halt when she caught a glimpse of Dara standing by a pillar as they went past. The train pulled up about ten yards ahead of him and since there was no one waiting to get off behind her, Lily stood for a few moments watching him without him knowing.

He was wearing a green casual army-style jacket with lots of pockets, and she was greatly relieved to see that his hair was not cut as short as she had feared. It must, she reckoned, have been damp or something in the hurling photo which made it look so different.

She observed him as he moved along the carriages, scanning the coaches for a sign of her. His face – quite serious and slightly anxious – was more familiar than she thought it would be after all these weeks. Then, as he moved closer to her door, she thought he looked even more handsome and attractive than she remembered.

She pushed the latch down on the door. It swung open and she stepped down onto the platform. "Dara!" she called, and as he came jogging towards her a wave of excitement washed over her.

He lifted her case onto the platform and pushed the train door closed. Then he turned towards her and pulled her into his arms and kissed her.

When they were both breathless, he held her at arm's length and looked at her. "Oh, Lily . . . Lily . . . I can't tell you how much I've missed you!"

"Good," she said. "Because I've missed you more than I could ever have imagined."

They walked out through the station, both talking at the same time and then stopping to let the other finish what they were saying.

"Is everything okay back at the house?" Lily asked. "Was it weird to be there without me? Were my mother and father okay?"

"They were grand," Dara told her. "Couldn't be nicer. Your mother asks me every ten minutes if I want anything to eat or drink. I've eaten so much I don't think I'll need anything for the next month."

"She was delighted with all the lovely gifts you brought over – that was very good of you."

He shrugged and pulled a face. "It was nothing, and what else would I do coming to stay with your family for a fortnight?"

"It was still nice of you." She reached out to touch the back of his head. "I was worried you'd had your hair cut really short. It looked very short in that photograph you sent me."

He smiled, slightly self-consciously. "I did get a few inches off it, but it grows really quickly."

"Good," she said. "It's nice now, but you suit it longer too. What did my mother have to say about it?"

"She just said I had a good thick head of hair." He gave her a sidelong grin. "To be honest, that was one of the reasons I got a bit cut off it. I didn't want to give the wrong impression the first time I met her."

Lily looked at him. "That hadn't crossed my mind. You're very thoughtful."

They went over to the ticket office to get Lily's single ticket to Rowanhill, talking ten to the dozen as they went. Lily was reassured that all was well between her family and Dara, but she knew she wouldn't feel relaxed until she had checked out her main concern.

They were walking towards the big board with the train

timetable on it to check what time theirs left, when she broached the subject that had dominated her mind. "And how was your journey over?"

"Grand," he said. "Long and boring, but no complaints."

"And how was Ava? How did you get on travelling over with her?"

There was a definite hesitation. "Do you want the truth?"

"Yes," she said. "I do . . ."

"I feel bad saying this, since she's your brother's girlfriend, she's nice enough, but . . . she's actually quite a boring person. Not the sort you can really talk to. Not a bit like you."

"Really?" Lily was relieved to hear him say that but curious. "But my dad and the boys all really loved her because she's always making them tea and fussing after them. I thought you might like that as well."

"Of course I do." A bemused look came on his face. "And she wanted to do the same on the boat. She brought a huge pack of sandwiches and cakes and everything for us. But anybody can do that. Your mother and my Aunt Carmel fuss about doing things like that all the time, because they're older and it's the way they were brought up. All that stuff about the best way to a man's heart is through his stomach. But Ava's only a young girl and she doesn't seem to have anything interesting about her. She doesn't really read for one thing. She was just flicking through a magazine or making comments about the other passengers and she knew nothing about music or films or anything like that."

"Oh . . ." Lily was beginning to feel much better.

"She's actually very limited," Dara went on. "When I think of how you and I filled five whole days in your college room and we still didn't get time to talk about half the things we wanted to. Just think of all the albums, all the books and all the films we still have to discuss." He gave a sigh. "The biggest discussion we had was what sort of chocolates we should buy to give to your brothers – not exactly riveting stuff!"

There was a tiny bit of her still not convinced. "But don't you think she's really attractive?"

"Oh, there's no doubt she's a nice enough looking girl."

Lily felt a little sting as she thought how unfavourably her own looks compared to Ava's, and wondered if Dara was just being nice. "Don't her looks and figure make up for all the other things?"

"No," he said. "They don't. It's like looking at a lovely picture. You can only stare at it for so long and you need something more – like an interesting personality. And that's what Ava is sadly lacking."

"Well, Declan seems totally besotted by her."

He took a deep breath. "I wouldn't want it repeated, but I don't think Declan knows her at all. I have a feeling that he had a certain image of her in his mind and it might not be entirely accurate."

Lily was really intrigued now. "What do you mean?"

"I mean that he has spent very little time with her –" He suddenly stopped. "I feel bad now. I shouldn't be talking about the poor girl like this. There's nothing wrong with her at all. I suppose it's just that having spent so long in her company – just the two of us – it just emphasised the fact that we're completely different types."

Lily now felt completely reassured, and realised that her fears about Dara becoming besotted by Ava had been completely groundless. She turned her attention to the train times.

"We have a train in a half an hour," she said. "Or we can catch the next one at four o'clock or even the one after that at six o'clock. What do you want to do? I know you've already had a bit of a walk around, so would you rather go straight home now?"

"How are you? Are you tired after travelling or do you want to have a couple of hours here?"

She looked at him. "I'd love to stay up here in Edinburgh. I'm not a bit tired, and once we get home we'll be with other people for most of the time."

"Brilliant! I was hoping we might get time to look around it together. I just had a walk along Princes Street and around the streets behind it. From what I've seen so far, it's even better than I had imagined. The Georgian buildings are amazing and so is the view of the castle."

She loved that he was so enthusiastic. "That's only the New

Town. If you've only been to that side of the city, you haven't seen anything yet." She smiled and squeezed his arm. "I can't wait to show you the medieval buildings in the Old Town." She halted and looked around her. "The phones are back in the main building where we got the tickets, so I'll just give my mother a quick ring and then we can put the case and things in left luggage."

He grinned at her. "You phone and I'll put the luggage in, then we'll be out all the quicker."

Lily pointed over to the wall by the taxi rank. "I'll meet you right there in five minutes."

34

Mona Grace hung up the telephone in the hall and then came back into the sitting-room to Ava. The Irish girl was sleeping at Sophie's at night and spending most of the day up at Mona and Pat's house. Declan had organised to get as much time off as he could while she was there, but there were certain coach and taxi runs that he couldn't get cover for.

"That was Lily," Mona said, smiling and shaking her head. "I'm not a bit surprised – they're going to have a few hours looking around Edinburgh this afternoon, and then catch the later train down this evening. They might as well. That way they won't have to pay for a separate train trip from here to see the city."

"It is a lovely day," Ava agreed, turning to look out of the sitting-room window.

"Lily loves Edinburgh and the castle and all the old buildings," Mona said, "and she'll be in her element to have a lad with her who likes that sort of thing. She studies history at college, you know, and she was saying that he likes all that kind of stuff too with him studying to be an architect." She paused. "Do you think you would like a trip up to Edinburgh one of the days?"

"I'm sure I would," Ava said. "It sounds lovely."

Mona tilted her head to the side. "And would you like the old buildings or would you prefer to have a look around the shops?"

Ava gave a little shrug. "I'm easy," she said. "Whatever Declan wants to do."

"Well, I'd definitely prefer the shops," Mona said. "I've been around the Royal Mile and all the streets leading up to the castle and if you've seen it once, it's more than enough. I don't know what Lily finds so interesting about it that takes her back there so regularly." She gave a little laugh. "It's not for the high fashion shops anyway. Lily is happier wandering around those odd kind of shops that the students like, and you wouldn't know what she would buy." She looked at Ava's classy buttoned-up lilac cardigan, her tight black skirt and matching stilettos and her discreet pearls and earrings. "I must say your own outfit is lovely – did you buy it in Ireland?"

"Dublin, in Clery's."

Mona recognised it as one of the better shops. "You can tell it's good quality," she said, nodding and wondering how a girl who worked in a bed and breakfast could afford such expensive clothes. "I must get Lily into Glasgow and buy her a few decent rig-outs for her teaching practice. She'll have to look the part if she wants the other teachers and the parents to take her seriously."

"She always looked lovely when I saw her in Ireland."

"Thank God for that at least," Mona said.

Ava glanced at the window again. "Did you hear how Seán is this afternoon? Is there any improvement with his flu?"

They hadn't seen him yet as he had taken to his bed.

"No, I must give a ring soon and see how he is. This is Eileen's night for going over to her mother's and Seán usually minds the kids. She'll probably have to cancel it if he's not well." She gave a sigh. "It's unusual for Seán to be sick. If he's no better in the morning we'll probably go up and see him."

A car pulled up outside the house and Mona moved to the window to see who it was.

"Talk of the devil! There's Seán's car now." She watched carefully as the driver's door opened. "Oh, it's only Eileen and little Susan."

As Mona rushed to get the door, Ava sat up straight and

smoothed her skirt down over her knees. A few moments later Mona, her daughter-in-law and two-year-old grandchild came into the sitting-room.

The small thin Eileen was dressed in her housework clothes of slacks, an old sweater of Seán's and plimsolls, her hair cut in a short, boyish style that spoke of tidiness and lack of time to manage anything longer. Her face today looked more pinched and harassed than usual.

"Excuse the state of me," she said, embarrassed when she saw how elegantly dressed Ava was, "but I've been up to my eyes cleaning the windows and the oven."

"Those windows must have the cleanest glass in Rowanhill," Mona laughed.

Ava stood up to shake Eileen's hand, towering a good six inches over her.

"I called yesterday and met Dara, but you were over in Sophie's," said Eileen.

"I was in bed," Ava said. "I had no sleep on the boat coming over."

"Begod, I know what that's like," Mona said. "Every time I go to Ireland it takes me a couple of days to recover."

"Next time I'll go on the plane," Ava said. "Declan said it's far easier and you don't miss a night's sleep."

"Oh, that's for sure," Mona said. "But I have to confess I'm not a lover of aeroplanes. I have the Rosary beads out from the minute I get on it to the minute I come off."

Eileen looked flustered when Mona asked her if she would have a cup of tea. "I can't stay," she said. "You're not going to believe it, I've just had a phone call to say my mother's been rushed into hospital."

"Again?" Mona said incredulously.

"The doctor says they'll definitely keep her in this time," Eileen said, making a grab at little Susan who was trying to climb up on the sofa beside Ava. "They'll have to do something. She can't keep on like this."

Ava bent forward to lift the child up beside her and then started playing with her.

"They'd be better taking the gall bladder out now," Mona stated. "I was the very same before they operated on me, hoping every attack was the last one, but it always came back."

"The only thing is, with Seán in bed sick, I've nobody to mind the kids to let me go to the hospital." She looked at her watch. "And I need to pick up Beth at school and take her straight to the optician's. I'm hoping she doesn't need glasses as she's a bit too young for that. They don't look a bit nice on girls, and she'd be forever taking them off and losing them."

"If she needs them she needs them," Mona said philosophically.

"So, I don't know what I'm going to do about the hospital if Seán doesn't rally round."

"Oh, I'm sure we'll sort something out," Mona said. "I could always go up to the house for a few hours."

"But it's your night for the Catholic Mothers' Association, and you've got that priest coming out from Glasgow to talk to you all."

"Oh, God," Mona said, clapping her hands on either side of her face, "can you believe it? I nearly forgot about that. We'll have to think of something else."

"What time is Lily due back?" Eileen asked. "She's always good with the children."

"Oh, it could be seven or eight. They decided to have the day in Edinburgh since it's fine."

Ava lifted Susan onto her knee and started jiggling her up and down. "Could I help?" she offered. "Declan has a taxi run out to the airport and he says he won't be back until after nine o'clock, so I won't be doing anything else."

"Oh, I don't like to ask you," Eileen said. "It's not fair – you're here on holiday, not to be baby-sitting . . ."

"I've nothing better to do," Ava said, "and I'm well used to children. I used to do a lot of child-minding for a family in Dublin."

Eileen looked over at her mother-in-law to see if she had any objections. "I don't like to take advantage."

Mona looked at Ava now, delighted that the girl had made the offer as she didn't want to miss Father McShane's visit. He was a great character, always telling jokes and he usually brought his guitar with him to give them a song or two. And besides, it would give Ava something to do while Declan was working.

"If you're sure," Mona said, "that would be a great help."

"It certainly would," Eileen said, smiling gratefully at Ava. She checked her watch again. "I'd better go and pick Beth up now."

*   *   *

Declan pulled up outside Seán and Eileen's house, to drop Ava off on his way to the airport.

"It looks lovely," Ava said, looking at the new two-storey house with the sweeping cream-lace curtains tied back with satin ropes on each window. It was different in every way from the grey post-First-World-War houses that Mona and Sophie lived in half a mile away.

"It's very good of you offering to look after the kids," he said, putting his arm around her. "I hope you don't mind us not going out tonight?"

"Not at all," she said, "I'm grand."

"We'll make up for it tomorrow," he told her. "I'm taking you shopping into Glasgow in the afternoon to get you a new rig-out and then we'll go for a nice steak dinner and on to the pictures. How does that sound?"

"Fantastic."

He kissed her on the side of the head and then she slid out of the car.

Eileen had the youngest child already in bed and little Beth had been bathed and was sitting up at the table in her pyjamas with a colouring book and crayons. Eileen was dressed up for her hospital visit in a matching pink dress and coat that was more suited to a wedding, and she had back-combed her short hair and put a tortoiseshell slide above each ear. The dress was fitted and emphasised how thin her figure was – it came just above the knee and had a fussy satin bow under the bustline.

"Your outfit is gorgeous," Ava told her. "It really suits you."

"Do you think so?" Eileen said, delighted with the compliment. "I got it for a First Communion and I thought I might as well get a wear out of it. I wasn't sure if it was a bit too much." She went over to the table to get her long cream clutch-bag. She opened it and took out her lipstick and compact. She powdered her face again and then reapplied her pale-pink lipstick.

"And, if you don't mind me saying, your house is lovely too. Your curtains and velvet suite and cushions all match perfectly."

Eileen's face lit up. "Oh, thanks – I'm glad you think so. Some people think you shouldn't waste time and money on furniture and decorating, but I think if you have to spend most of your life inside it, you might as well have something nice to look at." She made a little face. "Seán's mother thinks we're mad, and that we should have been content with a council house like theirs instead of saddling ourselves with a mortgage, but I want better for our children than we had."

"Well, you've certainly done well," Ava agreed.

"I'm not saying he's perfect," Eileen said, "but the one thing Seán Grace is, is a good and thorough worker." She waved her hand around the room. "He's decorated this place from top to bottom. He's very patient. He does whatever I ask." She then went on to explain all about the coving he had put on the ceiling and the ornate rose in the middle which held the small glass chandelier, and how he had wired the two matching crystal wall-lamps himself.

Ava listened carefully, making suitable comments of approval.

"You met him over in Ireland, didn't you?" Eileen asked. "That time when Declan got attacked by the bull."

"Yes," Ava said, her face serious now. "That was terrible. Poor Declan. Thankfully he got over it fairly quickly."

"They were all saying how good Seán was rescuing him."

"Did he tell you all about it?"

Eileen rolled her eyes and made a little disparaging sound. "Seán? Tell me all about it? That fellow would tell you nothing about anything. He's a man of few words, unlike the rest of his family. You have to drag every word out of him."

"Is that right?" Ava said. "I didn't really get to know him . . ."

"I'm not surprised, coming from that family. They're good in their own way of course, but I think he must have found it hard to get a word in edgeways when he was a child with the lot of them, and now he doesn't bother. He's at his very worst when he's with his family. He lets Mona say what she likes to him and won't answer back. She's forever criticising and making little digs about the way we keep the house, but it's like water off a duck's back to me. I'll do things my own way."

Ava gave a little smile. "I suppose everybody has their own way," she said diplomatically.

Eileen glanced at the clock and then said she'd have to go soon. She told her what time Beth should go to bed and that the child's bedroom was the first one at the top of the stairs.

"Actually," she then said, "I'd better show you where the rooms are so you'll know." She quickly went up the blue-carpeted stairs with Ava following behind. She stopped at the first door and turned back to Ava with a finger pressed to her lips. She pushed it open to reveal a pink-and-white bedroom with a single bed on one side of the room with a frilly pink nylon counterpane and matching pillow, and a cot on the other side with the sleeping Susan.

Ava glanced around the room, her gaze taking in the shelves full of toys and teddy bears, the old-fashioned rocking-horse and the large doll's house over by the window. She loved the lace curtains tied back with pink ribbon and the blue and pink rug in the middle of the room.

Eileen pointed to the cot, her face soft now and full of love. "She's out for the count," she whispered. "Hopefully, she won't waken until I get back."

She gestured towards the bed. "That's where Beth sleeps." Then she quietly closed the door.

They walked along the corridor.

"The bathroom is here in the middle," Eileen whispered, opening the door to reveal a clinically white-tiled bathroom with neatly folded towels stacked on two glass shelves, and a pair of fancier towels decorated with flowers on the side of the bath.

"This is lovely," Ava said.

"Do you think so? It's nice and clean but I think it's a bit plain. I was thinking of getting some nice marble tiles."

"Well, it looks lovely to me. Your whole house looks lovely."

Eileen glowed at the compliments. She then indicated to the room at the end of the corridor. "His Lordship is in there."

Ava just nodded.

When they were back downstairs Ava asked, "Should I take Seán up a cup of tea or a hot lemonade or anything? He might like a slice of toast."

Eileen shrugged. "I don't know if he'll have anything. He seems to have lost his appetite these last few days. If you hear him up, in the bathroom or anything, then you could maybe ask him then. If not, I'd just leave him sleep."

"Does he actually know I'm here?" Ava asked.

"Well, I told him I'd have to get somebody in to baby-sit to let me go to the hospital, so he knows that *somebody* will be here. I said I'd probably get Lily and her boyfriend if she was back home." She gave a little knowing smile. "I thought they might like a few hours up here on their own without anybody bothering them."

Ava smiled but said nothing.

"He's a fine-looking young fellow, that Dara, isn't he? I saw him yesterday just after he arrived. I think you had gone to Sophie's to get a few hours in bed. And his accent is lovely – and so is your own of course. It's not that clipped Galway accent that Mona has. Yes, Dara is lovely – it's just the hair." She shook her head and laughed. "For me, he'd have to get a decent haircut."

"So," Ava said, "if I hear Seán moving about it's okay to check if he wants anything?"

"Exactly."

Eileen then showed Ava where everything was in the kitchen to make tea, and where the bread and biscuits were and the cold meat in the fridge to make a sandwich. She showed her how to switch the television on and how to change channels, and then did the same with the radiogram. Then she lifted her handbag and car keys.

"I must go. Like I said, if you put Beth up to bed anytime in the next half an hour that will be fine."

"No problem," Ava told her. "You take your time and don't be worrying."

Eileen stopped on the doorstep. "You're very good. You're the kind of girl that makes me feel easy leaving the children. I feel they're in good hands."

"Oh, they are," Ava reassured her. "They are indeed."

Eileen hurried down the path and Ava closed the door behind her.

35

Mona opened the front door. "Here they come," she said, "the two explorers!"

"Hi!" Lily came up the path, beaming from ear to ear, Dara behind carrying her case.

"Well, did you leave any stone unturned in Edinburgh?"

"We had a great day," Lily said, following her mother into the house, "but my legs are killing me now with all the walking."

Mona's face suddenly became serious. Any mention of Lily's legs being sore brought back all the terrible memories of her battle with polio. "You shouldn't have overdone it like that. You should have come down on an earlier train."

"Och, they're not that bad, I'll be fine."

Lily gave her mother a big hug and a kiss and they walked into the sitting-room. "It's great to be back home."

"And it's great to have you back home." Mona motioned to the sofa. "Go over there now and put your feet up and rest them for half an hour."

"Should I leave the case down here or do you want it upstairs?" Dara asked.

"Upstairs, son, if you don't mind," Mona said. "You know where Lily's room is."

When she could hear him on the stairs she turned back to Lily. "Did you mention to him about your legs?"

Lily nodded. "I didn't make a big issue about it. We were talking about something on the phone a while back and the subject came up. I just told him I had polio when I was young and that I'd made a good recovery from it. I said that occasionally my legs still got tired when I did too much. He was fine about it, and he asked me a few times this afternoon if I wanted to go for a coffee and a sit-down. I can tell by the way he was that he's conscious of it and watching out for me."

"That's good," Mona said. "You can tell he's that kind of a lad." She suddenly remembered. "And you don't need to worry, nobody has said anything about his mother, I warned them all. But Dara mentioned it himself in passing. He was saying something about his sister doing exams and that him and his two brothers were all helping out in the house more to let her study. He just said she was hit the hardest when their mother died."

Lily nodded. "That's fine," she said. "I just didn't want him feeling awkward if it was mentioned or anyone else feeling that they had put their foot in it." She put her shoulder bag down on the table and then went to give her mother another hug. "What do you think of him?" she asked.

Mona looked as though she was going to make some funny remark, but then she stopped herself. "He's very nice," she said, "and very mannerly."

"Do you think he's nice-looking?"

"Will you go away out of that!" her mother said. "He's fine and he's obviously intelligent if he's going to the university in Dublin to be an architect."

"Well," Lily said, her manner skittish, "I think he's lovely-looking."

Mona trotted out one of her old sayings. "Beauty is as beauty does."

Lily laughed. "Talking of beauty, you're looking very well – did you have your hair done today?"

Mona's hand came up to pat the back of her hair. "I didn't have time. Sophie just put a few rollers in it for me."

"It looks really nice, as if you've been to the hairdresser's." She looked towards the kitchen. "Is my dad not in?"

"He's out on a coach run to Hamilton, and Declan's gone to the airport."

Lily took her jacket off. "Where's Ava? Is she at my Auntie Sophie's?"

"She's baby-sitting. Seán's not well, he's in bed with the flu, and Eileen was looking for someone to sit with the kids, and Ava offered."

"Isn't that good of her?" She heard Dara coming down the stairs now and lowered her voice. "What did you think of her?"

"Lovely – lovely girl, but as I said to you on the phone, I wouldn't have put her with Declan."

Lily nodded. "We must all be wrong."

Dara gave a light knock then came into the room.

Mona put her hands on her hips as though she were squaring up for a row with him. "Will you stop knocking on that door every time you come in! You're at home now, and just treat it the way you would your own."

Dara smiled at her. "Ah, you're very good."

Lily thought of the large rambling house that Dara was used to, and wondered what her mother would think if she knew he was used to living in a space nearly three times the size of theirs.

"Now," Mona said, looking at Lily, "I have your favourite pies here and some sausage rolls and bridies, and I've chips cut up and ready to cook."

"Oh, that would be lovely. I'll have pie and chips." She looked at Dara. "What do you fancy?"

"I don't mind," he said. "I can eat anything."

"I'll show you them," Mona said, going into the kitchen. She came back out with a plate with a pie, a long sausage-roll and the flaky pastry bridie. "The sausage rolls are the same as the ones you have in Ireland," she told him, "but the other two are unique to Scotland."

Dara looked first at the pie and then the horseshoe-shaped bridie. "They look interesting . . . have either of them got haggis inside them?"

Lily and Mona burst out laughing.

"No," Lily said, "There's no haggis in them! They're totally different things." She pointed to the round pie. "They're our Scottish traditional pies, and they have mutton in them." She indicated the bridie. "The bridies have minced beef in them and onions and spices. Both the pie and the bridie are best eaten with baked beans and HP Sauce."

"I'll do you one of each," Mona said. "And then you'll know the difference. Believe it or not, the haggis isn't so easy got here, but I'll order some from the butcher so you can try it before you go back."

"That's very kind of you," Dara said, winking over at Lily.

Pat came in just as they were sitting down to eat, and after shaking hands with Dara and kissing Lily, he came to join them at the table. "Well," he asked, "what did you get up to in Edinburgh today?"

Then, over the meal, they both gave Pat and Mona a rundown on all the places they had been and Dara told him about the things he had been most impressed with.

"Where do you start?" Dara held his hands out. "It's absolutely amazing. The only other city in Britain I've ever been to is London, but I think Edinburgh beats even that."

Pat was delighted to hear it. "The English always like to think they have the best of everything, but there's no comparison between Buckingham Palace and Edinburgh Castle. The way it's situated up on that rock is nothing short of spectacular."

Dara told him that they went right to the top of the Sir Walter Scott Monument and could see the surrounding area for miles. "That was magnificent, and then of course there's the Princes Street Gardens."

"That's my favourite," Mona said. "Especially the flower clock. It's absolutely beautiful."

Pat then went on to give Dara the full history of the clock, showing off his knowledge about how it was first designed in 1903 by a man named John McHattie.

Lily loved the way Dara listened so intently and didn't interrupt her father to say that he had read a leaflet he had got from the Tourist Centre which gave the exact same information. They then moved on to discuss the castle and the Royal Mile and all the old buildings. Dara had bought a book about the buildings and he went upstairs to get it to show Pat.

"We only got around part of Edinburgh," Lily told her parents as soon as Dara left the room. "So we're going to have a full day out again next week. In fact, I noticed that there's a youth hostel up on the Royal Mile, so we might even stay over."

Mona's face suddenly froze. "What?" she said. "Stay up in Edinburgh for a night on your own? I don't think that would look very good, just the two of you . . ." Her mouth formed a tight line and a red flush came over her face and neck. "What do you think, Pat? What do you have to say about the idea?"

"It's only a *hostel*," Lily said, annoyed at her mother's reaction and trying to keep her voice light-hearted. "It has separate dormitories for males and females, and they're even on separate floors. Do you not remember that I went away with the school to one in Inverness when we were in sixth year? There were boys and girls together on that trip."

"Indeed I do remember," Mona said, glancing over at her husband for backup. "But there were teachers there minding you."

Lily's eyebrows shot up. "But Declan went to a youth hostel in Loch Lomond with a group of his pals a few years ago, and that was mixed and they had nobody chaperoning them." She didn't say that she and Dara had discussed going for a night to Loch Lomond youth hostel as well – if she got past her mother with the Edinburgh one. They had two weeks' holiday and there wasn't a lot to do in Rowanhill – it would break it up to have a couple of nights away in more interesting places.

"Pat," her mother said, "you're keeping very quiet."

Pat looked at her. "Do you really want my opinion, Mona, or do you just want me to agree with you?"

Mona's mouth got even tighter. She glanced at the door in case Dara came in and heard the argument. It was hard enough for her dealing with Lily, without having to lay the law down with her boyfriend who she had only met. "I'd like to know what you think."

"Well . . . I think that Lily and Dara know their own business," he said, his eyes sliding away from his wife's. "It's nice for Dara to see a bit of the country and if they say the hostel has separate dormitories then I don't see what the problem is. They're both over twenty years of age, and don't forget that Lily lives away from home most of the time now."

Lily's spirits lifted. It was a big step forward if her father agreed, but a little niggling feeling told her that this was his way of trying to make up ground with her after the row back in Ireland.

"I know she lives away," Mona said, "you don't need to remind me about that, but while she's under this roof we're still responsible for her."

Lily gave an exaggerated sigh to lighten things up. "I'm a grown woman – you don't need to talk as if I'm not here." She put her hand on her mother's arm. "I can assure you that we'll be in separate dormitories in the youth hostel and that everything will be above board." She gave a little shrug. "I don't know what we're all getting so heated about. We only mentioned it in passing and it wouldn't be until next week if we did go." She looked over to the window. "If the weather's bad we probably won't even go at all."

She knew that, unless it was going to cause real trouble at home, she and Dara would go off for an overnight to Edinburgh, but by saying they might not, she was giving her mother time to get used to the idea. It wasn't as though she was asking to go and spend the night in a hotel with him or staying the night in a house alone. It was all above board – the hostel was very strict and they would definitely be sleeping in separate dorms.

Dara came down the stairs with his book and then he and Pat sat studying it and discussing the different buildings while Lily helped her mother clear the table and wash the dishes.

The youth hostel in Edinburgh wasn't mentioned again, and Lily pushed any anxieties away and kept her mother occupied by telling her all about her teaching practice that was coming up and the kind of school she would be teaching in.

"It's lovely they managed to get you a Catholic school," Mona said. "That will help you to get a job when you come back home after you've graduated."

"That's what I thought," Lily said. Her mother had already been presented with a situation that she didn't like and there was no point in telling her that she hadn't decided if she was coming back or not.

Later, when the conversation about Edinburgh and all its magnificence had been exhausted and Dara had discussed the Scottish bridies and pies with Mona over tea, all seemed fine between them.

It struck Lily how hard it was for her mother to shift in her way of thinking, and she hoped it would happen without any falling-outs. There were plenty of things she could have said to her mother, like the fact that Mona had come over to Scotland on her own, and who had chaperoned her when she met Lily's father? She didn't say anything like that because it would make her feel she was acting in a small-minded way herself and, more importantly, she didn't want to hurt her mother's feelings. She also didn't want her mother taking against Dara, thinking that he was having a bad influence on her. It was enough for the time being that she had her father on her side. She would wait and see how things panned out.

Then, she remembered their five days in her room in college and a shiver ran through her. If her mother found the thought of them staying in separate dorms in a youth hostel controversial, if she ever found out that she and Dara had spent five nights together in her college room all hell would break loose for certain. Lily knew that there would be no wriggling out of that – and however guilty her father felt, he wouldn't be able to take her side on that.

She took a deep breath to calm the fluttering anxiety and reminded herself why she had taken that risk. Spending time alone in Newcastle was the only way they would ever get to know each other properly, and as a grown woman, she had taken that decision and whatever happened, she would have to stand by it.

Lily's Aunt Sophie called at the house for Lily's mother so they could walk up to the Parochial Hall together for the Catholic Mothers' Association meeting. She sang Ava's praises and said how nice it was to have a young girl back in the house again to give a bit of life to Kirsty and Heather's old bedroom.

"Declan is lucky," Sophie said. "She's a lovely girl and she seems to have taken to Scotland in a big way."

"I think I heard him saying they're going into Glasgow tomorrow night," Mona said. "It will be nice for her to see a bit more of things than just be stuck in Rowanhill."

The two women left to go for their meeting, and as they walked up through the village, Mona mentioned Lily's plans about the youth hostel.

"What do you think?" she asked. "Did your girls do anything like that, or am I being old-fashioned thinking that it doesn't seem right?"

"God, Mona," Sophie said, "we had far worse than that. Don't you remember all the ups and downs with Kirsty and Larry? Fintan went mad when he found out that he was a good bit older than Kirsty and had his own flat."

"Now that you mention it, I think I do remember something."

If Sophie's memory was correct, she was quite sure that Mona had put in her tuppence worth at the time, but it was all water under the bridge now. Kirsty and Larry couldn't be happier, they loved their life travelling around the world on the glamorous cruise ships and seemed to have no plans as yet to settle down.

"Did you say it was a youth hostel that Lily wanted to go to?" Sophie asked.

"Yes, up in Edinburgh," said Mona.

"Sure the girls all went youth hostelling when they were at school – they're well run and quite strict with wardens. The boys in one dormitory and the girls in the other."

Mona's brow was knitted. "But none of them went with boyfriends."

Sophie gave a wry smile. "Well, as far as we know! Heather and Kirsty went with a gang of girls a few times to Oban and Pitlochry and places like that, and they came back skitting and laughing about boys that they met from Glasgow." She shrugged. "I'm sure there are rules that if the males or the females are caught anywhere near the other dormitories they're immediately expelled from the hostel and banned from the organisation. They're very strict. I don't think you have anything to worry about with Lily, and Dara seems a lovely boy."

"Too lovely," Mona said. "That's the problem. She's mad about him. I've never seen her like that over any other lad."

"Well, I can't see them coming to any great harm in a youth hostel," Sophie said. "And you're better agreeing to something safe like that than many a notion they might come up with."

After her mother had gone out, Lily suggested that they take a walk up to Seán's so that she could say hello to Ava. Having established Dara's complete lack of interest in her, Lily was able to relax now and remember all the nice qualities that she had first noticed in Ava. She felt she should make her as welcome in Scotland as Ava had made her family feel in Carraigvale. She also thought they should look in on Seán and see if he was recovering from his flu.

The new estate that her brother and his wife lived on was half a mile away, and they had to walk through the main street of the village to get to it.

"The good news," Lily said, as they walked along hand-in-hand, "is that I think we can go to Edinburgh and stay overnight without it giving my mother a nervous breakdown."

"That would be great," he said, "but don't push it if it's going to upset your mother. Your parents have been very good having me to stay and I don't want you to cause a strain because of me."

"She thinks you're great, it's me who's the problem. My father was fine about us going, and I think she's come round. At the end of the day, we are staying in a hostel in separate dormitories and it couldn't be more innocent. Who could say anything about that?"

He squeezed her hand. "One day," he said, "we won't have all this to worry about – we'll be together all the time."

But where? Lily thought. She wanted nothing more than to be with Dara but she knew he was tied at home with his family, and her mother was taking it for granted she would return home.

She hoped it would all sort itself out in the fullness of time.

36

Ava closed the door on the children's bedroom and stood outside it for a couple of minutes, checking that Beth was indeed fast asleep. She had read the little girl two stories from a fairy book and then told her a story that the nice nuns used to tell her.

It was about a special little girl who was found in a basket, who turned out to be a princess who had been stolen from her family.

It was a story that Ava now knew to be ridiculously childish, clichéd and full of fantasy, but that story had kept her going all those years in the orphanage. From the age of five – when she first heard it – until the age of eleven, she had scrutinised every visitor to the orphanage, wondering if it was one of her devastated parents coming to collect her.

She had also made sure she behaved impeccably in the convent, kept her bed and small wardrobe tidy and her hair and clothes always neat. As she grew older and was allowed to help in the kitchen, she did every task exactly as she was shown, and was always on hand to make tea for the nuns or priests and any visitors.

Whilst she got on very well with the adults around her, it was noticed that she found it difficult to mix with the other children. She didn't like the girls she shared a room with touching her things and she wouldn't borrow any of theirs. She had no interest in the younger children and did her best to avoid any contact with them.

Over the years she had refused offers from families to foster her, and when one determined family had taken her home for a weekend she had sabotaged the visit by refusing to eat or speak to anyone. Back in the orphanage she told them that the family were not as nice as they appeared, and had been screaming and fighting with each other and she had been terrified. The nuns were all fond of Ava and, since she seemed content to stay with them, they gave up trying to have her fostered or adopted.

Two nuns in particular grew very fond of her and took her for trips to Dublin and bought her nice cardigans and dresses from money donated to the orphanage. They also took her to the cinema and to funfairs in the park and Ava was content to pass the time with them until her real family came and found her.

Then, all her dreams had been shattered when one of the not-nice nuns overheard her telling one of the younger children that she was a princess who had been stolen. She had brought her into the back seat of the church and told her that the story was utter nonsense and for her to repeat it was a lie and a sin against God.

She had then told Ava that the silly story about the princess had been made up by some well-meaning nun when Ava was little, and had sprung from the fact that St Ava – on whose feast-day she had been left at the convent door – had in fact been the daughter of a king.

While her eleven-year-old mind was trying to digest the truth, the nun had then gone on to tell her that her real mother – the one who abandoned her – was no doubt a very bad woman who wasn't married and didn't want her.

Although she had gone about her duties in the convent in the same way, and showed no outward signs of the devastation she felt at having her aristocratic lineage ripped away from her, Ava changed from that day on.

She knew now that no one was going to turn up and sweep her off to a life of luxury. And worse still, she had to look back with regret on the nice families who had offered to give her a home in the better parts of Dublin, and know that she had refused the chance of a middle-class upbringing and a good education.

For weeks afterwards she'd had nightmares in which she was lying in a giant basket and being carried around by a tall faceless person in a black cloak. When the basket was eventually put down, and the person had disappeared, Ava would attempt to climb out of it. Each time she did so, she would find herself in a different, but always perilous location. Sometimes it was on a cliff edge looking out over the sea and at other times it would be on the very top branch of a swaying tall tree. The most frequent place that the basket turned up was in the bell-tower of a tall spired church. And each time when she got to the rim of the basket then she would fall – tumbling down, down through the air until she woke with a bump.

The nuns had got used to her screaming through the night and they had moved her into a single room to stop wakening the others. She also had to endure the other girls teasing her and mimicking her night terrors.

Gradually, the dreams eased off, and on the occasions when they did occur she was able to tell herself, whilst still within the dream, that it wasn't real and not to get upset about it.

And she had continued doing what was necessary to get by and to keep the nuns on her side. She had smiled and done all the tasks expected of her, made tea for everyone and looked for any chance that came up to secure herself a decent living when the time came to leave the convent.

When the chance of working and living in the superior bed and breakfast in Ballsbridge came up, Ava felt at the interview that the place was something like the houses she imagined she might have lived in. She loved going up the grand staircase and walking along the thickly carpeted hallway where her footsteps couldn't be heard.

And her meticulous work and willingness to give more than her stated hours had encouraged the owners – the O'Brien family – to take her under their wing and, like the nuns, treat her as more than a worker. It always helped that Ava looked more than she was, and the good-quality second-hand clothes Celine O'Brien gave her made her look like her employers.

She had worked there since leaving the convent at eighteen, and for the first couple of years things had worked out fine, but then problems arose. It was decided that a move from Dublin was the answer, and so the position in Carraigvale was found for her. That had worked for a while, but within a few months Ava found that rural town life was very limited and then the problems she had left behind in Dublin reared their head again.

And then Declan Grace had appeared, and had fallen for her in a big way, possibly offering a way out of Ireland and a solution to her current problems.

She had been looking forward to this trip to Scotland and hoped that something long-term might come out of it.

*　*　*

Ava walked along the hallway now, satisfied that the children were fast asleep. She went straight to the bedroom at the end. She stopped outside the closed door, listening for any sounds that would indicate that Seán was awake. Then, she tapped lightly on the door. She waited a few seconds and when there was no response she turned the handle and walked into the semi-dark room.

"Seán . . ." she said in a low voice. "Seán . . ." She stood silently and waited until he turned towards her.

"Ava?" His voice sounded bewildered.

She went to stand at the foot of the bed. "I thought I'd check if you wanted anything."

"My God!" He sat up now, leaning against the headboard.

She looked at him. His chest and the strong muscled arms she remembered were bare.

His eyes caught hers and he looked away, his hands straightening out the green counterpane on the bed. "I didn't know you were here."

"I thought Declan or your mother might have told you I was coming."

"I knew you were coming to Rowanhill," he said, running a hand through his sleep-ruffled hair, "but I didn't know you were in the house. Is Declan with you?"

"No, I'm on my own."

He looked at her again. "How come you're here? In our house . . ."

"Eileen has gone to the hospital to visit her mother and she needed someone to baby-sit." She lowered her eyes. "I thought you would be pleased to see me."

He shifted in the bed. "Sorry . . . I've just woken up." He smiled. "It's nice to see you. You arrived yesterday, didn't you?"

"Yes. I was sorry to hear you were sick. I was looking forward to seeing you. We got on so well back in Ireland."

He started moving the pillows behind him now as though trying to get into a more comfortable position. "I hope everything was okay after we left, you know, with that man who was annoying you?"

She said nothing for a few moments, then she gave a little sigh. "He's not given up. He's been down a couple of times, but thankfully Mrs Stewart was around so he couldn't make it obvious he was there to see me."

"You should call the police," Seán told her. "What he's doing is harassment and frightening you. It's a crime and he's not allowed to do that."

"I think the only way to get rid of him is to move away."

"Where would you go?"

"I'm not sure yet, but I'll decide soon." She waited for a moment and when he said nothing, she moved towards the door. "Would you like a cup of tea or something to eat?"

"No – no," he said, his Scottish accent sounding almost gruff. "You're all right."

"What about some Lucozade? Your mother sent a bottle down for you."

"I'm fine," he said, his voice not sounding fine at all. He looked at her again, his expression pained. "Ava, I feel awkward about what happened between us in Ireland . . . You're a lovely girl and it would be different if I wasn't married."

She nodded slowly without saying anything.

"You won't mention it to anyone?" he said. "It would cause terrible trouble all round – and God knows what Eileen would do."

There was a sadness to her smile. "Of course I won't say anything. I feel the same with Declan – I wouldn't want to hurt him. As you say, if things were different and you weren't married . . ." She paused, her voluptuous figure silhouetted in the doorway. "I think a cup of tea might help you feel better. The flu can take a lot out of you."

Seán hesitated, debating whether to stay safely upstairs or chance spending time with Ava down in the sitting-room. "I'm still not feeling great," he said, "so I might be best with the Lucozade if you don't mind bringing the bottle up." He felt it would be less awkward if he stayed in bed rather than sitting downstairs with her and not knowing what to talk about.

He felt a debt of gratitude towards her now for putting his mind at rest. He had been overwhelmed with guilt and anxiety since Declan told him she was booked on the boat to come to Scotland. Whilst she had been kind and helpful to everyone in Ireland – and whilst he was hugely attracted to her – there was something about her that had always made him feel a little uneasy. Something that told him Ava was too good to be true. Something that told him a girl so good-looking and so nice and helpful should be already married or at least spoken for. Like everyone else, he felt she could do a lot better than an ordinary fellow like Declan, and she certainly shouldn't be getting into dangerous situations with an ordinary married man like himself.

He wasn't totally oblivious to other women before he encountered Ava. In the past he'd had a couple of the looser local girls sidle up to him in the pub at the end of the evening, making it clear to him that they would be up for a one-night stand or even something more. He knew there was a certain type of girl who found his well-developed physique attractive, and there was one in particular – an old girlfriend from school, now divorced, who he'd only chastely kissed before – who had described when she was very drunk what she would love to do to him.

Seán had certainly been tempted, and had enjoyed the flirtatious late-night banter, but something held him back from any physical involvement.

Mainly, he thought, it was his feelings for Eileen, because there were times when he still saw flashes of the slim, elfin-faced girl from the big, expensive houses on the edge of the village he had pursued for months before finally pinning her down. And even though she got cross for the smallest of things and was over-fussy with the house, there was still that spark between them – the little glimmer that made him slide his arms around her waist as she stood peeling potatoes or playfully catch her when she came out fresh from the bath in her dressing-gown with a towel wrapped around her hair.

Most of the time he thought he was being sensible and mature by not giving in to any temptations, by being unwilling to put his neat and tidy life at risk – but occasionally he recognised it as fear. Fear of what would happen if he were found out. Fear of the wrath of his wife and his mother. Fear of letting go – of descending into deep dark waters that would take him way out of his sexual depth and experience. That night back in Ireland with Ava was the closest he ever came to that and it had haunted him ever since. And seeing her again had brought all those feelings to the surface again.

But he was pleased he had handled seeing her again so well. He felt relieved now that he had spoken to her, and even more relieved to hear that she felt the same about the incident back in the bed and breakfast. He was sure the recent weight of carrying that guilt had made him ill. He had never had such dull headaches or feelings of exhaustion before, and suspected it was caused, at least in part, by the sleepless nights he had leading up to Ava's arrival.

He heard her footsteps coming back up the stairs now and he lay back on the pillows. She tapped on the door and he called to her to come in. She opened the door with her foot as she was carrying the Lucozade and a glass.

She put the glass down on the bedside table, and then opened the bottle and started to pour it for him. "I'll leave the bottle here for you, in case you want more. You should drink as much as you can as it's easy to get dehydrated when you're ill."

"Thanks," he said. "You're very good."

The glass filled, she went to put the top back on when somehow the bottle slipped out of her hand and fell on the floor with a dull thud, the orange liquid splashing out on the light-coloured carpet and on the fancy quilted pale-green cover on the bed.

"Oh, Jesus!" Her voice was panicky. "How stupid of me! I'll go and get a cloth."

"It's okay," he told her. "It was an easy accident."

She ran downstairs and grabbed the two cloths that Eileen had neatly folded on the draining-board and a tea towel, then ran back upstairs quickly.

When she came into the room, Seán was already out of bed, barefoot, wearing only his pyjama bottoms, and busy mopping the mess up with a box of paper tissues he'd found on Eileen's dressing table.

"It's fine," he said. "I've got the worst of it mopped up."

"Let me do that," she said, briefly touching his elbow. "It was my fault."

Her hand on his arm was like an electric shock. He moved away from her and walked around the bed to stand at the other side.

Ava rubbed furiously at the bed cover and then, when she was satisfied most of it was gone, she got down on her knees to rub the carpet. As she did so, her tight black skirt rose up above her knees.

Seán turned away towards the window, his eyes closed and his hands clenched.

"I'll just rinse the cloth in the bathroom sink," she said, getting to her feet and going back out into the hallway.

Seán was still standing in the same spot when she came back in.

She looked over at him and smiled. "I think we've nearly got it. Thank God – Eileen would go mad – she keeps the house so perfect and lovely."

A picture of Eileen's tight flushed face came into his mind now as he remembered the row they had earlier that afternoon, when he told her he wasn't well enough to look after the children. She had ranted and raved at him, saying that she could never depend on him and that if had been *his* mother who was sick and in hospital that he'd soon be out of the bed.

Ava hoisted her skirt up to allow her to kneel again, and this time the hem rose up to reveal the tops of her black stockings.

Eileen rarely wore stockings these days or anything remotely sexy. It was either tights with skirts or socks with trousers. Most of the time she was dressed in old trousers and baggy jumpers for the housework she was obsessed with. It was only when she was going somewhere that other people might see her that she put on make-up and dressed up.

He watched Ava moving rhythmically in her tight skirt as she rubbed away the last of the stains, and then his gaze moved upwards to the soft lilac cardigan and he noticed the top three buttons were undone. And suddenly he was reminded of what she looked like with every one of the tiny buttons undone as she had in the sitting-room in the bed and breakfast.

The memory of her gorgeous full breasts, encased in a black polka-dot brassiere edged with lace, made him feel weak at the knees. He moved towards her, not quite sure what he was going to do . . . then he remembered the guilt that wracked him for weeks after he'd been in Ireland.

"That's enough now, Ava," he said in a hoarse voice. "You should go back downstairs now."

"I think it's fine, thank God," she said, in a cheery relieved voice. She moved from kneeling to sit back on her heels for a better view of the carpet and bed "Yes, that's fine." She put her hand over to the bed to lever herself up and as she went to stand one of her stiletto heels went to the side.

Instinctively, Seán moved to catch her, his two hands reaching for her arm. "Are you okay?"

"I'm grand," she said, looking up at him and giggling. "These high heels are dangerous." She put the back of her hand to her forehead, wiping away the slight dampness from all the exertion. "God, I've been very clumsy tonight." She got to her feet, and stood easing the hem of her skirt down over her knees. She looked at him and then she realised his face was strangely serious. "Are you all right, Seán?"

"I'm fine . . ." he said, looking away.

Her hands moved to the bottom edge of her cardigan and she tugged it down to straighten it. He watched as the fourth button strained across her generous breasts, threatening that it might just pop open.

And that was when he moved – when his hands came to cover hers and then encircle her waist.

She looked up at him.

"I can't help it," he said, "You are so beautiful!"

She moved backwards, until the back of her legs were touching the side of the bed. "No, Seán, we shouldn't! Remember what you said earlier."

He pushed against her and she could feel how aroused he was. "Nobody is going to know."

"But I don't want you to feel bad about us again, the way you did earlier."

His strong arms came on either side of her and he laid her down on the bed, then his hands moved to the bottom of her skirt. He pushed it upwards so he could see the top of her stockings and the taut black suspenders holding them up. "You are absolutely gorgeous," he said. He ran his hands over her legs and then he lay on top of her and kissed her full and hard on the mouth.

By that time Ava had given up resisting as she loved the feel of his strong arms around her. It made her feel protected and safe, the way she had felt the night that Seán had seen William O'Brien off.

The last button had just been opened on her cardigan and Seán was nuzzling his face in her cleavage when something made Ava struggle to sit upright.

"What is it?" he asked, seeing the alarm on her face.

"I thought I heard something . . ." Her hands came to cover her chest.

They both listened.

"I think it was the latch on the gate or something like that," she said.

Seán moved from the bed to go over to the window, pulling the cord on his pyjama bottoms tighter around his waist. "There's nobody there. It might just have been the neighbour's gate or the wind hitting the latch on the shed door."

He turned back and saw her hand move to refasten the suspender he had opened.

He quickly moved back to the bed and threw himself on top of her again.

37

Lily and Dara came towards the gate of her brother's house. They had walked quickly through the village huddled under her mother's umbrella, as the April night had suddenly turned cold and wet.

"My dad gave me a spare front-door key," Lily said, taking it from her jacket pocket. "Eileen lent it to him earlier on because he had to get one of Seán's car manuals. We'll let ourselves in so we don't wake the children."

"We might give Ava a fright just walking in," he said.

"We'll tap on the sitting-room window before we do. We often do that in each other's houses if the door is on the latch."

As they came up to the front door, Lily went to the sitting-room window and, shielding her eyes with her hand against the light, looked in. There was no sign of Ava but she gave a quick tap on the glass anyway. There was no response.

"I don't see her," she told Dara, "but I can see the television is on. She's either in the kitchen or upstairs."

She went to the door and slid the Yale Key in the lock and then turned it. The house was in total silence. "We'll keep quiet," she told Dara as they went in. "She might be upstairs trying to get the kids to sleep."

Lily shook the drops of rain off her umbrella outside the open door, then brought it inside and stood it in the brass holder behind the door. After closing the door over quietly, they went into the sitting room where the television was on but the sound turned down. Lily walked over to glance into the empty kitchen and came back shrugging that there was nobody around.

Then they both stood still as they heard a muffled sound from upstairs.

"She's up with Susan and Beth," Lily said in a low voice. She slid her scarf from around her neck and then took her jacket off and, after checking it wasn't too damp, threw it on the back of the sofa. "What do you think?" she whispered, waving her hand around the modern room.

"Fantastic," he said. "I can see what you meant about them being keen on decorating – it's like something you'd see in a magazine."

He went over to examine the television set standing on four long legs next to the radiogram. Eileen's parents had bought the TV set as a Christmas present, much to the consternation of Mona who thought it an outrageously expensive gift.

"They have all the latest models," he said. "They make ours seem ancient."

"It's well-known that Ireland is way behind the times," Lily teased, coming to put her arm through his. She gave him a peck on the cheek. "Why don't you take your jacket off?"

"It's a bit damp," he said. "I didn't like to say anything but the drips from the umbrella ran straight down on to me." He winked at her. "I'm not one to complain."

She felt the heavy army jacket, and there was a definite dampness. "Put it out in the hall," she said. "There's a long radiator there that Eileen uses to dry things on. It'll be fine by the time we go back home."

Dara went over to the door and quietly opened it. He stepped outside, took his jacket off and laid it along the radiator. Then, just as he made to go back into the sitting-room, the jacket slid off, the brass buttons making a clattering noise on the tiled floor. He went back and was fixing it more securely when he heard one of the doors opening upstairs and the sound of low voices.

He stood back to look up to the landing upstairs and saw Ava coming out of one of the bedrooms, pulling her skirt down and then beginning to button up her open cardigan.

Then, there was the sound of a man's voice and he watched her turn and stick her head back in the door she had come out of. Then he heard her say, "Stay here, I'll go down."

His eyes widened in shock as he took in what was happening. He was just deciding to move away, so as not to witness anything more, when she turned around and saw him at the foot of the stairs.

"Dara!" she said, smiling and fumbling at her buttons. She came to stand where the slatted railings of the wooden staircase on the landing shielded most of her top half. "I was just checking on the children and you won't believe it, I had a bit of an accident and spilled Lucozade all down me!"

Dara looked up at her and knew by her stumbling voice and flustered manner that she was lying. Then he remembered what Lily had told him about the night she had found Seán comforting her after the belligerent man had called to the bed and breakfast. Unless she had Declan hidden upstairs somewhere, he could see that you would have to be blind and deaf not to know what he and Lily had walked in on.

Lily, hearing the voices now, came out into the hallway. She went to stand by Dara.

She looked up to where Ava stood at the top of the stairs. "Hi," she said, in a loud whisper, giving Ava a little wave. "I hope we didn't give you a fright?"

Ava shook her head and mouthed the word, "No."

"How is Seán?"

Dara watched and could see Ava's hands trembling as she did up the top button on her cardigan. "I think he's still sleeping . . . I haven't heard any sound."

"Better to leave him," Lily said. "No sign of Declan yet?"

Again, Ava shook her head. "He said he would be back after nine."

"What about Beth and Susan? Are they asleep?"

Ava nodded. "Flat out. I was in the bathroom and then I was just checking on them when you came in . . ."

"I'll just have a wee peep in at them." Lily moved onto the stairs, and when she reached the top she turned to the right towards the children's bedroom – which was at the opposite end of the landing from the room Ava had come out of. And exactly where Dara knew it would be.

He looked back at Ava and saw her looking straight at him. They stared at each other without saying a word. He turned away and walked back into the sitting-room, leaving her standing at the top of the stairs. They both knew that he would say nothing. How could he arrive at Lily's home and turn everything upside down after only a couple of days? All his instincts told him that Ava had been in the bedroom with Seán and they had definitely been up to something they shouldn't have.

If he confided in Lily she would only get upset and, knowing the kind of girl she was, she would confront Seán and Ava about their carry-on. And then she would have to leave and go back to college, carrying all that upset with her, and leaving devastation behind her. And what about her parents? How about Seán's wife and their two little girls?

And how would Declan handle the fact that his supposed lovely, kind girlfriend had come all the way from Ireland just to be near Seán?

And then, Dara considered, what if he was in fact wrong? What if Ava had spilled something down her clothes and he caused uproar with Seán and all the family over something that turned out to be innocent? She had been pleasant and impeccably behaved on the long journey over from Carraigvale.

Weighing it all up, Dara knew he would have to keep silent about it. Just as he had kept silent about the older man he had seen Ava coming out of the cinema with. The man that his brother Frank said Ava had been kissing in a car late one night outside the bed and breakfast.

When he first met Lily in Ireland, he felt it was too soon to tell her any of this, afraid it would come across as malicious gossip, and he also hadn't been sure that Declan and Ava were going to keep up the romance. Being private himself, he had never been the sort to meddle in other people's business, but now he wondered if he had done the right thing by remaining silent.

He mulled it over and came to the conclusion that if he said anything about tonight it would be his word against Ava's – and he and Lily had a lot to lose if he was in fact wrong.

And even though Lily had had her own suspicions about them, if things erupted, there was a possibility he might lose Lily herself.

38

The first week went by steadily as Lily took Dara out on trips to Glasgow and over to visit friends for drinks in the nearby villages of Cleland and Wishaw. There wasn't a day that wasn't busy, as Lily's older brothers, Michael and Patrick, and their wives and children called down to the house regularly. They also invited Lily and Dara up to their houses for meals along with Declan and Ava.

Dara got on well with everyone, but a few times she felt there was a slight distance about him and she asked him several times if he was okay, and on each occasion he assured her that he was and brightened up.

Her mother had said nothing more about the youth hostelling, and when Lily broached the subject again, Mona just asked her what time they would be back so she would have the dinner ready for them.

Lily told her they were going on the Thursday morning and would be back Friday night which was Good Friday. "We'll get Mass in Edinburgh," she said before her mother had a chance to say anything. She also felt it would give Dara the option not to go if they were away from the family when the service was on.

Declan had taken most of the week as a holiday, and he and Ava went off during the day in the car. Once or twice they gave Lily and Dara a lift into one of the nearby towns, but they never suggested meeting up for lunch or a drink or anything like that. In the evenings that Lily and Dara were in the house, after dinner Declan and Ava either went out or went next door to Sophie's, and Lily began to wonder whether Ava liked being with her and Dara. If there was a problem, she decided, it had to be Ava, because Declan, who was easy-going and got on with everyone, didn't think that deeply about people.

Whatever it was, Ava kept herself more and more to herself. Any time she wasn't with Declan, she spent at Sophie's who was teaching her how to use the sewing machine.

As they travelled on the train up to Edinburgh on Thursday morning, Lily mentioned to Dara that she felt Ava had changed and wasn't as chatty and open as she seemed in Ireland.

He shrugged and said he thought she was one of those girls that you never really got to know. "I told you she had no conversation on the boat coming over," he said. "I live in the same town as her and I'm as wise as you are – you who have really only just met her."

They were sitting on a bench in Princes Street Gardens, eating sandwiches Mona had made and drinking bottles of Coke when Lily brought up the subject of Mass.

"I know it sounds like I'm being contrary, after saying I hate going to church," Dara said, "but I'll come with all your family on Easter Sunday, and I actually want to go to Mass tomorrow – not because it's Good Friday – but because it's my mother's birthday and her religion was important to her."

Lily took his hand and squeezed it, and when she saw the sadness in his eyes she wondered if that's what had been playing on his mind the last few days. "Well, we'll find the nearest church or we could go to the cathedral if you prefer," she said.

"Thanks." Then, looking straight ahead, he said, "There was a suspicion that my mother might have committed suicide. She had suffered from depression a few years before that . . ."

"Oh, God, Dara . . . I'm so sorry! I'd no idea . . . I didn't like to ask in case it upset you."

There was a silence, during which Lily was afraid to say the wrong thing.

"She had cycled down to visit a friend who lived by the canal." He turned to look at her, his dark eyes glinting with tears. "It was when we lived in Westmeath. It was a bad night, wet and windy, and when it was late and she still wasn't home my father rang down and the friends told him she'd left two hours before . . ." His voice cracked and he closed his eyes to compose himself. "Anyway, he drove down the town looking for her in all the usual places, the shops, the church and even the local pubs in case she was in chatting to someone." He shrugged. "Eventually someone was passing the canal and saw the marks from the bicycle tyre just at the canal edge. The Guards were called and –" He suddenly stopped, unable to speak. Eventually he said. "The details don't matter, and to be honest I never wanted to know them all, but she drowned."

Lily turned and put her arms around him. "I am so, so sorry, Dara. But from everything you've said it sounds like an accident . . ."

He nodded and buried his face in the crook of her neck. "It was terrible." Then after a while he sat up straight. "That's why we're all so protective of my sister, Rose. She took it really badly and was obsessed with trying to find out why my mother was depressed and why she would want to kill herself." He shrugged. "Maybe I'm deluding myself, but I believe it was actually an accident – she couldn't swim. My father and my brothers think the same too. The canal is treacherous and there have been a lot of accidents there between barges and people falling in." He sighed. "She had improved a lot in the last year or two, and the doctor had taken her off the medication. She was close to us all and had a lot to live for. I just can't imagine that she was so unhappy that she would take her own life." His eyes filled up again. "For ages afterwards I was really angry, thinking she had deliberately deserted us all. I felt really abandoned, the loss was so huge . . . it's hard to describe."

"I'd go by your feelings that it was an accident then," Lily said quietly. "And maybe over time Rose will come to realise that too."

He nodded. "I hope she gets into Tullamore hospital. It's the only one she wants. She's too nervous to live away from home, and she would have to do that if she was in a hospital in Dublin or Cork."

"She said there was another one nearby but she didn't fancy that one."

He closed his eyes. "Portlaoise. That's because my mother was a patient in the psychiatric ward for a while and people are funny about it."

"She's a clever girl," Lily said. "I'm sure she'll find a hospital that suits her."

"Yeah," he said, brightening up. "By the end of the summer she could be all settled with a job and leading a more independent life."

*   *   *

The youth hostel idea worked perfectly, and since the weather was fine they walked the length and breadth of the city, taking in all the old buildings and museums along the way. They stopped every so often for a drink or a sandwich and any time Lily needed to give her legs a rest. Dara loved the old rambling pubs on the Royal Mile and in Rose Street, as they were so different to the pubs back in Ireland. He enjoyed reading any information about the history of them or old photographs which were often framed and hanging on the walls.

While they were in one of the pubs, Dara rang home and had a quick word with his father and Rose. "They're grand," he told Lily. "And they both said thanks for ringing as it was a hard day for everyone."

The hostel just off the Royal Mile was better than any of the ones that Lily had been in before, with modern showers and plenty of cooking facilities. They didn't bother making meals as it wasn't worth shopping for two days, and instead ate in cafés or brought sandwiches or pies back to the hostel.

They found a lovely pub near the hostel where they spent the evening and had a ten-minute stroll up through the medieval streets before going in for the night.

They sat drinking coffee and when the time came for them to go to their respective dormitories, they were both very reluctant.

Dara held her hand across the table. "I'm going to feel very lonely without you, Lily. I wish we had booked into a bed and breakfast somewhere instead of having to sleep separately."

Lily looked alarmed. "We couldn't, they're really strict in Scotland. You have to be married. One of my friends went to a hotel in Glasgow with her fiancé and the owners demanded to see her wedding ring, and when she didn't have one, they told her to come back when she did." She started to giggle, thinking about it again. "She then made a bigger embarrassment of herself by showing them her engagement ring and the woman said it still wasn't a wedding ring, and it looked like something she'd bought out of Woolworth's!"

"So where did they stay in the end?" Dara asked.

"They didn't," she said. "They ended up coming home on the last bus. So much for their dirty weekend away." She couldn't stop giggling. "So we should feel lucky that at least we can stay in a hostel together."

"Yeah," he said, rolling his eyes. "You're not the one sleeping opposite the big American who snores all night."

Lily moved her head closer to his now. "Well, at least we won't be tempted . . ."

He caught her hand. "Wherever we are, I'm constantly tempted by you."

On Friday Lily said nothing about abstaining from meat, but when they stopped at a café for breakfast up near the castle, Dara grinned at her and said, "I suppose we'd better stick to eggs and fish today or we might get *eggs*-communicated from the church?"

They both laughed and the subject wasn't referred to again. At three o'clock they walked down past Waverly Station to St Mary's Cathedral for Mass and the traditional Good Friday 'kissing of the cross'. And then, when the service was over, Lily went with him to a side altar and they lit a candle for Dara's mother and another one each for themselves.

As they walked back to the hostel, Dara squeezed Lily's hand and said, "I lit that candle for us, asking that we would come back here in ten years' time, married and with our children."

Lily's heart soared, and for once she found herself lost for words. After a while Dara slowed down to a halt and looked at her.

"Are you okay?" he asked. "Have I just said the completely wrong thing? Am I going too fast for you?"

She shook her head, then she reached up on her tip-toes and put her arms around his neck. "I've never been so happy," she whispered. "I was just too scared to even think that far."

He kissed her, then he said, "Out of curiosity, what did you light your candle for?"

She rolled her eyes and laughed. "That my mother wouldn't make a big fuss again, when I tell her later in the week that we're going to a hostel in Loch Lomond!"

39

The early part of the second week flew by quicker than the first week did, the only pattern being that they would go somewhere during the day, were out most evenings, and last thing at night they would wait up until everyone else had gone to bed to have a kiss and a cuddle on the sofa.

Unlike the five days in college, sex hadn't been an issue over the two weeks. The physical circumstances of being in the house with so many other people made it impossible and in some ways it made it easier for them, as there was no choice in the matter. Sex was something they both told each other that they would look forward to when the time was right.

On the Tuesday night Lily asked Dara if he didn't mind entertaining himself the next day while she went to Glasgow with her mother. She explained that the shopping trip was something special they always did together when she came home, and she and her mother looked forward to it.

Dara said he had no problem at all, and would happily pass the day at home reading and watching the television.

Lily suggested that they ask Ava too, but she said she had already made plans to go with Eileen to visit her mother, who was still recovering from her operation.

"I'm glad they're getting on so well," Lily's mother said,

"because Eileen is usually so wrapped up in the house that she doesn't have much time for friends."

"It's funny that Ava's really taken to Eileen and the kids," Lily said, "when Eileen's quite a few years older. I thought her and Declan would spend more time with us."

"Ah, there's something about Ava that's older than her years," Mona said, "while you're still only a young scut of a thing."

"Mammy!" Lily said. "Don't forget I'll soon be a fully-qualified teacher."

"God help the children!" her mother laughed. "That's all I have to say."

When Lily got up the next morning, she put on her plain black sweater and pearls and a grey fitted skirt. She wanted her mother to enjoy the day as much as she did, and there was no point setting off on the wrong foot by wearing trousers.

Mona looked Lily up and down in approval. She was dressed herself in a nice wine-coloured suit with a sparkling brooch and earrings.

They caught the early train into town and when they arrived they started off at Arnotts Department Store at the corner of Argyle Street and then they walked up to C&A and Marks & Spencers. It was a pleasant, dry day and they both enjoyed the saunter around the shops and out in the street.

Whilst in Arnotts, Lily helped her mother choose a new raincoat and sandals and then they went into the restaurant and had coffee and scones. When they were going around the other shops, Mona said she would buy Lily some new outfits for her forthcoming teaching practice.

"I've got my new term's grant money through," Lily told her, "so I can afford to buy a few things myself without sponging off you and my dad."

They picked out a couple of summer dresses and cardigans to match, and a deep blue suit, which had a lovely skirt and a fitted jacket with three-quarter sleeves and a Peter Pan collar which really suited her.

"You look like a real teacher in those outfits," her mother said, a note of pride in her voice. "I think all you need now is a nice pair of cream sling-back shoes and a matching bag and you'll be perfect."

When they stopped at the Trees Tearoom for lunch, Lily kept her mother entertained with little stories about the children in the schools she had been in, and about all the projects she had planned for the coming term.

"There are times when I find it hard to believe you're actually going to be a teacher," Mona said, "when I think of the little devil you were when you were at school yourself! You never stopped talking and you nearly drove some of the teachers mad."

Lily just shrugged and laughed.

＊　　＊　　＊

When they came back from the hostel in Loch Lomond the following Thursday evening, Dara sat and had a glass of beer with Pat and Declan, and gave them a full report on the turreted country house, describing the sweeping staircase, the stained-glass windows and the huge ballroom.

Lily and her mother listened in, with Mona looking impressed as Dara reeled off all the architectural details of the building, and mouthing 'very clever' to Lily when he said something she thought was particularly interesting.

Pat told him that they should go up to Stirling Castle on his next visit to Scotland and, if they had time, travel as far as Inverness where they could see the Loch that the monster was supposed to live in.

Lily's eyes flicked from her father to Dara as they spoke, and she felt pleased they were obviously getting on so well.

"Oh, we have plenty of history here in Scotland," Pat said proudly. "And more again in London and places like York. I've never been, but they are places I intend to go and see sometime. I'm more interested now with Lily having told us all about the old places in York that she's visited with her college course."

Mona nodded. "They do great bus-runs from Hamilton down South and we're always saying we're going to go."

Pat looked at this wife and winked. "We will, we'll do it one of these summers."

"You could always come down to Newcastle to see me," Lily said, "and then carry on to York – it's not that far from there."

"We might just do that," her father said. "There's not too many of the old buildings in Ireland. There's only a few fine ones left, thanks to the English." Then, he caught Mona's warning eye. "But we won't say anything about that."

When Lily was helping to do the washing-up after the evening meal, her mother told her that they were having a family night out in a hotel in Motherwell on the Friday night.

"We thought it would give us all a nice night out to finish off the holiday," Mona explained, "since Dara and Ava are travelling back to Ireland on the Saturday night boat and you're back at college on the Sunday. They do a lovely steak meal and your dad and I will pay for you and Dara since you're only students, and Declan will pay for Ava since he's working."

"That's really good of you," Lily said, linking her mother's arm and hugging her. "Thanks for everything you've done. We've had a great holiday and it's given you the chance to get to know Dara."

"Oh, it has," Mona said. "And he's a lovely, lovely lad and he's so helpful about the house. He'd do anything you ask him, you can tell he's from a decent family." She paused. "How are you going to manage when you're both back at college and in separate countries? It's not going to be easy for ye."

"We'll write and phone, and we'll see each other in the holidays again." She paused. "And Dara might come over and see me in Newcastle some time."

"Oh well," her mother said, turning back to the sink, "that's up to yourselves . . . as your father said, you know your own business."

Lily suddenly felt a wave of emotion and she went over to her mother and put her arms around her. "You don't need to worry about me, Mum," she told her. "I'm not stupid."

Mona hugged her back but said nothing for a minute. "I can't help worrying," she finally said in a muffled voice. "And I worry about you most of all."

"I'm fine," she told her. "I love college and I'm looking forward to my teaching practice when I go back, and I know I'm lucky to have a career that I really enjoy." She kissed her mother on the side of the cheek. "And I'm really happy with Dara . . . I know it's difficult with him being so far away, but the one good thing is that he's not a distraction from my studies. If it was someone I was going out with at college and saw every day that would be harder, or if it was somebody from back home where I'd be running back here every other weekend. It's not ideal, but if it's the right thing, it will work out."

"That's true," her mother said. "And I don't mean to be going on to you – I know you're a grown woman and you need to make up your own mind." She halted, picking her words. "If you do think that Dara's the right one, then do what you need to do to make it work. Don't go settling for second best. Marriage is a long hard road even when you're with the right person."

Lily pulled back to arm's length now and smiled at her mother. Even though Dara had broached the subject of marriage when they were in Edinburgh, she knew it was still castles in the air. "We're nowhere near that stage yet. We've both got to finish our courses and we'll see what happens after that."

Mona smiled back. "Me and your dad were lucky," she said. "We might not see eye to eye all the time, but there's never been anyone else for me, and I'd like you to feel the same about the man you decide to marry."

Lily felt a great sadness rising up in her now. She gave her mother another little hug and then she went upstairs. She went into the bathroom and closed the door and then went to sit on the side of the bath, trying to fight back the tears. Had her mother really not known, all these years, that her father still had feelings for another woman? Had she never felt that his mind had been on someone else?

She had been tempted to talk it over with Dara on a few occasions, but she felt it would be a betrayal of her parents, and she didn't want him to look at them differently. She knew he saw them as the solid couple and family that Lily had always believed them to be.

She and Seán had never spoken about it since that night, and she wondered if he felt as she did, or whether he had completely forgotten about it.

And her father had shown no signs of being unsettled or unhappy at home. He had just been his usual self, working hard every day driving coaches and taxis and seemingly contented at home in front of the television or listening to the radio at night.

Maybe that was the way things really were, she thought. Maybe he was happy and wouldn't change things now. Even if a miracle happened and he was given the chance to marry that other woman. And then, maybe Seán had been right and it was all down to drink.

Lily stood up now and went to look in the mirror above the sink. Life was not at all straightforward, but she knew one thing for sure. She would only marry the person she truly loved, and if for some reason that didn't happen, she would rather be on her own.

40

Lily was pleased with the arrangements for the meal. It had been a while since the Grace family had had a night out together without it being for a formal occasion like a wedding or a christening. It had taken a bit of organisation for Lily's married brothers and their wives to get baby-sitters but they had all managed to come. Sophie and Fintan were also coming as they were always included in any family get-togethers.

They were all dressing up since it was a nice place, and Lily wanted to make sure that she and Dara looked their best. She had checked over the clothes he planned to wear, and then ironed the small creases out of the brown corduroy jacket that he had brought with him in case of something like this. She thought it looked lovely with his lighter brown trousers, small checked shirt and plain brown tie.

"You look like an architect," she told him. "I can just see you in your office standing over a pile of plans."

He laughed and told her she looked more like a model than a teacher in her short red dress and long stretchy boots. Lily said it felt funny going to something like this as an equal to the others. She had always felt much younger than her brothers and didn't feel they took her seriously, and she had never brought a partner with her to a family occasion before.

Dara was surprised and pleased to hear that, and told her that he had never brought a girl along to any family 'do's' either.

When they arrived at the bar in the small, family-run hotel, Lily could see that everyone had made a great effort. Her brothers were all in suits or smart jackets and Lily's sisters-in-law were in dresses or two-piece outfits.

Eileen was wearing the turquoise matching jacket and dress that she had bought for Susan's christening, and Ava looked very glamorous in a dark green fitted jersey dress with a wrap-over neckline which emphasised her bust.

They congregated in the lounge area, waiting for their table to be ready, and Pat went around the group taking their orders for a drink. Lily asked for a Bacardi and Coke, while her brothers' wives went for sherry, and Pat waited while Ava made up her mind. When she eventually decided to have the same as Lily, the men all gave her a little cheer.

"Now, lads," Ava told them, "don't forget I'm a good girl brought up very strictly by the nuns and I'm not used to drinking."

There was a slight awkwardness then as everyone wasn't sure whether to smile or look serious. They all knew Ava's background as she had mentioned it openly since arriving, and they all thought she was a great girl given her sad start in life.

Michael could always be relied upon to lift the atmosphere. "Don't worry about it, Ava," he said. "We'll keep working on you until you're as bad as the others."

Everyone laughed and, as they went back to their conversations, Lily thought that it was a strange thing for Ava to say out in front of everyone, and that she looked quite pleased with the attention.

Then, as she observed Ava going around chatting to all the women and asking the right questions about their children, she thought how well she seemed to have fitted in with the family and wondered what was going to happen to her and Declan. As far as she could see, at the end of this fortnight they still didn't seem to be any closer than they were at the start. Whereas, with herself and Dara, she felt they moved closer every day whether they were together or apart.

She looked for him now and saw he was standing at the bar with her father and there seemed to be a serious conversation going on between them. She also noticed her father knocking back a glass of whisky as they were waiting for the drinks order, a practice she knew a lot of men did to get a sneaky extra drink in without their wives knowing. She said nothing about it. It wasn't her problem and her mother was well capable of pulling her father up if she felt he had drunk enough.

When they both came back from the bar carrying a tray of glasses each, Pat announced that Dara had bought the drinks for everyone. And when her brothers began to say that it wasn't right and that Dara was only a student, he held his hand up and said it was nothing, it was just a little gesture of thanks to the family for the great welcome that they had all given him.

Eileen dug Lily in the ribs and said, "You've done well with him, good-looking and a great nature. When's the wedding?"

Lily laughed and said, "I think it's a bit early for that kind of talk," but she was pleased knowing that everyone liked him and assumed they were a serious couple.

Just as they were finishing off their drinks, another tray – bought by Pat this time – was brought around. Lily moved through the group, chatting to Sophie and Fintan and catching up with her brothers and their wives. She told them all about their trips to Edinburgh and Loch Lomond and then talked about the school she would be working in when she went back to college the following week.

Then, when everyone was starting to check their watches, the manager of the restaurant came through to apologise for the delay with their table, and explained that there had been some problem in the kitchen. He said they would be called in another ten minutes and in the meantime there was a waitress coming around with a complimentary sherry for the women and whisky for the men.

"Good God!" Mona said. "I'll have to take it easy with this next one or my head will be whirling. I'm no good drinking when I haven't eaten."

"Get a drop of lemonade in it," Sophie advised. "It will help to weaken it."

When Mona went off to the bar in search of the lemonade,

Sophie turned to Lily. "I meant to say that when Kirsty was on the phone yesterday, she said that there might be something coming up for you on the ship for the summer."

Lily's eyes lit up. "Really? Did she say if there was anything for Dara?" She took another sip of her sherry now, and could feel the warm, relaxing effect of the drinks she had so far taken.

"She didn't go into any great detail because it was a bad line and the long distance calls are very expensive – she just said she's sent a letter to your college address telling you all about it."

"That's great," Lily said, suddenly feeling all excited. She looked around to see where Dara was, as she thought it was as good a time as any to mention the possibility of the summer work. Over the months they had been getting to know each other, she knew she had been more cautious than Dara, and had waited for him to move things on to the next step. And although they had made references to spending time together over the summer, with Lily coming over to Carraigvale and he coming back to Scotland, deciding to spend the whole summer together was going to be the biggest step they had taken yet.

She looked around now and thought what a great buzz there was around the bar. People were beginning to move into the restaurant now, and she reckoned there would be a good crowd on the dance-floor later. Her brothers all loved dancing and so did her parents, and the type of band that was playing would suit them all.

She caught sight of Dara sitting at a table with her father, and could tell they were deeply engaged in conversation. She smiled to herself, and took another sip of the sherry as she walked towards them. Dara was facing her while her father had her back to her, and so, not wanting to interrupt them, she pulled a chair up behind her father and waited until they had finished.

"Explain again now if you don't mind," she heard her father say. "You're telling me your mother's not actually from Westmeath?"

"No," he said. "That's where my father's side – the Ryans – are from. We lived there until my mother died and then we all moved to Carraigvale when my father and my aunt were offered the running of the cinema. My Aunt Carmel knew the owner's wife. There were also two houses for sale, next door to each other, that were good and handy for working there. My father felt it was better to be near my Aunt Carmel as she was widowed too – years ago – and they could help each other out."

"True enough," Pat said. ""And you say your mother's family were originally from Ballygrace?"

Dara nodded, and Lily could tell by his face that he had already fully explained this. "Yes, just outside it. Between Ballygrace and Daingean. Her family name was Casey."

There was a silence and then Pat said, "She was a *Casey*?"

Lily noticed his strange tone and immediately wondered how much he'd had to drink. She watched now as he lifted his half-full tumbler of whisky to his mouth and threw it straight back.

"Am I right," he said, "in thinking your mother was Helena Casey?"

"Yes, you are indeed right," Dara's voice was low and shocked. "Did you know her?"

Lily's stomach did a somersault. *Surely not,* she thought, *Surely it can't be . . .* She saw her father's whole body stiffen and then saw his hands gripping the edge of the table.

"Yes," he said, his voice thick and hoarse. "I knew her well when we were young, God rest her soul . . . and she was the loveliest, finest girl I ever met."

Dara's face was expressionless now, and she guessed he might be wondering if her father had heard the rumours about his mother's death. She looked at her father and he seemed lost in his own thoughts.

"It's always nice to hear something like that," Dara finally said. "And I suppose it just shows you what a small world it is." He gestured towards Lily now.

"Can you believe it?" he said, looking straight at her. "Your father and my mother knew each other, and were actually good friends when they were young."

She could hear her father quietly muttering, "God rest her soul" over and over again to himself. Whether he realised she was behind him or not she couldn't tell.

Lily raised her eyebrows, affecting surprise. "Isn't that amazing?" Her face felt like a mask. She looked behind her. "I think," she said, "the table is ready now."

41

As she sat next to Dara at the long narrow table, trying to force down her dish of fancily cut melon, Lily felt as though she was sitting beside a complete stranger. He was no longer the person she had spent the last two weeks with or the boy she had slept in the bed beside in Newcastle. She now felt that Dara Ryan was a stranger to her.

And worse, he was the son of a faceless stranger who had caused her sleepless nights of knowing that her parents' marriage wasn't what she thought. The only saving grace about the situation was that the romance between Dara's mother and her father had ended a long time before Dara's mother got married and he and his older brothers were born. Thank God she didn't have the worry about her and Dara having the same father or anything totally weird like that.

Still, it was weird nevertheless: the fact that their parents had been in love linked her and Dara in a strange incestuous kind of way. She knew that wasn't a rational notion. There was no biological link between them at all. She was the result of her own parents – Pat and Mona – and Dara was the result of his. Yet the revelation had changed everything for her.

She sat there, trapped in the middle of a long table with over a dozen people around her. She wanted to get up and say she was going home, but she knew she couldn't possibly get away with it without giving some believable reason. For a few moments she wondered if she would feel better if she talked to someone about it, but there was no one that she could tell that sort of thing to. It was ironic, but the only person who would understand something like this was Dara – and he was the last person she could tell.

She looked along the opposite side of the table and she could see her father there, head bent, and appearing to concentrate over his food. He was bound to be reeling from the news that he had just discovered.

She tried to make sense of the situation, tell herself that none of this was Dara's fault, and that he wasn't even aware of it.

How would he feel, she wondered, if he knew that his mother and her father could quite easily have got married? If that had happened, neither she nor Dara would exist. Even as that thought came into her mind, a part of her knew it was sheer nonsense.

She glanced at him now, as he chatted away to her Uncle Fintan. He had suffered enough with his mother's illness and then death. How could she think of telling him this – even if they had never been a couple? What good would it do to make him feel as bad as she did?

And of course she couldn't let her mother know. She knew that if the subject came up, and if he was in the wrong circumstances, Pat might spill his true feelings out as he had at the funeral in Ireland.

Lily knew that this was something she would have to keep between herself and her father. She lifted her glass of water now and looked along the table, and her gaze fell on Seán. Should she mention it to him, she wondered? He had been more level-headed about the incident back in Ireland with his father than she had been. Would talking to him make her feel better? She would think about it. She would just get through the rest of the night and give herself time to decide whether the weird feelings about Dara would go.

* * *

There was a fuss made, as she knew there would be, when everyone saw the amount of steak that Lily had left on her plate.

"I'm full," she told them. "I got the biggest steak on the table."

"Well, we can't waste good sirloin," her mother said, looking at Dara, "I'm sure one of the lads will finish it."

Dara waved it away saying he couldn't eat another bite, and then the plate disappeared down the bottom end of the table to where Michael and Patrick were sitting.

There was another debate about young girls and their small appetites when Declan pointed out he had helped to finish Ava's steak off. Ava smiled and said nothing.

The desserts came and went and then tea or coffee with mints. Lily excused herself and went out to the ladies', but instead of going straight there, she went out to the front of the hotel for some fresh air. She stood for a while, and then, as she turned to go back in she saw Seán coming towards her.

The opportunity was too good, and the words just came tumbling out.

He listened intently as she told him the whole story about her father and Dara's mother.

"Jesus Christ," he said, shaking his head, "who would believe it? The coincidence is unbelievable. How did it not come out before now? How come Bridget or some of the other relatives in Ireland didn't say?"

Lily's face was white and stony against the cherry-red of her dress. "Well, for a start, I didn't tell any of them about Dara because I'd only just met him, and secondly, I don't think any of them put two and two together about the family, because Dara's mother had moved away from the area when she got married. I suppose if people live a distance away, it's easy to lose touch."

"That's true," Seán mused. "I can understand that – I don't know what's happened to half of the people I went to secondary school with."

"I don't know what to do about Dara now . . ."

Seán's brow deepened. "What do you mean?"

"About seeing him. It feels really odd knowing my dad was madly in love with his mother. That he wanted to marry her."

"What difference does it make? It's all water under the bridge." He made a little sweeping gesture and the way he did it told Lily that the drink had hit him a bit. "It happened years ago. It's nobody's business and nobody should care."

Lily looked over his shoulder now, checking that no one was around. "Dara's mother drowned, and some people thought she might have killed herself. She had been suffering from depression."

"God, that's hard," Seán said. "But that's the way things go sometimes." He looked at Lily now. "You're not suggesting it was because she lost my dad all those years ago?"

Lily looked away.

"Don't be so daft," he told her. "If she was going to do away with herself because of that, she would have done it at the time, not all those years later. My advice is to forget this. We're all humans and we make mistakes. The best thing is to put it all out of your head and don't interfere. So what if my father and his mother had a bit of a fling when they were younger? Big deal. It was a long time ago and our mother and father are ticking along as well as anybody else, and better than most."

"I can't help it – I just feel weird about the whole thing . . . and I don't know what to say to my dad."

"Say nothing," Seán advised. "It's an old girlfriend. For all you know he might have had half a dozen before he met my mother – and that's his own business. And have you thought that maybe my mother had boyfriends before she met him?"

Lily lifted her eyes heavenwards. "Okay, I get your point." She paused. "How is my dad? Does he seem any different since he found this out?"

"He's fine," Seán said. "He's in there telling some daft story about a coach company from Wishaw that he thinks is trying to steal some of our school contracts." He reached out and touched Lily affectionately on the nose. "Stop worrying and get back in there." He grinned and made a few moves as though he was doing The Twist. "The band is on and the dancing is ready to start."

42

Lily was relieved that she had spoken to Seán, and she knew what he said made sense. But even so, she still felt confused about the whole thing.

How could she be so madly in love with someone one minute – feel as though he was her other half – and then feel as though he was a stranger the next?

She went into the ladies' and touched up her make-up and hair, and was glad that she looked better than she felt.

She didn't need to use the toilet but she went into one of the cubicles and shut the door and just stood there, trying to working out what she was going to do.

She closed her eyes and took several deep breaths and then she told herself she was being really stupid. Whatever happened and no matter how she felt about this, it was nothing to do with Dara, and it wasn't his fault.

She remembered how sad he looked the previous Friday when they'd gone to Mass for his mother's birthday. He'd had enough to deal with losing his mother and he was still trying to help his sister and the rest of the family through that.

He had done nothing wrong and he didn't deserve her to turn all funny on him on the last night of their holiday together. He had been lovely to her family, and up until this weird turn of events he had been the best thing that ever happened to her.

She decided now that she would do whatever it took to get through tonight and until the time he left for Ireland tomorrow. She would go back to college and give herself time to work all this out, and, hopefully, she would soon be able to see the situation the way that Seán did. Hopefully, Dara would turn back into the boy she loved with all her heart again.

She came out of the cubicle now and went to check herself again in the full-length mirror on the back of the door. Then, she took another deep breath and went back out towards the restaurant.

The tables had been separated into smaller ones, and moved further back to allow more room for the dance floor. Dara was standing at the bar chatting to the men, while the women had congregated around two of the tables. She looked towards him as she came in and gave him a smile and a wave. His face lit up and he came towards her.

"Are you okay?" he asked, putting his arm around her.

"I'm fine." She smiled so hard her face almost hurt.

The lights dimmed and the band struck up the opening bars of Roy Orbison's "Pretty Woman" and then the evening moved into a higher gear as all the women from their group took to the empty dance floor, her mother making the most noise.

The extra drinks earlier on meant that no warming-up period was needed. They threw themselves enthusiastically into dancing, laughing and talking loud to be heard over the music.

Lily danced with all the women to begin with, laughing and carrying on and trying not to think. Then, after a few numbers Dara came over to join them and the women all clapped when he started dancing along with them, and started calling to the other men to get up.

"Isn't he a great dancer?" Sophie said loudly, tugging at Mona's sleeve to watch.

Dara covered his face playfully and turned away as though embarrassed.

Eileen leaned back into Lily and said, "Is there anything that man doesn't do right? How did you find him?"

Lily smiled and shrugged and carried on dancing.

Within a short while the floor was packed as people from the other tables got up to join them.

At various stages during the night, some of the women commented on how the drinks had gone to their heads, and sat down or went across the room to where double doors opened on to an outside veranda.

Lily danced until her legs were tired and then she and Dara sat down and watched the others for a while. At one point he pulled his chair close to hers and put his arm around her.

"This time tomorrow," he said, "I'll be on the boat back to Ireland. It's going to feel very strange without you."

"I know," she said, leaning against him.

"What are we going to do? When do you think we can meet up again?"

"I'm not sure," she hedged. "I can't think any further than this teaching practice at the minute."

He bent his head close to her ear so no one else could hear them. "I could come over to Newcastle at the end of May. If I get my head down from now with my studies and save what I get from working in the cinema, I think I could make it over for a few days. I'd do it even if it was just for a weekend. I could fly next time."

She looked up at him. "It sounds great ..." And then she turned her gaze away so he couldn't see the sadness in her eyes. "We can check out dates and then we'll chat about it when we're both settled back into a routine."

"Great."

From the way he was talking, it was obvious that Dara hadn't noticed any change in her, and she was grateful for that. She was trying very hard to seem normal, and she thought it might be helped by the fact that he, like everyone else, had had a few drinks. He certainly wasn't drunk and neither was she – she had drunk nothing but lemonade since the meal – but she knew from experience that the alcohol slowed everything down and the more subtle things were missed.

A slow number came on and they got up to dance, and then Lily felt someone tapping her on the shoulder. It was Eileen.

"Me and Claire are going home now in a taxi . . ." She gestured towards Michael's wife. "I rang home and the baby-sitter says that Susan has been crying for the last half an hour. It's probably only her back teeth coming in, but I don't want to take a chance. The baby-sitter is only a young girl and I think it would be best if I got back." She turned back to Claire. "I don't think it's a bad idea going now, as we've had more than enough to drink." They all laughed, then Eileen pointed over to Seán who was standing chatting to Declan and Ava. "Keep an eye on him, Lily – I don't want him falling in the door and waking us all up."

Lily nodded. "We won't be much longer. It will probably only go on for another hour at most." She smiled. "It was a great night, and I'll see you both before I go on Sunday."

Eileen looked at Dara. "I might not see you tomorrow before you go, but no doubt we'll see you soon. Have a safe journey back."

"Thanks," Dara said, smiling warmly at her. He shook her hand and then Claire's and they both looked delighted. "I'll probably see you over the summer."

"You must like Rowanhill," Claire said, "if you're happy to spend your summer holidays there."

"Oh, you never know what we might do," he said, teasing them.

As they continued dancing, Lily decided she wouldn't say anything to Dara about working on the cruise ship. She would wait and see what was in Kirsty's letter and then see how she felt after that.

Some more quick tunes came on and then everyone was up on the floor again. Lily was pleased to see her father and mother and Sophie and Fintan were up jiving together, and she thought that Seán had been right. Her father looked happy enough and was laughing at something her mother had said.

She noticed then that Declan seemed a bit drunk and when he bumped into her for the second time she told him that he should sit down.

"I'm fine," he told her. "I'm just going to go out to the gents' and then I'll have a wee walk out at the car park to freshen up." He said something to Ava and then went off, leaving her to dance with Seán.

Lily thought that Declan wasn't himself at all. He had got quieter as the week had gone on, and he hadn't chatted much to herself or Dara. She shrugged it off. He'd never had a serious girlfriend before, and maybe he was off form because he didn't want Ava to go back to Ireland or something like that.

A short while later Lily noticed Seán and Ava had disappeared, and she thought they must have gone with Declan.

When the dance finished, Dara took both of Lily's hands in his. "Can we go out to the veranda for a few minutes?"

"Okay," Lily said. "Are you feeling very hot?"

He didn't answer. He just kept hold of one of her hands and led her towards the veranda. When they got outside the door, Lily thought it all looked lovely with small outdoor tables and chairs, and colourful plants in tubs and window boxes.

Dara pointed to a bench down at the end of the veranda. "Will we sit for five minutes? I've actually something I want to give you."

When they were sitting he put his hand into the inside pocket of his jacket and brought out a little blue velvet bag with a black ribbon. "I bought this in Edinburgh," he told her, "and I was going to give you it tomorrow when I was leaving, but I thought I'd like to see you wearing it while I'm here."

Lily's chest tightened. "You shouldn't have bought me anything . . . you've bought me loads of things, all the books and records."

He put a finger to her lips. "This is different . . . open it."

She untied the fine black ribbon and then loosened the top and then she lifted out a small jeweller's box. She opened it and caught her breath when she saw a silver Claddagh ring with a black onyx stone for the heart.

"It's beautiful," she said. "It's absolutely beautiful."

"I wanted to get you an engagement ring, but I know it's too early with college and everything. And I don't want to give our families a heart attack. So, I'm giving you this to wear until I have the money to buy you a decent ring at the end of the summer. By then you'll have been back in Ireland and I'll be back over here and nobody will argue."

Tears suddenly filled her eyes and she rubbed hard at them. This was something she had been almost afraid to hope for – and now she was afraid to take it.

"You don't need to say a thing," he told her. "And you don't need to wear it until you get back to Newcastle. I know they'll all probably tease you and make a laugh out of it, and you might not want all that attention. It's something just between you and me." He bent to kiss her now. "But I would like to see you trying it on while there's just the two of us."

Lily took a deep gulp of the night air, and then slid the ring on her finger. It fitted perfectly. "It's beautiful . . ." she said again. "And it's so good of you to have bought it for me."

He tilted her chin to look into her eyes. "I bought it because I love you."

Lily looked back at him, and willed herself to see him as the old Dara again. "And . . ." she finally whispered, "I love you."

43

When Lily went off to the ladies' to wipe the smudged mascara from around her eyes, Dara went down the steps of the veranda and into the garden.

He found it strange that everything would change from tomorrow and that he would be back in Ireland on Sunday. It had been a good two weeks and, after meeting more of Lily's family, he was more convinced than ever that things would work out for them.

Her parents and brothers had been great. The only one he wasn't sure about was Declan, who, Dara felt, was slightly awkward around him. He wasn't taking it personally, as he suspected Declan's distant manner might well be down to the stress of dealing with a girl like Ava. It wasn't that noticeable in a crowd, and he hadn't mentioned it to Lily, but he had a definite feeling that Declan wasn't as keen on him as the others were.

His instincts still told him there was something going on with Ava and Seán. He had noticed her constantly watching him in the bar and then in the restaurant, but it wasn't his business. It might not be anything serious and it might all settle down. He really hoped that Ava wouldn't be on the scene long, because he instinctively knew she was trouble, and the last thing he wanted was to see it brought to the Grace family's door.

That aside, all was going well with him and Lily. When they

broke up for the summer, they had another year of being students –
another year of travelling to see each other – and then they could start
to make plans. He envisaged them engaged by the end of the summer
but apart from that he wasn't sure. He could try and find summer
work for Lily back in Carraigvale or Tullamore so they could be
together. Maybe even working in the cinema or one of the local bars
or shops. He could work something out. He felt sure that this would
be the last year he would have to spend the summer at home, as Rose
would be a nursing student somewhere after that. He couldn't desert
her until she had her exam results and her place in a hospital.

Once she was settled, everything would change. He would take
a room in Dublin so he wouldn't have to come home mid-week or
every weekend. Lots of his university friends shared houses, and he
would find a decent one so that Lily could come and stay with him
during the half-terms. They would be engaged by then and he had
a feeling the way things were with her parents now, that they
wouldn't object to her visiting him.

If things continued they could start looking at things on a more
long-term basis. He knew that there would be problems about
work for Lily in Ireland if they got married, as National School
teachers needed to be fluent in Irish.

His own degree was fine and he could work anywhere in Britain,
and from what he had seen of it, he wouldn't have a problem with that.

These were all things they could sort out.

He was just walking back toward the veranda steps when he
heard voices above him and when he looked he saw it was Seán and
Ava. His heart sank.

He didn't know whether to cough to let them know he was there
– and say a few friendly words on his way back into the hotel – or
whether to move further down the garden until they went back in.

Then they suddenly moved away from the doors to stand just
above where Dara was in the darkened garden. He had stepped
back, intending to call a greeting to them, when he realised from
their low, urgent tones that they were arguing.

The last thing he wanted was to be involved in any more
incidents to do with Ava.

Then he heard her say quite clearly, "I don't want to go back to Ireland and I don't want to move over here to be with Declan. I want to be with you!"

"You've got this all wrong," Seán said, his voice cold and sharp. "What happened between us was never meant to be serious."

"You never said that back in Ireland," she snapped. "You said if I ever needed anything all I had to do was get in touch."

"But I never thought it would turn out like this." He suddenly stopped and went over and closed the verandah doors so they couldn't be heard, then he guided Ava by the arm down to the right-hand corner of it.

"What would have happened," she demanded, "if we'd gone any further and I'd got pregnant? Did you think of that? I have no family and no one to fall back on. Would you have expected me to do what my mother did and hand a baby over to the nuns?"

Dara stood with his hand over his mouth, willing them to go back inside.

"Don't even think of that," Seán said. His voice was firm but there was a note in it that sounded as if he was just trying to be reassuring. "There's no chance you could be expecting, I made sure I stopped well before that could happen."

"But if it had happened . . ." she was crying now, "if I was, would you come away with me?"

"Ava, talk sense!" Seán's voice was angry now. "That's not going to happen. I made a mistake with you twice and it won't ever happen again. And I know it takes two to tango, but in all honesty you practically forced yourself on me both times."

"Oh, that's a terrible thing to say! You don't mean it. You're just saying it because you're worried about Eileen."

"I'm saying it for both our sakes!" He was lowering his voice again, trying to get through to her. "You're going to get on that boat and go back to Ireland tomorrow, and you're going to forget all about me and all about Declan. It's not fair the way you've been stringing him along just to get to me. He's a decent lad and he deserves better."

"I can't help it! He is nice but you and me are more similar. I can tell by the way we clicked in Ireland. And anyway, I think Declan has changed a bit. I think he's noticed something and he's gone off me."

"Jesus Christ, Ava!" Seán groaned. "We need to let this go now. You're a lovely girl but what's done is done. I'm not getting involved any further. I've a wife and kids to think about. I'm going back inside and we're going to act as if nothing has happened and you're going home tomorrow."

"And what if Eileen found out?"

"Aw, Ava, don't threaten that! You promised she wouldn't from the start. You're a lovely-looking girl and you could get any man. Don't waste yourself on a married man who can't give you all the things you deserve."

"Lots of people get divorced."

"Not me," Seán said. "I love Eileen and the kids."

"I'm willing to wait. Declan said he could get me work in one of the local hotels. I could get work in here. We could see each other and then when the time is right, we could be together properly."

The verandah door opened.

"No, no," Seán said. "You're going home tomorrow."

Then Dara was startled when he heard Lily's voice. "Who's going home tomorrow?" he heard her say in a light-hearted tone.

There was a silence and Seán said, "We were just talking about the boat and the weather and that kind of thing . . ."

"Is Dara around?" Lily asked.

He took his chance to move out into the main part of the garden.

Lily moved to look over the veranda and spotted him. "You're there!" she said, waving down at him.

He came around the front and up the stairs. "I had a walk down in the garden while I was waiting for you . . ."

Seán's face was expressionless, but Ava's face was tight and cold, knowing she had been caught for the second time.

She whirled around to look at Lily. "I was actually telling Seán that I'm *not* going back to Ireland tomorrow, I'm staying for a bit longer." She took a deep breath. "Seán doesn't know that I had a problem on the boat coming over. I told Declan about it the other night, and he understands."

"What do you mean?" Lily said.

Ava gestured towards Dara. "He'll tell you."

Dara looked at her in shock. "What are you going on about? What problem? You never told me anything about a problem."

Ava was shaking now. "Keep away from me!" She moved over to Seán and buried her head in his chest. "Don't let him near me!"

"Ava," Lily said, suddenly understanding, "what are you saying about Dara?"

Then Declan appeared at the doorway, his hand leaning against the jamb of the door to steady himself.

"I'll tell you what she's saying about Mr Architect Dara." His voice was slow and slurred. "She's saying that he got her into a quiet part of the boat when there was nobody around and tried it on with her. I was mad but I never said anything because I thought it was only a kiss – she only told me the full extent of it tonight."

"This is absolute nonsense," Dara spluttered. "I never laid a hand on her." He shook his head and looked from Lily to Declan. "I know what this is all about – I know exactly why Ava doesn't want to go back to Ireland, and it's got nothing to do with me."

Lily put her hands on either side of her head. "I don't understand any of this." She went over to take Dara's arm. "What's going on? You never told me there was any problem on the boat coming over."

Declan's face was twisted. "Well, he's hardly likely to tell you that he tried to force himself on my girlfriend!"

"What?" Dara's voice was a roar. "I never laid a hand on her! That's a really serious accusation!" He looked at Ava. "Tell the truth – tell them I never laid a fucking hand on you!"

Lily flinched at the anger in his voice and his language. She'd only ever heard him swear when he was joking before. This wasn't like the Dara she knew.

He jabbed a finger in Ava's direction now. "This lady is leading you all on a bit of a dance here. Now, I don't want to say something now that might cause a far bigger row among you all, but she needs to take back this accusation. I was never in any quiet part of the boat with her and I never laid a damn hand on her."

Ava started to cry, clinging harder than ever to Seán. "I'm not travelling back with him – I'm not going back tomorrow!"

"No, you're not travelling back with me," Dara answered. "You're nothing but trouble and I don't want you anywhere near me."

Declan clenched his fist and moved as though he was going to hit him, but Lily swiftly went between them. "You're not going to start a fight over this," she told him firmly. "Whatever it is can be sorted."

"There's only one person here who can sort all this," Dara said. "And that's Ava." He looked at Lily, then Declan, then at Seán. "As I said earlier, I know exactly why she's doing this and why she doesn't want to go back to Ireland, but if I tell you all it will be like a bomb going off in the middle of the family, and I don't want to do that."

Seán disentangled Ava's arms from around his neck and moved her towards Declan, then he stood with his back against the wall and his gaze on the ground.

Lily took Dara's hand now and guided him back into the restaurant. The band was playing a slow number and the floor was packed.

"What are you talking about?" she asked, on the verge of tears. "Tell me, so I understand." She looked around and then she spotted a table in the faraway corner. "Let's go over there where we can talk quietly."

They sat down opposite each other.

"I feel as if I'm in a nightmare," Dara said. "If I tell the truth I'm going to involve other people and cause ructions, and if I stay quiet, it looks as thought I'm guilty of what Ava has accused me of."

"Tell me about the other people."

He looked at her. "Okay, but you're not going to like it." He took a deep breath. "Do you remember the night we went up to Seán's house last week?"

"Yes," she said. "The night Ava was on her own."

"Do you remember my jacket getting wet and you telling me to put it on the radiator?"

Lily nodded.

"Well, I saw Ava coming out of Seán's bedroom with her top completely open and pulling down her skirt."

"No . . ." Lily was shaking her head. "Seán wouldn't do that."

"It's the truth," Dara said, his manner abrupt and defensive. "I didn't tell you at the time because I'd a feeling you might say that, and I don't blame you. You want to think the best of your brothers. That's why I put it to the back of my mind." He stabbed a finger on the table. "Until tonight. I went down into the garden while I was waiting for you to come back and then Seán and Ava came out onto the veranda and they were arguing."

"What about?"

"About Ava not wanting to go back to Ireland because she's in love with Seán."

"This doesn't make sense! She hardly knows him."

"Ava doesn't make sense," Dara told her. "There's something not right about the girl. And it's not just here that this has happened. Think back to the incident in the bed and breakfast when the man appeared and Seán had to sort him out. Didn't you tell me afterwards that you got a shock when you walked in on them, but that Seán and Ava convinced you that she was just upset?"

Lily nodded, feeling uncomfortable as she recalled the row with Seán afterwards. Then, she noticed a figure coming towards them. It was her father.

His face looked dark and grim. He pulled a chair out at the table.

"I hear we have a bit of a problem," he said, his eyes darting from Lily to Dara.

"It's Ava," Lily said. "She's been saying things about Dara . . ."

Dara looked straight at him. "It's not true. Not a word of it."

Pat turned his gaze to Lily. "The girl is so upset she's just fainted. Declan has had to take her back to the house in a taxi."

Dara sighed and pushed his hands through his hair. "I wouldn't be surprised if she's faking it. I don't believe a word that she says."

Pat looked at him. "Well," he said in a quiet, slow manner, "there's more believe her than believe you . . ."

Lily looked at Dara and then looked at her father and once again had the weird feeling about the woman who linked them. "We need to get this all sorted out."

"It's already sorted," Pat said, pushing his chair back and standing up. "There's a room booked here for you tonight, Mr Ryan," he said in a low, even tone, "and in the morning I'll drop off the rest of your stuff. After that you can head off to Glasgow for the boat back to Ireland."

"Daddy, that's not fair! I don't believe Dara's done anything wrong!"

Dara looked at her. "There's been enough arguments, Lily. Your father is right – I think it's best if I just go straight from here."

"Come on, Lily," her father said. "We've got taxis waiting outside." He walked off towards the door.

Lily closed her eyes. "All this can't have happened . . ."

"But it did," Dara said, "and you're the one person who knows what has happened. Everything I've told you about Ava is the truth."

Lily looked at him with tears in her eyes. "You might have made a mistake. If I go now and tell everyone what you've said about Seán and Ava, God knows what will happen!"

Everything about him looked resigned. "I know . . ." He nodded towards the door. "You better go, your father is waiting."

44

On Sunday evening, when she was settled back in her college room, Lily walked across to the refectory and into the area where the mail pigeon-holes were. She went to the box with 'G' pinned above it and sifted through the piles of letters, and found she had three letters with her name on them. The largest envelope contained a small catalogue from a company that sold maths materials for schools, the second was an invitation to an art exhibition in Newcastle and the third – an airmail letter – was from Kirsty.

She put them in her shoulder bag and then went into the refectory and picked up a salad and a glass of milk. She chose a table for two by the window where she was less likely to be disturbed and settled down to read the letter.

The first page was all about Italy and the places they had stopped off at, and Kirsty described the shops and the fashions there. She said the weather was lovely, not too hot, and perfect for sight-seeing on their days off.

On the second page Kirsty said that she had been making enquiries about staff vacancies, and she was delighted to say that there was a summer job for Lily working in a brand-new fashion shop that was opening on their ship starting at the end of June. So far, she said, she hadn't found anything definite for Dara, but she would keep looking.

Lily felt a weight lifting off her shoulders. This meant that her long, empty summer was all sorted and she could now start to make plans. Plans that no longer included Dara.

She couldn't bear to think about what had happened now. Couldn't face the thought of analysing the rights and wrongs of last Friday night. But at the centre of it all she knew that Dara was innocent. She knew in her heart that he hadn't laid a hand on Ava, and she knew he was right about all the business with Seán and Ava. But the effort involved and the upset it would cause to unravel all the strands was too huge.

She knew, of course, that if the horrendous coincidence hadn't come out about her father and Dara's mother that she would have done whatever it took to save their relationship. She would have risked all the devastation and the rows that would have happened in the family. Risked telling Eileen, and risked Eileen not forgiving Seán for his carry-on with Ava. And she would have even risked her father and mother never speaking to her again for causing all the disruption.

But the sickening truth about her father being in love with Dara's mother had come out and she had been unable to see beyond it. Her love for Dara was now tainted and there was no point in dragging everyone else down when she felt their relationship couldn't survive.

She turned back to the letter. She would write back tonight to Kirsty and tell her she definitely wanted the job in the fashion shop.

She would also tell her not to worry about finding a job for Dara, that things had changed and he would be staying at home and working in Ireland for the summer. She knew that Kirsty might hear what had happened through her Auntie Sophie or Heather or someone else in the family, but she couldn't face writing it all down now. It would mean having to think it all through and face all the facts. She would tell her the full story when the right time came.

She was heading out of the refectory when she met Pamela and Bill Toft coming towards her, their arms wrapped around each other.

"Did you have a good time in Scotland, Lily?" Pamela asked.

Lily pinned a smile on her face. "Great, thanks."

"And Dara? How did he like it?"

"He loved it," Lily said, a stabbing feeling in her heart. "We had a brilliant two weeks." And they had, she thought, up until that very last night.

She had watched the couple as they walked away, laughing and chatting as she and Dara had done only days ago. She wondered at how life could change in such a short time. Just a half-term ago, Pamela was so depressed it looked as though she might even lose her college place, and yet, there she was, happier than she had ever been – with the unlikely Bill.

She suddenly felt a huge sense of loss as she thought about the special thing she had found and then lost with Dara. She knew it was far more than the easy relationship that Pamela and Bill had. It was far more than most people ever found in their whole lifetime. And the saddest thing was that Lily knew she would never find it with anyone else again.

Tears blinded her as she walked back to her room.

* * *

By the end of her first week of teaching practice Lily was exhausted. She had to be up before seven each morning to have breakfast over and have all her stuff ready for catching a college coach into Newcastle at quarter to eight.

It left early as it did a circular route of all the schools that the students would be working in, dropping them off in ones and twos outside the school gates.

All the others doing teaching practice in her year were in the same situation, all running around in the mornings carrying briefcases and folders and large pieces of coloured cardboard with things stuck on them for displaying in the classrooms.

Lily spent her nights correcting books, checking over lesson plans and sorting out all the materials she needed for her lessons the following day. And she was grateful that her hectic schedule left her little time to agonise over what had happened with Dara. During those busy periods she somehow managed to put her sadness into the little box at the back of her mind where all the difficulties in her life lived. And she forced herself to shut out the beautiful memories they had built together in Ireland, Newcastle and Scotland.

All her energy now went into her teaching.

She had discovered that she had one particularly clever boy in the class and three slow children, and it was hard work catering for them as well as the other thirty-odd pupils. The main subjects like English, Maths and Spelling were fine, as the bulk of the class all worked from the same books, while Rhys, the clever boy, worked from a secondary school book and the slower children had books from the younger classes. When she looked at Rhys's maths book for the first time, she had felt slightly panicky wondering if she could remember the more complicated things like square roots and algebra, but she relaxed when the class teacher had smilingly handed her the answer book.

Naturally, Rhys knew more about the Vikings than Lily did, and was disdainful of the books she had given them to choose from and the worksheets she had prepared, telling her they were far too easy. She was relieved that the rest of the class had all seemed happy with any work she had given them, and when she checked their exercise books she could see from their answers that it was pitched at the right level.

She gave the three slower children extra attention at the break-times, and quietly explained anything they didn't understand. She praised their efforts, and told them that they just had to do their best, and not to worry if they didn't write as much as the others.

On the third day of the Nordic project, the class teacher had quietly taken Rhys out and given him extra maths instead of the project. And even though everything else was fine and the other children were all behaving well for her, and knuckling down to their work, Lily felt a failure, and thought it made her look as if she wasn't coping.

She talked to Ann and Beryl about it coming back on the coach from school, but they were teaching younger classes and were more worried about children who wet themselves or burst out crying without explanation.

When she arrived back to college that evening, she went straight to her room and dumped all her bits and pieces, then she ran across to the lecture rooms to see if she could catch her teaching practice tutor. As she walked along the corridor, Gerard René came out of one of the rooms.

"Hey, Lily," he said, smiling at her. "I haven't seen you around since you got back. How was your holiday? Did you have a good time?"

"Yes, thanks," she told him. "But my feet have hardly touched the ground since I got back with my teaching practice."

"It will get easier," he told her. "Things always do when you get used to them – when it becomes more routine."

They chatted for a few more minutes and she felt better after it. As he walked away, for a brief moment she considered calling after him and asking if she could talk to him about what had happened between her and Dara. She knew he would listen carefully and give her an honest, considered opinion.

But a weary, hopeless feeling had descended on her just thinking about it, and she didn't.

Mrs Hall, her teaching practice tutor, came up with some good suggestions for Rhys. She told Lily to go across to the college library and sort out a selection of secondary-school level history books which had sections on the Vikings. Then Mrs Hall advised her to sit and work out a list of comprehension questions related to the books which the boy could work on. She also gave her a few lighter alternative lessons like word-searches relating to Viking words, or jumbled-letter spellings that Rhys could make for the other children to do.

Buoyed up by all the suggestions Lily went back to the library and worked until nine o'clock.

When she came back across the green and into the house, carrying a bag-load of books, Ann met her in the hall.

"Dara phoned an hour ago," she said. "And he said he'll be in the cinema between ten and half-past if you want to ring."

Lily nodded and smiled. "Thanks," she said. "I'll catch up with him later."

She didn't phone him that night nor the next. She would wait, she decided, until the weekend. By that time maybe she would feel better and be able to sort things out in her mind.

45

Dara tackled Lily's changing attitude in a letter the following week.

"*I can tell by your voice on the phone and the difference in the letter I got from you yesterday that your feelings have changed,*" he wrote. "*You are entitled to that if you've just fallen out of love with me. But if it's because of what happened in Scotland then that's a complete tragedy and it means you are not the person I thought you were either.*" Then, with tears in her eyes, she read, "*Do you remember what I said about the journey over with Ava, about her being boring and not very clever? Well, I was wrong; I now think that she's cleverer than the two of us put together. She's so clever she's made you believe that I did something that I didn't do. And it wasn't something trivial that can easily be forgotten. It was a dreadful accusation.*"

He also said he wondered how things were going in Scotland with Ava still there, and he warned her to expect more trouble.

Lily closed the letter, unable to read on.

She had only spoken to her mother the previous evening, and Mona had told her that Ava was staying in Scotland for the time being, and that she had got herself a live-in job in the hotel they'd had the meal in. Apparently Mrs Stewart, back in Carraigvale, had been more than understanding, and said the other girl who sometimes worked there would be glad of the extra hours.

"Ava is a hard worker," her mother had said, "and having a place to live means she's not totally dependent on the romance with Declan." When Lily had said nothing, her mother had said. "I hope you're not still bothered about that Dara fellow? I know it was upsetting and hard on you the way it all came out, but you're better finding it out now, than further down the line. And don't feel bad, Lily. He had us all taken in. We all liked him, even your dad."

"I'm not bothered about him," Lily had said in a flat voice. "It's more or less over between us, but from what I know of him, he would never have done what Ava said."

The following night she sat down in the library and wrote Dara a letter back. She told him that she was having a very pressurised time with her college work and teaching practice, and that the awkwardness between them was upsetting her. She said from the tone of his letter that he obviously felt the same, and she thought it would be best if they had a bit of a break from writing or phoning each other. She wasn't saying their relationship was completely over, but just that they needed a break. She said nothing about falling out of love with him or anything about Ava or her family.

Then, just before she sealed the letter, she took it back out and added a

PS. *"I know we hadn't made any real plans for the summer, and just to let you know that I've been offered a job on Kirsty's cruise ship and I've accepted it. I hope you understand, but you know that it's something I've always dreamed of doing."*

* * *

As the weeks moved on, and Dara's letters became shorter and less frequent, Lily let the girls at college know that things had not worked out with them. She didn't go into any great detail and, since they had all experienced relationships coming and going, they didn't pressurise her for any further details.

Pamela and Bill's romance had obviously become more serious, helped by the fact they were in the same school every day. Bill had become a fixture in their house as he came every night to work on lesson plans with Pamela.

About four weeks into their teaching practice, Ann came rushing onto the coach to tell Lily that one of the younger male teachers in school had asked her out.

"He is gorgeous," Ann said, "and really big into sport, and he's asked me to go to a dance with him."

Lily was delighted for her and sat and listened as Ann went into raptures about what a great teacher he was and how the children loved him, and how fantastic he looked on the playing field in his shorts.

When she got back to her room that night, it dawned on Lily that she was now the only girl in her group that didn't have a boyfriend. She was surprised that the thought didn't really trouble her. She knew she wasn't going to meet someone now or in the near future. The intense months she'd had with Dara had been wonderful, and being in love with him had taken over her whole life. She couldn't imagine anything being better than what they had – and yet, it still hadn't worked. It had all burned out in just a few short months. All the wonderful physical passion – the hopes and plans, the trust and love.

Like a beautiful firework, it had all just fizzled away.

It hurt so much to think of it that Lily didn't think she could ever go through that again.

＊　＊　＊

The college had no half-term break before summer, and only had the bank-holiday weekends. Lily told her mother she was too busy with school to come home for a long weekend, but she would see them for a few days before jetting off to Spain with Kirsty and Larry.

"We'll have to get Sophie to make you a few nice fancy dresses," Mona said. "You need to look well – a lot of millionaires go on these cruises, you know."

"Kirsty has told me not to worry about clothes," Lily explained.

"We're about the same size and she says I can borrow her sundresses and hats and things. She said the ship is gorgeous, but the dress isn't as glamorous for the staff as it is for the passengers, and that I'll be mainly wearing a uniform for work in the shop."

For the June bank holiday break, Lily went down to London with Ann and Beryl. They booked into a cheap hotel near King's Cross and shared a three-bedded room. They went to see a show one night and to a Chinese restaurant the second night. Then, as they were on a guided tour of the Tower of London, Lily remembered Dara saying he had been in London and she wondered if he had been to any of the places she had seen. She could picture his enthusiasm about the old buildings, the wonderful bookshops and the Elizabethan pubs, and she knew she would have enjoyed it ten times more if she had been with him.

Ann had asked her about him on the train back to Newcastle. "Have you heard from Dara recently, or are you not in contact at all?"

"He sends the odd letter," Lily said evasively. "He has exams this term and a project to hand in so he doesn't have much time."

There were other times when she couldn't help but think of him. There was a night in the Students' Union bar when a band was playing Donovan music. And then there was another night when the two pretty third-year girls who had tried to chat him up asked Lily what had happened to him. She had just shrugged and looked at them, her face expressionless, as if she wasn't sure who they were talking about.

As the Seychellois lecturer had told her, everything about school had got easier and by the second month she was in a regular routine and enjoying it. Lesson planning had become more instinctive to her, she marked her books more quickly and confidently and she knew every child in her class individually. She knew exactly what she needed to sort every evening for the following day, and she spent her weekends writing up her notes and observations.

Her teaching practice tutor had paid regular visits and she had been given good reports on each one.

"You're a natural teacher," Mrs Hall had told her on one of her final reports, "and it's not everyone who is. It's also obvious to me that the children all really like you, and that's a huge part of it, because the key to learning is through relationships. The school will be giving you an excellent report too."

Lily was delighted and relieved, and felt it validated her choice of career. And she realised that she enjoyed the variety of lessons that she taught, and thought that maybe it was just as well she hadn't trained as a dance teacher. She might have found teaching the same things over and over boring. Maybe, like a lot of things in life, it just wasn't meant to be.

When her last day in school came, Lily was taken aback when the head of the school and the class teacher organised a surprise farewell party for her. The children brought in cakes and buns their parents had made, and the head provided sandwiches and a glass of wine for the teachers. They also presented her with a beautiful pen set.

But the highlight of it all was when the headmaster had taken her to the side and said that if he had a vacancy the following year when she qualified, he would be delighted to have her as a full-time member of staff.

She still hadn't decided what she was going to do when she finished, or where she was going to go, but she thought she would keep the offer at the back of her mind just in case.

Lily phoned her mother that night with the news of her first-class teaching report, and after heaping praise on her, her mother said everyone was looking forward to seeing her, and that it seemed ages since she had been home. Then she said that she had a bit of news. She told her that the romance was all off between Ava and Declan.

"Good," Lily said, "because I certainly don't want to see her when I come home."

"Now, don't be saying that. She's a nice enough girl and she was always helpful."

Lily was curious in spite of herself. "Why did they break up?"

"I'm not sure what's happened," her mother said. "Declan has been very quiet about the whole thing. You know what he's like – he's not the easiest to get information out of."

"Do you think she'll stay in Scotland or go back to Ireland?" Lily asked.

"You'd never know," Mona said. "She's a hard worker and from all accounts the hotel people are singing her praises. Your father was talking to the manager there recently, and he was saying that she couldn't do enough for the guests and to help the other staff out."

"That's always been her way," Lily said. "That's how she got to know us all back in Ireland."

"I suppose so," Mona said, thoughtfully. "While she's lovely and everything, she's the type of girl you could never get a handle on. To be honest with you, I don't feel I know her any better now that I did from the first day I met her."

Maybe, Lily thought wistfully, Dara had been the only one who really knew her.

46

The teaching practices all finished in early June and then there was only one week left of the term, and then college was finished until the last week in September. With the pressure of exams and reports behind them, there was a feeling of excited but nervous anticipation, especially amongst the third years who were finishing college and hoping to start their full-time teaching careers in the autumn.

Lily had mixed feelings about breaking up for the summer. She was certainly excited about all the travelling she was going to do, but she had an empty feeling when she thought about saying goodbye to her friends, and knowing she wouldn't see them for over two months. And although she had a great sense of relief at finishing her teaching practice, she had felt sad saying goodbye to the children and staff she had grown to like.

She made her final goodbyes to her friends in Newcastle Railway Station – all heading off in trains going in different directions – and was delighted to see Pamela and Bill going down to London together to work in a children's camp for the summer.

As she walked over the bridge to her platform, dragging her heavy case, Dara came into her mind and the lovely day they had spent going around the city.

As always, when she thought of him she had a hollow feeling in the pit of her stomach. She still couldn't imagine herself with anyone else.

When she arrived back home she noticed that a great deal of decorating had been done in her absence, and she could tell that her mother was waiting for her reaction. Lily told her how lovely the new wallpaper and curtains were, and as she opened the door of her bedroom, she knew her mother's heavy footsteps on the stairs signalled a need for further praise for the new white wrought-iron bed and the white wardrobe and dressing-table and the small daisy-print bedding. Eileen who had a good eye for such things, Mona told her, had picked everything out for her.

"It's gorgeous," Lily said, "but you shouldn't have spent all this money on doing up my room when I'm hardly here."

"You've only one more year and you'll be back home for good," her mother reminded her. Then, she had looked Lily up and down. "I think you're looking a bit peaky. You've been working too hard. You need a bit of mollycoddling at home before you set off to all those foreign countries."

Lily had smiled and then given her anxious mother a hug.

When the door was closed Lily was left in the quietness of the room to unpack her clothes and washing, and a few favourite books and records she didn't want to leave in her room at college. She had left most of the things that Dara had given her, like the books and the picture of the Ha'penny Bridge, as she didn't want any reminders of him while she was in Scotland. The only thing she'd brought with her was the Claddagh ring, as she was afraid it might get lost.

As she moved around, hanging things up and putting things away in the shiny new drawers, she had a feeling that she would never get the full use of this room again. From now on she would only use it as a guest.

Somewhere along the way, she had come to realise that she had outgrown both the house and living as part of the family. She would not be like Declan who was heading up to thirty and still at home. But even as she knew this, she had no idea where she actually wanted to be.

Later, her father came up to her room to see if she liked the new wallpaper he had hung and all the new furniture. As he was leaving, he stopped at the door and told her how proud he was of the great reports she had had from college.

Then he had looked her in the eye and said, "Are you okay in yourself, Lily? Your mother thinks you're a bit quiet or something."

She told him she was just tired after a hard term in school and was looking forward to the cruise.

"Good," he said. "You deserve a nice break after all your hard work and after the unfortunate business earlier on."

Lily had looked away towards the window. They had never really discussed the way things had finished when she was last home. They had just come back after the night out and then her father had taken Dara's stuff to him in the hotel, and he hadn't been mentioned again.

Everything had been about Ava – not upsetting the poor girl any more, not talking about Dara because it would only remind her about the awful incident on the boat. All the family had just danced around the subject, until it had been time for Lily to go back to college.

And her father had never mentioned Helena Casey again. She still felt uncomfortable when she thought about Pat's drunken ramblings back in Ireland, but she had taken a leaf out of Seán's book and put it away in the back of her mind where all her uncomfortable thoughts lived.

As she mulled it over now, Lily felt there were an awful lot of things that her family had recently swept under the carpet. Of course it was the easy way out. As Dara had told her, if some things were said, it would be like dropping a bomb in the middle of their ordinary, decent family.

In that first afternoon home, various members of the family appeared and she began to catch up with all their news. Declan was pleased to see her and told her he would pay for new luggage for her cruise, since her old suitcase was too battered and bruised from all the trips to Newcastle to be allowed on a posh liner. Lily thanked him, but sensed an awkwardness underneath his joking banter that she knew was to do with Ava.

When Eileen and Seán and the two little girls appeared, her mother lingered at the door as though waiting for something.

Lily found it hard to look Seán straight in the face. He was bound to know that Dara had told her all about Ava, but he had obviously put it behind him. He was lucky, she thought, that he could live with a guilty conscience so easily.

They chatted about the new regular taxi run that Seán was doing to the Law Hospital, and about the small playhouse for the garden that he had just erected for the children. Then they all held their breath, as Susan demonstrated how she could now walk from the sofa to the chair without hanging on to anything.

Just afterwards when they had given the child a cheer, Lily saw her mother gesturing to Eileen.

"And there's another little bit of news," Eileen said, looking across at Seán. "We'll have a new addition to the family before Christmas."

Lily looked from one to the other. "Another baby?"

"Yes," Seán said, taking Eileen's hand in an unusual gesture of affection. "And we're absolutely delighted."

* * *

Kirsty and Larry had already been back at their apartment in Motherwell for a month and were well rested and ready to head for the high seas once again. When Lily went to their place on the Thursday night for a meal and drinks, to hear all about her new job, she thought they both looked great with their expensive clothes and tanned skin. Larry poured them all a glass of cold Italian white wine, then he told Lily all about the brilliant new Glasgow band – Dynamite – who would be the main alternative entertainment to Kirsty.

"They are fantastic," Kirsty told her, "and Larry was lucky to have signed them up earlier in the year, because they're fully booked to play in big venues all over Scotland and England when they finish the cruise contract. They were even on a children's TV programme recently as they've got fans from school age to grannies."

Larry nodded in agreement. "They've got what's called 'mass-appeal' and most bands don't have that." He then showed Lily brochures of the band with black-and-white photos of them captured in front of a cruise liner in Beatles-type poses.

"They play everything from rock to soul to ballads," Larry went on. "And they're so good even Kirsty comes to hear them on her nights off."

Lily had studied the brochure and thought the lead singer with his blonde hair and cheeky grin would definitely be a draw to the females on the cruise.

Kirsty then gave her brochures about their cruise ship, *Mediterranean Contessa*, and a brochure about the elegant ladies' on-board shop Lily would be working in.

"Now, I've already explained to you that it's not all glamour for the staff," Kirsty reminded her. "We have our own recreation mess and our own staff restaurant, and our sleeping quarters are on the lower decks. Everything really is separate for the staff and very different from the facilities the guests have. It's the same rules basically as working in a high-class hotel."

"I understand," Lily said. "You don't need to worry. I'm not going to go barging into areas I'm not supposed to. I'll know my place and I'll stick to it. I know the guests are paying a fortune for the cruise."

"They are," Kirsty said, smiling. "You are very lucky to be working in the shop. You'll be walking through all the guest recreation areas and the pool, and the bars, and of course you'll be beside all the other shops. I was delighted to get you that job because it's one of the better ones and much nicer than working in the kitchen, because you would have little or no contact with the guests. And, as you can imagine, it's hot in there all the time especially with the Mediterranean weather."

"You don't need to worry about a thing," Lily told her. "I'm just looking forward to being part of the staff, having the lovely weather and being able to see all the places when we have a day off."

Kirsty winked at her. "You've got it. And if you get fed up at any time, just think how it would feel to be stuck in a shop in Rowanhill or Glasgow on a dull, wet, freezing day!"

Lily spent ages going through the brochures reading about all the places they would visit when they set off from Rome. Then Kirsty took her into the spare bedroom which had three walls with fitted wardrobes and told her to pick any dresses and accessories she would like for the cruise. "It's all summer wear on the cruise," she told her. "Apart from the odd thunderstorm we're guaranteed temperatures well in the seventies and eighties. It's a bit cooler at night so you might want to bring a cardigan or a light jacket."

As she searched through the rails of colourful dresses, Lily pictured all the sunshine and beautiful countries ahead and felt her spirits rise.

Nothing would be the same without Dara, but it was the best she could hope for.

47

When Lily came downstairs in her dressing-gown on Friday morning, her mother was waiting for her, dressed in her usual sombre black skirt and white blouse for her housekeeping work with the Parish Priest.

"Seán rang a few minutes ago to see if he could drop off Susan for a couple of hours. Eileen had an ante-natal appointment and she's taking Beth with her. I told him I was working, but I didn't think you would mind looking after her."

"That's fine," Lily said. "I'm not going out anywhere."

"He said he'll be here in half an hour."

"I'll be ready. I had a bath last night before going to bed so I won't need one this morning."

She had some tea and toast and then she washed up and went upstairs to get dressed. She was just coming down the stairs when Seán knocked on the door and came in carrying a sleeping Susan wrapped in a pink blanket. He put a finger to his lips and then he went over to the sofa and laid her down. He arranged a few cushions around her and then put another small blanket over her.

"Thanks," he said. "It's good of you to have her. I know you're busy getting ready to head off on Monday."

"It's fine," Lily said. "I'm well ahead. Have you time for a cup of tea or coffee?"

He checked his watch. "Aye, go on," he said, smiling at her. "I'll have a cup of coffee made with milk. I've got about twenty minutes before I need to pick up the next fare."

He started talking while Lily had her back to him at the kitchen worktop, pouring the milk into the pan.

"Lily, I have a few things I need to tell you. I never got the chance to say any of this before and I'm no good at writing it down." His voice was rushed and strangely formal. "I want to say thanks to you for keeping quiet about the thing with me and Ava. I'm sure Dara told you all about the stupidity that happened back at our house, and then all the stuff he heard at the hotel that night."

Her stony face told him she knew, and he sighed deeply.

"I know it wasn't fair on you, especially after the row you and me had over the same thing in the bed and breakfast in Ireland and, believe me, I'm sorrier than you will ever know."

Lily put the milk pan onto the gas ring then slowly turned around to look at him.

"I just want you to know it's all over . . . and that I feel bad she caused all that trouble between you and Dara. It's been on my mind ever since."

She listened in silence, watching him now as he closed his eyes and swallowed hard.

"You know that thing she said about him was all lies."

"Of course I knew that," Lily said, her voice cold. "I knew he would never do that."

Seán turned away from her gaze now to pick at the edge of the Formica kitchen table. "I couldn't speak out because if I did she would have told Eileen and everyone what had happened."

"And what did happen exactly?"

Seán went towards the window, folding his arms over his chest. "It wasn't as bad as she would have made out, but I'm not proud of myself. I behaved badly and there's no getting around it."

Lily waited.

"She came into my bedroom and, well . . . things just happened. She's a good-looking girl and Eileen's not always the easiest. But I did stop it just before it got completely out of hand."

"You're an absolute fool," Lily said in a low, contemptuous voice. "And you let Dara be the scapegoat for you. You let everybody believe he had attacked her."

"I didn't know she was going to say that about him, honest to God . . ." When he turned around she could see there were tears in his eyes. "I didn't know what she was going to say next. Things were just coming out of her mouth. Just before that, she was going on about telling Eileen, and saying rubbish about us running away together. She was even asking me what would have happened if she had been pregnant, when in fact I never went that far, thank God." He looked up at Lily. "But she would have gone all the way – she didn't care about Declan or Eileen or anybody."

"And neither did you," Lily snapped, "or it would never have got to that stage. It goes without saying what you've done to your wife – and it's terrible what you've done to Declan." Her voice was full of disdain. "You've made a total fool out of him. You know that, don't you?"

He nodded.

"But the worst thing is what's happened to Dara," she said. "The one man who wasn't a bit interested in Ava – he could see straight through her stupid head. He told me she wasn't what she was pretending to be, even before they came over, and I knew he didn't want to travel with her."

Seán shook his head. "Please believe me, Lily – I had no hand in her coming over. I gave her no encouragement, and in all honesty I stayed away from her for the first few days because I didn't want to see her. I was hoping her feelings for Declan were genuine. I would never have made a move towards her if she hadn't come up to the bedroom." He put his hands over his face. "I'm ashamed of myself for a million reasons, but the biggest shame I feel is that Dara and you got the brunt of all this. That it broke you up. He's a decent lad, the best you'll get, and I wasted that for you by not speaking up." He made a muffled sound. "I've never done anything like that before and I swear to God I never will again. I just couldn't speak up or she would have spewed the lot out to Eileen and my mother

325

and father. I couldn't risk it, Lily. Do you understand? I didn't want to lose my wife and children."

Lily was silent. It was exactly as Dara had told her. And somewhere inside her – it was exactly as she knew. She looked at Seán's shoulders heaving up and down now, and she knew there was no point in making a terrible situation worse. Like Dara, she wouldn't rock the boat. Seán had learned his lesson and she would safely bet he would never be tempted again.

"You don't need to worry," Lily said in a weary voice. "I'm not going to say anything. At least you had the decency to tell me."

He took a hanky out of his jacket pocket and wiped his eyes. "I knew I was taking a chance confessing all this, but I couldn't have slept easy without telling you." He came over to her now, all blustery and awkward, and put his arms around her. "Thanks, Lily, I appreciate it and I know I don't deserve it."

She put her arms around him now and they just stood for a while in a miserable silence. Then Lily moved back, smelling burning, and when she looked at the cooker the milk had boiled over and was burning on the gas flame.

"For God's sake, that's all I need!" She quickly moved the pan off the ring and straight into the sink. She ran cold water on it and left it steeping. She went to get fresh milk.

"Leave the coffee," Seán said. "It doesn't matter."

She ignored him and went and got fresh milk and poured it into another pan and put it on to boil. "What about Ava?" she asked. "She might still tell all of this."

"No, she won't. That's one of the reasons I can tell you all this now. She's gone."

"Gone where?" She suddenly thought of Dara and her heart sank. What if she went back there telling all her lies? "Has she gone back to Carraigvale?"

"Nope. She's done a moonlight flit to England with the manager of the hotel."

Lily looked at him open-mouthed. "I don't believe it …"

Seán shrugged. "A bigger mug than me. He was only married

two years, and he's run off with the bar-takings and the money that was in the hotel safe."

"Oh, my God!"

"They were carrying on within weeks after she started there. They were seen together on a number of occasions in his car. Then the night porter saw the pair of them putting suitcases in the boot the night it all happened."

"How do they know where they've gone?"

"I don't know all the details," Seán said, giving a weary sigh. "Someone said he has a brother down in London and maybe they've just put two and two together." He shrugged. "But they've definitely gone."

"Does Declan know?" She glanced over at the milk and when she saw it was starting to bubble, she lifted it off the cooker and on to the worktop.

He nodded. "I think he guessed that she wasn't going to stick with him when she first came over. She was always making excuses not to be on her own with him." He looked at the floor. "Declan told me that himself after you went back to college, but what could I say? At that time I was living on a knife's edge, waiting on her telling Eileen everything. He had a good idea that something was going on because she started saying she was working all the time, and my father and everybody told him she was making a mug out of him. Eventually, Declan just phoned her up at work a few weeks ago and said it might be best if they just forgot all about it."

Lily poured a large spoonful of Camp coffee into the two mugs, then poured the hot milk in on top and stirred. She could hardly take in this latest turn of events. "Did she say anything?"

Seán shrugged. "I don't know, but he's been quiet with me. I wouldn't have put it past her to say something out of spite. But so far he hasn't said anything, and now she's gone I'm hoping he'll forget about it."

"Poor Declan," Lily said. "But he's probably come out of it all lighter than you and me." She handed Seán his mug and lifted the other herself.

He took a sip from it then gave her a half-smile and said, "Is there any chance of a spoonful of sugar?"

Later, as he was heading out the door, he turned to Lily and hugged her again. "You'll never know how sorry I am. Is it too late for you and Dara?"

She closed her eyes and leaned her head on his shoulder. "It is," she said. "But that's more my fault than anyone else's. I should have stuck up for him more but . . . there were other things going on at the time."

"Are you still in touch with him?"

Lily shrugged. "Occasionally . . . I haven't heard from him for weeks."

"That's a pity, but then you can't blame him. Anyway, I'm going to tell my mother and father and Sophie about the lie Ava told about Dara. I've thought it all out. I had to think up something that wouldn't hang myself with Eileen, but would let everyone know that Dara did absolutely nothing wrong. I've decided to tell them that I met up with her by accident in a pub in Motherwell one night when she had a few drinks, and she broke down and told me everything. I'll say it was weeks after the big row, when it was too late to do anything – and that I didn't want to hurt Declan's feelings."

"But won't they ask why she picked on Dara?"

"I'll say something like she fancied Dara and made up the story to get back at him for not being interested in her."

Lily shrugged, uneasy at the prospect of more lying. "I don't know how believable that sounds. Why would she tell you all that?"

"I'll work something out that sounds believable. Something like she made a pass at me then started crying, asking why all the decent fellows rejected her. If I say I had a few drinks myself and don't remember all the details, they won't quiz me too much. It shouldn't be too hard now they know she's done a bunk with the hotel manager."

"What about Declan?" Lily asked.

Seán shrugged. "She obviously didn't rate him. I don't want to go on about it any more, but even back in Ireland she was more after me than him."

Something clicked in Lily's mind. "Can I ask you one thing about Ireland? Was it you that I saw with Ava in the reception on the first night? At the time I thought it was Declan, but now I think it was you in the blue and green shirt."

He looked at her for a few moments and then he nodded. "I know . . ." he said, his voice cracking. "I know exactly how bad it makes me look, doing that to my own brother. I can only look back on it and think that I was trying to prove something to myself. I've gone over and over it in my head and all I can say is I've learned from it. God strike me down dead, but I'll never do anything like it in my life again."

Lily shook her head and sighed. "You have to live with your conscience, Seán," she told him. "But whatever you do, sort this out as best you can."

"I will." He swallowed hard. "I'll fix it, Lily. I promise."

After he left, Lily sat down in the chair opposite the sleeping Susan and went over everything Seán had told her. Half an hour later she was still going over it, and each time she did, she realised that there was only one thing she could do. She was going to have to write to Dara and tell him that the truth had come out and everyone was sorry for what had happened – as she knew they would be when Seán explained it all to them.

And then she would tell him that she was the sorriest all.

If she had been braver, then she would have phoned him and let him hear her saying the words, but too much time had passed. For all she knew he might have a new girlfriend by now, and she just might make things even worse for him.

Enough damage had been done and she couldn't take that risk.

48

Lily's first day on the *Mediterranean Contessa* flew by. After arriving at Rome airport, Larry had guided them over to a waiting black car which then took them out to Civitavecchia, where the port was and where the cruise ship would start its two-week voyage from and return to. Lily would cover the route three times in her six weeks.

She would work every day when the ship was afloat, and have time off when it pulled in at ports, to allow her to explore the various places. This, Kirsty and Larry had pointed out, was the reason they worked on the cruises as it gave them a chance to see amazing places, enjoy fabulous weather while working and getting paid for it. It also meant they saved money on the running costs of their large apartment back in Scotland. They explained that it wasn't all glamour, and was the type of work you only did for a number of years, while you were young and fit enough to handle all the travelling and the constant packing.

After Larry had organised for their luggage to be delivered to their cabins, he then led them onto the ship to show the waiting crew their various documents. Then, a uniformed staff member had led them through a series of narrow corridors that all looked the same, and then down two decks, using iron stairs, to reach the staff quarters. Larry and Kirsty were shown to their double cabin and they let Lily have a quick peek inside.

It was smaller than most double-bedrooms but, as Larry demonstrated, it had everything they needed. There were wardrobes and cupboards built around the bed and small bedside cabinets and lamps at either side. There was a dressing-table-cum-desk with two chairs. There was a shared toilet and shower-room just a couple of doors down which Kirsty said was cleaned daily.

Lily's twin-bunk cabin was at the very end of the long corridor – and was as small as Kirsty had warned her. When she arrived in the cabin, she met Valerie Cox who was waiting for her, and discovered she would be sharing the small cabin with the tall, red-haired, cheery-looking girl and working with her in the shop. Valerie was from Liverpool and was more nervous about starting than Lily was.

"You're lucky having your cousin working on the cruise," she told Lily. "I'm terrified to move out of here in case I go to the wrong deck or talk to somebody I shouldn't. All the officers look really strict in their uniforms."

"You'll be fine," Lily told her, sounding more confident than she felt. "Kirsty said she'll call for us in ten minutes and that we should get changed into our uniforms and then she'll take us up to the shop."

They had a look around the tiny cabin and discussed which bunk they would have, and how they would divide the space in the fitted wardrobe and the shelves inside. There were also shelves inside for their cases and shoes.

Lily was relieved that the two white blouses and the black skirt she had been told to bring were still perfectly pressed, thanks to the tissue paper that her mother had packed them in. Valerie's clothes hadn't travelled quite so well, but Lily assured her that the creases in her blouse would fall out after she had been wearing it for a while.

Kirsty arrived a short while later, looking very sophisticated in a floaty green and white dress and jacket and white high-heeled shoes. She advised the girls to tie their hair back and put on a bit of make-up and lipstick – but not too much – and then she had taken them up to meet Mrs Maddox, the manageress of Ladies First, the on-board shop where she would be working for the next six weeks.

On the way to the shop Lily saw what Kirsty meant by the staff and guests being totally different. The glamorous women she saw were like none she knew. She had only ever seen women dressed the way they were in films, with beautiful dresses and bags, and some of them in wide colourful trousers and tight tops and scarves tied around their hair. The men were all very smart too, many in blazers and light-coloured trousers or shorts. And most of the men and the women were wearing sunglasses.

Mrs Maddox was a tall, elegant woman in her forties, dressed in a tight-fitting black jersey dress and a triple strand of pearls, with her dark-brown hair swept up in a bun. Her eyes were made up with a grey-blue eye-shadow and she wore a bright red lipstick. She looked Lily and Valerie up and down and then she nodded in approval, and thanked Kirsty for bringing them.

"I'll call in to your cabin to see you when you've finished work," Kirsty told them and then she was gone.

Mrs Maddox locked the door and put the Closed sign showing to the outside and then she came back to stand in the middle of the shop.

"Now girls," she said, in a low but clear voice, "before we start looking at the things we sell or learning how to use the till, or any of those matters – I want to tell you the number one rule. It's something you will no doubt have heard before – but it's worth repeating." She looked first at Lily then after a few moments, she turned her gaze to Valerie. "We must remember that the customer is always right, and no matter how they act towards you, you must treat them with the greatest of respect. Is that understood? The guests who are on this ship have paid a lot of money for good service and that's what they will expect."

Lily and Valerie both assured her that it was perfectly understood.

"And you address each of the ladies, regardless of age, as 'madam'."

She then moved into action taking them around the rails of dresses and suits, blouses and slacks and showing them where the price-tabs were on each of the garments. She explained about the different sizes and then showed them to the stock cupboard at the back where any spare sizes were kept

She then went to the shelves that were positioned between the hanging racks, and showed them the perfectly folded sweaters and T-shirts, and the handbags and scarves.

Lily and Valerie followed Mrs Maddox to the changing-rooms – three large cubicles at the back of the shop, with purple velvet curtains and heavy gold tie-backs. There was a gilt-edged chair in each one and a large gilt mirror. Lily thought she had never seen such a glamorous shop or changing-rooms before, and smiled when she caught sight of herself in the ornate mirror.

The manageress then brought them both behind the counter and explained how to use the till and where all the receipts should go, and what bags they should use for the different items. She told them that for today all three would work together, and then after that they would work to a rota system.

When the doors were opened, the women started to drift in, mostly in twos but sometime in a group and sometimes a woman came in on her own. Some spoke and acknowledged Mrs Maddox and the two girls, but mostly they just browsed around and ignored them until they wanted to buy something. Lily and Valerie were positioned at opposite ends of the shop with their hands clasped behind their backs. If anyone approached them or looked as if they were in need of help, they had to say, "Can I help you, Madam?"

At one point Lily felt as though the floor beneath her feet was moving, and then she realised that the ship was now actually afloat.

When she sold her first handbag and packaged it exactly as Mrs Maddox had shown her, and then rang it up on the till, Lily felt a surge of satisfaction. After that, it was simply a case of repeating the same thing again and again.

At lunch-time, Kirsty arrived at the shop and took the two girls back through the shopping area and the leisure deck where the sophisticated guests were sunning themselves on deck-chairs and sun-beds.

She was surprised to see there were quite a lot of children on board, as they passed a play area with miniature houses, see-saws and a variety of sit-in cars and tricycles. She thought how wealthy and privileged their families must be to afford to bring them plus the women in uniforms, who Kirsty said were nannies.

As they moved through the luxurious bar, Kirsty told them to keep a nice smile on their faces, and acknowledge anyone who spoke to them, but the main thing was not to stare or gawp at the guests.

The staff deck was a different kettle of fish. When Kirsty held the door of their recreation area open, Lily was relieved to feel the friendly buzz in the place, and felt her shoulders relax for the first time that morning.

As the three of them walked in, she glanced around the big, open room and could see people of all ages and types, and immediately she sensed that there were quite a few eyes on them. Kirsty guided them to a table over by the window, where they could look out onto the sea.

"This is where you will eat and spend any time off when the ship is moving." Kirsty explained. "There's a games room over to the side with things like darts and billiards and table-tennis, and there's a cupboard full of board-games."

She went on to tell them that the small staff shop, which was over in the corner, sold books and magazines and all the basic things they might need like shampoo and sanitary towels and bags of sweets.

When they went up to collect their lunches, Lily was reminded of the refectory in college as she lifted a tray and then queued to order her food. There was a good variety of food including hot chicken dishes, fish and roast potatoes and chips, and the usual salads. There was also a selection of sandwiches and pastries. Kirsty told them that a similar buffet was laid on both during the day and in the evenings, as the staff all worked different shifts.

Lily came back to the table with her chicken meal and a glass of Coke, and they sat eating and chatting. Every time the door opened they looked up to see who was coming in, and whether it was uniformed staff or the others working in shops, kitchen or entertainment.

At one point Mrs Maddox and another well-dressed lady, who Kirsty said was the manageress from the perfume shop, came in and they sat at a table on the other side of the room eating sandwiches.

"Ah, here's Larry," Kirsty suddenly said, waving him over to the table. "He's been down in the cabaret bar listening to Dynamite going through their rehearsals."

Lily looked up and saw him standing with four lads around her own age, all dressed casually, and then she recognised the blonde lead singer she'd seen in the entertainment brochures. When she saw them heading over to the table, Lily felt her face and neck start to flush. She wished she knew Valerie well enough to whisper something or kick her under the table, as she would have done with Ann or Beryl or her friends from school, whenever they saw attractive boys. When she was younger and at home, she would have said something to Kirsty, but she was trying to give her older cousin a good impression of her as a worker, and didn't want to come across as giddy and boy-mad.

Larry introduced the four boys to Lily and Valerie, and as Lily shook their hands, she thought that each one of them was attractive in their own way. The band members were all from Glasgow and had formed just over a year ago.

They chatted to the girls for a bit and then left them to go and get their own lunch. As they left the table, Bobby King – the lead singer – smiled and winked at her and said he'd have a good chat with her later.

She thought about him as she went about her duties in the shop that afternoon, and it crossed her mind that he was the first male she had felt any interest in since Dara.

She knew that Dara should have received her letter by now, and she wondered how he would react when he read it. She had written to say how everyone in her family now knew exactly the type of dangerous person that Ava was, and were all very sorry that they had believed the awful things she said about Dara. The incident at the dance had happened so quickly and in such a dramatic way that they hadn't had time to digest it all. And of course Seán's dalliance with Ava had further complicated things, and meant he couldn't speak up that night without his wife and family finding out.

She had explained that Seán had had to embroider the truth quite a bit to save losing Eileen and the children – especially now that another baby was on the way. But, she wrote, he had managed to get the main point about Dara's innocence across to her father and mother and everyone else who was there that night.

Lily said she hoped he could find it in his heart to forgive them for treating him so badly. She then went on to write about Ava's subsequent disappearance with the married manager of the hotel in Motherwell, which just proved how completely lacking in scruples she was.

She wished him well with his summer plans, and said that she had lit a candle in her local church and said a prayer that Rose had got the hospital place she wanted.

A few times she had thought about mentioning the link between her father and his mother, and explaining if that hadn't happened how different things would have been. But she felt he'd had enough to deal with, and there was no point in making him feel as weird as she did when she first heard about it.

Of everything that had happened, she knew it was the one thing that had caused the emotional shutters to come crashing down in her heart. To think that the person she loved was the son of the woman her father had been besotted with! How cruel a coincidence for life to throw at them! Even all these months later, it still made her feel strange to think of it, and she had to confine it once again to that dark place in her mind.

She finished off by saying that by the time he received the letter, she would be on the cruise ship and sailing around the Mediterranean.

After work, when she and Valerie were having a coffee in the staff canteen and going over the day's events, Bobby King came over to sit with them. He was dressed in his stage suit – a modern black collarless jacket with a studded white collar showing at the neck. His blonde hair was lightly oiled back so that the side wave stayed in place, and Lily noticed that he was wearing a lovely fresh citrus-smelling cologne.

He told them all about the record deal the band were in the middle of negotiating, then told them about the brilliant new manager who had got them the countrywide tour starting in the autumn.

"Of course we're very grateful to Larry for the stint here on the ship," he said, "and it will mean we're well rehearsed and ready for our big breakthrough."

Valerie had been very impressed. "It sounds as though you'll be rivalling The Beatles soon."

Bobby had put his fingers in a gun-shape and pointed at her saying, "Not *rivalling* The Beatles – taking over from them!"

Lily had smiled and said, "I suppose you have to be confident to make it in show business."

He had then given a lop-sided smile. "Well, some of it's a bit of bluff – it certainly ain't easy. You think you're on the verge of a breakthrough and then nothing happens. A bit like snakes and ladders."

Lily warmed to his honesty now, and liked the familiarity of his Scottish accent. "Well, Larry and Kirsty have spoken very highly of the band, and Valerie and I can't wait to hear you."

"Oh, they're great, and Kirsty's some singer herself. She can sing anything! She should be on television by now."

"Hopefully she will be," Lily said. "Like you say, it's a matter of getting the breakthrough."

"We're doing two shows tonight," he told them. "Why don't you get Larry or Kirsty to sneak you in backstage? That's the only way you'll get to hear the band playing, because they have all these stupid rules that the staff aren't allowed to sit in any of the guest bars or in the cabaret."

When Lily knocked on Kirsty's cabin later, she told her how well her day had gone in Ladies First and then she asked her what the chances would be of going backstage to hear Dynamite playing.

"I'll have a word with Larry, but I think if we're careful not to draw too much attention to you then it should be okay. If anyone asks, I can just say you're helping out with my stage costumes or something like that. The crew are usually okay with Larry and me but, as you can imagine, they have to be fairly strict, because if they let one member of staff in they would be inundated with complaints from everybody else."

Lily understood and said she would keep a very low profile.

It didn't work out that night, but the following evening Kirsty told her to be ready around ten o'clock as Dynamite were wrapping up the night's entertainment.

Bobby had been back and forward to the staff area and any time he saw Lily at her breaks from the shop or after work, he came over to chat with her and have a cup of tea or a Coke. On a couple of occasions, they went out to sit on the deck or have a walk around it if it wasn't too hot.

He was amazed when she told him she was training to be a teacher, and said she didn't look older than a teenage schoolgirl, and then asked her if she had a mortarboard and cane. She laughed at his suggestive humour, and enjoyed chatting to him and the other band members. And when they had a go at the table-tennis, she actually felt like she was back in school as she and Valerie joked and carried on with them. It was a different kind of fun from the sort she and the girls had at college – and certainly different from the way she and Dara had enjoyed things – but it helped lighten the heavy feeling she carried within her.

When she told him she hoped to see the band on stage that night, he asked her for a request that he would play especially for her.

"I'm not sure what kind of music you play? What are your usual numbers?"

"Well, don't forget it's all middle-of-the-road stuff for the cruise," he told her, "because loads of the guests are retired."

He started rhyming off a dozen or so well-known songs and then Lily stopped him.

"That last one, the Jim Reeves," she said. "'Welcome To My World'. I know he's a bit old-fashioned and everything, but I think it's a lovely song."

Bobby shrugged. "He goes down well with all the cruise audiences anyway."

He leaned forward and said in a conspiratorial manner, "Half of them must be bloody millionaires to afford the prices in the cocktail bar." He made his eyebrows meet in the middle. "I think I should try and chat some of the older-looking ladies up, and see if I can get one to die and leave me her fortune."

"You're unbelievable," Lily said.

He blew her a kiss. "Not as unbelievable as you."

49

Lily got dressed with great care, so that if she was spotted by any of the crew they might take her for a guest. She wore a yellow silk dress, with little grey dots and a low neckline, that Kirsty had loaned her with a pair of silver sandals, and Valerie had helped pin her hair up into a more sophisticated style. When she had finished her make-up, her friend said she looked older and more sophisticated with the grey eye-shadow and peach lipstick.

Lily helped Valerie to get ready, and it was agreed that Kirsty would take Lily for a while and then Larry would bring her back and Valerie would take her place.

Kirsty took her through more back corridors she had never seen, which meant they met very few people along the way. When they arrived in at the stage entrance, Lily couldn't believe how big it was, and when Larry brought her to the side of the stage where she could see into the cabaret ballroom, she was almost speechless. It was the most luxurious place she had ever seen, and reminded her of the old Hollywood films, with sweeping staircases covered in blue and gold carpet and circular tables with flowers and candelabras. The guests were all dressed in evening wear with dinner suits and long flowing dresses. Some of the women had floral headdresses on.

Kirsty laughed and said she had felt exactly the same when she first saw the cruise ships, and weren't they lucky to work in such fantastic surroundings.

There were dressing-rooms at one side of the backstage area, and when Lily wandered round, she saw that Bobby and the band were just getting ready to go on. When she saw him, Lily went over to speak to him and wish him good luck.

"I'm sorry, darlin'," he told her, holding his hand up, "but I don't like anyone coming in here before I go on stage. I need to psyche myself up and I can't do that if I'm chatting rubbish."

Lily had immediately backed off and apologised and said she would see him later. Although she knew it wasn't meant personally, she still felt snubbed and more than a little out of her depth, not knowing the way the entertainers worked. She went back to the place at the curtains where Larry had suggested and stayed put until the band came on.

She watched them take their place before the curtains went up, Bobby at the stand-up microphone, and the two guitarists and the drummer. She noticed Bobby's white clenched knuckles and the way he shut his eyes, and she realised with a start that he was actually very nervous. It was something she hadn't expected because he was so cocky and confident, and to see him standing there so serious and intense made him seem like a different person.

Then, they started the opening bars for Cliff Richard's "Summer Holiday" and the guests all started cheering and clapping. They repeated the bars until everyone was quiet again, and then Bobby moved to the microphone.

His sweet but strong voice filled the huge room, and if Lily closed her eyes he sounded exactly like Cliff. She stood mesmerised watching him until the end of the song, and then waited while the audience gave him a thunderous applause. The reaction seemed to energise Bobby further and as the band moved into "Twenty-Four Hours From Tulsa" she could tell that he was a star on the rise.

Each song relaxed him more and after half a dozen he had the microphone in his hand, and was walking around the stage introducing the band and encouraging the audience to send requests. He came back to centre-stage and then, after glancing over to the corner where Lily was standing, he started singing "Welcome To My World".

After half an hour or so, Lily was sorry when Larry indicated that she had to leave, but she smiled and moved quickly. They stopped for a minute at Kirsty's lovely big changing-room to wish her good luck on her first night, and Lily felt almost star-struck when she saw her cousin dressed in a shimmering black and gold dress, moulded closely to her body and then at the bottom flouncing out into a fishtail of sparkling black net.

"We'll bring you down another night to watch Kirsty," Larry said, smiling lovingly at his wife.

Later that night, Lily and Valerie were up in the staff mess room discussing their second day in the shop and saying how well it was all going, when the band came through. Bobby had changed into a short-sleeved white shirt and was wearing casual trousers. Larry came in afterwards and congratulated them and then bought them all a drink.

"The boys deserve it. It's thirsty work up on that stage," he said, placing a tray of lagers on the table for the boys and two Babychams for the girls. "They've been waiting all evening for this. The Contessa is stricter than the other boats about the staff drinking and they won't even let them have a shandy before going on stage."

Lily looked over at Bobby now, and watched as he gulped half the glass of lager down in a few mouthfuls. They sat and chatted and had a few more drinks and then Kirsty said she was heading to bed.

Bobby moved over beside Lily. "How about a little walk out on the deck before you go? It's a lovely night and the fresh air might help you to sleep."

She looked over at Valerie, and could see the drummer was already asking her.

"Okay," Lily said.

On their own, Bobby was less showy and he chatted easily to her like the boys she knew back home. He told her all about his family in Dennistoun in Glasgow, and talked about how he started singing around the small clubs when he was just a teenager.

She found him friendly and interesting and he was full of funny stories. When she said she was tired, he walked her back to her berth, and then he moved to give her a passionate kiss.

Although she was half-expecting him to make some kind of an overture, the intensity of the kiss caught her by surprise, and she was almost overwhelmed by it. It was strange, she realised, to have anyone so physically close to her other than Dara, and she had to steel herself against drawing away and hurting his feelings. She said a quick goodnight and told him she would see him tomorrow and then went inside.

She had hardly closed the door when she dissolved into floods of tears.

She undressed and took her make-up off, crying all the while, and was glad that Valerie was still walking around the deck with the drummer.

She climbed up onto her top bunk and buried her damp face in the pillow, then cried until her body was heaving up and down. Eventually, it all subsided and she lay back, staring up at the ceiling.

What had happened, she asked herself. Here she was on a fabulous boat, basking in constant sunshine, travelling from one exotic port to another, and meeting a gorgeous, talented young man who was obviously attracted to her. It was like a romantic story in a magazine. And yet there was something missing. And no matter how hard she tried to deny it, and tell herself that it was all wrong, something deep inside her was yearning for the person who was the other half of her.

The person whose heart she had broken.

50

After the first week on board a pattern began to form.

They would have two or three days working and then the ship would pull in at a port and they would have the day and night completely free. And, as Kirsty had forecast, every day was sunny and hot and Lily spent part of her lunchtime and every evening sitting up on the deck. Sometimes she sat with Valerie or Kirsty and Larry, but more often she sat with Bobby.

She had got past the initial awkwardness of kissing someone else other than Dara, and had given herself a good talking to about the whole situation. The hardest thing for her was knowing that she would probably never meet anyone like Dara again. Anyone so like herself.

The chances of coming across someone who ticked all those imaginary boxes again was hugely unlikely. The appreciation of the same music, the books, the films, even the old buildings. In the eighteen months before she met Dara, and in all the years before, she had never met anyone like him. Never met anyone who came close.

And yet there was nothing wrong with all the nice fellows in her college, they just weren't right for her. Even in such a short space of time Lily knew that she had been lucky to come across someone like Dara Ryan. To meet another man like him might well be asking for too much.

343

But, she decided, she had a long life yet to live. She wasn't yet twenty-one and she couldn't live the rest of her life like a nun.

She would have to throw away the imaginary list and adapt to meet whatever lay in the future for her.

*　*　*

As the weeks wore on, Mrs Maddox no longer seemed the formal, stern woman the girls had met on their first day. The shop had been a roaring success and the two girls had a natural way with them which helped the customers feel at ease and more inclined to try things on.

Every day they had to go through into the stock room and replenish the rails, and the manageress said she would have to re-order all the more popular lines. She said the company that owned the shop would be pleased and she would make sure to give good reports on the work that Valerie and Lily had done. She had relaxed more and now chatted to them when the shop was quiet. She told them that she was divorced, and since she had no children and no ties she decided to see a bit of the world. "You're a long time dead," she said. "And you have to take your chances while you can."

Lily had taken her boss's advice to heart and had taken the chance to visit as many places as possible when the ship came into port.

Over the weeks she had seen Naples, Capri, Venice, Sicily, and when they disembarked in Livorno, she and Bobby had taken a tour of Florence and Pisa along with Larry and Kirsty.

Initially, Kirsty had teased her for spending so much time with the singer, but gradually she had stopped and now saw them almost as a couple. Lily enjoyed Bobby's company and felt she had got to know him much better. He had the same sense of humour as her brothers, and he was generous buying her little souvenirs from the various places they stopped at. He bought her a bracelet made from local gemstones from Venice and a leather purse from Florence.

Their nights on the deck together became longer, and had it not been for the lack of somewhere to be alone, Bobby would have pressed for their relationship to become more physical. Whilst she liked him a lot and found him very attractive, six weeks on board a ship was too short a time for her to take any big steps in that direction.

And although he was attentive and had a good way with women, Lily did have a few reservations about him. She had now seen him perform on a number of occasions, and she had noticed that he still couldn't relax before a performance and at times she found it painful watching him look so angst-ridden. And she felt their differences when he teased her for acting too much like a teacher – for getting too engrossed in books, or for suggesting they visit an art gallery or anywhere that wasn't in the mainstream tourist areas.

He was quite happy spending hours on deck working out the lyrics of new songs he was writing and constantly looking for her opinion of them, but when she brought the subject round to her work with children, she noticed his eyes glazing over.

On the last week of the cruise, when the ship dropped anchor at Barcelona, Kirsty suggested that she and Lily have a day to themselves. Valerie had planned to go off with the drummer, and Larry was meeting up with an old friend who had moved out to Spain.

They dressed up in bright trousers and colourful tops and wore their sunglasses, and Larry and several others remarked how glamorous they looked and how they could pass for sisters. They both laughed, happy with the comparison.

They had a few hours around the shops, and Lily picked up a nice scarf for her mother and leather wallets for her father and Declan, and bought some small ceramic pieces to give to her married brothers and their wives.

When they were sitting having lunch and sharing a bottle of Lambrusco in an outside café, Kirsty asked her if she would be seeing Bobby when she got back home.

"Do you know, I haven't even thought that far . . ." She was silent for a few moments. "I like him. I like him a lot, but when I take the time to think it through, I don't honestly see how it would work out."

Kirsty took a sip of her wine. "I suppose he has all those tour dates coming up and you're in Newcastle."

"That's part of it," Lily said. "But I don't think we're really that suited. Don't get me wrong, he's a lovely guy, but when we get off the ship I don't think we've enough in common to keep us together. He's not like . . ." She halted and corrected herself. "Bobby is really talented and I think he could make it big, but I think he needs to concentrate on his music career and not have anything that will distract him for the next couple of years. And I need to get on with my college work, make sure I pass all my final exams and then start looking for a teaching post."

Kirsty studied her for a few moments. "You never told me what happened with Dara."

Lily looked up sharply, although her eyes were hidden behind her sunglasses.

"I heard all about it from my mother," Kirsty said. "She was very worried about you, and sorry that things went so wrong. She told me all about Declan's girlfriend and the lies she told."

Lily took a deep breath. "That Ava was a disaster." Her voice was suddenly strained. "I still can't even bear to think about it."

Kirsty reached over and touched her hand. "I didn't mean to upset you. If you don't want to talk about it, that's fine."

Lily sipped her wine and sat in silence watching the people going up and down outside the café, and then suddenly the words came tumbling out.

"I loved him, Kirsty. He was different to anyone I've ever met . . . I still love him."

Then she told her cousin everything, from how they met in the cinema, their letters and phone calls and she even told her about Dara's visit to Newcastle. Kirsty offered no comment or criticism, she just sat and listened.

"Everything," Lily said, "was going perfectly well between us until that vicious Ava ruined things." For a moment she contemplated telling Kirsty the whole story about Seán and how Declan had been made a fool of – but she stopped herself.

She had no doubt that Kirsty was completely trustworthy, but she felt that to say anything would forever put a question mark over Seán and Eileen's marriage and she felt it wasn't fair. They and their children deserved another chance, and who was she to deprive them of that?

"And is it too late?" Kirsty asked. "Surely if Dara knows that the whole thing was cleared up . . .?"

"I wrote to him and explained it all before I left," Lily told her.

Kirsty's face brightened up. "There might be a letter waiting for you when you get back!"

Lily shook her head. "There won't be. He's been hurt too much by everybody including me. I didn't stick up for him that night and I let him go back to Ireland without saying a proper goodbye. I was terrible to him."

"Contact him the minute you get home and tell him how sorry you are. Don't let him go. You'll never meet anyone like him again."

"Oh, I know that . . ." Lily looked down at the table, as two large tears slid down her cheeks. "I haven't told you it all, Kirsty. I haven't even told Dara . . ."

Kirsty leaned forward, lifted the wine bottle and filled their glasses up. "We've all afternoon," she said, "and I'm listening."

Ten minutes and several paper hankies later, Lily finished the saga of her father and the love of his life, Helena Casey. Then she told Kirsty that her father's old flame was Dara's mother.

"My God!" Kirsty said, sitting back in her chair. "What a coincidence! The chances of you two meeting up!"

Lily nodded sadly. "The thing is, Dara's mother suffered from depression and some people think that she might have committed suicide. I thought about that later and wondered if it was because she had never loved her husband. If maybe that all those years she had suffered, wishing she was with my father."

Kirsty considered it for a few moments. "I doubt it very much. People can have depression for all sorts of reasons, and from what you've said, it sounds far more likely that it was an accident. You said Dara told you that she had been fine for a few years before she died. I think that tells you everything."

"But what if . . ."

"What *if* anything? I think you've been reading too much into things that aren't connected."

Lily took her glasses off for a moment to rub her red-rimmed eyes with a tissue. "But don't you think that the whole thing between my father and Dara's mother is too creepy and weird for us to be going out?"

"You're not suggesting that Pat's Dara's father or anything like that, are you?"

"Not at all. Apart from the fact that it happened years before either my dad or his mother were married, he has two older brothers and he looks like his father and he's got the exact same thick head of hair."

"Well, what's the problem?"

"The fact that they went out together and we're boyfriend and girlfriend . . ."

"But it's kind of romantic in a way." Kirsty wrinkled her brow and then smiled. "I'm sure in a lot of small places that situations like that could happen very easily. Just think about it. And you often hear about two brothers going out with the same girl, or two sisters going out with the same brother." She laughed. "Well, maybe not often, but it's not unheard of." She shook her head. "Lily, it was over twenty years ago. Why do you care?"

"Because," she said, "I'm afraid that Dara will always remind me that my father didn't really want to marry my mother."

Kirsty looked at her incredulously. "Why on earth would you think that? They have their ups and downs, but your mother and father are as happy and devoted as any couple I know." She patted Lily's hand. "And look at the lovely family they have together and their beautiful grandchildren. Are you really going to tell me that all that means nothing?"

Lily took a deep breath. "I never thought about it like that."

"And even if your mother wasn't your father's first choice," Kirsty said, "lots of people marry their second and third choice and end up happy enough. Life isn't all straight lines, Lily. Look at me and Larry. You were too young to realise, but my father wasn't a bit happy when we were first going out, but we stuck with it and look at us. I couldn't imagine being without him. We do everything together and he's the absolute love of my life. Dara sounds like yours. Why on earth would you walk away from him?"

"Because of all this . . . He doesn't know."

"Well, get a bloody paper and pen and write and tell him! Tell him the truth about all this and see what he says. If he's okay about it then I don't see why you should let it bother you. If he thinks it's all too weird then at least you'll both agree."

Lily bit her lip. "Do you really think so?"

Kirsty smiled at her. "I certainly do. Get writing tonight and he'll have it by the time you get back to Scotland next week."

51

After she had posted the letter, Lily felt as if a ton weight had been lifted off her. She had no idea how Dara would react but at least they would both know she had been completely honest with him.

It had been hard finding the words, but after three drafts she had somehow managed to pull it all together. She had given the final version to Kirsty the following morning, and she had looked it over and said it explained things perfectly. Then, before she had a chance to change her mind, Kirsty put a Spanish stamp on it and posted it in the staff mailbox.

Later that evening, after she and Valerie finished work in the shop, she went looking for Bobby and had the honest chat that she felt was necessary with him.

He seemed surprised that she thought they needed to talk about anything, and thought it was okay for them to continue as they were until the last night.

"I thought you were enjoying us being together," he said, a hurt note in his voice.

"I was," Lily said, "but we need to be realistic. There's no way that the romance can continue when we leave this ship. We're probably never going to see each other again, and I think that it's only making things harder on ourselves when we know it's not going to get any more serious."

Bobby had reached out and touched her hair. "Are you sure about that? I'd like it to be more serious. I've been talking to Johnny, and we were thinking if we did a wee bit of juggling about with the cabins for the last week, that maybe I could come up to yours and Valerie could go to mine with Johnny." He looked into her eyes. "What d'you say? It would be a lovely memory to take away with us. A great way to end the summer."

"Are you serious?" Lily asked.

"Deadly," he said.

She started to laugh. "Thanks for the offer," she told him. "I'm very flattered. And I have to say I do like you a lot, Bobby – and I think you're a terrific performer – but let's just say a summer fling is not my style."

"Aw, don't say that!" He reached out and took her hand. "I really, really like you, Lily."

"I'm sure it's my loss," she said, "and I'm sure that in the future when I tell all my friends I turned down the famous Bobby King, they'll all think I was mad. Who knows, I might even think it myself."

"I would hate you to have any regrets . . ."

"I'll live with it," she said. "Whereas I couldn't live with a meaningless fling. It's just not me."

"It's a pity. We get on so well together. And it wouldn't be like that. I would really try to see you again. I'll always get back to Glasgow between my dates."

"It wouldn't be enough," she said.

He grinned at her then. "I was hoping I might get a chance to see you wearing the teacher's mortarboard with the cane in your hand."

She wagged her finger at him, like a teacher would do to a naughty pupil. "Have you heard of the Everly Brothers?"

He looked at her as though she was mad.

"Well, they have a song," She started to sing. "*Dream, dream, dream . . .*"

He looked at her and then he put his arms around her and kissed her on the lips and said. "You are a case, Lily."

* * *

The final week on the ship flew by. Mrs Maddox was sorry to see the two girls go and told them it had been a pleasure working with them. She also told them they could pick anything in the shop at a fifty per cent discount.

"I'll probably get shot for doing it," she laughed, "but I think you two helped bring a lot of the sales, so I think you deserve it."

Lily was glad everything had worked out, but also glad it was only a summer job. At times she had found it very boring and repetitive, and couldn't imagine doing it day in day out, and it made her all the more grateful to know she had something more fulfilling planned with her teaching career.

Lily thought carefully about what she would buy as the clothes were so expensive. There was no point in buying summer clothes as she had loads of them and the weather wasn't likely to be that great in Scotland or Newcastle. After discussing it with Kirsty she bought herself a lovely soft blue cashmere sweater that she knew she would get the wear out of.

* * *

Since they had got to know a lot of the senior crew by now and were on friendly terms with most of them, she and Valerie sneaked backstage most nights to hear Kirsty and Dynamite perform.

Valerie had fallen hard for Johnny, and she told Lily she was going to do everything she could to keep the romance going when they finished on the ship. She had no job or ties waiting back in Liverpool for her and Johnny had suggested she join them on the road as the wardrobe girl, looking after their stage outfits.

Lily wished her good luck and told her to send her postcards from all the cities they played in. "And make sure all the bands sign the cards," she told Valerie. "Because I'm sure their signatures will be worth a fortune one day!"

Each night Lily heard her cousin singing, she got a lump in her throat. She was so proud of her, and even more so since she had another long-playing record due out for Christmas. After next year, Kirsty had told her, she and Larry were going to have a break from the cruise ships and do some tour dates in Scotland and England to promote her new album. Lily said she hoped they would come to Newcastle and she would bring a whole coach load to the city to see them.

On the final night, Lily and Valerie stayed in the wings to hear Dynamite's last performance. They had added a few new numbers to their list and the girls were enthralled listening to them. As she watched him, Lily thought how beautiful Bobby's voice was, and as he sang "Yesterday", she was sure he was even better than Paul McCartney.

They got a thunderous round of applause when they finished it, and then, continuing the theme, the band struck up another slow, mellow number. Lily thought she recognised the opening bars and stood with her brow furrowed, trying to guess what it was.

And then, Bobby's pure, clear voice started singing, "*Oh, my love, my darling, I've hungered for your touch . . .*"

Lily caught her breath. She closed her eyes and suddenly she was back in her college room lying in Dara's arms.

She tried with all her might to hold back the tears.

52

When Lily stepped off the plane in Glasgow on a Saturday afternoon, the sun was shining, although it felt freezing compared to the temperatures they had left behind in Rome.

Seán collected her and Kirsty and Larry, and he chatted all the way back to Rowanhill, asking Lily lots of questions about the cruise ship and wanting to know about all the places she had seen.

When they arrived at the house, there was a crowd of her family all waiting to welcome her home. Everyone commented on her lovely tan and said how the sun had brought out the blonde tints in her hair.

She gave out her presents and showed them the brochures and pictures she had, and then everyone asked her all the same questions that Seán had, and she repeated all the same answers.

They all had tea and sandwiches and cakes, and then her brothers and their wives and children left in dribs and drabs until there was only Lily and her mother and father left.

"You certainly sound as though you saw a bit of the world," her father said. "And fair play to you. You've seen an awful lot more than me and your mother did."

"Ah, sure, I'm no good on planes," her mother said in a resigned voice, "and I don't suppose I'd be any better on one of those big fancy ships."

"Did they have bingo on it?" her father asked, winking over at Lily. Mona loved the odd game in the church hall.

Lily grinned and shook her head. "The posh gamblers go to the casino."

"Ah well," Pat said, clapping a hand on his wife's shoulders, "it's horses for courses, and I don't think me and your mother would fit in with a casino crowd. The bingo and the odd flutter on the horses suit us fine. Isn't that right, Mona?"

Her mother looked up at her father and then they both laughed.

Lily caught the tender look and she remembered what Kirsty had said about them being happy in their own way, and she realised her cousin was right.

"Oh God," her mother suddenly said, "I nearly forgot . . ." She got up from the sofa and went over to the mantelpiece. She lifted a long, thick airmail letter and handed it to Lily. "This came for you yesterday."

Lily took it from her, and she knew without looking at it that it was from Dara.

There was a silence and then Pat Grace stood up. "Lily . . ." he said, his tone not quite as sure as normal. "I think I owe that young Irish lad an apology. Seán explained what really went on . . . and that none of the things Ava said about him were true."

Her mother got up to stand beside him. "I think we all owe him an apology."

She looked at the envelope in Lily's hands. "I don't know what we can do about it now . . ."

Lily shrugged. "I don't know myself."

"He's a decent lad," Pat said, looking at his wife. "And he's from a decent family. I told you I knew his mother when we were young?"

Mona nodded. "Poor lad, losing her so early . . ."

Lily looked at them both and once again had the feeling they were much closer than she had ever understood.

Upstairs, in the privacy of her bedroom, she opened the letter, and as she slid the pages out her hands were shaking.

53

Dear Lily,
Thanks for writing again. I received your letter from Spain this
morning. It sounds like you've had a fantastic trip and I'm so glad
it went well for you.

It was an amazing experience, and I envy you having seen cities
like Rome and Pompeii. I suppose that's the boring architect in me
coming out!

Lily paused to take a good deep breath. Thank God he had
replied, and thank God he hadn't been horrible to her, because she
knew it was what she deserved. She steadied her hands and read on:

I've had a fairly ordinary summer here – a typical wet Irish one
– but thankfully, it has been productive enough.

Rose, unfortunately, didn't get her place in the local hospital, but
the good news is one of the teachers persuaded her to apply to some
of the hospitals in London and Manchester. At first she wasn't
keen, but she gradually came around to the idea and has three
interviews over there next week. If she gets a place, of course we'll
all miss her, but we think it will be good for her and she can always
come home at the holidays and get a job here when she's finished.
My aunt in London has said she would be delighted to have her live
with them if she gets one of the hospitals in that area.

Now I have all the small-talk over, I have to confess I felt very strange when I got your letter explaining the real reason as to why you distanced yourself from me in Scotland. I can only imagine how you felt when you found out our parents had been in love, after your father had made that terrible confession to you – and then you had to deal with accusations about me and that dreadful deranged girl. I'm still reeling about that news of your father and my mother – and, like you, I can't believe that such a coincidence should have happened to us. I'm still trying to work it out in my mind, and it's the last thing I expected you to tell me.

I felt the same shock as you did when I read it, and, after thinking about it, I understand how you were feeling before the situation with Ava blew up. I just wish you had told me at the time and we might have been able to make some sense of it together. I certainly would have told you. But then, I suppose it shows you weren't as sure of our relationship as I was and that there was a basic lack of trust in me. I think that's the most hurtful thing.

Lily's hand came to her mouth, and tears filled her eyes. She went and got a hanky and had to wait a few minutes before she could start reading again.

Regarding Ava – when I got your first letter saying she had disappeared to England I felt a great sense of relief as I had been worried she might come back to Carraigvale and spread her vicious lies. For a while I just let it simmer, but it ate away at me, and I felt I had to do something. She had ruined the best thing in my life and I needed to understand more about it. I decided to pay a visit to the bed and breakfast and have a chat with Mrs Stewart. To say it was a revelation is an understatement.

Apparently the older man who we thought had been harassing her – O'Brien – had suffered at her hands as well. She'd been involved in a long-term affair with him since working in his hotel in Dublin – no surprise there, now we know what she's like! When his wife became suspicious about another woman, they decided it would be better if it ended and Ava moved away, and that's when he contacted Mrs Stewart to find her work. But of course it didn't end there as we know.

Mrs Stewart knew nothing about the affair, and Ava of course was very good at hiding it, but eventually O'Brien said he thought it best to end it completely. He felt bad about Ava and gave her a thousand pounds, and initially she seemed fine. But, after a while, she contacted him again asking for more money and threatening to tell his wife and family about their affair. Apparently the hardest part was that his two teenage girls adored Ava, and his wife had been very fond of her too, and he just couldn't face them finding out. It's too long to go into all of it, but the upshot is the night he came to the bed and breakfast he gave her more money, and said if she didn't leave him alone he had no option but to go to the Guards and tell all. And of course you know what happened after that. She had met your brothers by that time and thought she saw a better option. It's good news that she's since moved on, and I'm glad she went without telling everyone about Seán's lack of judgement over her, especially since there's another baby on the way.

All I can say about that night is that it was a complete nightmare for me and for your family. They had been so good and welcoming to me, and it must have been a shock when the seemingly perfect Ava made those horrendous accusations.

I could go on now and say I wish you'd trusted me and stood by me, but I know you've done your best to explain that. Enough said – it's my problem now.

Lily, I must finish off now, as I'm up early. Apart from working in the cinema in the evenings, I've been working in an architect's office up in Naas. It's been good experience for me and it's helped pass away a difficult summer.

I appreciate you writing to me and I know it must have been difficult.

I'll finish by saying you will always have a special place in my heart and I will treasure the memories of the wonderful times we had in Newcastle and Edinburgh. I wish things could have been different.

If you ever find yourself in Carraigvale again, you will probably still find me in the cinema!

Love, Dara

Ten minutes later, Lily was still sitting there, frozen in her sadness. How could she have been so wrong? How could she have hurt him so badly? There were no answers. She could tell it was all too late.

Eventually she moved. She would go to her aunt's and find Kirsty. Maybe if she talked to her and showed her the letter, she might somehow start coming to terms with the loss.

The loss of the best thing in her life.

54

On a Friday morning a few weeks later, Lily stood by her bedroom window, taking a breather from her packing. She was going back to college on Sunday to start the final year of her teacher training course. And while she had enjoyed the time after the cruise with her family, she was ready to get back to her independent life.

She turned back to her wardrobe, and went to a shelf to lift the blue cashmere sweater she had bought from Ladies First. She smiled as she put it in the case. She had already received two postcards from Valerie, one from London and one from Birmingham – and both signed by all the members of Dynamite. Bobby had written a short line by his signature – *See you in Newcastle in October!* He had remembered her saying that she would bring a crowd of her college friends if he ever played there. She would surprise him by keeping her promise.

She heard the door going and then Seán shouted up the stairs to her.

She went to the door and called, "I'll be down in a minute." He probably needed her to look after the children again.

She put the lid down on her case, pleased she was nearly done, then she closed the wardrobe door on all the bright, summer dresses and tops she wouldn't wear until the following year. It had been a long, boring job sorting out her autumn and winter clothes for the coming term. But in a way, she was glad to let go of the last reminders of the long, eventful summer.

She went down the stairs, trying to think if she had remembered everything she needed. She could hear Seán's voice, chatting away, and the sound of the children laughing.

She opened the living-room door, and suddenly found herself rooted to the spot. There, sitting on the sofa, was Dara and his sister, Rose, and standing beside them were her mother and Seán.

Dara stood up. "Hi, Lily, I hope we haven't given you too much of a shock, but Rose and I were up in Edinburgh, and I thought since we were that close we would call in on you."

Lily looked at him, unable to speak.

He glanced anxiously at his sister. "She had an interview at one of the big hospitals there and there's a good chance she's going to be offered a place. They more or less confirmed it yesterday."

Lily looked at Rose and when she saw the beaming smile on her face, she found herself able to move. "Oh, Rose," she said, going over to give her a hug. "I'm delighted for you."

Rose looked all embarrassed and pleased at the same time. "I'm delighted too. I loved Edinburgh, it's absolutely fantastic. Dara had told me all about it, but it's even nicer than he said."

"Now, Rose," Lily's mother said, moving towards the kitchen. "You must be dying for a cup of tea." She pointed at Seán. "I know that fella's always looking for one. Come on in and tell me all about the hospital and everything."

The three of them disappeared into the kitchen, closed the door and left Dara and Lily on their own.

Lily came to sit on the chair opposite him. "I don't know what to say . . . I can't believe you've come."

He gave a wry little smile. "I can't either. I nearly didn't."

They looked at each other in silence, and then huge tears filled Lily's eyes.

"I'm so, so sorry," she said.

He nodded his head slowly, saying nothing.

"I spoke to Kirsty," she finally said. "And she thinks the thing about my father . . ." She swallowed hard. "She thinks it doesn't matter, she thinks I made too much of it."

He glanced away, looking towards the window. "I talked to my brothers and they said the same thing. Then I got the letter from Seán just the day before we came over."

"From Seán?" Lily repeated. "Seán wrote to you?"

"Yes, and he gave me his phone number and asked me to ring him. I spoke to him yesterday morning. After he finished apologising again, we talked about the thing between my mother and your father, and he just said that it was twenty-odd years ago and what did it have to do with us? It made me feel better." He looked back at her now. "What do you think now?"

"I feel the same now. I only wish I'd talked to you about it at the time . . ."

There was another silence, and then something told Lily that there might just be the tiniest chance . . . She moved towards him and when she saw the vulnerable look in his dark brown eyes, all the feelings she had ever had for him came rushing back.

"Oh, Dara," she said, putting her arms around him. "I've made some terrible mistakes, but I've never stopped loving you – not for one minute!"

He waited for a few moments then he held her at arm's length and looked directly into her eyes. "And I still love you."

"What," she asked, "will we do?"

"I think," he told her, "it's called, 'start all over again'."

She felt a moment of pure joy. "That would be wonderful. And I promise I'll never, ever let you down again."

There was just the smallest glimmer of humour in his eyes. "You better not." He looked down at her bare hand. "Have you still got the ring I bought you in Edinburgh?"

She nodded. "It's upstairs. I couldn't wear it. Every time I looked at it I started to cry."

"Well, I'd like you to start wearing it now, so that when you go back to college, you'll be reminded of me every day."

"I'll wear the ring because I love it – not because I need a reminder. You've been with me every day since I last saw you."

"And you've constantly been with me." His hands tightened on

362

hers. "Do you remember what I said about buying you a decent ring at the end of the summer? Well, I have the money all saved, but maybe we should give it time to see how things go."

She lifted his hands and kissed them. "I promise that things will go exactly as they should. I'll make sure it." She looked up into his eyes. "When will I see you after this?"

"We go home tonight," he told her. "We're flying back from Edinburgh. Maybe I could come back to Newcastle in a few weeks' time. What do you think?"

"I think that would be wonderful. The sooner the better." She stopped, trying to take it all in. "And it's such good news about Rose. She looks so relaxed – more confident somehow."

"She is. And a lot of that is down to a good teacher who took a bit of time with her." He smiled. "You see – you teachers really can make a difference."

"I'm delighted for her, and I'm so pleased it might be Edinburgh."

"So am I," he said. "Because I've been looking at jobs over there for when I finish."

"You've been looking at jobs in Edinburgh?"

"I know it's all a bit early, but you have to think ahead." He touched her face. "I'm sure you would like to come back to Scotland, and there's a lot more work for me here than there is in Ireland. What do you think?"

Her eyes lit up. "I think it's brilliant . . . And I think you're very clever for coming up with it."

After spreading her wings so far, she hadn't really considered coming back to Scotland – as in coming back to Rowanhill. But Edinburgh was a different matter. A thrill ran through her at the thought of living there every day. It was near enough to visit her family regularly and they would also be beside Rose.

"We'll never go through a summer like this again," Dara said.

"From now on," Lily said, "we'll spend every summer together – and we'll see all those beautiful places that felt empty without you."

He looked into her eyes and then he held her close.

If you enjoyed
Summer's End by Geraldine O'Neill,
why not try
Sarah Love also published by Poolbeg?
Here's a sneak preview of Chapter One

SARAH LOVE

Geraldine O'Neill

POOLBEG

CHAPTER 1

Tullamore, County Offaly

September, 1964

When the morning sky gave enough light to see clearly, Sarah Love checked her watch. She slid out of the narrow single bed and walked barefoot on the cold, cracked linoleum over to the old wardrobe. She opened the door inch by inch, wary of the loud creak it made when opened quickly.

She tucked a long strand of white-blonde hair behind her ear, then carefully lifted out the heavy hanger. It was weighed down with the long white lace wedding dress she had been working on for the last few months. She often did alterations and made items for local people, but this dress was different. It was the first wedding dress she had made – and it was her own.

She hung it on the outside of the wardrobe and then sat back on the bed, scrutinising it for any flaws. So far, she had found none. The pattern had been ordered through a shop in Dublin and then she had waited two weeks until it arrived from London. It had been worth the wait. No bride in Tullamore would have a dress like it. She still had a few small details to finish – loops for the pearl buttons on the back and the cuffs, and some small white roses to sew on the neckline. But she had plenty of time. The wedding wasn't for another two weeks.

A door creaked somewhere in the cottage and then the familiar rattling in the kitchen told her that her brother James and his wife Martina were up. It would be another half an hour or so before she would feel comfortable about joining them.

When Martina moved into Loves' cottage eighteen months ago, she had made it perfectly clear that she liked to have the mornings alone with her husband. When Sarah joined them, the stilted conversation indicated that Martina didn't want her sister-in-law around until she and James had their first cup of tea together and eased themselves into the day.

At the beginning it had upset Sarah, being made to feel like an unwanted lodger in her own home. But there was nothing she could do about the situation. As the oldest and only boy in the Love family, James had been left the cottage and she was now living there under sufferance.

She had endured it, and in a few weeks she would have her own kitchen and would be sitting down to breakfast with her own husband every morning.

Sarah wondered whether it was worth starting work on the dress now or whether she should wait until after breakfast. She glanced at a book on the cabinet by her bed, and then her gaze moved to the sewing table beside the window with her collection of needles and threads, and the new boxes of trimmings for her dress.

She went over to the wrought-iron stand where she washed every morning. She lifted the white tin jug and poured water into the basin. Then she took a bar of soap and washed her hands in the cold water and dried them on a rough towel. She wouldn't risk marks on the white material.

As she worked away, stitching the satin rosebuds around the neck of the dress, Sarah lost herself in the details of her wedding day. She rehearsed every minute of the morning from leaving the cottage on James's arm until she was walking up the aisle with her two friends, Sheila Brady and Patricia Quinn, walking behind her in the pink dresses she had made for them.

Then, she saw herself standing at the altar beside Con Tierney – the local lad she had been courting for the last three years. They would take their vows in front of nearly sixty people, and after that they would go to Butler's Hotel for their wedding breakfast.

Later on that evening they would take the train up to Dublin, and spend their first night together in a small hotel in Bray.

Sarah's thoughts always came to a halt after that. She couldn't begin to imagine herself and Con alone in the hotel room for a whole week. Herself and Con in a big double bed for the first time. She supposed she would just handle it like every new bride. Take it a night at a time.

When she decided that it was safe to venture out into the kitchen, Sarah finished the rosebud she was on, hung the dress back up, slid her feet into her slippers and went into the kitchen.

Martina was over at the stone sink, washing the plates and mugs.

"Good morning," Sarah said. "It doesn't look too bad out."

Her narrow-hipped sister-in-law turned towards her. "Are you on a split shift in the hotel today?"

"I finish at four and then I'm back on again at six for the evening."

"We need flour and tea."

"I'll get them," Sarah said. "But can it wait until tonight? I wasn't going to come home because Sheila invited me to have dinner out at their house." Sarah's old school-friend lived with her elderly parents in the middle of Tullamore and was always happy to have Sarah's company for a few hours.

Martina turned back to the sink without answering, the way she often did.

Sarah's chest tightened. "We're not that short of tea and flour, are we?" She went over to check the flour bin. "There's enough for three or four loaves, and the caddy is half full."

Martina took up a linen teacloth and began to dry the wet cups and plates.

Sarah waited for a few moments, to see if there would be any more to the conversation. There wasn't. The silence hung in the air, making her wonder if she should change her plans and come home with the tea and flour during her afternoon break.

Then, she caught herself. If her brother's wife wanted her to bring the things home, she could ask like a normal person. Trying to read Martina's mind had got her nowhere in the past. Her moods were so changeable that Sarah could cycle all the way back home with the flour and tea to be met with a bemused half-smile.

Having a nice hot meal put down to her in Sheila's welcoming house was a far better option. She put the kettle back into the middle of the range to boil and then cut two slices of brown bread and buttered them.

As she poured hot tea into her mug, she looked over at Martina who was now scrubbing the sink. "Will I pour you a cup of tea?"

The scrubbing continued for a few more seconds. Then eventually she said, "No . . . I've had enough."

Sarah lifted her plate and mug and headed towards her bedroom where she could relax with her breakfast.

"Thank God the timing has worked out well," Martina suddenly said.

Sarah halted in her tracks. "Timing for what?"

"The wedding . . . we're going to need your room."

Sarah turned to look at her.

"We've a baby on the way now, so we'll need more space."

Sarah's face broke into a smile. "That's great news!" She turned back to put her breakfast things on the kitchen table. "You both must be delighted."

Martina leaned against the sink. "I suppose we are . . . I'm still getting used to it."

"It'll be lovely for you to have a baby around the house." She suddenly noticed her sister-in-law's pale face. "Are you feeling okay?"

"I'm not too bad."

"Do you feel sick in the mornings? Do you know when it's due?"

Martina's face tightened. "I'm grand – I'm not making a big issue of it and I don't want you to be going around telling everybody."

Sarah caught her breath at the assumption. "I wouldn't say a word until you –"

"It's private business," Martina continued. "And I'm keeping it in the family for the time being. I've my mother warned to say nothing for a while, and I'm not telling the sisters yet because they're nothing but a pair of yaps."

"Well, I'm delighted for you and James." Sarah lifted her mug and plate. "I'll be in the room sewing until it's time to go to work."

"Sarah . . ." Martina said. "Have you decided what you're doing with your hair yet for the wedding?"

"I've had a chat with the hairdresser," Sarah's voice was deliberately light, "and she's going to try the head-dress with my hair loose or up in a bun."

"You've far too much hair for a bun," Martina stated. She narrowed her eyes. "I thought you were going to have a good bit cut off it?"

Sarah shook her head. "I never said that. You suggested it to me last week and I told you then I didn't want it cut."

"Please yourself!" Martina snapped. "I just think you're going to look like a ghost in a white dress with all that whitey hair around you. If you had it cut to an ordinary shoulder length, the head-dress would sit better."

"I'm not having it cut." Sarah went into her bedroom and closed the door. There were a lot of things she wasn't confident about, but the one thing she knew was that she had nice long hair. Since she was a little girl, people had commented on the colour and the fact it was so long she could sit on it. Occasionally she found herself on the receiving end of snide remarks from other girls. She remembered being teased by two particular girls in school, that even though she didn't have pink eyes, the colour of her hair meant she was half-albino.

When she came home crying, her father had told her that they were only jealous of her unusual, beautiful hair and she must learn to ignore them. Sarah now recognised that same jealousy in Martina and was determined to ignore her advice.

* * *

The hotel dining-room was busy at lunch-time as it was a market day for the farmers who had travelled earlier in the morning into the town. Sarah went back and forth to the kitchen carrying plates of cabbage and bacon, roast beef and chicken. She then brought out dishes of potatoes and vegetables and jugs of gravy. This was followed by apple tarts and trifle.

When the rush quietened down, her time was spent clearing tables and setting fresh tablecloths and cutlery for the evening meals. It was hard work, but the hotel was a nice place to work in, and she was more grateful for it than ever since Martina had moved into the house. The staff were cheery and friendly, and there was always a bit of banter in the kitchen with the other workers.

Sarah could find herself working anywhere depending on how busy things were. She was often asked to come in on a Friday or Saturday morning to help with the bedrooms after the commercial travellers, who usually stayed mid-week, had departed. She found the work in the bedrooms satisfying, and enjoyed looking at the shiny sinks and taps and freshly ironed sheets on the bed when she had finished. But any time she had a quiet minute to herself, Sarah drifted off into daydreams about the dresses she was making and the ones she planned to make after her wedding. At some stage in the future she would love to work for a good-quality dressmaker where she could spend all day working on the small details that made a garment stand above the rest.

That was one of the things that she and Con had in common – dreams for the future. He worked as a painter and decorator, and had plans to open his own shop one day, selling wallpaper and paints and, further down the line, carpets and furniture. He had saved up and bought a van in the last year, so that he could travel further afield, and often worked late into the evening.

Over the last few months, Con had been busy doing up the small cottage just outside the town where he and Sarah would live. It was within easy cycling and walking distance for work. An old uncle had left it to him and his three brothers. Con had given the others the price of their fares over to England and a bit extra to tide them over until they got settled in jobs, and they had willingly given him the run-down cottage.

Sarah had made curtains for all the windows while Con had plastered and painted and hung wallpaper. Over their year-long engagement, they had saved up and bought rugs for the stone floor and had put a new range in the kitchen for cooking and to keep the place warm, and a sturdy pine table and chairs.

Now that it was almost ready to move into, Sarah was doing

her damnedest to keep out of it until they were married. Con had a different view of things. He would have been happier if they would meet up in the cottage regularly to do – as he called it – "a bit of courting". But once they had got somewhere on their own, Sarah found out that the kissing and cuddling wasn't enough for him.

She had walked out on him on several occasions recently, once when he had tried to take her blouse off, and on another occasion when he had forced her hand on top of a part of his body that was out of bounds for a single girl.

"If you don't stop this carry-on, I won't come down here any more when we're on our own," she had warned him. "It's only a few more weeks until we're married. Don't go spoiling things now."

He had gone stomping off out the back door and down into the overgrown garden. Ten minutes later he had returned. "I'm sorry, Sarah," he said. "I promise it won't happen again." He'd run his hand through his dark hair. "It's just that you're so lovely. It's only natural I can't stop thinking about you. Every night recently, I keep imagining what it will be like when we're actually married." He'd gone over and stroked her hair, then he had pulled her close and murmured in her ear. "I keep thinking what it will be like with your long blonde hair hanging down over your face and your breasts – like Lady Godiva."

"Don't!" The picture he described terrified her. "If there's any more talk like that, there will be no wedding."

Con had reassured her that he would keep his hands to himself until they were married, but the incidents had made Sarah wonder whether she actually loved him, because she had felt nothing but panic on both occasions. It worried her, because in most other ways they got on fine. Con had a good nature and locally was held in high regard, although he was inclined to be a bit loud when he'd had a few drinks.

She'd had to bite her tongue on a few occasions when he got carried away, enjoying being the centre of attention and hogging the conversation. If it continued when they were married she would have to have a serious word with him about it, because she didn't want to be one of those wives who sat in the background afraid to speak out. The other area of concern was more intimate. She had heard from friends that when you really loved somebody the sex thing came naturally. She hoped they were right. She would find out in a few weeks' time.

* * *

Sheila had a corner cleared for Sarah at the cluttered old kitchen table, and the two girls sat chatting as Sarah ate a pork chop, fried potatoes and cabbage. Sheila had had her own meal earlier, and now sat opposite her friend eating a slice of apple tart. As usual, her elderly parents were seated at either side of the fireplace, "like two bookends" as Sheila often wryly referred to them.

Every time Sarah visited they would be in the exact same spot, sometimes dozing and sometimes chipping into the girls' conversation, although their poor hearing often meant they got the wrong end of the stick. Most of the time they all rubbed along together, but there were often occasions when Sheila felt the lack of privacy in the house. The only place she could have brought Sarah was into her bedroom, but her mother and father would have seen it as odd, and couldn't imagine that the girls would have anything to talk about that couldn't be said in their presence.

"How are things going for the wedding?" Sheila asked. "It's not long now."

"Grand," Sarah said smiling. "I've only another few evenings' work on the dress and it's finished."

"What I've seen of it, it's absolutely beautiful," Sheila said, "and I'm delighted with the bridesmaid dress. You made a lovely job of it. I don't know why you don't go into it professionally."

A slight tinge of embarrassment came into Sarah's cheeks at the praise. "I think Patricia was pleased with her dress, too."

Sheila rolled her eyes. "Well, if you can please that one, you can please anybody! She's the fussiest girl you could come across."

"Oh, she doesn't mean any harm," Sarah said. "It's the way her family are. They just worry about every little detail."

"The last time we were over at your house together, she kept going on about the dress being too loose at the front, and it looked perfect on her. She was breathing in and trying to grab handfuls of the material but there was nothing to grab." Sheila sucked her breath in through her teeth. "I'd swear to God she's only saying it to make the point that I'm stouter than her."

"Ah, she wouldn't do that," Sarah said, wrinkling her brow. "In fairness, she has lost weight. I'd say she's gone down about half a stone between the first fitting and the last. She came over one night last week and I took it in a bit at the side seams, and it looks better now." She paused for a moment. "I didn't think she looked too well, between the loss of weight and looking very pale."

"Patricia's the lucky type that's more inclined to drop weight than put it up." Sheila looked down at her half-eaten apple pie and shook her head. "I think I'd better start cutting out the sweet stuff or you'll be letting the seams out on mine as opposed to taking them in."

"You're grand as you are," her mother commented loudly. "It's better to have a bit of weight on you than to be looking all thin and pinched like Patricia Quinn. Her mother is the very same – you'd wonder if they ever eat a bite at all."

"Men like a woman with a bit of meat," Jimmy Brady chipped in.

Sheila clapped a hand over her mouth to stop herself from laughing out loud.

She leaned across the table and whispered to Sarah. "You can't say a word in this house without it becoming a free-for-all!"

Sarah smiled. She was well used to the Bradys' ways, as she was with her friend Patricia's family. Both families were very pass-remarkable. Patricia's mother was forever commenting about Sheila Brady, saying would the girl never think of getting out for a bit of a walk to lose the weight around her hips. Behind all the comments there was no real malice, and Sarah usually let it all wash over her with a smile.

"How is the little cottage coming on?" Mrs Brady asked.

"Grand," Sarah told her. "We've the inside more or less finished. It's all papered and painted."

"Oh, you're lucky having a man that's good around the house," the old woman said. "Con Tierney can turn his hand to anything."

Sheila gave a low giggle and whispered to Sarah. "I hope he

keeps his hands to himself before the wedding . . . I've heard a lot of men find it harder the nearer it gets." She was not speaking from personal experience, as she had never had much luck with lads.

"He'll keep his hands to himself all right," Sarah whispered back. "I've warned him if he doesn't there won't be any wedding!"

"And no better woman to put him in his place. He's a changed lad since he met you."

Sarah suddenly felt uncomfortable at the way the conversation had turned. She knew Sheila meant no harm, but her chatter had touched a raw nerve. She changed the subject to something more inane, and tried to put Con's reputation as a ladies' man before they met out of her mind.

She spent over an hour at Sheila's, cycled back into town to collect the items that Martina has asked for, then headed back to the hotel.

She would keep busy for the next few hours, serving meals and clearing and setting tables for breakfast in the morning. When she got back home around ten that night, she would go straight to her room to continue working on the rosebuds and button loops on her dress. She would then cross off another day on her calendar – counting down to her wedding.

Another day less until she was gone from the home she was no longer welcome in.

•◆•

If you enjoyed this chapter from
Sarah Love by Geraldine O'Neill
why not order the full book online
@ www.poolbeg.com

•◆•

POOLBEG WISHES TO

THANK YOU

for buying a Poolbeg book.

If you enjoyed this why not
visit our website:

www.poolbeg.com

and get another book delivered straight
to your home or to a friend's home!

All books despatched within 24 hours.

POOLBEG

WHY NOT JOIN OUR MAILING LIST
@ www.poolbeg.com and get some
fantastic offers on Poolbeg books